1

SPECIAL DELIVERY

The swarthy man on the moped rode into the middle of the rundown estate. Parking in the forecourt of the tower blocks that surrounded him, he looked at his mobile phone to double-check the time and address. Cameron had delivered here before, but tonight he had an uneasy feeling. It wasn't the regular order and it had been a different voice making the call.

But it was his last delivery of the night and he couldn't wait to get away from here. Taking off his helmet and linking his arm through the strap, he took off his thick leather gloves and picked up the pizzas on the back of his bike. Shivering slightly, he looked around and pulled the collar up on his jacket to keep warm. It was no wonder people wanted their food delivered to their doors in this shitty weather. It was freezing and still damp from the rain.

Looking up, he saw that the windows of the grim tower blocks were lit from inside. Usually he would see people on their balconies smoking and shouting to each other from one tower block to the next, but not tonight. It was midnight and there wasn't a soul around. At least that gave him hope. At least no one would steal his moped.

Passing the burnt-out cars, he walked to the lift and pressed the button. This place gave him the creeps and the darkness didn't help, but his boss at the pizza shop had convinced him to go. When the lift failed to arrive, Cameron considered ringing the customer to come and pick up the pizzas from the forecourt, but considering what was buried in them, he thought better of it. If it wasn't for the money he was going to make tonight, he would have reconsidered walking the twelve flights of stone steps to get to his destination. The spicy smells from the pizzas made him feel hungry and reminded him that he hadn't eaten yet.

Breathless from climbing the stairs, he knocked on the door. The porch light above the door was broken and so was the neighbour's. It was nothing unusual in this place. Slum city, some people called it – personally he'd seen better slums.

This place was known for its violence and drug dealing. It surprised him that his Albanian boss wanted to take over this place and use it as his own turf. People like this always stuck together. They didn't want to do business with foreigners they didn't know; it was a known fact.

When the door eventually opened, he was nearly blasted away by the sudden burst of music that greeted him.

The customer who opened the door wasn't known to him, making Cameron's hackles rise even more, and a frown crossed his brow. But he was warmly greeted by a man wearing only a T-shirt and boxer shorts, which made him feel easier, and it sounded like there was a party in session, which was why they wanted the food and anything else he had hidden under the pizzas. Squinting slightly, he could only see the outline of the customer's features, especially his bushy beard but, given the state of the customer's undress, he could only presume what kind of private party was going on.

Hoping to make himself understood above the noisy racket, he

First published in Great Britain in 2022 by Boldwood Books Ltd.

Rotherham MBC	
B54 059 065 0	
Askews & Holts	30-May-2022
AF	£8.99
RTCLS	

A CIP catalogue record for this book is available from the British Library.

Paperback ISBN 978-1-80280-066-1

Large Print ISBN 978-1-80280-067-8

Hardback ISBN 978-1-80280-065-4

Ebook ISBN 978-1-80280-069-2

Kindle ISBN 978-1-80280-068-5

Audio CD ISBN 978-1-80280-060-9

MP3 CD ISBN 978-1-80280-061-6

Digital audio download ISBN 978-1-80280-062-3

Boldwood Books Ltd
23 Bowerdean Street
London SW6 3TN
www.boldwoodbooks.com

held out the square parcel and nodded. 'Pizza, the one with the extra topping is at the bottom.' Moistening his lips, he waited for some kind of acknowledgement from his customer.

'How much is it, laddie?' the thick Scottish accent of the customer bellowed out towards him.

Doing his best to make himself heard without shouting, Cameron smiled. 'A hundred pounds for the extra topping.' Avoiding eye contact, he looked down at the floor. He knew it wasn't the usual amount, but it was late and he was tired. He felt it was worth something extra for coming to this hell hole at this time of night.

The barely dressed customer scratched his beard and cocked his head to one side. 'That's more than usual, isn't it?' Pausing for an answer, he held out his hands for the pizzas, but Cameron stopped him and stepped back, squeezing the parcel firmly towards him.

'It's the delivery charge. Money first. Do you want it or not?' Furtively he looked around to see who was nearby, hoping this wasn't going to be some kind of ambush. It had been known in places like this.

'Just give me a second, laddie, and don't be so tetchy, my wallet is through there, I don't keep it in my underwear.' The customer laughed, while stressing the point by looking down at his underwear. 'Let's not be silly now, you've given your price and I'm prepared to pay it. Just give me the parcel to shut this lot up. I have a lot of hungry people in there, waiting to liven up the party with a few extras.' He winked and laughed again.

Eyeing the jovial Scotsman up and down, it was clear to Cameron he'd had a few drinks. Reluctantly he decided to hand over the parcel. He didn't want an argument and, given the noise coming from inside, he didn't want a fight on his hands from anyone at the party. Shivering with the cold, he could see his own breath as he spoke. 'Okay.' Rubbing his hands together to keep them warm and wishing he had kept his gloves on, he stood on the doorstep while the guy disappeared into the flat, leaving the door wide open. Cameron felt he was maybe being over-cautious; surely if the man wasn't going to pay him, he wouldn't have left the door open. It was just this place, it was enough to put anyone's teeth on edge.

Once inside, the guy threw the pizzas on the sofa. 'I'll just be a minute, laddie,' he shouted over the music to placate the man waiting at the door. Opening the pizza box at the bottom of the pile, a larger than normal packet of cocaine as promised lay beside a gun. Turning the music up a little louder, the man – nicknamed Jock – hastily looked around and reached for an old, discarded T-shirt he had worn earlier in the week. Wrapping the T-shirt around the barrel of the gun, he walked down the hallway. Shaking his head and laughing, he walked closer to Cameron, waving his wallet in the air, his T-shirt wrapped around the gun in the other. 'Sorry about that, it was in my trousers in the bathroom. I suppose you want a big tip for climbing those stairs and waiting for me.' The man winked and laughed again, putting Cameron at ease.

For the first time that night, Cameron smiled. It seemed he had been wrong. Smiling back in the hope of getting a tip as well as what he was creaming off the top from the cocaine he was delivering, he waited for the guy to open his wallet.

Quickly raising his gun, Jock dropped his wallet on the floor and grabbed hold of Cameron's jacket. Pulling him forward, he pressed the gun to his forehead. 'We've had enough of you selling your shit and creaming it off the top, making me look bad. You're a dirty thieving bastard, just ask your boss, laddie.'

Panicking and trying to struggle free, Cameron looked both ways down the hallway. There was no one around, and he thought about making a run for it. But when the guy pressed the gun against his forehead, he knew it was too late. 'There's no point in shouting, laddie, no one is going to hear you, let alone give a shit!'

As he fired the gun directly into Cameron's forehead, the T-shirt burst into flames, almost burning his fingers as the kid dropped to his knees and slumped to the floor with his eyes wide open. The bullet had gone straight through Cameron's head and the blood was minimal; just the open hole in his forehead from the bullet to show he was dead.

The shot could hardly be heard above the music, but Jock knew that if anyone had heard anything, they wouldn't come out to investigate. They were all safely tucked up in their own homes. Any minute now, someone would be coming to help him get rid of the body, but he wanted to save them the trouble of climbing the stairs to his flat. Lifting the pizza guy up, he dragged him towards the rail on the balcony. The safety rails surrounded all the flats to supposedly stop people from falling over, but in this case Jock heaved Cameron's limp body up and threw him over the balcony. Instantly he regretted his decision, as the sound of a car alarm burst into action, blaring out its horn. He looked over the balcony and saw the flashing lights of the car beneath him in the forecourt with the dead man lying on his stomach, spreadeagled over the top of it.

Trying to think, he scratched his beard and looked around as people opened their front doors, illuminating the blocks of flat from the lights in their hallways, to see what was happening. Shit. This wasn't supposed to happen, Jock thought. The balconies around him seemed to be filling up with people, standing and staring over the railings. When he had been asked to do this job, the idea of getting some free cocaine for a couple of days had appealed to him but now, in the cold light of day, realisation stepped in and he felt afraid. What was he going to do now? He was supposed to wait for the Undertaker's men to come and collect the body, those had been his instructions. His heart sank, and he knew he was in trouble now. He could hear a woman's voice screaming and echoing around the estate, and running inside, he slammed the door behind him. He needed something to calm his nerves. He knew he had totally fucked up and the consequences would be fatal. The fear of the police investigating the murder didn't bother him; it was the people who had instructed him to do this job that worried him. They had no mercy and just as easily as they had instructed him to murder the delivery driver, someone would be instructed to kill him. The boss who people knew as the Undertaker would see that he paid dearly for this calamity.

Opening the plastic bag containing the cocaine from the pizza box, he used the handle of a discarded spoon nearby and dipped it inside the bag. Jock sniffed the powder in his nostril and did the likewise with the other. Wincing slightly, he rubbed his nose with the back of his hand. Now he felt better. They had been very generous with the size of the bag they had given him. He had been paid well. The burning sensation in his nostrils made him wince again, with pain this time, and his nose started to bleed. Suddenly, his whole face felt as though it was on fire. Feeling lightheaded, he sat down on the sofa to steady himself. His eyes were watering and he was finding it harder to breathe. Gripping his chest, he lay back on the sofa. A black curtain of unconsciousness overcame him as he closed his eyes.

* * *

'Look at my car! There's a dead body on top of it.' The woman was in floods in tears. Wrapping her dressing gown tighter around her, she ran around the car looking at it. 'Somebody call the police! Do something. Someone help me, I'm not a well woman', she shouted to the crowd. Everyone shifted their feet and turned to look at each other awkwardly. The woman's husband came rushing out towards her, his jaw dropping at the sight before him.

Although it was dark, he could see a body sprawled on top of the small Fiat Panda, with one arm hanging aimlessly down the windscreen. 'Is he alive?' he shouted to the onlookers. 'Has no one had the common sense to call a bloody ambulance? You over there,' he shouted to a young man standing nearby. 'You're tall, have a look up there to see if he is breathing.'

'It's only a fucking Panda, mate, not a lorry. If you're so concerned, why don't you have a look?' the young man shouted back at him. Everyone was shouting to each other and presuming what had happened.

'It looks like he fell off the balcony,' someone shouted.

'Yeah, he was probably pissed,' someone shouted back.

As the noise of the crowd escalated, a figure emerged who immediately quietened everyone down. 'Don't worry, you lot.' Fin waved his hands in the air to attract attention. Everyone on the estate knew him and seemed pleased at his intervention. Fin was in his mid-thirties; he had turned up at the estate one day to stay at his friend Beeny's for the night while they were having a rave and just never went home. He was the local scrounger and drug dealer and was always hanging around street corners selling whatever he could get his hands on. It was a love-hate relationship between the estate and Fin, which was short for 'Fingers', because he always had his fingers in every pie or in someone's pockets.

Fin knew what had happened, but wanted to make some sense of it to this hysterical woman. 'These balconies are a death trap, especially to kids.' He could see that they were all nodding their heads and agreeing with him. They followed his lead and moaned about the tower blocks, which in turn took their minds off the trouble in hand. 'I'll call the police, you lazy bastards,' he shouted, waving his mobile in the air. 'What's the matter, don't you want to use your own mobile credit?' Stepping away from the crowd, Fin dialled a number. 'Daz, it's gone tits up around here. There's a dead body on top of a car. I'm supposed to be calling the police.' There was no answer on the end of the phone and then the line went dead. Fin realised he'd said enough. Now he had to attend to some damage limitation.

'Did you call them, Fin? What did they say?' The panic-stricken woman rushed towards him and grabbed his arms, shaking him. 'What is my insurance going to say? I need photos, they won't believe me when I tell them what's happened!'

'Of course they will bloody believe you, you stupid cow. There's a dead body on your car and the police are on their way. You'll get a crime number and their report. For fuck's sake, get off my arms, this jacket's designer!'

Again, the woman burst into tears, waiting for sympathy, but none came. Everyone was as shocked and surprised as she was, enthralled by the whole thing without paying attention to her tantrums. Falling to her knees for effect, she shouted to the crowd again, 'I use that car to get my husband to the hospital for his regular check up. He's ill, you know, and I've got arthritis!' Holding up her hands to the ever-growing crowd to prove her point, she burst into tears again.

Fin rolled his eyes up at the night sky; he was bored now. He was doing his best to pacify everyone, but he was running out of things to say. 'It will all get sorted, Mrs Mack, believe me. As for your husband, he's had that mobility scooter for ages but I've never seen him use the bastard!' Turning to the crowd, he shouted out, 'Have any of you lot seen him use it?' Some started laughing. They knew Mrs Mack always had something to moan about, especially her lack of money. She knew the benefits system better than the people who worked there. 'When your old man hears the mobile shop hoot its bloody horn, he's like a marathon runner.' Fin was rousing the crowd as best he could. He didn't know what else to do; this had turned into a catastrophe.

'For a bloke with a bad back, you've got six kids. It doesn't hurt when he's climbing on top of you, does it?' another woman from the crowd shouted. It was becoming mayhem, but Fin was playing for time. Surely Daz would send someone to intervene soon.

Mr Mack then started pointing his finger at the crowd and arguing about their accusations regarding his disabilities. Fin felt better now. At last they were all arguing between each other. His abuse towards Mrs Mack and her husband had done the trick. There was nothing like a bit of good old shit-stirring to distract the crowd.

Mr Mack held a hand to his lower back, feigning pain. 'Take some photos, love. Just as back-up. I would but my back is starting to ache. I think I'll go indoors and have a lie down.' Mr Mack left his wife and the crowd baying for his blood and went back into their ground-floor flat.

Reaching into her dressing gown pocket, Mrs Mack took out her mobile phone and took a couple of photos of her car with the dead body on the top of it. A nearby woman, who had been watching the proceedings, put an arm around Mrs Mack's shoulders to console her. Leaning closer to her ear, she whispered, 'I wouldn't do that. It could be bad for your health. Go back inside and have a cup of cocoa with something in it to warm you through. All this will get sorted soon enough.'

Wiping her tear-stained face with the arm of her soiled dressing gown, Mrs Mack turned to the woman beside her, and for a moment both women stared at each other. 'Maybe you're right. It is cold out here. And I'm just a bit shook up by it all. You understand, Maggie.'

'That's the ticket, love, you go and have a nice sit down and I will pop you a wee dram around in a minute. It will make you feel better.' Smiling to reassure Mrs Mack, Maggie soothingly put her arms around the woman's shoulders. Maggie knew everyone would take notice of her. She was one of the estate's longest-standing residents.

'Bloody hell, you lot! Old Mrs Mack has got a better mobile phone than me. I thought you had no money?' Fin looked at the gathered crowd again in disbelief and shook his head.

Scowling, Maggie turned to him. 'Shut it, Fin – considering Fin stands for Fingers, I thought you would have stolen a better one by now. What is your real name, anyway? Did your mother give you one, you waste of space?' she spat out.

Fin instantly stopped shouting out. Maggie was a force to be reckoned with and she had friends in high places, or in very low ones. It depended how you looked at it.

Seeing his subdued look, she felt better. Walking Mrs Mack to her front door, and changing her voice, she soothingly patted Mrs Mack's arm. 'We'll sort it, love. Don't worry. You and your husband get some rest now.'

Once Mrs Mack had taken her advice and gone back into her flat, Maggie walked back up to Fin. She was in her late fifties, skinny, with jet-black hair tied in a ponytail to cover the greying roots. The lines around her mouth seemed to encroach even more into her sallow skin as she pouted and poked Fin in the shoulder. 'Shut your mouth and get everyone back into their flats or I will rip your head off and shit down your neck. You're making things worse!' The glare that followed the sentence sent a chill down Fin's spine. Even though he called her Morticia Addams behind her back, she was a feisty old woman.

'Sorry, Maggie.' Glancing around, Fin suddenly felt embarrassed. Maggie was a real hard case and didn't offer empty threats. He'd seen her hit bigger blokes than him, and he knew she would punch him in front of everyone here. Which would ruin his 'hard man' status on the estate if they knew he'd been hit by a woman. Sometimes, she really got on his nerves.

'Show's over, folks,' Fin shouted, 'police are on the way, everyone back home and hide your stolen goods before they come knocking.' He laughed and then turned to Maggie for approval.

'Better leave it to the grown-ups now, Fin,' she muttered, and walked towards her own flat to get the whisky she had promised for Mrs Mack.

Quickly the crowds started to scatter. If the police were on their way, that could mean trouble. The dead man on the top of the car seemed irrelevant now. They'd had their sport for the night. Time for bed and to make sure that anything that didn't have a receipt was carefully hidden away!

Fin's mobile started to ring. Answering it, the instructions on the end were clear. 'Go to Jock's flat. I'll call you back.' The line went dead again. Why did they want him to go to Jock's flat? That uneasy feeling made his stomach turn somersaults. Waiting until he felt it was safe to go there without being seen, he made his way up the flights of stairs. He hadn't known Jock long, but he was a pain in the arse, always scrounging cocaine and he owed money everywhere.

That was how Fin had heard that Jock was doing some temporary work with the Albanians who ran the pizza place. They had tried selling their stuff on the Undertaker's turf and it had got to the boss man's ears about Jock doing some trading for them on the side. The anonymous man known as the Undertaker ruled most of Glasgow. The worst part was that no one knew who he was, or what he looked like. It sent chills down Fin's spine, wondering if it was the guy next door or someone he stood at the bar in the pub with. A lot of the drug drop-off points and prostitution rackets were run from local cemeteries. Basically, they were nice quiet places without too many prying eyes. That is why they nicknamed him the Undertaker: it sounded better than just 'the boss'.

He seemed to have eyes and ears everywhere and no sooner did you step out of line, you ended up paying the consequences. God knows how he found out the most intimate of secrets, but he did and that was the scariest part of all. Whoever he was, he was someone to be feared; he had no mercy. There was a long chain of dealers, and Fin knew, being a street dealer, he was at the bottom of the pile. They all had their own point of contact to answer to, but that was it. This so-called Undertaker had run this place for nearly ten years without anyone knowing who he was. The previous bosses had succumbed to horrible torture and even death to get rid of them from his turf while he was taking over. Someone must know him, Fin had thought many times. But they were all keeping their mouths shut and the thugs and the street soldiers who served out the beatings he ordered were not people to ask or mess with. They were all hardened criminals from around the area, who did this mystery man's bidding.

That was why Jock had been set up – to make a point to the Albanians that trading on their turf was a big mistake. One of their own was supposed to have been left dead for them to find. Instead, he was lying on top of Mrs Mack's car!

Fin didn't know what he was going to find when he went to the flat, but his gut instinct wasn't good. There was music still coming from inside, so he pushed the door open a little, looking for any sign of life. Taking a deep gulp, he started tentatively walking down the hallway, towards a light that was on in the living room. And that's when he saw Jock's lifeless body. Stunned, he stood there, just looking. Then he started sweating and rubbed his face with his hands. The last thing he wanted was to be found by the police with a dead body. Jock was lying on the sofa, his head at an awkward angle. Fin had seen people unconscious before, but it was pretty clear that Jock was dead. There were blood stains under his nose which had now dried and from what Fin could see, the man had choked on his own vomit – it was all down his shirt and on to the sofa. Seeing him lying there made Fin feel sick himself and his heart was pounding in his chest. Quickly looking around to see if there was anyone else in the flat, he could see there was no one. But he could see a packet of cocaine beside Jock. Fin was tempted to take a sniff himself but thought better of it. After all, if it had done that to Jock, what the hell was in it?

Instead, Fin looked around for Jock's wallet and found it in the back pocket of the man's jeans. Emptying the contents into his own pocket, while consoling himself that Jock wouldn't need the money now and whoever found him first would only do the same thing, he put the empty wallet containing only Jock's driving licence (which informed Fin that Jock's real name was Matthew) back where he'd found it. Turning the music system down so as not to draw attention to the flat, Fin decided it was time to leave. On the way out, he tripped over something and, looking down, saw a gun with a burnt T-shirt lying beside it. Pulling his sleeve down over his hands, he emptied the bullets out of it and then wiped the fingerprints. Shutting the front door behind him, he breathed fresh air into his lungs. Once downstairs, he walked around to the big skips that were at the bottom of the rubbish chute from the flats. Taking the gun, Fin smashed it against the floor again and again, breaking it into pieces. Then he went along to each of the five skips and dropped a piece of the broken gun into each of them, along with the T-shirt.

Fin's mobile rang just as he was about to go into his own flat. 'Is he dead?' Fin had heard the same cold, calculating voice before, but he knew not to ask questions.

'Yes, boss.' Fin was about to tell him about the gun and the cocaine beside Jock, but decided not to. This wasn't his problem. He'd done more than was expected of him.

'You've done well, Fin, you will get your rewards in heaven.' The line went dead again. Fin wasn't sure what they'd meant by that comment, but it gave him the creeps. It felt like someone was watching him.

* * *

The next morning, when everyone looked out, Mrs Mack's car had disappeared and, unknown to the people on the estate, so had the delivery driver's moped, which in all of the mayhem no one had noticed. There were no traces of the accident, and it was as though it had never happened. Everyone was surprised that they hadn't heard any police sirens or ambulances, but no one wanted to push it any further. Fin and Maggie both knew this was the job of the Undertaker. Fin knew that as soon as he made the call, the chain of authority would pass the message on to the so-called 'cleaners' who would step in to hide any trace of evidence left behind. It would be as though you had dreamt it. These men were professionals who could hide bodies and make people disappear.

Maggie knew it would all be tidied away and brushed under the carpet and had made it her job to put everyone at their ease again and spread the word that they didn't need to send an emergency ambulance because they knew it was a dead body they couldn't save. It all sounded feasible and no one questioned Maggie. They all agreed that whoever it was had been drunk and had clearly just fallen over the balcony. Thankfully, with all of the shouting going on last night, no one had noticed the bullet hole in the man's head. It had also helped that it was dark and he was lying face down on the car and, as much as everyone was being nosy, no one wanted to take a closer look at the corpse.

Jock, the annoying druggie, whose flat was permanently full of misfits and who always had his music blaring out, much to the annoyance of the estate, apparently had upped sticks and left without a backward look. People were surprised, but not shocked.

Whenever he was in rent arrears or owed money, he usually skipped town for a while.

Then Maggie popped in to see Mrs Mack. 'How are you, Mrs Mack? I hope you're feeling better after last night. I wondered, do you still have those photos you took of the accident on your mobile phone?' Maggie pursed her lips as she broached the subject.

'Oh yes, Maggie, and look at this, it looks like the guy who fell had a hole in his head. He must have fallen on something on the way down.' Bringing her phone to life, Mrs Mack showed Maggie the photos. Both women squirmed at the gory sight.

Only Maggie breathed a sigh of relief, thankfully Mrs Mack was an idiot. It was obvious to a blind man that it was a bullet hole through his skull. What the hell did she think had happened?

'The police haven't been to see me yet. I would have thought they would have been by now. They have taken the car away. How did they do that without the keys?' Mrs Mack's stupidity surprised Maggie. You only had to ask any five-year-old on this estate how to unlock a car and it would be done in the blink of an eye.

Mrs Mack put on the kettle and nervously wrung her hands. 'Something is wrong, I know it. Why haven't the police been in touch, Maggie?'

No police had been and no ambulance had picked up that dead man. Maggie hadn't lied when she said she had seen everything. She had indeed been there when the tow truck had taken away the car and body away. She knew they were going to be crushed. Now Maggie had seen the photos, she had to give the instructions she'd been given to Mrs Mack. They were incriminating, it was definitely a murder, without a shadow of a doubt.

'Before you do anything, Mrs Mack, love, you need to do as I say.' Maggie led her to the kitchen table and sat her down. Taking two mugs off the hooks, Maggie proceeded to make them both a mug of tea. 'You need to go down to the telephone box on the corner.' Raising her hands, Maggie shook her head, as Mrs Mack tried to interrupt her. 'Don't ask questions, just do as I say. It's for your own good. You know the old telephone box?' Giving a weak smile, Maggie waited for a response before carrying on.

Mrs Mack was still in her dressing gown. In all of Maggie's years here, she had never seen her wear anything else. Maggie doubted she had done a day's work in her whole life.

'Yes, I know where you mean, but what has that got to do with me?' Puzzled, Mrs Mack put two teaspoonfuls of sugar in her tea and stirred it.

'If you want all of this sorted out, you will do as I say. Go there right now and wait. Don't tell Mr Mack where you are going. Just do as I say.' Pressing the urgency upon her, Maggie stood up. She had delivered the message and it was up to Mrs Mack now. As the two women looked at each other, Maggie was thankful that the penny seemed to drop at last.

After Maggie had left, Mrs Mack wrapped her dressing gown around her, tightening the belt more securely as she left the flat and headed for the old telephone box through the estate on the main road.

No sooner had she stepped into the old telephone box, she could hear a telephone ringing, but knew it wasn't the one in the box – that hadn't worked for ages. Following the sound, she looked down at the concrete floor and saw a mobile phone, lighting up and springing into life. Nervously she picked it up. The voice on the other end was calm and articulate, giving her instructions. 'Leave your mobile phone with the photos you took in the telephone booth. Take the one you are holding with you, it's new. The box on the floor has fifty pounds in it for taxi fares until your car is ready and delivered to your door in two days' time. Do not contact the police or your insurance company. Let that be the end of it. If not, I have this number and I know where you live. The other options are not so generous.' Then the line on the other end went dead.

Mrs Mack's hands began to tremble and she looked around, peering out of the dirty glass on the windows mostly covered with graffiti now. She squinted her eyes to get a better view. There was no one around, apart from the usual passers-by, but no one suspicious, although she knew someone must be watching because the telephone had rung the moment she had stepped into it. She was afraid, but followed the instructions, and leaving her own mobile phone in the telephone box, she picked up the new mobile phone and the box containing the money, opened the door and left.

As promised, two days later when she got up in the morning and opened the curtains, a car was parked outside her ground-floor flat. A gasp of astonishment left her lips. It looked as good as new. Looking even closer at it, she realised it was new and was even better than the one she had owned before, although it was the same colour and model.

Beads of sweat appeared on Mrs Mack's forehead as she stared at it. Going to inspect it, she saw the keys had been put through her letterbox. She picked them up and went outside to take a better look. A cold shiver ran down her spine and she looked up at the flats to see Maggie standing there with her arms crossed, watching her. Both women exchanged glances and then went back inside their own homes. The matter was over. The problems were solved.

Fin had kept a close watch on Jock's flat. He saw a skip outside on the forecourt with council workers throwing his furniture in it. Fin wasn't sure if they were real council workers or not. Just because they wore those luminous jackets and overalls didn't mean a thing around here. All he knew was that the word was being spread that Jock had gone to Edinburgh and so nobody thought any more of it. The matter was over, dead and buried, you might say.

2

GOING STRAIGHT

The grey high-rise tower blocks standing side by side seemed to block out the sun and cast a shadow over the estate. The washing blowing on the makeshift washing lines on the balconies of the flats created strange shapes and patterns on the pavements, almost like monsters.

This estate was a city of its own in the heart of the East End of Glasgow and the people who lived there had their own language and lived by their own rules. It was known particularly to the police and outsiders for its drug dealers and crime. This was Legoland. Floor on top of floor of flats squared on top of each other. Nothing here worked properly and no one from the council would come to fix them. The old tenements opposite them did nothing to brighten the place up and buses never went past the end of the road after 5 p.m. Taxis refused to go there in case they got mugged. This was Steve's home, and it was all he had ever known.

Walking in front of the tower blocks and tenements, shouts and laughter rang out from the broken windows of a car, shattered by fire. Steve raised his eyebrows and cocked his head to one side to get a better view. Bending down, he looked inside the burnt-out Fiesta.

Three kids were playing in it, pretending to be racing drivers. He'd done it himself once upon a time, which brought a half-smile to his face. Nothing had changed in the last three years since he had been in prison. 'Go on, piss off. You'll hurt yourselves,' he shouted.

'Fuck you, mister,' the eldest boy of the three shouted. He was sitting behind the steering wheel, pretending to drive. He was around ten or eleven and raised his middle finger at Steve.

'What's your name?' Steve shouted through their noise.

'What's it gotta do with you, mister?' Again, the stubborn boy who was trying his hardest to act tough in front of his younger mates glared at him.

'This burnt-out car could blow up and cause you harm. Just listen to me, eh, laddie. Go and play somewhere else, and don't use that tone with me, you little shit, I'm looking out for you.'

'Don't bother. My dad does that!' There was his answer. Rolling his eyes up to the sky, Steve looked up at the tower block in front of him. As it met the sky, he searched the windows and balconies for his home, but everything looked the same and he wasn't sure which was his. It was obvious the charred remains of the car held much more interest for the boys than what he had to say, and shrugging at their comments, he stood up straight and walked towards the centre of the estate, clutching his few belongings in a plastic bag with the HMP emblem stamped on the front of it. It didn't seem a lot for a lifetime, but it was all he had.

'Oy, Stevie! Is that you?' The echoing shout from above surprised him and he scanned the balconies again to see who it was.

'Over here, you moron,' Fin, his old friend, shouted again.

A smile crossed Steve's face. Seeing his old friend jumping up and down, waving both arms in the air to attract his attention, made him feel better. Waving back, he cupped his hands around his mouth and shouted back. 'What floor are you on?' Fin was always in someone else's flat, especially if there was free food or drugs available. It was always sensible to ask him where he was before you started the long walk up the stairs.

'Fifteen, but the lift isn't working. Come up. Some of the lads are here. Come and have a few beers.' As Steve looked up, he saw some other friends of Fin come out and join him on the balcony. They had all been at school together, but that seemed like a very long time ago now.

Steve had served three years for possessing a firearm and dealing drugs, and Fin and the men with them that night had walked away scot-free. Fin had been under orders to help set him up, he knew that now, but time and time again he wished Fin had tipped him off in some way, considering they were old school friends, but it was obviously a chance Fin wasn't prepared to take. But the man who ran all the operations in Glasgow had been severely pissed off with him and he would have made Fin pay for it too. It was survival of the fittest, and the last thing Steve wanted was the blood of his friend on his conscience.

Everyone saved their own skin so they could live to deal another day. He had been a dealer. He wasn't bitter, they all took that chance and knew to keep their mouths shut. The man they called the Undertaker ran this whole estate and beyond. This was his turf. And everyone knew he'd killed more people than cancer. No one knew the man's real name and, to be honest, it was for the best they didn't.

Traipsing up the stairs was taking its toll. He'd done his best to keep fit in prison, but now he was challenged by a hundred stone steps. The steel door that was left wide open for him was nothing new. All drug dealers had steel doors with a hatch in the middle where they handed out their drugs and took the money. It was supposedly to hide their faces, but the main reason was to stop people kicking the door in or shooting at it. Which was a frequent occurrence and an occupational hazard.

The ambush by his friends was a welcome home indeed for Steve. They shook their cans of lager and opened them, spraying the fizzy drink over his head. 'Here, you can have this one to drink.' They were all laughing and patting each other on the back.

'How was it, Steve? Shit place, that prison. Been there myself a couple of times. Everything okay? We solid?' Fin frowned as he spoke the words. His voice was low in front of his friends, but he knew Steve would know what he meant. He wanted to know if he had said anything and if there was any bitterness between them. Pushing back his wet, lager-stained hair, Steve shook his head. 'Everything's okay, Fin. It's over now. Mates.' Holding out his hand, he shook Fin's.

'Good one. Because I knew you were coming out sometime this week and I have a job lined up for you. If we'd have known the exact date, we could have lined up a couple of willing lasses to give you a proper welcome home. Don't suppose that dick of yours has seen much excitement lately apart from your hand, has it?' Everyone laughed and Steve felt like one of the boys again. Part of the gang.

A couple of men Steve didn't recognise were sitting in a corner, spaced out from the drugs. They had smoked roll-ups for so long their fingers were yellow with the stain of nicotine. Steve guessed there was more than tobacco in the roll-ups. It was definitely some form of weed, it smelled like an opium den in here.

'I've only just got out, Fin. What do you mean, you have a job for me? Doing what? I have to see my probation officer on Monday and I'm keeping my nose clean while I'm wearing this tag.' Rolling up his trouser leg, Steve showed them his ankle tag. He was also under curfew, which would restrict his activities day and night and give his whereabouts to the authorities. Steve's heart sank. He did need a job, but he wanted more than this. He had served his last prison sentence. He wanted more for his family now. It was just this estate, it was like quicksand, no matter how hard you fought, it kept dragging you back in. Steve wanted no part of it now. He was older and wiser and wanted to lead a proper life with normal people. That is if Sheila, his wife, would keep her promise and give him a final chance at their marriage.

With only a Celtic flag pinned across the windows to block out the light and a faded, mottled sofa with the sponge coming out of the rips in the arms that had probably come out of a skip somewhere, Steve suddenly saw the place for what it was. He'd spent all of his life here and this flat was the place to be, but suddenly it had lost its grandeur. The small wooden coffee table in front of them all still had traces of the lines of cocaine they had been sniffing. Their pupils were enlarged and they were rambling on. This had been paradise once, and he had been just the same. He just hadn't seen what the rest of the world saw. It suddenly dawned on him how much he'd changed. He'd given up the drugs, even when they were offered in prison. Maybe, he thought, he had just grown up?

Football was an important part of the estate. You were either blue or green, and God help anyone who went into the wrong part of the stadium at a match. There had been wars over the colours of the shirts. You were either Celtic or Rangers. There was no in between.

In answer to his question, excitedly, they all shouted at once. 'To pizzas!' Raising their cans in the air like some kind of salute, Steve looked on. This was weird.

'We're all working at the kebab and pizza shops around the area. One is on the main road. All up front and legitimate!' Fin turned to his friends and they nodded at each other seriously, then burst out laughing. 'On the face of it, Stevie, everything is above board. The boss has bought quite a few shops around here. Let's be honest, they were all derelict shitholes, but it makes life easy to sell the gear. It definitely beats standing around in the rain,' Fin laughed.

'The delivery guys on their mopeds and the shops are all legitimate, but you can sell some gear on the side and make it worth your while. That's what you need to do, Steve. Get a legitimate job to keep your probation officer happy and off your back. And pizzas it is, Stevie! The rest is easy peasy.' Fin turned to each of his friends and gave them a high five. Their spirits were high, as though the world couldn't touch them. Sighing, Steve remembered when he had felt that way once. It seemed weird but prison had opened his eyes. He'd seen the world for what it was. He had too much to lose this time around.

In his last letter to his wife, Sheila, he had promised to go straight. She had said this was his last chance or she was moving away and taking his two kids with her. He wanted them out of this shithole too, but preferably with himself alongside them. He owed Sheila that. She had stood by him all this time.

He knew who they meant by 'the boss' and instantly he felt the bile rise in his throat. They all spoke as though they knew this so-called gangland boss, known as the Undertaker, but no one did. The mystery was part of the fear he instilled in them. Everyone knew all of the orders came from above via messages left at the cemeteries or mobile phones, different levels of decision makers doing this man's dirty work. He had his fingers in every pie and resorted to regular beatings to keep them on their toes. Some people had even wondered if it was a woman. That was the whole point, no one knew. That was what made him so deadly. No one could sweet-talk their way out of a beating or charm their way up the promotion ladder. The Undertaker wasn't interested. All he wanted was his money, although in fairness he paid a good wage for your services, which is why the majority followed order. When you were told your money would be there, it always was. Shaking his head, Steve tried his best to wriggle out of Fin's proposal.

'Nah, I don't think so. I think my probation officer already has a job lined up for me. They said as much.' Steve was trying to be polite while refusing their offer, and he drank back his lager and stood up. But Fin and his friends just burst out laughing again. They were high on drugs and alcohol and there was no point in trying to make sense out of their garbled conversation. This was beginning to get on Steve's nerves.

'Steve, we know you, daft bugger. We've sorted the job for you. You're to start at the pizza shop on Monday. Nice and early, now.' Again, they all thought it was hilarious, as they laughed and slapped each other on the back.

Shocked, Steve sat down again. Narrowing his eyes in confusion, he asked, 'What do you mean, you've sorted it? You mean you've set me up... again!' Watching the smiles drain from their faces, Steve was glad they knew what he meant. 'For God's sake, Fin, I have just done three years in prison, because you helped set me up for robbery. You didn't have the balls to tell me what plans your boss had in store for me and now you're handing me to them on a plate again. Will you never learn, you fucking Judas!' Angry and upset, Steve couldn't believe his ears. He'd only been out of prison a few hours and yet his fate was already decided. Steve the fall guy, again.

'No, Steve, I wouldn't do that. This was the Undertaker's idea. Maybe he feels he owes you. I thought you would be pleased.' Stammering, Fin looked down at the floor. 'I thought you said there was no bad feeling between us. That we were good?'

Sighing and rolling his eyes up at the nicotine-stained ceiling, Steve nodded his head. 'So what has he got planned for me this time? He won't be happy, Fin, until I am pushing up daisies. No wonder they call him the fucking Undertaker! We are mates, I owe you lot. You gave me a job dealing with you and drugs when I was an addict, but I don't see it the way you do. That bloody phantom you call the Undertaker doesn't think he owes me anything! No offence, Fin, but I don't intend going back to prison. Sheila will wash her hands of me. I'm not prepared for that.'

'It's a legitimate job, Steve. Go and see for yourself. There is money to be made on the side, but if you don't want to that's your business. It's a job, mate,' Fin pleaded. He was the one who felt he owed Steve. He had pleaded to get Steve this job at the pizza shop. It was where a lot of the drugs were sold. Each pizza had its own special priced topping and the addicts knew what they were. 'It's a regular wage for Sheila and the kids. What else are they going to find for an ex-con like you? For fuck's sake, Steve, unless you have a winning lottery ticket in your pocket, you're fucked!'

Although Steve could see Fin's reasoning, he was still unsure. It was a job and a regular wage and Sheila would be pleased about that. Surely that would give her some hope that he was going straight and trying to start afresh? And what job would his probation officer find him? What was there for a man in his thirties with a criminal record? Steve knew Fin was right, but he didn't want to admit it. Taking an even bigger sigh, he nodded his head and gave a weak smile. 'Okay, Fin, thanks, I'll take the job. But I want no part of any other dealings. That okay with you?'

Sheepishly, Fin looked at his friends. 'Yeah, sure, Steve, whatever you say. Come on, it will be a laugh and you'll get fed as well. You look like you need a few good pizzas inside of you. Fatten you up a little like Beeny here. He eats more than he sells.' The tense atmosphere disappeared as they all burst out laughing again.

Steve still had his reservations. His friends seemed to think this was a great adventure, but he couldn't make his mind up whether they were stupid or so off their heads on drugs they couldn't see the woods for the trees. He'd already been caught dealing and taken the rap for it. He now knew it had all been a set-up. Night after night, he'd gone over it in his mind. He'd upset the Undertaker by not shooting another drug dealer on his turf.

But it had been a young kid and Steve hadn't seen the point in killing him. The kid hadn't been to blame; all the main dealers used kids to stand on the same street corners or park benches for hours on end. Kids couldn't be prosecuted and they were cheap labour. The biggest factor was that they were so terrified by the street dealers, they wouldn't dare say anything. For a day's work they would maybe get ten or twenty pounds and they thought they were millionaires.

When it had come to the attention of the Undertaker's street dealers that others were dealing on his turf, he had wanted his competition killed as a warning. But when Steve had seen the kid riding his bike round and round on the corner, he knew he couldn't do it. He was only around ten years old, and Steve was no kid killer.

Instead, Steve had threatened and frightened the young boy. He'd taken his bag of drugs and money and felt that was enough. But only seconds later, he heard the engine of a car start up – the street dealers in charge of the young kids who were always watching. Steve had run as fast as possible down side alleys to escape his pursuers, who not only chased him but were shooting at him, too. Thankfully, their cars couldn't get to him, but he heard the screech of the car and then the doors bang. They were going to chase him on foot.

Seeing a back window of a house open, he had climbed inside and fallen into the kitchen, banging his head on the sink. A woman screamed when she saw him, but he put his hand over her mouth and told her to be quiet. She had nodded and he had headed for the front door. In the wake of further screams from the woman, this had given him time to escape.

Now, three years on, he realised it hadn't been enough to please the Undertaker. Whoever he was had not been pleased when it was reported back that he hadn't killed the young kid. The only appeasement was the bag of drugs and, of course, the money he'd taken from the kid. Steve had helped himself to some of it, but had decided to hand the rest over. He'd taken one hell of a beating for his lack of judgement. He couldn't remember how many men had ambushed him that night. But he could remember the pain. His jaw had been broken and he'd thought that was the end of it, but it wasn't, much to his regret.

Next he'd been ordered to do a raid on the house of a well-known drug dealer in Edinburgh. It was some rich guy's house, full of cocaine and whatever else you could get your hands on. He, Fin and these two friends sitting before him had agreed to do it. They had been tooled up with guns, which was the usual thing. To be a dealer in Glasgow, you needed a gun, just in case. After donning balaclavas, they had watched from the car they had stolen for the man and his wife to leave the house so it would be empty.

Once they had broken in, they had separated into different rooms and ransacked the place. But no matter how hard they searched, behind skirting boards, false walls, the webbing underneath the sofas, there were no drugs to be found. Absolutely nothing.

Instead two police cars pulled up, followed by the police banging and shouting at the door. They had driven up to the house without their sirens, purposely giving no warning. They had been tipped off, that was for sure.

When the police had handcuffed him, Steve had been surprised to hear them report that there was no one else in the house. Fin and his friends had fled, leaving him to face the music alone. He'd been arrested for possession of a gun, breaking and entry and he had filled his pockets with jewellery and money he had found in the bedroom. On top of that, there had been the cocaine they'd found in the inside pocket of his jacket. Steve never used cocaine and he certainly hadn't put it there, and he knew right then that this was a 'set-up' and he had walked straight into it. When they checked the car outside and found it was stolen, he was charged with that as well.

Steve had just shrugged and accepted his fate. There was nothing else to do. But to make things worse, he found out that someone had shot the young kid on the corner anyway. It had all been pointless, but at least Steve didn't have that on his conscience.

He didn't blame them. He blamed himself. Only he had got himself into this situation. The Undertaker was pure evil. This face-less man had no conscience. Kill or be killed, and he didn't care who got hurt. He never seemed to get his hands dirty, he paid everyone else to make him rich.

When Steve's case had gone to court, he had entered a guilty plea and kept his mouth shut about his friends. But facing Sheila had been the worst. The look of disappointment on her face when she had visited tortured him. To make things worse, she had brought the kids, too. Who would want their kids visiting them in prison? Sheila had made her point. This was his last chance.

Now, three years on, with a tag on his ankle, he listened to Fin and his friends telling him of their good fortune while his mind wandered. It was time to leave. He'd heard enough. It was time to face the music and see Sheila. Part of him felt pleased that he could tell her he had a job. Although his heart sank. He couldn't go back-wards. He just couldn't.

'I've got to go, lads. It's been great catching up.' Standing up, he shook their hands in turn. Fin held on to his hand a little longer. 'No hard feelings, Steve. I'm sorry, man.'

Reaching out, Steve hugged him to reassure him. He knew Fin had been threatened to do this. Everyone knew and heard about the Undertaker's tortures. It made even the hardest of men wince. It was said that if you ever met the Undertaker, that would be the last time you saw daylight. It was a death sentence. Although, many nights Steve had lain on his bunk bed and vowed he would find this mystery man. He had imagined what he looked like. Small, pathetic, balding. Or tall and fat. He had probably passed him in the street a million times and didn't know who he was. He couldn't fathom it out. But he was determined to look him in the eye one day and revenge would be his.

3

MOBILE SHOPPING

Pensively, Steve knocked at his own front door. He wasn't sure what to expect from Sheila; it had been a long time since they'd seen each other, although their letters and drawings from the girls had been frequent. But this was the cold light of day. Hearing the sound of the bolts sliding across the inside of the door made him feel nervous and his hands sweaty. It was like going for a job interview, and although Sheila had agreed to give him a second chance once released from prison, he knew he was on borrowed time.

Running his hands through his damp hair, he suddenly regretted meeting up with Fin and his friends. He'd been sprayed with lager and stank of it. His clothing was also wet, not exactly the first impression he wanted to make.

With the door chain on, Sheila looked through the small gap to see who it was. Once she saw it was him, she opened it wider. There was no warm greeting, no arms thrown around his neck with the welcome home he had envisioned in the darkness of his cell. Already Sheila was on her guard, standing there with her brown hair tied back into a ponytail, no make-up and her arms folded. The blue V-neck jumper she was wearing had something in the form of food spilt on it. He could see she had made no effort for his home-coming, probably on purpose to prove a point. The worst part of his criminal lifestyle had been the disappointed look in her eyes when the police had searched their flat for the hundredth time and had even ripped the filling out of the pillows and cushions. Her lovely home had been trashed, time and time again. He knew he had a lot of grovelling to do to make this work.

Looking him up and down, she dramatically sniffed the air, which he knew was a sarcastic way of saying he smelt of booze. 'You're home, then. I see your loving family wasn't your first port of call?'

'I bumped into Fin on my way and him and his friends sprayed me with their lager as a welcome home,' he stammered. He'd already started the day on a bad footing with Sheila. He wasn't sure now if she would let him in or tell him to go back to where he'd come from. She was right, of course; he'd been thoughtless and selfish as usual.

'It's good to know your mates come first. I expected you earlier. Don't the prisons throw you out early?'

'I had to go to the local police station first to let them know I was home. I have to report there daily and then there are no buses that come here...'

'Enough, Steve, I think I can fill in the gaps. Well, you'd better come in. I'll make some tea. That is if you're still thirsty,' As she walked away, Steve's heart sank.

'Daddy!' As he took a deep sigh of relief, his two daughters came running down the hallway to greet him. Penny, who was eight, threw her arms around his neck as he bent down to greet her. Sweeping Sharon, who was six and hardly knew him, up into his arms, he hugged her and kissed her cheek, while squeezing Penny's hand. This moment was what he had waited for. The worst part of being a prisoner was missing your children and not being part of their lives, secretly hoping they wouldn't forget you.

'How's my wee lassies?' he laughed while still being slobbered all over by kisses and hugs. Penny tugged at his arm and pulled him inside the house. Consumed with guilt, he looked at his daughters as they pulled him into the kitchen, shouting to Sheila that Daddy was home. They had grown so much. He was surprised they recognised him, and he felt his heart would burst on hearing their excitement at seeing him. He never wanted to leave them again. He was determined this time. His life had been one catastrophe after another and Sheila had always stood by him, ever since they had been childhood sweethearts at the local comprehensive. But he noticed that she looked tired and haggard now, much older than her twenty-seven years. His time away had clearly been hard on her and Steve was determined to make amends.

As he sat down at the kitchen table, Penny opened the plastic bag from the prison with the few possessions he had in it. 'Did you bring us some presents, Daddy?'

Again, Steve could have kicked himself. It hadn't occurred to him to buy some sweets for the girls. He'd been given a voucher for his train ticket and the only money he had was what was in his wallet when he was arrested.

All he could see of Sheila was her back as she made the tea. The house looked sparse. It had the basics but it was obvious she had sold a lot of stuff to manage on the meagre benefits she received. Even the washing machine was gone.

'I've got a job. I start Monday.' Breaking the silence after the girls' excited voices, he was trying his hardest to get through to Sheila. Her shoulders looked tense. He hoped this would be good news.

Turning around with two mugs of tea, Sheila looked at the girls bouncing around Steve. 'Go to your room, girls. I want to speak to your dad alone.' Waiting for them to leave, she sat down at the table with her tea. 'What kind of a job is it?'

'It's at the pizza shop on the main road. I start Monday. I'm not sure what I'm going to be doing yet, but it's a start.' Picking up his tea, he took a sip, without taking his eyes off Sheila. He wanted some kind of reaction from her, some kind of emotion. Even if it was only shouting. Anything but this awkward silence where they were skirting around each other.

'I presume your probation officer sorted that out for you?'

Steve nodded, deciding it was better not to mention that Fin had set the job up for him. Suddenly they were interrupted by the noise of a car horn. It continued for a minute or so, and jumping up, Steve was about to go to the window to see where it was coming from when Penny and Sharon raced back in. 'The van is here, Mum.' Jumping up and down excitedly, they held out their hands.

'You promised,' Penny shouted. Smiling for the first time since he arrived, Sheila picked up her purse, took out a few coins and handed them over. 'Tell him I will pay him the rest on Thursday when I get my benefits.' Nodding, Penny took Sharon's hand and ran to the front door.

The van horn was still blowing in short spurts and Steve could hear people shouting over the balconies and the banging of doors. Pulling back the net curtains, he peered out. All he could see was a white van and yet people were running towards it.

'It's the mobile shop, Steve.' Sheila interrupted his thoughts. 'It comes every day.'

Confused, he looked towards her and then back through the windows. The side of the van had been converted and from what he could see it had a shutter fitted that rolled up, showing a serving hatch. People from the estate were scrambling towards it, queuing patiently for their turn. Others were shouting over the balconies, asking people queuing at the van to ask him to wait. It was chaos. Steve was amazed, people were walking away from it with bread, milk and other groceries. He spotted his own daughters standing in the queue. 'How long has that been coming?' he asked, not taking his eyes away from the window.

'About a year. Just as well, really, with no buses it's one hell of a walk to the shops. There are a lot of pensioners in these flats. At least if you run out of milk you know he's coming. It saves a lot of hassle. And he sells ice-cream.' Nonchalantly Sheila nodded, trying to justify the girls' excitement.

'Maybe I should go down there with the girls. Are they safe going down there alone?'

'Why?' Sheila snapped. 'You weren't here last week to escort them or the week before. They will be okay.'

'I can't do right from wrong, Sheila. Are you constantly going to be throwing my past in my face? What was the point in saying you would give us another chance if you're not prepared to? Can't we just move on?'

Brushing back a lock of hair that had escaped from her pony-tail, Sheila nodded. She was tired of fighting. Tired of living hand to mouth. She was also embarrassed about what her husband had come home to. This wasn't the family home he had left. It was stripped bare and her wedding ring had been pawned so many times she'd lost count. 'Sorry, Steve, it's just going to take some time getting used to you being home again.'

Footsteps stampeded down the hallway and Penny and Sharon returned, holding up their paper sweet bags. 'He sent you this and this,' Penny said as she handed over two tins of baked beans and a note for Sheila.

'Who in their right mind would bring a van full of money and groceries onto this estate, let alone give them credit?' Laughing out loud, Steve shook his head in amazement.

'Well, they've managed so far,' said Sheila while looking at the hastily scribbled note.

Suddenly it dawned on Steve who was behind this act of kindness. This scam must be owned and run by the very people he was trying to avoid.

'He said the tins were three pounds and he will put them on your bill.' Penny passed on the message and then happily ran to her bedroom with Sharon and her small bag of assorted sweets.

'You're going to pay three pounds for two tins of beans? You've got to be joking, Sheila.'

'He has overheads, like petrol and stuff, and it's convenient,' Sheila snapped, defending the mobile shop, and opening the drawer, she took out the tin opener. 'And at least that's dinner sorted.'

Steve couldn't believe it. The relief in Sheila's face when she saw the two tins of beans made him angry. Christ, was this what they had come to? He couldn't contain his outburst. 'But they are half the price of that in the shops,' he shouted.

'Yes, they are, Steve, but the supermarkets don't give you credit!' Sheila shouted back. 'How do you think we've managed all of this time while you have been getting three meals a day? The benefits don't go that far. I have bills and clothes to buy. God knows they are always growing out of clothes and shoes. Mind your own fucking business, Steve. Remember this.' Snarling, Sheila pointed a warning finger at him. 'It's not just the police you're on probation with!'

Silenced and stunned by her outburst, Steve drank his tea, which was nearly cold by now. Sheila was right. He had to agree.

She'd had to survive without him. Now was not the time to start an argument over a couple of tins of overpriced beans.

'I'd better go and get washed and get out of these clothes.' Picking up his plastic prison bag, he headed to their bedroom and dropped the bag on the bed. All that was inside it was the suit Sheila had brought for him to wear in court and his best shoes. The clothes he was wearing were what he'd had on the night he was arrested. Curiously, he opened the wardrobe and a smile crossed his face. His clothes were still in there, which surely meant Sheila hadn't totally given up on him. Clean shirts hung on the hangers and fresh underwear that he could see had been newly washed and ironed was waiting for him in the drawers. He was pleased. She had looked forward to him coming home and made an effort after all.

After their beans on toast, Sheila disappeared while he played with Penny and Sharon and watched television. When she walked back into the lounge, he was shocked. She was wearing make-up, a short leopard print skirt and a flimsy top and was pulling on her denim jacket. A big smile crossed his face, now that was what he was hoping for!

'I'm dropping the girls off at Betty's for a couple of hours. I have to go out,' was all she said.

'Going out? Dressed like that?' This was not what he had presumed. He thought the outfit was for him and taking the girls to a neighbour would give them some time together, but going out?

'Where are you going dressed like that?' Confused, he couldn't help raising his voice.

'Out. I won't be long. Make yourself at home.' Beckoning the girls to her, she instructed them to get any dolls they wanted to take with them.

'Why Betty's? Why can't they stay with me? Have you got some bloke you're meeting, because you're not dressed for the bingo, are you?' Shocked and disappointed, Steve stood up. This had been one shitty homecoming and now she was off to meet some boyfriend. For fuck's sake, could it get any worse?

Ignoring his questions, she nodded. 'Okay, if you're staying in, you can look after them. I won't be long. I work some evenings.'

'Doing what?' Suddenly the penny dropped. 'Oh fuck, Sheila, you're on the game, aren't you? Have you turned to prostitution now, is that it?' Upset and angry, he started shouting, 'You're going to leave me and go and screw some guys. Bollocks! Well, you don't need to go anywhere now. I'm home. I've got about thirty pounds in my wallet. We can survive on that until the benefits come through.' Walking towards her, he pulled at her arm to stop her leaving.

Sheila's face burned with shame and embarrassment, but Steve couldn't stop himself.

'You've been leaving my daughters with neighbours so you can turn tricks? Does everyone on the estate know you're a prostitute? Oh, my God, I can't believe this. Well, you can take that shit off your face. You're not going anywhere!' he demanded.

'Don't you accuse me and don't shout at me,' Sheila snapped back. 'Yeah, I'm a tart and you're a criminal. So that makes two of us!' Their raised voices got louder and louder and Penny and Sharon stood in the doorway, watching with sad faces. Trying to hold his temper, Steve looked at them. They both looked frightened as they held their toys, cowering near the doorway.

'It's okay, you two. We're just having an argument over the television. No one is angry. Go to your room and put your nightgowns on, I will be there in a minute.' He tried soothing the situation, but inside he was boiling mad. He wanted to slap Sheila for this revelation, but he had to keep his cool while his young daughters were listening.

'I've got a job, Sheila, this stops now.' He was trying to be reasonable and lowered his voice. 'The past is the past.'

Sheila followed suit and lowered her own voice. The last thing she wanted was to upset her daughters. 'But you won't get paid for at least another week, Steve. In the meantime, who is going to top up the money on the electric meter? I have debts, I need to pay them off. Don't you dare look at me like that, Steve, you're no bloody angel!' Tears streamed down her face. 'You got us into this mess and it's been up to me to get us out of it. By any means, fair or foul.' Pointing her finger at her body sarcastically, she looked at him. 'This was the only thing I had left to sell! Do you think this was my life's vocation? Oh yeah, when I was at school, I dreamed of being a prostitute to put food on the table while my husband was in prison,' she shouted accusingly. She was starting to raise her voice again, to make her point. She had been left with nothing and two young daughters to bring up. She hadn't been able to get a job, given their age. Her family had disowned her a while back when they found out she was standing by him. She needed him to understand, not accuse her. There were other things she hadn't told him, but she knew she would have to. She felt sick to the stomach having to admit this, but sometimes you had to do the unthinkable to survive.

The fallout from the anguish he'd caused stabbed at his heart. He hadn't really thought about her struggle while he had been in prison, he'd been too engulfed in his own problems.

'The rent is paid while you're on benefits and here—' taking out his wallet, he threw what money was in there at her, 'here's your bloody electric money. I'm not having everyone knowing my wife is a prostitute and I'm her fucking pimp!'

'I have to go, Steve.' More tears flowed and she smudged her make-up while wiping them away. 'I have my list.' Taking out a piece of paper from her pocket, she waved it in his face. Steve snatched it from her and read it in confusion. There were names on it, but some of them were women's names. Baffled, he looked at her. 'You're turning tricks for women?' He couldn't believe it.

'No. That's where I meet my punters. It's the names on the head-stones in the cemetery,' she blurted out.

Sitting down, Steve rubbed his face with his hands. He couldn't believe what he was hearing. 'You're meeting punters in a cemetery? Who do you owe money to, Sheila? It's the Undertaker, isn't it, he's been running the prostitution rackets around here. Well, he did before I went inside, I used to drive them around. Don't you remember? And you said you would never be caught dead doing something like that,' Steve spat out. 'I doubt a lot has changed. If anything, he seems to have expanded. It's the cemetery link, I'm not stupid, he's the one you owe money to. He and his whole gang have got their hooks into you.'

'I don't know who it is, but he's kept us fed. This is how I get my credit at the mobile shop and it's better than standing on a street corner, waiting for a punter to pass by.'

'That's the piece of paper Penny brought back with those pathetic beans, isn't it? I thought it was the bill or something.' His ears were ringing with this devastating confession. It had to be the bloody Undertaker! He couldn't swear to it, but who else could be running a prostitution racket around here? Although the mobile shop was an addition. Steve was supposed to be working for him on Monday. He must be laughing his socks off. The bastard! Steve knew he was being swallowed up by hate for this man and at the moment, whatever happened in his life, he felt this Undertaker guy was at the root of it. He blamed him and his circle of greedy, corrupt bastards for everything and it seemed that even now his life was being ruled by them. He'd had years to fantasise about finding him and exposing him, killing him, even.

'If I pay what I owe him when my benefits come through, I have nothing left. When it was suggested to me, I felt this was my only option. I have to go, Steve, they will be waiting for me.' Turning around, she headed for the door.

Swallowing hard and doing his best to hold back his own tears, he knew she was right. It was all his fault. He'd destroyed lives. Or rather, the Undertaker had. Whoever he was, Steve mentally vowed to himself that he would pay for this.

'I'm coming with you... you can't walk around the estate dressed like that and God knows who you're meeting.'

Pointing at his leg, she grimaced. 'What, with that tag on your leg?' she reminded him. 'Anyway, we get picked up and dropped back off. It's safe enough.'

Again, he was surprised. 'How many of you are there?' Raising his eyebrows in amazement, he waited for an answer.

'Take a look around you, Steve. How many women are on this estate? Do your fucking sums, Mr High and Mighty.' Running down the hallway, she opened the door and slammed it behind her before he could catch her. He shouted her name, but it was useless. He couldn't run after her because of his tag and the girls were in the bedroom and he could hear them crying. Fuck, he thought. He didn't know what to do. He felt helpless.

Running to the balcony, he knew it would take a few minutes for her to get down the many flights of stairs to the forecourt of the estate. But from where he stood, he could already see women similarly dressed, all meeting up in the darkness. Eventually, he saw Sheila join them and then a black hearse pulled up alongside them and they all got in. Steve felt sick and kicked the wall. There was nothing he could do, it was past his curfew time and the last thing he wanted to do was break the rules on his first day out.

Mentally, he could see the reasoning behind it. The clever bastards! No one around here would say anything about a hearse picking up a bunch of prostitutes and no one would blink at a hearse driving through the cemetery gates. Whoever was behind this had it all worked out.

Punching the wall hard, Steve felt better until he saw the blood run down his knuckles from the scrape and his hand throbbed. So that was it: the mobile shop was a prostitution racket that preyed on penniless mothers. Steve felt like low-life scum. He'd kept his mouth shut at the trial and done his time in prison and yet he was still paying for it. His whole family was paying for it.

The only thing left to do was rinse his hand in cold water and try his best to soothe the girls.

After a few stories, they both fell asleep. The television was on in the lounge, but he wasn't really watching it. He was nervously pacing the room and looking out of the window like a cat on hot bricks. His troubled mind was running away with him. If this was the work of the Undertaker, Fin would know all about this. And yet he'd never said a word when he'd seen his old friend earlier. And Fin clearly hadn't helped Sheila out with money as he'd promised he would. He'd been the selfish, two-faced snake as always. Well, he would remain friends with Fin and hopefully that would lead him to the Undertaker, this almighty man who destroyed lives. His mind was on Sheila at the cemetery. Hell, he didn't even know which cemetery it was. Suddenly he heard the key in the lock, and he ran down the hallway to meet her.

'Sheila,' he blurted out, 'I've been worried sick! Are you all right? We need to talk. We can work this out.'

She avoided his face and looked down at the floor. 'Leave me alone, Steve. I need a bath and by the looks of it, you need some ice for that hand.' She shook her head. 'How are you going to work with that? Leave me alone, there's nothing to talk about.' She was tired and upset, and she had mud on her knees and skirt from kneeling down giving blowjobs in the cemetery. The last thing she wanted was another shouting match. 'By the way, you're on the sofa tonight,' she called to him over her shoulder as she walked to the bathroom.

Steve let her go. He could see she was distressed and he didn't want to make things worse. He felt like shit and his hand throbbed. He didn't realise how bad things had been for Sheila whilst he'd been inside. But he was determined that now he was out, things were going to change for his family. He'd make sure of that. Whatever the price. He had a lot of making up to do and putting an end to this horror story was his one and only goal.

4

THE SCOTTISH QUEEN

Clouds of dust flew into the air as the red E-Type Jaguar sped along the long gravel drive towards the front main doors of the Tudor mansion in Dorset. Nick Diamond got out of his car and surveyed his parents' home. It was a lovely mansion, but situated in the back end of nowhere. He detested cattle and sheep and it seemed that was all there was on offer here. Nick loved the London nightlife and it was much more to his flamboyant taste. Straightening his tie and making sure his tie pin was straight, he walked up to the large oak doors, which were instantly opened by the family butler, Peters. His distaste for Nick was well hidden under his professional stare. 'Mr Diamond. We didn't expect to see you today, sir.'

'Why not? This is my parents' house, isn't it?' The grin that spread across Nick's face was more sarcasm than question. Throwing his car keys into the air for the butler to catch and park his car properly, Nick walked inside the house.

Swallowing hard, Peters caught the keys and nodded. 'Mr Diamond. Your grandmother is here.'

A genuine smile and gleam in his eyes lit Nick's face up. This usually meant fun.

Raising his eyebrows, he smiled again at the butler. 'Well, this really is worth coming for. Nana, all the way from Scotland. She will be as mad as hell... let the entertainment begin, eh, Peters.' Rubbing his hands together with excitement, Nick strode forward, then stopped. 'Tell me. Has she scolded you yet?' Nick's laughter seemed to echo down the hallway.

Peters was already waving towards another member of staff to give the car keys to the chauffeur. He hated Nick's arrogance, he always had. But his family were good people and fortunately Nick didn't visit too often. But his grandmother was a real matriarch. She hated everyone apart from Nick, who could do no wrong in her eyes.

Glancing into each room as he walked down the hallway, Nick spied Gladys, the maid, who seemed to have worked there forever. 'Where's Nana?' he mouthed to her. Pointing to a room across the hallway, Gladys almost smiled. Nick blew her a kiss as he opened the drawing room doors and walked in. He was a flirt, but then he always had been.

'Nana, you look more beautiful each time I see you.'

'Oh, shut up, Nicky. I have been dragged here to Dorset kicking and screaming. Why would I want to leave Scotland to come to a place like this? All farmers and thieves. I watch the TV, I know these things. Sheep shaggers, the lot of them!' she grunted. Cocking her head to one side, she waited for her usual kiss on the cheek.

'I believe that's another county, Nana. Or so I've heard.' Oozing with charm, Nick couldn't help laughing out loud. 'So why are you here?' Leaning down, Nick kissed his grandmother's cheek. They had always been close and she was still as sharp as a razor and didn't suffer fools gladly. A Glaswegian born and bred, she hated stepping outside the borders to mix with 'those English!'

Rolling her eyes his way and squeezing her lips together in a pout, she pointed her thumb towards the dining room. 'That mother of yours thinks I don't know she has arranged a surprise birthday party for me... who the hell wants to celebrate the fact they are eighty? Not eighty-year-olds, that's for sure. And that wife of yours, what's her name again?' Letting the smile creep across her face, she stared at him.

'You're a minx, Nana. I've been married to Patsy for fifteen years and you're saying you've forgotten her name? You just don't like her and that's fine. But you're still my number one girl. Here, have a drink.' Pouring her a whisky from the decanter, he handed her a glass and sat down opposite her.

'What's that? I thought you were going to pour me a drink. That looks more like a sip. For God's sake, laddie, pour your nana a proper drink.' Bringing the decanter over, he put it on the table at the side for her to help herself.

'Why are you so dressed up in your best suit?' She looked closely at her grandson, who was wearing a dark Savile Row suit with a white silk shirt. His light brown hair was just below collar length, but long on top, giving him a fly-away side fringe. His large green eyes, surrounded by long, dark eyelashes, were like two emeralds in his well-chiselled face. He was a handsome young man, that was for sure.

'I always wear suits for work, Nana. If I don't, no one would take me seriously. I'm a solicitor, after all.' Wagging his finger at her, he couldn't help laughing. 'I can't wear my old denims or my tartan kilt to do that now, can I?' His warm, low laughter was infectious and she smiled. 'How is sunny Scotland, anyway? What have you been up to before you were captured by the English and brought here?' He winked.

'Nick! You're home. I didn't hear you come in.' Hearing his mother's shout, Nick turned to greet her.

'I did call out but I was hypnotised by this beautiful woman.' He turned his head and winked at his nana.

Nick's mother, Victoria, was flustered as she kissed him on the cheek. 'I'll get some coffee, have you eaten? I didn't realise you would be coming so soon. And for the record, that beautiful woman sitting there talking about me behind my back has done nothing but moan since the chauffeur brought her here. For God's sake, Nana, with all your complaining you would think I'd asked you to walk from Scotland.' With a deep sigh, his mother walked away to order some refreshments.

'Why does she need a big house like this, Nicky? Your daddy worked hard to pay for this house, but ten bloody bedrooms! And servants! Who the hell does she think she is? A hard day's work would kill her.'

'Oh, Nana, that tongue of yours is as sharp as ever.' Nick couldn't stop laughing. 'Mum has the title, but no money. Dad made a lot of money, but sadly not the title to get him into the circles he wanted. Mum introduced him to all the right people who would use him as their stockbroker. It's even Stevens, I would say. It suited them both to swap one for the other.' Mumbling under her breath, Nana reached for the decanter and poured more whisky into her glass. She made her feelings known, no matter what. She didn't approve of the way Victoria lived.

'They were happily married, Nana, you know that.'

'Maybe, Nicky, but she's always been a stuck-up cow. And she hasn't always been that blonde, you know, my guess is she has it done that colour to cover her grey hair.' Giving in to his charming smile and warm laughter, she laughed, too. She enjoyed winding them all up, but only her beautiful grandson Nicky could see the funny side of it. Everyone else groaned and just put up with her. 'Why a nice Scottish man like your father would want to marry an English woman is beyond me. I knew it would be trouble when he went to London to work in that exchange, she was like a ferret up a drainpipe when she spotted him. Don't forget, Nicky.' She wagged her finger in his face. 'You're a Scotsman too. It's in your blood. You're one of us. That posh accent of yours doesn't fool me.'

'Mum insisted I went to a posh private school, Nana, and speak properly. The Queen's English.' He knew he had just thrown the bait to make her angry. This was sport indeed.

'And what queen is that? Her English one or my Mary Queen of Scots. Poor woman. She suffered at the hands of her lot!'

'Nana, I doubt Mum had anything to do with that. And you weren't even there. For God's sake, you're not that old, are you?' Raising an eyebrow, he cocked his head to one side and raised his arms to defend himself, as her cushion went flying towards him.

'Now I've hurt my hands. It's my rheumatism, Nicky. Look at my fingers, all gnarled up and bent. I used to be able to play the piano as a girl. That medicine you gave me the last time you came to visit helped me a lot. Eased the pain, it did.' Their eyes locked for a moment, but nothing was said. Some things were left unspoken, but Nick knew she meant the marijuana he had given her. Sometimes he wished he hadn't, because she was always asking for more.

'Being coy doesn't suit you, Nana. I know what you mean.' Looking up, he grinned broadly and winked at his nana. 'Here's afternoon tea.' Changing the subject quickly, he waited for his mother and Patsy, his wife, who had turned up the day before for their usual shopping trip, to be seated as the maid put down the tray of tea and coffee, with the usual scones and sandwiches. Waiting until they had been served, Nana went on to complain how cold it was in the large room and everyone sweated as the maid put more logs on the log burner.

'Well, Patsy, my love. How are things in the beauty salons?' Nick dutifully asked his wife who was sitting beside his mother on the sofa. Mentally he felt the two women looked like twins. It was obvious they both shopped at the same stores – their Chanel suits and pearls made them look like a pair of bookends.

'Business is good, Nick, thank you. You would know if you ever found the time to come and see for yourself.' Although her voice was polite, there was an undertone of sarcasm to her words.

'Bloody beauty salons. Only ugly people go to them. Why would Nicky want to go to one?' Again, Nana jumped to Nick's defence. 'And when are you going to give Nicky here a son and stop messing around in them shops of yours?' Nana's tongue lashed out, as sharp as ever, and she knew she had hit a nerve in Nick's wife.

'When Nick is around long enough to give me a child, Nana, I will let you know.' The smile was sweet, although Patsy's voice wobbled slightly. Nana's comments had cut deep.

Nana pouted her lips, making the lines around her mouth look even deeper. 'In different cultures, a man would be allowed to take a second wife if his first wife wouldn't give him children.' Satisfied at making her point, Nana took a huge bite of her cream scone and jam.

Victoria patted Patsy's knee to comfort her. She was also sad there were no grandchildren, but fate had dealt them both a bad hand. 'Oh, for goodness' sake, Nick. You've put the whisky decanter near Nana. No wonder she is being more spiteful than ever. Ignore her, Patsy, and you, Nick, try standing up for your wife once in a while. That might make a lot of difference.'

Nick could tell his mother was angry. This conversation about children had gone on far too long. Patsy had wanted tests, but Nick had refused – he didn't want to know if it was him who couldn't have children. And even though Nick was the one in denial, it was Patsy who always got the blame. Especially where Nana was concerned. A wave of guilt washed over him, and he avoided Patsy's stare. He felt guilty, he had deprived Patsy of children. He was the one who refused to see a doctor, or even discuss adoption. Thankfully, over the last few years, she had stopped talking about it but he felt helpless when his nana sniped at Patsy. He felt like a coward but said nothing. Patsy rarely contradicted his nana and accepted her comments without betraying him or blaming him in the process. Seeing the disappointment in his mother's face, he blushed slightly.

Picking up the decanter, Nick's mother put it back on the cabinet. 'Enough now, Nana,' she warned. 'You've had your fun and insulted everyone but Nick. But now, enough is enough.' Wagging her finger in the old woman's face, making her point, Victoria was angry. 'I will not have any more arguing.' Victoria had put up with Nana for years and the two women had come to a truce. That was until Victoria's husband had died last year. It seemed to have made Nana even more bad-tempered.

Victoria was determined to keep her husband's mother in the family, although it was hard sometimes. She had asked her time and again to live with her, but she had insisted on staying in Scotland. And to make matters worse, it was on one of the worst estates in Glasgow. It was a hellhole, but dynamite wouldn't get her out of it. It was her home, where she had raised her family, and she saw it in a totally different light to everyone else.

Nana just glared at Victoria and then looked towards Nick, who she hoped would take her side, but instead he shook his head with distaste. 'You are your own worst enemy, Nana,' he shouted across the room towards her. 'I love you, you know that, but one day that sharp tongue of yours will slit your throat. Our married life is our business, the same as your married life was yours. I don't want to hear any more of it, thank you,' Nick snapped. The smile from his face dropped suddenly and he threw her an icy glare, his green eyes glazing over as they bore into the old woman.

Lowering her head, Nana realised she wasn't only hurting Patsy but Nick as well in discussing their family. Or rather the lack of it. She knew she had overstepped the mark, because Nicky never snapped at her like he just had. She felt remorseful now. The last thing she wanted was to upset him.

Clearly upset, Patsy left the room in disgust and, jumping up, Nick followed her and stopped her in the hallway. 'Patsy, did you get the money?'

'I knew that's why you had come. It certainly wasn't to see me or that old witch through there! Yes, I got it and yes, I'm laundering it. As instructed. I wonder how your wonderful nana would feel about her beloved Nick being a crooked solicitor. Dear God, save the self-righteousness for those who are interested,' she spat out at him, shrugging him off.

'Don't be a silly girl now, Patsy.' Nick's face flushed with anger and his green eyes pierced her own. 'You'll get your share. What do you think pays for all of those fancy shops of yours, eh?' Nick glared at her. 'Just keep your mouth shut and show some respect. She's an old woman, after all. Now get back in there, drink your fucking tea and be polite.' Looking up, he saw Peters walking towards them. 'What the fuck do you want?' Nick rasped.

Peters looked towards Patsy and then turned and walked away. It wasn't his place to interfere, although he too hated Nick's arrogance.

Seeing the anger in Nick's face, Patsy nodded and struggled to free her face from his grasp. Both of them were breathing more heavily than normal. Emotions were high and tempers had risen. Patsy had been concerned about Nick lately. He had changed so much over the last few years. Nick was a cold, calculating man, who seemed to be permanently on edge these days, with his temper always at the surface. Luckily, he wasn't the kind of man to lash out at women, just a few harsh words, but something was obviously troubling him. She wished he would confide in her more, he seemed very distracted and very troubled. On the face of it, everyone presumed they were the perfect couple, but underneath the surface, being married to Mr Wonderful had proved to be a nightmare. Everything had been okay until he had been the defence solicitor for some drug baron, worth a mint. She didn't know all of the details but suddenly Nick had changed. Whatever had gone on between them had proved profitable to both sides.

After that case, Nick had money rolling in that he didn't know what to do with. He'd bought all kinds of businesses and laundered money through them all, including hers. Patsy knew whatever it was Nick was involved in, he was up to his neck in it.

The pair of them walked hand-in-hand back into the drawing room to sit with his mum and nana. There was tension in the air and tears were brimming on Patsy's lashes; Nick's face and neck were flushed.

'So, Nana. What would you like for your birthday?' Victoria tried her best to change the subject and ease the situation.

'I want to go home.'

'Come on, Nana, darling.' Nick knew she was stubborn and hardly a kind word left her lips these days, but he hoped he could charm her around.

'Well, if you're asking, Nicky.' She was slurring slightly, because even though Nick's mum had taken away the whisky, Nana had her own whisky flask underneath the shawl around her back. 'I'd like my bingo back.' She nodded.

'Bingo?' All of them looked at each other and echoed each other's surprise and shrugged. They knew she was as mad as a box of frogs, but this was something new.

'Yes, my wee ladies. My bingo.' The more she drank, the more her Scottish accent seemed to get thicker and thicker, to the point where they could hardly understand her.

Frowning, Nick asked again. 'Nana, I don't understand. Tell me about your bingo, why can't you go?' Glancing around the room, everyone shrugged. They had no idea what she was talking about.

'The community centre!' she shouted. Her face was flushed from the whisky and now she was shouting, her ruddy complexion made it worse. 'Every Thursday afternoon with my pals, my bonnie lad. It's all gone now. Council won't fix it.' She actually looked sad about it, the whisky was making her maudlin. Sitting there in her chair beside the log burner, her mind seemed to wander back to better days.

'Why do you insist on living on that council estate, Nana? Come and live here with us.' Victoria's voice softened. As much as she hated the old woman, she felt sorry for her, too. She was a strong, independent woman and had been someone to fear in her younger days. Her harsh, ginger hair was now mixed with stone grey, and her face was weather worn and lined. They had made sure she was never short of money, but she liked to fend for herself. So they topped up her pension account by drip-feeding money here and there so she wouldn't notice. She'd lived on Thistle Park Estate for sixty years and everyone knew her. It was a lot to ask for a woman of her age to give up her roots and change her lifestyle.

'My pals, Vicky lass. I want to be with my pals. I live there and I will die there...' Her words drifted off and suddenly she was snoring. The whisky had worked its magic and she was asleep.

Victoria put a blanket over Nana's knees and put her finger to her lips, indicating they should leave the room and let her sleep.

Standing up, Nick put his hands on Nana's shoulders and squeezed them lovingly. He loved the old woman; she seemed to be the only one who understood him. And he had fond memories of the school holidays he had spent with her in Scotland. Walking quietly out of the room, he turned and looked back. Seeing her dozing, he smiled to himself and pondered her words. He would like to do something for her in her twilight years. She wouldn't leave Glasgow and live here, but maybe he could give her something she badly wanted. She had always looked after him, maybe this was her dying wish. Her bucket list, who knows. On the other hand, she had just handed him a money-making scheme that he would never have considered before. His business mind was working overtime as he watched her sleep. He could hear the snoring coming thick and fast, but she had given him an idea. And everyone knew Nick Diamond would do anything for his nana!

The supposedly surprise birthday party Victoria and Patsy had organised for Nana was a great success. Everyone brought presents, even though they knew she would turn her nose up at them. But they all joined in with the celebrations and wished her a happy birthday.

The huge dining room and adjoining conservatory were full of people Nana didn't know. She sat at the table, bored, with only her whisky to keep her company. Sticking her rheumatic finger into the icing on the cake, she scooped it up and licked it, while the guests looked on, wincing at the sight. They definitely didn't want to take any home with them!

'You look like you're enjoying yourself, Nana... not,' Nick laughed, and pulled up a chair beside her, putting his arm around her shoulders and hugging her. 'I take it you're not impressed by all this.' Waving his hand in the air at around the sea of faces before them, he spied her sad face. He'd already realised that the only reason she was rude to people was to hide her sadness. The best form of defence was attack, isn't that what they say?

'I don't know these people, Nicky. Who are they? What do they know about me? Why do they want to celebrate an old woman's birthday that they hardly know? I'll tell you why, Nicky. For free drinks and food. To come to this great big show house and feel posh for the night.'

Changing the subject, Nick tried to comfort her. 'Tell me more about this community centre of yours, Nana. It sounds like an interesting place. What happened to it?'

The spark seemed to come back into her eyes as she thought of home. 'Don't you remember it, Nicky, laddie? The Christmas parties that were held there for the wee ones and someone off the estate dressed as Father Christmas. It was a magical place. Do you remember when you were a wee laddie, your father dressed up as Father Christmas and set up a small grotto for the wee ones. You had that elf's costume on with those bloody green and white striped tights.' Laughing out loud, she gripped his hand and wiped a tear of laughter from her eyes, 'I still have a photo of you with those tights on and those cardboard pointed ears we made.' Again she couldn't stop laughing.

Now it was Nick's time to reminisce as it all came flooding back. And he roared with the laughter. 'Oh, God, Nana, yes. How embarrassing. For God's sake, don't show anyone those photos. I remember that all too well. It was hilarious.' He hadn't thought about it for years, but now he remembered it well. He'd had good times there when he was a kid, but that was all behind him now. He'd fitted in with his parents' or rather his mother's ideals for him. He'd attended the private schools and fulfilled his parents' wishes by becoming a solicitor. His life was so very different now.

'So what happened to it, Nana?' curiosity and sentiment made him wonder.

Nana's Scottish drawl dropped to a whisper as she furtively glanced around the room full of guests. As she leaned closer to Nick's face, the smell of whisky almost knocked him out. 'Like the rest of us, Nicky, old age. The place fell apart – paint was peeling off the walls and some of the plaster had fallen off. That old kitchen they had, you know the one where all of us old women used to cook Scotch broth for the homeless, to warm their bones, well, it had to pass some kind of hygiene tests and of course it failed. I don't suppose the hole in the roof helped either,' she laughed, nudging him in the ribs. 'We used to organise clothes swaps too. Coat hangers were held up by nails in the walls with someone's old clothes hanging on them, but it didn't matter. It was a real place for the community to gather, you know?' For the first time that evening, Nana seemed to be enjoying herself. Taking another sip of whisky, she beamed. She was all smiles. Her once sad eyes sparkled with excitement.

'Clothing on nails in the walls.' Raising his eyebrows and laughing, Nick shook his head. 'And you wonder why the plaster fell off.' The pair of them burst out laughing. Other guests turned around to see what the amusement was. Victoria looked across the room and smiled. Whatever Nick had said to lift the mood, it had worked. At last Nana was smiling, laughing, even. Victoria breathed a sigh of relief and took a sip of her champagne and carried on talking to her guests.

'I'd hug you, Nicky, but my rheumatism hurts my fingers. You know how bad it gets. I need something to ease the pain.' Nana rubbed her rheumatic hands together.

Nick paused. He had always thought of his nana as a wily old woman, and he knew exactly what she was hinting at. Maybe he should have given her some earlier to keep his mother happy. It might have helped her efforts at the party. Looking around to see who was watching, he put his hand in the inside pocket of his jacket and reached out and squeezed Nana's hand, kissing it for effect, sliding the little plastic bag of marijuana into her palm.

Quickly, she grasped it tight in her hand then bent over and made the pretence of scratching the back of her leg, while slipping the small packet into her shoe. Again she smiled and gave a slight nod to Nick.

'I'd better do the rounds and say hello to the other guests. I hope you're feeling better soon, Nana.' Standing up, he flashed a smile at her and picked up his drink.

'I'm feeling better already, Nicky,' she giggled like a naughty schoolgirl.

'I saw that.' Patsy sidled up to Nick and whispered in his ear. 'Dealing in your mother's house? That's a novelty.'

'It's medicinal, Patsy, you know that. I should have given her it earlier, she might have smiled more.'

'And you just happened to have a packet on you? Don't make me laugh, Nick. I know you. Remember that.' Kissing his cheek before she walked away, Patsy painted on her best smile and thanked everyone for coming. It was getting late and everyone was itching to leave. They had done their duty by Victoria by turning up and that was enough.

At last the house was empty and the staff were clearing away the remnants of party poppers and plates of half-eaten cake. Victoria kicked off her shoes and sat on the sofa opposite Patsy, brushing away a streamer from the shoulder of her pale pink bolero jacket, which highlighted her blonde hair. 'Well, that went better than expected. Where's Nick?'

'I think he's gone up to see Nana and say goodnight. She went up before all the guests had left.' Victoria nodded and yawned, while stretching out her legs on the sofa. 'It's nearly midnight, time I joined her upstairs to Bedfordshire.'

'Me too. Do you fancy a nightcap before you go?' Walking to the drinks cabinet, Patsy poured them both a brandy. They were both shattered. It had been a long day, with little to show for it, but they had done their duty by Nana, even if she hadn't liked it. Patsy was playing for time. She knew what was going on upstairs and why Nick was taking so long. 'Has she ever been a nice woman, Victoria?'

Victoria let out a warm deep laugh and nodded her head. 'She must have been once because she got married! But she was a very pretty woman when I first met her. With her striking red hair. She reminded me of Lulu, you know, the singer. She was a petite little thing and those big brown eyes and long lashes of hers were to die for. Of course, I was never good enough for her darling boy. Mothers and sons, eh?' Victoria could have bitten her tongue. It was a feeling Patsy would never feel. 'And me being English as well didn't exactly make the path very easy. She's actually a very nice woman when she puts her mind to it. Just not to me or you!' They both burst out laughing.

* * *

'Right, that's it, Nana. Open the windows while you smoke it.' Nick had rolled the marijuana into a joint for Nana and he was also smoking a cigar. His mother hated smoking in the house, but the smell of his cigar would at least disguise the smell of Nana's marijuana.

'I will, laddie. I usually put it in my morning coffee, but this is better. Thank you, Nicky, my boy.' Taking his face in both of her gnarled hands, she looked at his handsome features and gave him a peck. He was her whole world. 'I love you, Nicky, you know that. You've always helped me.'

'I love you too, Nana. Now don't forget, open the windows and don't leave the end of that thing in the ashtray where the staff will find it. Sweet dreams, Nana.' With that, he blew her a kiss and left the room. Walking down the hallway, he entered his own bedroom. He was shattered. All that pretence in front of his mother's friends had worn him out. Pulling at his tie, he loosened it and took it off, undoing the top buttons of his shirt.

'You okay, Nick?' Patsy came into the bedroom, sat in front of the mirror and started taking off her make-up.

'Yes, just tired. What about you?' Sitting on the edge of the bed and taking off his shoes, Nick watched his wife. He hadn't looked at her properly for a long time. They both had busy lives and sometimes they just met in the hallway of their home as one was leaving and the other one was coming home. But looking at her now, she was a beautiful woman, he acknowledged to himself. She was tall, slim and had long dark hair that fell around her shoulders. He watched her slip out of her dress and let it drop to the floor, displaying a silk slip. He could feel a stirring inside him that he hadn't felt for a long time. It seemed like an age since he had held her in his arms. Standing up and walking towards her, he slipped his arms around her waist.

Surprised, Patsy looked up and met his eyes and their lips met. This was the loving, charming man she had fallen in love with. Their arguments were soon forgotten. They were both busy people, with busy lives. She knew they were both feisty passionate people who rubbed each other up the wrong way at times. But sometimes, like tonight, Nick rubbed her up the right way and this was the kind of passion she loved about him.

'Is that why you asked me if I was tired?' Patsy murmured as she nuzzled his neck and met his lips again.

'Maybe, do you mind?' His voice was low and husky, filled with desire. Slipping the straps of her camisole over her shoulders, he let it fall to the ground, displaying her nakedness. His hands roamed over her body as they held each other. Sweeping her up into his arms, he walked her over to the bed and laid her on top of it, quickly pulling off his jacket and ripping open his shirt, letting the buttons fly in opposite directions.

Patsy laughed like a schoolgirl as he pounced on top of her, searching for her lips, tweaking her nipples as her legs wrapped around him. As she felt the hardness of his passion, their kisses became more ardent and their excitement for each other's bodies was heightened with each stroke and caress. This would be a birthday party to remember!

* * *

Breakfast the next morning was a happy affair; even Nana forced a smile. Everyone was in high spirits and Patsy and Nick were like two love-struck teenagers. 'What's your plan for today, Mum?' Nick buttered his toast and waited for an answer. He felt he should ask and make conversation, they had hardly spoken since he'd arrived. He'd had an idea during the night and, although he had business to attend to, he didn't want to look like he was just running out of the door at the first opportunity.

'Well, I'm going to make sure Nana gets home safely. Thank you for coming, Nick, it's been a while since you've been home and you know I like to see you. You're still my son, after all,' she reminded him. No one else noticed the tension in the room between them. Victoria felt this charade was becoming tiring and wanted to end it.

Charmingly, Nick smiled through gritted teeth. 'I'll make more of an effort in the future.' Avoiding her stare, he turned towards Nana. 'And you, Nana. I'll come and see you soon too.'

Victoria sat back down at the table. 'What about you two love-birds? What are your plans?'

Nick cleared his throat as his mum poured more coffee. 'I have a meeting with the accountant today and then I'm in court this after-noon. Only a couple of cases, nothing special.' Nick brushed off his day nonchalantly.

'I have to go and check on the salons,' Patsy butted in. 'The builders are a little slow with the fittings for the new one and so I'm going to see them today. Maybe we could have dinner this evening, Nick?' Patsy smiled and squeezed his hand under the table. Her expectations of another night like last night excited her.

'That sounds good to me.' He winked at her and blew a kiss, catching her meaning. He felt satisfied. It seemed to him that all of the women in his life were happy and busy. Now it was time for business.

No sooner was breakfast over, he said his goodbyes, knowing that as Patsy had driven herself she didn't need a lift. Hugging his mother, he went over to Nana. 'I've popped a couple of things in your bag. One is for your rheumatism and the other is to buy yourself something you don't need,' he whispered in her ear.

Victoria waited while he did the rounds. 'Come on, you two, what are you whispering about?' she laughed.

Quick as a flash, Nana looked up. 'We're discussing the plans for your eightieth birthday party!'

Everyone burst out laughing, it was far too much to ask Nana to keep up the niceness for more than an hour or so. 'No doubt you will be there, Nana, I'm banking on it.' Victoria shook her head and poured some more coffee, leaving Patsy to wave Nick off at the door.

'Later, darling,' Patsy whispered. 'Drive carefully.'

'Wear something nice, Patsy, it will give me something to think about all day.' With that, he walked to his car and sped off down the driveway.

Now Nick had placated everyone, he could get back to his thoughts. He had tossed and turned all night, working out his plans for Nana's community centre. It was just what he was looking for. He needed to see his accountant, that would be his first port of call and the rest he would work out from there. His mind was working overtime as the ideas flowed through his brain. Without realising it, Nana had just provided the golden goose.

'Come in, Nick. Sorry to keep you waiting. Coffee?'

'No, Tom. It was just a quick consultation I wanted. Nothing major, strictly off the record.'

'I'm your accountant. Everything is strictly off the record,' Tom laughed. 'Take a seat.'

Nick drummed his chin with his fingers as he looked into Tom's eyes. Tom had been his accountant for a long time and he trusted this man. They had made a lot of money together. 'I was just thinking about charity donations. Is it right,' Nick continued, 'that charity donations are tax deductible?'

Tom nodded, doing his best to follow Nick's lead. Keeping up with him was the hard part. Looking towards the frosted glass door in his office and then glancing at the pile of folders on his desk that needed his attention, Tom wanted to finish this meeting as soon as possible.

Tom watched Nick in his well-tailored grey suit and black silk shirt. The top buttons of his shirt were open, showing his tanned chest. He didn't particularly like Nick Diamond, he felt he was arrogant and hid it behind a charming smile. On the other hand, Tom had to admit, Nick was an excellent businessman who brought him in a lot of revenue. They had never been friends, although they had known each other for years and he knew a lot about Nick, just by looking through his accounts, and knew there was more to him than met the eye.

He was paid well for his services, but there was that edge to Nick that unnerved him. 'As a solicitor, Nick, you know that. But, if you want it confirming: yes, charity donations are good for tax purposes... why?' Confused, Tom sat back in his chair and straightened his black tie. He knew Nick would know all of this, apart from anything else he would have done his homework before he got here.

'As you know, I have a few businesses here and there and so does my lovely wife Patsy, but how would I go about making a donation to refurbish a community centre in Scotland? Glasgow, to be precise.'

'A community centre?' Tom was very confused and coughed to clear his throat. Reaching for his water jug, he poured himself a glass. 'Well, I presume this community centre is owned by the council? Isn't it their responsibility? I don't understand...'

'You know I have some contacts in Scotland, Tom, and I hear they are having trouble regarding their community centre. It's the heart of the community and yet it's been left derelict. No wonder there is so much crime around if the kids have nowhere to hang out and the pensioners are lonely because there is nowhere to meet.' Nick sounded concerned about these people, which confused Tom even more. He was astonished at Nick's compassion to his fellow man! He knew Nick was a sharp-minded businessman, who always had an angle, but this was a side to him he hadn't seen before – maybe his assumptions about him had been wrong. Deep down, he was jealous of Nick, he didn't deny that. Fate seemed to have smiled at him. Whatever rundown business he bought always ended up thriving and his wife was beautiful. Tom liked Patsy, even though she had the same fiery temper as Nick – on her it looked beautiful, when her face was all flushed and her business head was firmly on. Maybe his dislike of Nick was based on his own insecurities.

Listening to Nick's crisp, articulate voice float around the office still confused him, he didn't understand what he was asking of him. Nick was a lawyer, he had all of the answers, so why was he going through Tom?

'Tell them to contact the council for funding – that should sort it out.' Tom smiled and shrugged. He felt he had answered Nick's question and held out his hand to shake Nick's. This conversation was going nowhere. It was time to end it.

Nick remained seated and ignored the proffered hand. 'The council won't touch it. It's been rundown for a long time. It's basically derelict.' Nick laughed for effect. 'It's my nana from Scotland, Tom. She would give her heart and soul to have the community centre refurbished so she can meet with all the other grannies. I would like to do this for her, but I would also be doing it for the community. Surely that would be worth something in a charitable donation?' Frowning, Nick looked at Tom for assurance. His smooth, articulate voice filled the room with authority. He liked watching Tom squirm. He was an expert accountant who knew the system and how to claim for everything in expenses, and he knew his place. But as a man, Nick felt he had no backbone. Day in, day out, Tom sat in his office, adding up other people's money – mostly Nick's!

He had no ambition, which is why Nick knew he could trust him with this matter. Nick mentally laughed as he watched the puzzled look on Tom's face. He didn't look any further than his columns of numbers. He was the right man for the job.

Shrugging, Tom shook his head. 'As I say, it's council property, Nick. It's up to them to refurbish their own property. Unless they were selling it, of course. Is it for sale? That would be a different matter. If you bought the place and donated it to the community then that would be a huge tax matter.' His curiosity roused, Tom nodded his head. 'Give me the details and let me look into it for you. I'll get back to you in a couple of days. If they wish to sell, do you want to buy?'

Nick let the smile spread across his face, showing an immaculate row of white teeth. He hadn't thought that far ahead; he'd only thought about having it decorated to make it useable again. But buy the place? That was an even better idea! 'If the price was right, Tom. Yes, I would consider it. The things we do for families and love, eh?' Looking at his watch, Nick stood up. 'Well, I have kept you long enough. And I have to represent some poor old sod in court. See what you can find out for me, will you? I will get all the information together for you and email you later today, if that is okay.' Nick shook Tom's hand and left the office. As he walked down the stuffy corridor, Nick punched the air. Buy the community centre. Lock, stock and barrel! Now that was a bloody good idea!

* * *

Although he was still tired from the party, along with the drive back home to London from Dorset, Nick had to be in court. He was shattered but work was work. He had a few court cases to deal with at the magistrate's court, and one particular case he had a keen interest in, which is why he didn't want to adjourn it.

On arrival at the court, Nick headed for the coffee machine, when he heard a voice. 'Mine's a black coffee, Nick, if you're buying!' Alan, another solicitor, shouted while he was at the vending machine.

'Have this one, it's all hot water anyway.'

'So, Nick, we need to talk. Walk with me. Your client is as guilty as hell. What are you prepared to settle on?'

'At worst, Alan, a suspended sentence. At best, dismissal. The evidence is weak and your witness is questionable.'

'You have got to be kidding me. It was assault, fair and square. How it never got to crown court is beyond me. It bordered on GBH, you know that. Why do you defend all of these druggie losers? Where is the money in it? Or has that silver spoon in your mouth made you feel charitable to the undeserving?' Alan scoffed and took a sip of the boiling black water they called coffee.

As the pair of them bantered, Nick looked up at the crowded corridor and saw his client and nodded to acknowledge him.

'My client is here, Alan. I can't see yours. I would check the toilets if I were you, otherwise I get my dismissal. And for the record, as you're making so much money as a solicitor, don't you think you should invest in some decent suits? That one has seen better days.' Nick's voice dripped with sarcasm.

'True, but who buys yours? Mummy had her credit card out again, Nick?' Alan shot back at him, but it was too late to get a reaction. Nick was already greeting his client and heading into court. Inside the courtroom, everyone was waiting and there was still no sign of Alan's client. The magistrate sat tapping his pencil and after a few minutes spoke up.

'I see your client hasn't turned up. I will adjourn this case for twenty-four hours. I suggest you contact Mr Morris and find out if he wishes to continue his case against Mr Diamond's client.' Turning to the clerk of the court, the magistrate asked if any messages had been left. The clerk shook his head.

Red-faced and apologising for wasting court time, Alan picked up his briefcase, thanked the magistrate and walked out. Nick pulled at the sleeve of his own client and steered him out of the court.

'Phew! Thank you, Mr Diamond. I owe you one. Do you think he'll turn up?'

'I doubt it.' Nick raised one eyebrow and nodded while shaking his client's hand. 'And indeed you do owe me one, James. I'll be in touch.' After seeing his client off, Nick couldn't help but to walk up to a forlorn Alan. Nick smugly stood watching Alan squirm under his gaze. Seeing his cocky face drop and burn with embarrassment in front of the judge was worth its weight in gold.

'Twenty-four hours and counting, Alan. You really did look like a prize prick. At least all of my druggie losers turn up. And for the record, I wasn't born with a silver spoon. It was made with pure diamonds!' Laughing loudly, Nick turned and walked out. He had better business to deal with. Next was the prison. It was his weekly visit and he didn't want to miss this either, although he cringed inside at the prospect.

* * *

'I'm here to see my client, William Burke.' After the usual checks, although they knew him well, the prison warder led Nick through the long corridors and up the worn, grey stone stairs of Wandsworth prison. It was an awful looking prison and carried the reputation to go with it. The overwhelming stench of disinfectant greeted him first. Then the sound of keys jangling and the noise from the prison made him cringe. It gave Nick chills just walking through all those doors being locked behind and in front of him.

At last, he was led to an open room, which resembled a school dining hall. His client, known as Billy, was sat at a table in the middle of the room. This was the one place they could speak freely. As Billy's solicitor, he was allowed to be alone with him while the guards stood outside the door.

'Mr Diamond, it's good to see you.' Billy winked at him. 'Did you bring any smokes?' The huge burly man looked up at Nick in expectation and held out his tattooed hand.

'Of course, here.' Opening his briefcase, Nick took out a couple of packets of cigarettes and laid them on the table. Along with those, he also had an open packet which Billy could smoke while they talked so as not to waste the extra packets. Cigarettes in prison were gold dust and a great bartering tool for whatever you wanted. They were better than money.

Although, since the smoking in enclosed spaces ban the prisons still had a few smoking rooms left for special cases, and all of the officers felt that Billy was a special case. Normally, the routine would be to escort him outside to the yard for a cigarette break. Billy was a chain smoker, and to take his cigarettes away was like taking a dummy from a baby. It would cause nothing but hassle and result in a fight. Once the officers had spoken to the governor of the prison they had all agreed to turn a blind eye and use one of the few smoking rooms they had left. Nick felt this was more of a concrete cupboard with a glass slit for a window, the only air conditioning which in his opinion never worked. Nick's sharp brain often wondered if the grating for the air conditioning was used for the officers to eavesdrop. It wasn't unheard of but they couldn't use it. that was entrapment.

Quickly lighting one up, Billy savoured the nicotine and blew the smoke into the air. 'This place is a shithole, Mr Diamond. Over-crowded and the food is crap. When are you going to get me out of here? I want to go back to Scotland.'

'I know, but it's easier for us to meet here. I never said it would be the Hilton hotel, but by rights, if and when they move you it will be to a Category A prison. Would you rather have that? I've had you transferred to a Category B prison, Billy. That on its own is an achievement. Anyway, how did Steve enjoy his first day at work in the pizza shop? Have you heard anything through the grapevine yet?'

Ignoring his complaints, Nick wanted the information he had come for. Nick didn't like Steve. His dealings with him, although indirect, annoyed him. He disobeyed orders and thought he knew better, and he wasn't paid to think. He was paid to do as he was told. Shit stirrers like him caused trouble and unrest amongst the workers and that was the last thing Nick wanted. He felt the best thing to do was offer a hand of friendship. A truce. Steve would end up dead in a gutter somewhere, Nick was sure of it. He'd make damned sure of it!

'He's okay. Keeping his head down out the back, clearing away and stocking shelves. About all he's good for. He's a spineless rat, Mr Diamond.' The rest of the sentence was an outburst of Glaswegian dialect which was too fast for Nick to follow, but he knew it wasn't complimentary.

A smug grin crossed Nick's face. 'Keep your friends close and your enemies closer, Billy. I've just been representing a friend of yours. James McNally, I hope everything is sorted there. Mr Morris has twenty-four hours to turn up before the case is dismissed.'

'McNally is a bastard! I don't know what your interest in him is, but I sorted it. Morris will have to take the cling film from around his face first and dig his way out if he wants to be there on time, Mr Diamond.' Giving him that knowing wink, Nick was satisfied.

'Jock isn't our concern any more either,' said Billy. 'He was taking too much of what he was supposed to be distributing. A dead weight. That is why I suggested we send a strong message to the Albanians who want to deal on our turf. One sniff too much of that stuff and Jock would be mouthing off. Nobody will be surprised he's gone, he always changed addresses when he was in trouble. Slimy rat.' Once again, Billy spat venom but Nick ignored him. He was used to Billy's ramblings now and he was getting sick of it.

'I'm about to arrange a dookit. It will take a couple of weeks or so, but I think it will be worth it in the long run. It will possibly need some help from you and your inmates, but that is what we pay them for, after all. Do you think you can arrange that?'

'A dookit?' Billy was surprised. 'Is that the Scottish in you coming out? A swanky London lawyer going back to his roots. How do you know what a dookit is? In one of those fancy dictionaries, is it? Aye, we can help with that, not a problem. I checked my bank account, everything is in order, Mr Diamond. Let's just carry on as normal, then.'

Nick smiled at this brute of a man. 'I thought everyone knew what a dookit was? A messenger service. A pigeonhole, that's the kind of thing, isn't it?' Nick grinned. 'Anyway, don't you trust me, Billy?' Billy might be a criminal, but he wasn't stupid. He might not trust Nick completely, but he knew he could make his stay behind bars even longer if he wanted to.

And why should Billy and his acquaintances trust him? Because he was a wealthy solicitor who only had their best interests at heart? Not a chance! It was because Nick could change their lives when they were facing a long stretch in prison. Every contact of Billy's that he had put forward had begged and pleaded with Nick for his help. And Nick had been like their priest. All of them had confided their innermost secrets to Nick and then Nick had worked his magic and greased palms amongst barristers, who didn't put up a fight for their own clients. Evidence had gone missing or the barrister had slipped up and not given their final speech in court as convincingly as he could have done. It had all been so easy. Money talked, and Nick was like their guardian angel. Favours passed amongst his colleagues, which in turn bought their silence. His colleagues' reasoning was simple. Why should they give a shit about a few drug dealers? They meant nothing to them and these low-lives would only end up behind bars one day, anyway.

But Nick saw another use for these men. And his grip on them was simple. Sometimes, the simplest things are the best. These men were the fall guys for his own criminal gain. He was an innocent man. All he had done was listen and with each confession these men had made to him, informing him where they had hidden money or a drugs stash, or possibly even committed a murder, Nick had recorded their guilt on his mobile phone and made duplicates of the recordings to be used as blackmail. His mobile had been recording when he had stepped into the interview room to be alone with them. He'd made sure they had given their full names before he started the recording so there were no misunderstandings. As shocked as they were, this kept them all in line, should they ever feel like disagreeing with him. Considering he had offered them a copy, they knew there were more. This was a sting in the tail they hadn't expected.

He had even told them that there were copies kept with his will, should anything happen to him, with strict instructions that they be handed over to the police. So it would be pointless killing him. He had warned them that it was better that he stayed alive, for all of their sakes, and they could all make money. They cursed him, of course, but they also knew that kind of information could put them behind bars for life, or worse still, let their criminal associates find out they had grassed them up. And everyone knew the penalty for that was death.

Nick's cool composure hid the anger rising inside him. Looking up at the door, he could see the prison warder looking through the pane of glass. Spying him, Nick opened his briefcase and took out some paperwork. After all, that was what he had come for. While they talked, it looked like they were discussing Billy's pending court case.

'I do trust you, Mr Diamond. Sorry. Your brain plays games with you in a place like this.' Billy took another drag of his cigarette and looked down at the table, almost subdued. He knew Nick held all the cards and there was nothing he could do about it. Life was okay in prison and, as long as he ruled it, it was even better.

He could get his hands on anything the other prisoners wanted. He'd been in prison so many times, they were like homes to him, and what was more he knew an awful lot of other prisoners in other prisons who owed him favours. 'I need three more of those mobile phones. I know it's not easy, but I'm sure you will find a way. And plenty of credit. The men can make their calls home, which they pay dearly for, and I have one for business. Can you top up the one I have already?'

'That's not a problem,' Nick nodded. He liked the mobile phone scam they used. It gave him full contact with Billy and if Billy was ever caught with it, the excuse was easy, he'd simply been contacting his solicitor. What could be more innocent than that? That is what the telephone records would show and Nick would be clear of all suspicion.

Taking another drag on his cigarette, Billy blew the smoke into the air as though in thought. Watching him intently, Nick paused. He knew Billy had something on his mind and usually it was of benefit to him. 'Use Midge's pigeons,' Billy whispered. 'He's been training them. They know the way from Scotland to this shithole. Hell, if they can find their way to Spain and back, shitty London is not a problem.'

Nick frowned; he had never heard this man mentioned before. 'And just who is Midge?'

'Midge is a good friend. You know him, he's helping run the mobile shop on the estate. That was a good idea of yours, by the way. It's making a lot of money.'

Remembering, Nick nodded. 'Oh, yes, Midge. He's doing a good job by all accounts. People need credit and they also need drugs. And we can give them both, Billy!'

'Just how many businesses are you going to buy, Mr Diamond?' Billy laughed.

'Billy, if you're doing well in business, you should always invest in another. That's how the supermarkets end up with a chain of them.' Nick could see Billy wasn't interested in the business side of things. Only himself.

'Well, you are going to have to think of another way of getting the phones in to me here. Sewing them into dead rats and throwing them over the prison walls is beginning to catch the eye of the warders. For fuck's sake, they will think there's an infestation. Thistle Park doesn't have as many rats as this place!' Billy roared with laughter and banged the table with his fist, which almost shook with the weight of the shovel that Billy called a hand. His hands were huge and fat, with sausage, nicotine-stained fingers. They made Nick feel sick. Nick looked up at the small viewing window, which was basically a spy hole on the cell door and saw the guard looking through again.

'Pipe down, you overgrown idiot. You're attracting attention.' Angry at the outburst, Nick's face flushed and his green eyes flashed with anger.

Billy looked behind him and saw the guard watching them. 'Sorry, Mr Diamond.'

'Now. Tell me more about Midge. I can't go to the mobile van, it's too suspicious. So how do I find him?'

Billy grinned. 'I'm not sure what his real name is. Everyone calls him Midge because of his wee size. He's one of those midget blokes. About three and a half foot. But he is one crafty criminal and great for getting into windows and the like. Aye, Mr Diamond. His hobby is racing pigeons, they go all over the place and God knows how they do it, but they all find their way home.' Smiling and stifling his laughter, Billy's shoulders shook as he nodded at Nick.

'For the record, Billy, it's dwarfism,' Nick sighed, correcting him and mentally thinking what an ignorant oaf the man before him was. How he had got through life amazed him. 'How would his pigeons carry mobile phones?'

Leaning forward and propping his elbows on the Formica table while lowering his voice even more, Nick was intrigued. Pigeons dropping mobile phones?

Billy sat back, enjoying the attention. His face beamed a satisfied smug expression. 'They don't drop them on the ground, Mr Diamond. Fuck, that would be a waste of time. They fly directly to the window. Now, Midge is no fool when it comes to pigeons and we have been practising. I put food out for the birds outside my windows and Midge has been putting weights on their legs to strengthen them. They do it all the time, it's not cruel or anything. By God, that boy loves those pigeons more than anything.' Billy grinned again.

'So how long have you had this scheme up your sleeve without telling me?' Raising his eyebrows, Nick was slightly annoyed. Billy always kept something in reserve, but his cocky attitude was beginning to annoy Nick.

'Och, a couple of months, laddie. You're not the only one with brains, you know. Stop getting your knickers in a twist. I'm telling you now, aren't I? Trust me, it will work. If not, well, I don't get any mobile phones. It's just as well it's not the early eighties, the mobile phones back then were like bricks. We would have needed a bloody ostrich for one of those.' Billy laughed, although he could see his light-hearted banter was not impressing Nick. Shrugging his shoulders, he leaned forward and lit another cigarette.

His chain smoking was beginning to make Nick's eyes water. Feeling agitated and anxious to get out of there, Nick wanted to end this visit. Billy was becoming more addled in the brain by the day. It was clear he was taking far too many of his own drugs that he sold in prison. 'Look, I'll sort the phones out and we'll talk more when I know more for certain. In the meantime, how do I get the mobile phones to this Midge? I meet no one, Billy, you know that.'

'Your usual place, Mr Diamond. Margaret Heap.'

'Very well, I'll speak to you in a couple of days.' Putting the unused paperwork back in his briefcase, Nick stood up and waved to the guard at the window to let him know he was finished.

'What about my court case, aren't we going to talk about that?' Shocked at Nick's dismissal, Billy's eyes widened. He was desperate to get out of there, but each time there was a hearing, there was always some excuse to prolong it.

'Not today, Billy. Rest assured, everything is in hand and your money is safely in your bank account, as you know.' Nick pointed his finger at Billy's face. 'I didn't put you here, Billy, you did.' Billy had irritated him and now he knew most of his contacts, Nick felt he didn't really need him any more. 'I'm just trying to help you out, but that takes time.' Seeing Billy's face drop made Nick feel better. He enjoyed reminding him who was in charge. He needed taking down a peg or two, but at the moment he was very useful and that was all that mattered.

7

PROBATION

Watching the clock on the wall as he stacked up more pizza boxes, Steve took his time. It was only fifteen minutes to the end of his shift and then he could go home. He didn't know if Sheila was going out again tonight. He hoped not, but they didn't discuss it. He felt sick to his stomach and had envisioned all kinds of things she was doing, but it only ended in an argument when he tried stopping her. He didn't like arguing in front of the girls and he knew how humiliated Sheila was that he had found out her sordid secret. Their lives were a mess, although at the moment, as long as they trod carefully around each other, things were calmer. Although he was on probation, his biggest problem was his probation with Sheila. He loved her, he always had. Nothing would ever change that. Sometimes it would be great if life was just black and white, but it wasn't.

He'd seen some of the old dealers he had hung around with come into the pizza shop. They had looked his way and sometimes nodded but didn't speak to him. Some of the old customers he had distributed to came in and just sat on a bench near the supervisor

Fatso Paul's counter. The counter was L-shaped and Fatso Paul had his own cash register and serving side.

Steve knew why they were there. They were picking up their allotted drugs to sell. He had done it so often in the past, he couldn't judge them. The dealers were paid on commission. They were given a fixed quantity of drugs and the price to charge and they would get a percentage of the takings. It was good business if you knew where to sell, and in the past he had. He had made a lot of money out of it and pissed it all up the wall or sniffed most of it up his nose. He'd been a fool and he knew that, and all he had was regrets. The only regrets he didn't have were Sheila and the girls. He'd let them down too many times and, as tempting as it was to resort to his old ways, he didn't want to do it. Some nights he'd lain awake thinking he should go back to dealing. He could clear all their debts easily, and it might even get this mysterious Glasgow boss off his back. He felt certain that this Undertaker and his men hadn't called a truce. They were playing for time, thinking he would be stupid enough to trust them again. And then what?

Steve wanted to laugh when he saw the customers come in and not ask for anything. They just took a seat on a wooden bench in front of Fatso Paul's side of the counter and waited for him to hand over a pizza box and take their money. That side of the counter was all cash. The main counter took cards, for any unsuspecting customer who actually wanted a pizza!

The clock eventually moved to the hour and Steve walked to his locker. Looking up, he saw his replacement getting changed. He was about to start a conversation with the man when Fin burst into the back. Steve found it strange that neither his replacement nor Fin spoke. There seemed to be some tension in the air. Possible rivals as to who got the best stash, Steve thought. Everyone wanted promotion in the dealing game. The better the product you had to sell, the more commission you made. It was plain and simple, but you had to prove that you were a good seller first.

'Home time, Steve. Get your apron off!' Walking past Fatso Paul's counter, they were both handed carrier bags, each containing a couple of pizzas or doner kebabs with chips. It was a bonus on their wages and Steve was pleased for it, at least it saved money and put food on the table.

'Is that it? Don't we get asked what we want?' Fin chirped up. He was showing off for Steve's benefit, but Fatso Paul wasn't having any of it.

'You want to choose off the menu, you little shit? Then you pay the full price. Give them back if you don't like them.' Fatso Paul was not impressed by Fin's cocky stance. If anything, it irritated him.

Glancing at Steve, Fatso Paul looked at the carrier bag he was holding. 'You don't want yours either?' Raising his eyebrows, he waited for an answer.

'No, that's fine with me. Thank you. I really appreciate it.' Steve knew better than to upset him. He was built like a brick wall. He never smiled and had conversations with himself while carving the doner meat. Steve steered clear of him – he felt he was very strange. Something not quite right in the head. The best way was to appease him: thank him and bugger off. Satisfied with his politeness, Fatso Paul turned around and filled another carton of chips and handed them to Steve.

'What about me?' Fin interrupted.

Scowling, Fatso Paul took the carrier bag off Fin without saying a word. Fin winked at Steve and smiled. 'It's all in the charm, Steve, mate.' Looking up at Fatso Paul, Fin grinned. 'I think I will have some of those chicken pieces. He'll sort my order out, Steve.'

Flabbergasted, Fin's jaw dropped when he saw Fatso Paul empty the contents of the carrier bag containing his free food into the bin.

'What are you doing? That's my dinner!' he demanded.

'No, it's not.' Fatso Paul's Greek accent seemed to get thicker as he got angrier. Steve had noticed that earlier in the week when one of the assistants had turned up late with a host of excuses. And in the end Paul had hurled a long string of Greek sentences and punched him so hard in the face the man had fallen back and nearly left his imprint on the plastered wall. He lay there unconscious and Fatso Paul had walked around the counter and poured a can of fizzy drink over him to stir him. 'It's okay,' he shouted. 'He's coming around, leave him there to rest for a while.' Everyone had done as ordered, as the man on the floor staggered to his feet, almost crawling. Waiting for the same thing to happen again, Steve backed away, pulling Fin's sleeve, and casting him a furtive glance to shut his mouth. Fatso Paul smiled directly into Fin's face. 'That's not dinner, its rubbish. Now go!'

Fin was no fighter so, accepting his fate, he swaggered out of the shop. He'd messed up and he knew it. Fatso Paul had friends in higher places than he did. Fin could have cursed himself. It was time he learnt to shut his mouth sometimes, he knew that, but the drugs he took didn't help. They made him loud and stupid, which was why he would always be a street dealer.

Walking out of the shop, Steve breathed in the fresh air. He stunk of chillies and tomatoes from the pizzas. Fin slapped him on the back and dangled his arm around his shoulders. 'Give us a chip. He's stingy, that fat bastard!'

Pulling a bag of chips out of the carrier, Steve offered him the bag. 'I wouldn't upset him, Fin, and you don't have to impress me. We're not kids any more. Christ, I'm middle-aged and so are you. It's time you started taking a proper look in the mirror!'

'Yeah, yeah. Tell it to the hand.' Ignoring his advice while digging his hands into the bag to take out a mountain of chips to stuff his face with, Fin carried on, 'Well, Steve, that's your first week over for you, your probation officer is happy, Sheila and the kids are happy. What about you?'

'It was better than I expected. Thanks for putting a word in, I appreciate it. Exhausting, though. Christ, people eat a lot of pizzas and kebabs around here. Does no one cook any more?' Putting a wisp of hair behind his ear, he took the proffered cigarette from Fin. 'I suppose, working in a food shop, I should have my hair cut.' Stroking his ponytail back, he looked in a shop window as they walked home.

'Nah! That's your signature tune, Steve. You've always had long hair. What with that and that old parker coat of yours, you're known as the hippy of the estate. Look at you, it doesn't matter how smart you dress, you still look like you've just stepped out of a commune.' Fin laughed. 'You're just out of touch, mate – you need some proper designer jeans and a leather jacket like mine.' He laughed. 'Do you want to meet later at mine for a few beers?'

Steve nodded and took a drag on his cigarette. 'Yes, I'd like that.'

'I have to pop to the shop first, but I'll see you in a couple of hours, yeah? I'll tell the others Sheila is letting you out.' Taking another handful of chips, Fin crossed the road, then started running up the opposite side of the street.

Knowing of old not to ask, Steve presumed he was meeting a dealer for something. It wasn't his business any more. He wanted to stay clean and get this tag off his leg! Walking along, swinging his bag, Steve almost laughed at Fin's comment about Sheila letting him out. To start with, he couldn't stay anywhere for long, not with this tag on his leg, and secondly, he doubted Sheila cared.

He felt Sheila was just waiting for him to let her down again and end up back in prison. She had no faith or trust in him any more. Deep down, she probably hated him, more than she hated herself. He wanted more than anything to get off that sofa and back into her bed, but he didn't push it. She was being groped by men nightly, the last thing she wanted was to come home to her safe haven for it to happen again.

The work at the pizza shop was simple enough, all he did was stack boxes and make sure there were enough bags of chips for chefs to cook. A couple of the chefs were obviously related to Paul the Greek, and they had been decent to him, although he knew they were all on their guard about saying anything to him. The Undertaker had seen to that, he was sure of it.

Night and day, that man played on his mind. Only once had he spoken to him. Well, he presumed it was the Undertaker. The chilling voice on the end of the telephone was something he would never forget. The voice wasn't Scottish. It was English, but the Queen's English. Each word that had been spoken had been crisp and articulate.

Steve shuddered when he remembered his time in prison. It had been harder staying off the drugs inside than it had been on the outside. Drugs were rife in prison, everyone knew that. He had been beaten up on a regular basis until, in the end, the prison had put him in solitary. He didn't tell Sheila any of this. It wasn't worth upsetting her any more. He could handle prison, he had been in and out most of his life, not only for dealing but robbery and GBH too. This had been his life for nearly thirty years. A week on the outside wasn't going to change things. He had to prove himself to everyone. What he really wanted was to get away from the area where he was known for his past. He would always be the ex-con Steve in this part of Glasgow.

* * *

Just as the florist was closing, Fin burst through the doors. 'I need a bouquet, any one will do. As cheap as you like,' he shouted at the woman as she was carrying buckets of flowers back into the shop.

'Hold your horses, laddie, let me put this down first. Janice will serve you.' Looking Fin up and down, she thought he looked like a pimp in his fancy sunglasses and leather jacket. 'You've only just made it before we close.' Picking up another bucket, the shop owner pushed past him and made a point of giving him a dig with her elbow.

'Well, I thought if I came late I would get some of your dead ones. Flowers don't last forever, you know.' Fin looked around at the buckets of flowers. Poking around in a bucket of carnations, he felt the petals and squeezed and poked them around a bit. 'These look half dead. They won't last until tomorrow. I'll give you a couple of pounds for a bunch.'

'You cheeky bugger, my flowers are all fresh, thank you very much! And stop pulling the petals off or I will charge you for them as well. Anyway, I thought you said a bouquet?'

'What's the difference? Flowers are flowers. Come on, lady. Give us a discount, it's the end of the day.' Doing his best to charm his way into the florist's affection, he flashed a smiled.

'That smile wouldn't be half so bad if you actually had white teeth. Or even more of them. I'll give you six carnations for three pounds and that's the ones you've just pulled the petals off,' she scoffed, ignoring his flirting.

Ignoring her slight, Fin nodded. 'Done! Wrap them nicely, will you, so they don't look like fish and chips. I've seen your flowers before.' He couldn't resist having a dig back at her after her insults. Fishing for the money in his pocket, he laid it on the counter.

'If you don't like them, don't have them.' Wrapping the carnations roughly in some floral paper, she handed them over and took the money off the counter, handing it to young Janice, who was cashing up the day's takings. The well-rounded florist stood there with her hands on her hips, waiting for another comment from Fin. She could see by the baseball cap turned backwards and his damned mirrored sunglasses that he was the kind of person who had to have the last word. Seeing him turn to walk out, she heard it.

'Fat cow,' Fin muttered under his breath as he left the shop. Looking at his watch, he saw he only had twenty minutes. Taking the three mobile phones out of his pocket, he pushed them deep into the bunch of flowers. As far down to the bottom of the paper as he could manage, then he ran as fast as possible to the cemetery. The gates were closed, so he climbed over the top. The jump from the top sent him sprawling on the floor, making him wince and hop a bit on his aching leg. He picked up his flowers and mentally crossed his fingers that the mobile phones were okay after climbing over the gates.

Running around like a madman, Fin searched for the grave marked Margaret Heap. He bent over, holding his stomach, trying to catch his breath. It felt like daggers stabbing in his sides as he tried to breathe. Finally, he found the grave and laid the flowers down. Looking around, he saw no one, but he knew someone would be watching and waiting for him. Walking slowly to catch his breath, he jumped at the large wrought-iron gates and climbed over them again. Landing on his back, he banged his head and felt a warm sensation which he presumed was bleeding. Reaching up his hand to touch the back of his head, he saw the blood on his fingers, but it wasn't much. Lying there on the ground for a couple of minutes to catch his breath, Fin was angry with himself. If he ever had to do this again, he wouldn't dawdle with Steve. He would get here a lot earlier and not climb those bloody gates!

Picking himself up, he looked around and swiftly walked home. Whatever was going on, he didn't want to be spotted. He'd done his job and taken the money and the note that had been left in his locker, and that was enough. He'd even gone so far as to eat the small piece of paper with the instructions written on it. They had been simple: *Margaret Heap RIP*. He knew what cemetery it was, because that was his contact point with his dealer as well as the pub. But he wouldn't be looking for a headstone in Chalkie's shitty pub, that was for sure.

Fin was right, someone had been waiting for him and was watching him. Waiting for him to leave, she chuckled when she saw him fall flat on his arse. Served him right, he was nothing but an upstart and his gran would be mortified if she knew how he'd turned out. Everyone presumed that his gran was his mother who had had him late in life, but she wasn't.

At some point, Fingers Fin, as he was known because of his permanent shoplifting, had been dropped off at his gran's house and no other family was ever mentioned. When she had died, he had never informed the council and even had the cheek to keep collecting her benefits. He had no shame.

Stopping at Margaret Heap's graveside, the person watching picked up the flowers. When she got close to the caretaker's hut, she unwrapped the flowers, took out the mobile phones and threw the flowers in the bin. Taking off the green council jacket, she left it on the door handle, where she had found it. Then she parked the bin at the side. Everything was in order. As the daylight faded, she walked towards the side gate and left. Fortunately, the rusty lock had not worked properly for a long time, but as no one ever used this entrance, apart from the caretakers, no one had bothered to fix it. She would pass the phones on to Midge as planned when the mobile shop came, and he would give her the money she had been promised for collecting them.

'Maggie! What are you doing all the way out here? I thought it was you.' Maggie almost jumped out of her skin when she saw Kim from the launderette.

'Oh, I just had an errand to run.' Trying to compose herself, Maggie held on tightly to her bag containing the mobile phones. Kim was a gossip, everyone knew that. She had to make her alibi plausible. 'Look, Kim. I had to pop to the doctors, ladies' problems, you know what I mean?' Giving Kim a knowing nod and a wink, Maggie moved towards her and linked her arm. 'I would rather no one knew about it, if you know what I mean...' Maggie gave her arm a squeeze.

Frowning, Kim's face showed concern, but she knew better than to pry. She had been lucky to get this amount of information from Maggie. She was a closed book.

'I had better go, it's starting to get dark and the buses don't go up to the estate any more.' Waving, Maggie walked on. Her heart was pounding in her chest. She wished she hadn't agreed to pick up the mobile phones, although she didn't know what they were for. There had been a delivery for her the day before, which had contained a note that had given her instructions about collecting the mobile phones and making sure no one saw her. It had said that if she wouldn't do it, she was to hang a single T-shirt on her washing line. She hadn't dared put any washing out all day, in case whoever was spying on her got the wrong message. The note had also said they would pay her £500 for her trouble. All she had to do was pass the phones on to Midge who worked in the mobile shop, and once she had done that he would pay her.

Maggie knew she was in deep with whoever had contacted her, but whoever it was seemed to trust her, which made her feel safe. This wasn't the first thing they had asked of her, but anything they asked never put her in danger and £500 was a bloody lot of money. Whatever favours they asked of her, they were always prepared to pay, even though she owed them much more and would be forever grateful to them.

* * *

'Hey, Steve, are you in?' There was a bang on the door, and when Steve opened it, Fin stood there with a six pack of lagers. 'It's getting late, so I thought I had better pop around to see you. What time is your curfew?'

Steve's heart sank. He was pleased to see Fin, but he didn't really want him around. He always seemed to bring trouble with him and that was the last thing Steve wanted.

'Is Sheila not in?' Without invite, Fin walked in and through to the lounge.

Embarrassed, Steve shook his head. 'Erm, no, she's popped to a friend's so I'm babysitting.' He smiled. How could he tell Fin she was on the game? He didn't even know which cemetery she was at – even when he had asked her, she said she didn't know until they got there so there was no point in asking.

Even though he had been pensive, Steve enjoyed his catch-up with Fin. They talked about their school days and had a few beers. The pair of them avoided discussing the night Steve had been arrested and Fin had done a runner, leaving him behind to face the music. Steve had never grassed Fin up; it wasn't the done thing, and the consequences could have been worse than what he had faced already. As usual, Fin was boasting about his girlfriends and his sordid sex stories. Some were imaginary and others were usually prostitutes, although this time Steve felt he couldn't throw stones at glass houses. After all, where was his wife now?

Looking at the clock, Steve realised the time and knew it was time to get rid of Fin before Sheila got home. He started to yawn. 'Blimey, Fin. I'm not used to having a few beers. I can't take my drink any more,' he laughed. 'It's been a long week, I'm ready for bed.' He knew it sounded abrupt and rude, but he was starting to panic inside. He didn't want Fin seeing Sheila in her hooker's clothes and make-up, and usually when she came home her knees were muddy or grazed. He was embarrassed, not only for her but for himself. Watching his wife go out and sell her body and doing nothing about it while she paid off their debts – that was how other people would see it.

'Yes, sure, give you a few more weeks and you will be able to finish that whole pack off on your own. You need to get back into the swing of things, eh, mate? Anyway, you never said how your first shag was after all that time in prison?' Fin laughed.

'Fuck off, Fin,' Steve laughed. He felt on safer ground now. That was Fin's sense of humour. He always thought with his dick in mind. Nothing had changed. Steve couldn't help laughing. 'Why the hell do you think she's gone out? It's to give her a rest!' As the lies rolled off Steve's tongue, he could only wish they were true.

Still laughing as Fin left, Steve closed the door and took a sigh of relief. The only thing to do now was put the kettle on and wait for Sheila to come home.

* * *

Anxiously, Maggie waited for the sound of the mobile shop horn. Running out of the door to get there first, she stood there while the shutter went up. Almost throwing the mobile phones that were carefully wrapped in a small towel under the hatch without being seen, she waited. 'For God's sake, hurry up,' she snapped. Hearing her voice, Midge stuck his head through the hatch. 'Have you got something for me?' she enquired.

Midge handed her a box of cornflakes, which confused her, until he gave her an icy stare. 'Here's my customers,' he shouted while rubbing his hands together. Taking the box, Maggie walked away and, once inside her flat, she put the box on the table and felt disappointed. That was until she saw the Sellotape along the top of the opening. Curiously, Maggie stripped away the Sellotape and grinned. Through the plastic containing the cornflakes, she could see a stash of cash. Kicking herself as she counted out the money, she realised how stupid she had been. Of course no one was going to hand over that amount of money in front of other customers! Talk about giving the game away. She had been so anxious and nervous, she hadn't been thinking properly. Picking up the money, she kissed it.

8

THE PAST IS THE FUTURE

As Nick walked into his apartment, the telephone was ringing. Picking it up, he could hear the accountant on the other end babbling on. 'What is it?' Nick snapped. After his long day, he didn't need any more aggravation. He just wanted a nap and a shower before Patsy came home.

'Mr Diamond. I checked out that community centre you were asking about. You were right, it's a derelict building – are you still interested?' the accountant asked tentatively.

Nick's mood softened. Hopefully this was good news. 'Yes, I'm still interested. I knew it wouldn't be up to much. So who did you speak to and what did they say?'

'In short, Mr Diamond, the council are prepared to sell it. It's going to cost them too much money to fix and they feel when they do it's only going to get trashed by the residents again. In simple terms, they want it off their hands and if someone is mug enough to buy it, they can have it.'

'You're the accountant. Is it worth what they are asking for it?'

'I think you need to get a surveyor on it first. They have their own but personally I would request an independent one. And the final price would depend on that report – they are currently asking for £80,000, but I think you could get it cheaper. I also told them it was going to be a charitable gift to the community and that made them feel better. But it has hardly any roof, so it's probably got damp – I can't say how much it will cost to sort it out. Keep in touch and let me know what you think.'

Nick was beaming. That was the best news he'd had all day. After thanking Tom, he put the telephone down and punched the air. Nick liked it when a plan came together and by the sounds of it, this one was going to be worth its weight in gold. What's more, it was legitimate.

Now all he had to do was work out how to get rid of Billy. The truth was that he was never going to be released from prison. Over the last eight years, Nick had learnt more than enough from Billy, who was stupid enough to spill his guts with all of his bravado. Nick had taken over the running of things and now Billy was surplus to requirements. Nick's new client, James McNally, had friends in low places and he owed him a favour or two. Billy would be well and truly out of the picture in no time.

Nick lay flat on his back, spread-eagled on top of the bed in the coolness of the bedroom, staring at the ceiling as the fan rotated above him. As it cooled his body, he let his mind wander. Had it really been eight years since he had befriended Billy Burke? He cast his mind back to that fateful day, when his world had been turned upside down in a moment...

It had been one of the few times that Nick and his mother had sat together in the family home. He loved his mother, but being away at school for most of his life hadn't created a close bond between them.

'Nick, I want to talk to you,' she had said that day. 'I need to speak with you while we are alone.' She called him into her own private parlour, away from the prying eyes of the staff. As she sat pouring coffee from the porcelain coffee set, with its small dainty cups and saucers, Nick had waited. There was usually a reprimand of some kind when his mother wanted to be alone with him, but for the life of him this time he couldn't think what it could be.

Handing him the cup and saucer, she took a breath. 'What I am about to tell you isn't good, but it needs to be said. Your nana doesn't know what I'm about to tell you, but it seems the past has suddenly become the future.' Her voice was subdued.

Curious now, Nick put down his cup. 'You make this sound like a confession, Mum. What is it?'

'I wasn't prying, son. Really, I wasn't,' she stammered. She was nervous and didn't know where to start, but she had no option. 'I saw your work files in the study and noticed you have a new client. William Burke, is that right?' Avoiding his stare, Victoria looked down at the carpet.

'Yes, he's a new client. I've been asked to take on his defence. But why should that concern you?' Nick asked.

'You can't defend him, Nick. You just can't! The man is... well, he's your father!' Victoria blurted out the words she had kept a secret for many years. She was ashamed of her past but she felt it might solve the problem of children between Nick and Patsy, who were still childless. Early on in their marriage, Patsy had talked with her about adopting a child, although she seemed to have given up on the idea now and her salons were her babies. Over the years, they had both accepted the fact; it was only Nana who kept bringing the subject up. It was her own venomous weapon against Patsy. Victoria wasn't even sure they wanted children. They were both busy people with busy lives. She also hoped it might make Nick feel better. It obviously wasn't him, because there was nothing wrong with Billy Burke's ability to produce children, that was for sure. It seemed he could make kids at the drop of a hat. Nana was so sure that there was nothing wrong with her side of the family and yet Victoria knew she had never got pregnant with her husband, Nana's son. Victoria was afraid. What if Billy remembered her and realised Nick was his son? She needed to tell him first and get him to listen. Depending on what lies and poison Billy would spin, she could lose her only son forever. Nick's whole life was based on lies, she needed to tell him her side of the story while he was there to listen.

Stunned, Nick had sat there. His head had felt like it was going to burst. He felt sweaty and loosened his tie for fear of fainting. Surely this was a bad joke? His mother had continued talking and although he could see her lips moving, he wasn't taking in what she was saying. The man he loved, his father, was not his father at all and his mother was nothing more than a deceitful slut!

His mouth felt dry, and he could feel a lump rising in his throat. 'Why are you telling me this now? That is, if it's even true?' Hopefully, he had searched her face for some kind of indication that it wasn't true.

'We hadn't been married that long,' she continued and reached for the cigarette box on the coffee table. The lighter was a block of square glass. It was all very classy but now mentally Nick felt how tacky and tarty his mother looked, dressed in her two-piece pale pink suit with matching shoes. She had always portrayed the lady of the manor, but it seemed it had all been a lie.

Now she had started, Victoria had wanted to finish, no matter what he thought about her. 'We'd gone to Glasgow to visit Nana. Your father and I had argued. The same argument that Patsy and Nana have about children. I know how Patsy feels, Nick,' his mother stressed. She reached out for his hand, but he didn't move. His beautiful green eyes bore into her coldly. 'In the end, I stormed out. I was very upset and in floods of tears as I ran down that stone staircase to the bottom of the flats. At the bottom, I bumped into Billy. He had grown up with your father, they were friends. We all knew each other, so seeing that I was upset, he took me to his flat. I didn't see anything wrong in it, I had been there before.' Victoria looked up. She waited for an outburst. Nick's face was set in stone as he listened to his mother's confession.

He felt crushed. His whole life had been a lie. His mother had built the family unit on a lie. He was disgusted but, more to the point, he was hurt. Fighting back the tears that were brimming in his eyes, at last he spoke up. 'So this man offered you tea, sympathy and a good fuck to pass the night away and make you feel better. I can guess the rest, don't bother going on. Does my father know? Or rather, the man I thought was my father! Does he know?'

Victoria's face was burning with shame, and she shrugged. 'We've never discussed it.' Bursting into tears, she reached for a hanky. 'Once I was pregnant, it seemed to solve a lot of problems. You were the solution. I'm sorry, Nick, I really am.' Tears rolled down her face and her hand was trembling as she tried to hold her cigarette. She didn't like smoking in the house, but this was one of those times when it didn't matter. 'To be honest, I don't remember having sex with him. We'd had a few whiskies, and then the rest seems muddled.' She sniffed and blew her nose.

'Did you ever love me? Or am I, as you say, the solution to your problems?' Shaking his head, Nick stood up and wandered around the room a little. He was lost for words. 'So you recommend that Patsy go out and fuck one of my friends, do you?' He laughed, sarcasm dripping from his mouth. He wanted to hurt his mother and make her feel some of the pain he was feeling now.

'Oh, for God's sake, Nick, don't ever doubt my love for you. You're my baby, my little boy. I love you very much and so does your father.'

'Why are you telling me this now? Do you want absolution or something before you die?' he shouted, which turned into hysterical laughter. 'There's no need to tell me this, unless it's for your benefit.'

'There is, Nick. After all, Diamond isn't a common surname. Billy will put two and two together when you defend him. He's not a stupid man. He'll remember that night, I'm sure of it. I don't know if it ever crossed his mind, or indeed if he thought about it ever again. But on the slim chance that he does, I don't want him telling you or taunting you. I would rather you heard it from me.'

'Do I look like him? What kind of a man is he?' Curiosity was creeping in for Nick now.

'No, you look nothing like him. There is no resemblance, not even in manner. You are very much your father's son, Nick – the man who raised you and loved you. Even though Billy and your father were friends, they both went their separate ways regarding the law. Your father wanted to better himself. He had ambition where Billy had none. He hung around in the wrong crowd. If he was a law-abiding citizen, you wouldn't be working out his defence, would you?' Keeping her voice as calm as possible, Victoria knew what Nick was thinking. He hated her and there was possibly no way of ever making this right. But he was a man now, whatever he did regarding her husband or herself was his decision.

'I ask just a couple of things of you, Nick. Please don't bring that man back into our lives,' she pleaded. 'And please try to understand and forgive me. It was a stupid mistake.' Brushing away another fall of tears, Victoria's face was now red and puffy.

'You're in no position to ask any favours of me!' he shouted. 'You're a lying fucking whore!' It had turned into a heated argument and his mother had begged him to lower his voice, in case the staff heard him. 'I'm leaving,' he half screamed at her, ignoring her pleas. He picked up his briefcase and stormed out of the room and got in his car. His head was spinning. Stopping his car at the side of the road, he sobbed. The pain felt like knives stabbing his stomach and he felt sick, as his shoulders shook with each sob that wracked his body. Although he was a man, he felt like a child again. Life was cruel.

Once back at his London apartment, Nick had poured himself a stiff drink and swallowed it back. Then he poured himself another one. He wanted to get drunk. He wanted to blot out what his mother had told him. His life had fallen apart in one conversation.

Looking down at his briefcase, he had seen Billy's folder and picked it up. He was curious now and wanted to meet this man – his father. Pouring another drink, he sat down on the sofa and opened the folder. Page after page became one court case after another. This was his heritage? A criminal who had spent most of his life in prison at one time or another. Now Nick was intrigued and Billy's newly appointed lawyer, he was in a good position to meet him. Fate was a strange thing, he decided. He hated the man already, but curiosity spurred him on.

The sound of the mobile shop's horn blowing as he entered the forecourt of the flats sent shivers down Steve's spine, but his daughters jumped with excitement when they heard it. He didn't want them using it any more, but Sheila hadn't told him exactly how much money she still owed them. He was glad it was payday as it seemed to lighten the mood and he could pay off something of what she owed.

She still disappeared some nights, but they didn't talk about it. He felt like a pimp and didn't like that feeling. Sheila had begged him not to go down to the mobile van and cause a scene when he had threatened to sort this mess out once and for all. She had come up with all kinds of arguments that made sense but didn't make him feel any better. She had stressed that he was on probation and if he started a fight, he could end up back in prison and she would be back to square one. His hands were tied.

'Go and get some pick 'n' mix sweets, girls, and get your mum some too, she likes those, though God knows why.' Handing Penny a ten-pound note, he watched her run with all innocence out of the door, hand in hand with Sharon.

Watching over the balcony, he saw the usual queue at the van. It was the same old faces, day in and day out, and it depressed him. He didn't want to go down there for fear of what he would do. At last, he saw Penny and Sharon making their way back into the flats.

'Where's my change?' Standing there with his hand out, Steve waited for Penny to hand over what was left of his money.

'There isn't any. The man said he would take it off your bill. Here's Mum's sweets.' Running into the lounge, Penny and Sharon sat down to watch their favourite cartoons. His whole body sank as he sat down into the chair at the table.

They were no better off. Thankfully, the pizza manager had given him a couple of pizzas, which was usually a bonus for the people who worked there. Ten pounds out of his wages had just disappeared in a puff of smoke. Looking at the white paper bag on the table with Sheila's sweets in, he put his hand in and took one. He needed some kind of sugar rush. He noticed a blue felt tip pen mark on the side of the bag. It was only a dot, but it made him suspicious. He didn't know why, but he felt a sense of foreboding. Emptying the contents of the bag onto the table, he looked at it in despair. There was a small plastic bag in it with two pills inside. Looking at them closely, he didn't know what they were, but he knew it was drugs. So that's why the bill from the van was so high! Sheila was on drugs and he had never even noticed. God, what a fool he was. He must be the laughing stock of the estate.

As though on autopilot, he started making some chips for the girls' tea to go with the leftover pizza. At least there was food on the table. He heard the front door open. Sheila was struggling through it with two large plastic bags of freshly washed clothes. She was complaining about the number of stairs she had climbed and how heavy the laundry was.

'Why didn't you ask me to take it? I could have dropped it off on my way to work and picked it up on my way home.' Wanting to sound as normal as possible in front of his daughters, he gave her a weak smile. 'It must give you quite a headache, sat there in the wash house for so long and then the long walk home. Here, take something for your headache.' Reaching across, Steve put the two tablets on the table in front of her with a freshly made cup of tea. 'I'm sure these will help.' Tongue in cheek, Steve hid his sarcasm as best as he could, although inside he was blazing with anger.

Stunned, Sheila sat there and picked up her mug of tea. 'Not now, Steve, I don't need it. All you have done since you got home is complain. Why did you ever bother coming back?' Picking up her tea, she stormed off to the bedroom and slammed the door behind her.

'Is Mummy okay?' Penny looked up at Steve as she poured tomato ketchup on her chips. The worried look on her face made him feel guilty.

Ruffling her hair, he laughed. 'Of course she is. Mummies just get grumpy sometimes after a long day, especially after carrying those bags up the stairs,' he lied. He knew he had to do something about this and there was only one man he could turn to for help. Fin would be up to his neck in this, he knew that for sure.

After an hour or so and more cartoons, Sheila emerged from the bedroom. The uneasy silence between them as she slammed around the kitchen and got the girls washed for bed made Steve wish she had stayed there. He knew there was going to be another argument and waited patiently for the girls to go to bed. But he had to get to the bottom of it. All he had faced since he got home was secrets and lies.

'Not going out tonight, then?' he asked with the same coldness he was greeted with.

'None of your fucking business. It's my business! You never considered me while you were robbing houses and being a street distributor with your drugs, did you?'

'How long have you been on them, Sheila?' His voice softened. She always threw his past in his face and he knew he probably deserved it. 'What are they? What are the pills?' he pushed. 'I thought we'd agreed to make a fresh start.'

Her face flushed with embarrassment, she had no real reasons, just excuses. 'They are whatever they can get their hands on, Steve. Sometimes diazepam, opioids and amphetamines. That kind of thing,' she confessed. 'I tried my best the first year you were in prison, but after that I became fed up of living hand to mouth. Those tablets make me feel better, even for a short time.'

Sitting beside him on the sofa, Sheila felt deflated and buried her head in her hands. She had hidden so much for such a long time, she didn't know where to start. She had never intended to be an addict, it just kind of crept up on her. When she told one of the women on the estate how she was struggling mentally and physically, she had given her one of her own pills to make her feel better. And after taking a couple more, she'd been told that if she wanted more, she would have to pay for them like everyone else.

She had been climbing the walls with anxiety and depression. It hadn't occurred to her to see her doctor. She thought it would make her look like a bad mother and not able to cope. She was afraid social services might take the girls off her.

'The woman on the estate.' Sheila held her hands up in submission. 'She obviously told the mobile shop about me and he started giving me the pills on credit. They are called pick 'n' mix because you never know what you're going to get! Everyone around here knows what a pick 'n' mix is – except you, Steve. The woman who gave me that first pill, she's a distributor for them and that's how they rein you in. They drip-feed you one every now and again until you depend on them. Isn't that how it's done? That's how you distributed them, wasn't it?'

'Yes.' Bowing his head in shame, Steve knew it to be true,

because he had done the same thing when he was a street distributor. It was the worst act of kindness you could give someone. Helping them become an addict until they owed you their life. For the first time since he had been home, Sheila put her arms around him and hugged him. Tears rolled down her face. She had needed him, and he hadn't been there, and she had crashed! She had been in dire straits and these druggies had been the only people supposedly trying to help her.

'This unknown woman you speak of.' He trod softly, not wanting to upset her again. And to be honest, he was enjoying being in her arms. 'I presume she was a friend of Fin's?' With his arms around her so tightly, he couldn't see her face. It was her shoulders and back he was talking to. This seemed to make it easier for her. She didn't want to look him in the eyes and confess. Feeling her nod her head and sob, he felt satisfied. If nothing else, they were breaking down the barriers between them and that was a start. He wasn't starting his shift until the next afternoon, and he decided, as Sheila lay in his arms that night, that he was going to go down to the mobile shop and tell them where to shove their sweets!

* * *

The next day, Sheila popped out and Steve nervously waited for the sound of the horn. As predicted, it came at midday, echoing around the estate. Running down the stairs, he ran to it and was the first one there. He didn't recognise the man serving behind the makeshift counter. It wasn't one of the old crowd. Angrily, he stormed up to the front and shouted. 'Oy, you bastard, stay clear of my wife and kids. We don't want your overpriced shit and we owe you nothing. You've been paid back threefold!' Reaching up to the open shutter that was the counter, he pulled on the man's shirt, pulling him downwards and closer to his own face. 'Do you hear me, you bastard? Stay away from my family,' Steve spat out. He was angry. The man looked at him in ignorance as though he didn't understand him. The queue behind him was getting longer by the minute and people were tutting and waiting for him to move on.

Turning to the crowd behind him, Steve shouted, 'Do you lot really want the wrong bag of his pick 'n' mix sweets falling into your kids' hands? Are you all fucking crazy, you drugged-up bastards?' No one answered him. If anything, they looked bored with his outburst. Turning back to the man at the counter, Steve was shocked to see that he was suddenly looking down the barrel of a shotgun. At the side of the man whose shirt he had grasped was what looked like a ten-year-old boy pointing a gun at him. Instinctively, Steve let go of the man's shirt and stepped back.

'Fuck off, mister, and take your big mouth with you,' said the boy holding the gun. On closer inspection, Steve saw it wasn't a child, but a very short man. The face was much older, possibly late twenties or thirty, but he could barely see over the makeshift serving hatch. No one could see him behind the counter unless he wanted to be seen, and this was one of those times.

'So pull the fucking trigger if you want to!' Steve shouted. 'That is unless you need Snow White and your six other mates to tell you what to do.'

'Fuck off, Steve, you're not wanted around here. No one wants you here.' The slow words of the man behind the counter echoed in Steve's brain. He knew his name and yet they had never met. Pointing the gun downwards to the concrete floor, he fired it. The explosive sound made everyone run in opposite directions for cover. Dust and concrete flew in the air as Steve threw himself to the ground and curled up into a ball to protect himself. He knew the next shot would be for him, but it didn't come.

'We're closed for today. We'll be back tomorrow.' With that, the shutter to the serving hatch was pulled down and the van drove away.

'You interfering bastard, now look what you've done,' someone shouted at him. The crowd turned on Steve. They were shouting and spitting at him as he lay there helpless. As he tried to stand up, one man came up to him and kicked him in the face, hurling him backwards on to the floor. As he curled himself up into a ball again, kicks and punches were rained upon him by this pack of dogs, until eventually they all started to retreat and left him lying on the floor, covered in blood and cuts. Doing his best to stand up, Steve staggered to the main flight of stairs that led up to his flat. With each step, he felt a stabbing pain in his side. He knew his rib was broken. With the back of his sleeve, he wiped the blood from his face, so that he could see more clearly. Feeling the tenderness in his nose, he knew that was broken too. Cursing himself for being so stupid, he almost threw himself through the front door and into the bathroom. Stripping off his torn, bloodstained clothing, he knelt in the bath and turned on the shower spray, letting the cool water flow over his burning body. He was exhausted, puffing and panting as he watched the crimson water turn pink and flow down the plug hole. He knew he had only made things worse for Sheila and the kids.

They would be ostracised now. All he did was make her life hell. Tears flowed, making the swelling in his eyes hurt more as snot and blood fell from his broken nose. He couldn't miss his afternoon shift at work. A day missed was a day short in his wages and his probation officer would want to know why. Either way, he was stuffed. How he was going to get through his shift was anyone's guess.

* * *

Walking through the kebab shop doors, Steve saw Fin look up from the counter first. Seeing his cuts and bruises, Fin just nodded, which was unusual for him. Normally he would have made some comment or joke about it, but not today. He looked agitated and put his head down and carried on cutting up the salad.

There were a couple of customers waiting for their orders who spied him as he lifted the shutter of the counter to walk through to the back, but nothing was said. Even the manager ignored him as he sliced the kebab meat from its spit. His heart sank. He knew he was going to be sacked for coming into work like this, but he'd had no other option. Standing at his locker and opening it, he felt something press against the back of his head. He could feel someone behind him but couldn't turn around because they pushed him forward into the metal lockers, squashing his face against them so he could hardly breathe. He heard the gun click as they loaded the barrel, and hot breath burned at the side of his neck.

'You have just cost everyone a day's takings, you son of a bitch,' the voice in his ear rasped. 'Your wife's interest has just doubled to make up for the loss.' Trying to struggle free and turn his head, the person behind him slammed it harder against the lockers, almost squeezing the life out of him. 'Don't even think about it. If it was up to me, I would shoot you, but this is your final warning. No more trouble. If you don't like it around here, then fucking leave with our blessing. But be warned. No confessions, Stevie boy. You have a lot to lose. Very nice pretty daughters you have.'

The whispered words rang in Steve's ears. He had gone too far and now his family was being threatened. The pressure from the man behind him eased and he heard footsteps and the back door shut. Inwardly shaking and leaning with his head still on the lockers, he turned his head slightly, but there was no one around. He was helpless. There was no one he could turn to for help. He had been better off in prison; at least Sheila and the girls had been safe.

'You okay, Steve?' Fin's voice broke the silence and their eyes met. He looked worried and put his hand on Steve's shoulder. 'We're mates, Steve, and I've done my best to help you but I'm not sure I can help you again. I got you a job to keep your probation officer happy. I've paid my debt to you. All you had to do was play by the rules and keep your gob shut, but your pride and ego wouldn't let you. Everyone knows Sheila's on the game. What's the big deal? You don't miss a slice off a cut loaf! My woman does it all the time, brings in good money, too – at least she gets a lie in and a smoke. Better than turning up here night and day. Time to wake up, Steve. This is life and unless you win the lottery, you're fucking stuck here.' With that, Fin turned and walked away, leaving Steve weak and powerless as he slumped to his knees on the floor.

'Can you ride a moped?' The manager stood in the doorway as Fin was leaving.

Doing his best to stand up, Steve nodded. 'Yeah, why?'

'Because you're on deliveries now at one of the other shops. Get your stuff and get out of here. Here's the address. At least the helmet will cover those cuts and bruises.' He threw a piece of paper, which landed on the floor beside Steve.

Steve wasn't sure if it was kindness or the manager just didn't want him there. Either way, he knew he was back to dealing drugs, just like before. Taking a deep sigh, he nodded at the manager. Once again, he'd brought misery on his family.

THE PENDULUM

'I have a nice surprise for Nana. Something to make her happy before she dies,' Nick laughed across the table to Patsy. He wanted to break the news about the community centre to her before she heard it from elsewhere.

Not saying any more as the waiter poured their wine and took their orders, Nick felt he could speak more freely once he'd left. Sipping his wine, Nick waited for Patsy's comments.

'What kind of a surprise?' The last thing Patsy wanted to do while having a nice dinner with her husband was discuss his nana. Sipping her wine, she waited. For Nick to spring it on her like this usually meant it would be something she wouldn't approve of.

'That community centre she was talking about – I'm thinking about buying it.' Taking a gulp of his wine, he waited for the outburst. He knew she wouldn't be happy. After all, this wasn't just a box of chocolates. He was going to buy a community centre in Glasgow just to keep his nana happy!

'You're doing what? Why, for God's sake? I thought she said it was closed, a bloody dump. Why are you buying it?' Shocked and angry, she picked up the bottle of wine and poured some more into her glass. 'How much is that going to cost?'

Nick sat there while Patsy fired all kinds of questions at him, all of which he was prepared for. He knew the way her mind worked after all these years and was ready for the onslaught.

'It's a good charity scam. I've spoken to the accountant and he agrees. Very good for tax purposes, I believe.' Nonchalantly, Nick laid on the charm, smiling at her over the candlelit table.

'Don't make me laugh, Nick. Since when have you been interested in charity? Scam, yes, charity, definitely not Nick Diamond! All of this so she can play bingo, are you crazy? Do you think I buy that?'

'If nothing else, Patsy, the land is worth the money, although I believe there is a clause in the sale which says I can't sell it for five years to any house builders. It's an investment, Patsy.'

'And who is going to pay for the upkeep of this investment? You're giving them a community centre and who pays the lighting and the heating bills?' she snapped. 'Is that why we're having dinner, so you can soften me up with this shit news?'

'Eventually it will pay for itself. And no, darling, I've brought you here to have dinner with you and spend some time with you.' His smooth, velvety voice wafted across the table towards her.

'Do you know how much something like that costs, Nick? And then there is staff. Who is going to pay their wages? You haven't thought this through at all, have you? You're so impulsive sometimes, Nick,' she scoffed.

'I thought you liked it when I was being impulsive? I've never heard you complain in the bedroom,' he winked at her, his green eyes glowing in the candlelight. 'It's all tax deductible, Patsy, and I'm sure the residents will find some way of holding jumble sales and stuff to keep the place running. After all, it benefits them.'

A grin crossed her face; she liked Nick's spur-of-the-moment sex sessions. It made life interesting. Taking another sip of her wine, Patsy thought about it. Frowning, she considered the options. 'You could always rent the centre out to people. There are those aerobic classes and things.' The more she thought about it, she reasoned to herself maybe it wasn't such a stupid idea. Yes, there were tax reasons, but it might in time turn a profit. People always wanted to hire a hall for something or other. 'If you got onto the council, you might be able to get volunteers to work there. Say, for instance, on community service. It would save them picking up litter off the streets. I could look into it if you like. When are you thinking of starting this venture? More to the point, how much are they asking for it?'

Nick liked Patsy's business brain, he always had. He felt she was getting slightly carried away. But, for now, he would let her think what she liked. 'Not as much as you think. I know a man who has builders on hand. Okay,' he laughed and held his hands up in submission. 'They are all ex-cons needing work and they're willing to work hard for it, but it's a wage for them and a job well done for me. It's much better than getting some overpriced cowboy firm in.'

He had dropped his bombshell and she had taken it much better than he had expected. 'Well, it's going to take some time and money, but we both know that isn't a problem and to get it into any kind of order that resembles a community centre shouldn't take too long.' Shrugging, he picked up his glass again and took a drink, while spying her over the rim of his glass.

Cocking her head to one side and raising an eyebrow, Patsy looked at him. 'And I suppose you would find a way to launder money through it, Nick?' Her sarcasm was more than visible to him, but he ignored it.

'Anything is possible, I suppose,' he laughed, portraying a row of pearly white teeth. Then they both burst out laughing. As the waiter came back to the table and brought their starters, Patsy looked at her husband. He was a very handsome man and he knew it. His light brown hair seemed to highlight the green of his eyes. They shone like two emeralds in his sun-kissed face and finely chiselled features. He was tall and slim with strong, muscled arms. He always went to the gym or swam, and took great pride in his appearance.

His Savile Row suits fitted to perfection with his silk shirts and pearl buttons. He was definitely a ladies' man: charming, witty and funny. That's how he had been when she had met him. But in recent years, he had changed. Suddenly he was buying pizza and kebab shops in Scotland, of all places. She could never understand why he never bought them in London. After all, that was where they lived! He had told her it was cheaper than London and that had been the end of it.

They had both bought her beauty salons, but Nick suddenly seemed to have large amounts of cash that he needed laundering through them. She never asked where the money came from, she didn't want to know, and he had never felt the need to tell her. If she knew, that would make her an accessory to the fact. Whatever it was, she knew it wasn't legal. If it was, why did he have to launder it?

Day after day, she would put money into the cash register and print out receipts for a service to an invisible customer so that she could launder it. After all, as Nick explained to her one day, while giving her careful instructions on how to launder the money, 'a taxable receipt, Patsy, is legal money, and who knows how many customers you have coming in a place like this?' For whatever reason, she had gone along with it. Eventually, it had got too much, and she had bought another salon. Now he was doing it through his pizza shops. They had often argued about it, but Nick's temper soon rose and she had stopped asking questions.

She remembered when she had loved him dearly – she still did, but these days they were more like business partners. Fifteen years of married life seemed to bring complacency. Sex was just a bonus, although a very nice one. He was an excellent lover.

Interrupted by the waiter, they waited while their starter dishes were taken away and their lobster thermidor was brought out. This was the house speciality and the waiter served the lobster and garlic sauce with all of the pomp and ceremony he felt it deserved.

'That looks delicious.' Patsy smiled and gently kicked Nick under the table, prompting him to comment on the dish.

Taking her lead, Nick looked up and smiled. 'A feast for the gods. My compliments to your chef'. Not wanting the interruption to last much longer, now that Nick felt he had Patsy all softened up and prepared to hear him out without a fuss, he picked up his fork and tasted it. 'Delicious, as always'. Nick gushed. Graciously, the waiter poured more wine and walked away.

Picking up her drink, Patsy took a sip of her wine and smiled at him, while running her tongue over her moistened lips seductively.

'Does your nana know about this yet, Nick?' Feeling slightly heady with all the wine, Patsy realised she'd drunk far too much too quickly. The dinner and the ambience were working, she had come around to Nick's way of thinking. Maybe this was legitimate. Wonders never ceased.

'No, darling.' Leaning forward over the table, Nick reached for her hand and kissed the back of it. 'I wanted to discuss it with you first.' The velvety tones of his voice floated towards her once again, she couldn't deny him anything when he was like this.

'I appreciate that.' Her voice was low, almost a whisper. She didn't care about the community centre. She wanted her husband now! He was a very sexy man and for once she had his full attention. Looking across the candlelit table at her husband, she admired his good looks and charming ways. After a few more mouthfuls she put her fork down, deciding that she didn't have an appetite for food. Her appetite was for Nick. 'Have you had enough to eat?' she winked, letting a smile spread across her face. 'Shall we go home?'

Instantly knowing what she meant, Nick put his napkin on the table and indicated to the waiter that he wanted the bill. Realising he'd won Patsy over, he smiled. At least now she wouldn't complain and life would be easy. Seeing the desire in her eyes, it seemed he had one last thing to do to seal the deal and then it would be back to business.

* * *

Yawning, Patsy turned over in bed and nudged Nick. 'Nick, love, wake up, I can hear your phone ringing. Are you the duty solicitor tonight?' She pulled the duvet up further around her head.

Bleary-eyed, Nick looked at the clock. It was 2 a.m. Shit! He'd forgotten to turn off the mobile in his briefcase. Normally he made a point of putting it on a low vibrate. Cursing himself, he threw back the duvet, got out of bed, and reached for his dressing gown.

'You go back to sleep, Patsy, I'll sort this,' he whispered, but then he realised that thankfully she had already drifted off.

Opening his briefcase, he saw his private mobile flashing up an unknown number. Instantly he knew who it was. 'Yes?' he snapped.

'It's Billy.' The hushed whisper on the other end of the mobile chilled his bones. He was becoming a burden. 'I'm just letting you know I got the phones. Midge's carrier pigeons have worked a treat. Four days and four mobile phones. Thanks, son. You think a lot inside this place.' There was a deep sigh on the end of the phone. 'I was thinking back to when we first met. Do you remember? We've come a long way since then and made a lot of money. I will be out of here soon and now Jack Diamond is dead we can let everyone know that I'm your real dad. We make a great team, son.' And then the line went dead.

'Fuck!' Nick was angry at himself and clenched his fist so hard his knuckles went white. He hated Billy Burke and wanted him dead as soon as possible in the most gruesome way he could think of. He'd waited years and become a multi-millionaire draining that fat bastard, and now Nick held all the cards he would chew him up and spit him out. He poured himself a drink and sat down. It was torture. There were no bars but he felt he'd served a seven-year sentence in prison and he'd earnt every penny he took from Billy while listening to his whining, demoralising insults. Nick was visibly shaking with anger – he needed to compose himself so as not to alarm Patsy.

Pushing his hands through his hair, Nick poured himself another whisky and gulped it back in one. Switching the mobile off and locking it away securely in his briefcase, he decided to go back to bed. His mind was working overtime and the last thing he needed was for Patsy to get out of bed to see if he was okay, when it was obvious he wasn't. There was nothing he could do now. Just a few more months to sort the plans for the community centre, and he would be finished with Billy Burke once and for all.

Peering over in the darkness of the bedroom to Patsy's side of the bed, he could see she was asleep and soundly snoring.

Thanks, son. The words rang in his ears and he wanted to shout out loud. All this pent-up anger and tension was driving him crazy. Nick felt sick. Sometimes he wished he had never told Billy that he was his son. It had been a foolish and vain thing for him to do. On the other hand, it had been a profitable few years, and maybe knowing he was his son had made it easier for Billy to trust him. Who knew what that drugged-up animal thought! How dare he call him son! Billy coming out of prison and exposing him as his son could not be allowed to happen. Nick would be a laughing stock, and his whole family would be disgraced.

Lying in the darkness with his arm under his head, Nick's mind was in a whirl. He would have to bite his tongue a little bit longer. Billy bloody Burke, aptly named after the famous grave robber from Edinburgh, had fantasies coming out of his ears. Nick decided it was all the drugs he was taking. Either that or being cooped up in a cell made him fantasise about his life on the outside.

The night was still; only Patsy's steady breathing as she slept beside him could be heard. Billy's words echoed again in Nick's mind as he thought back to their memorable first meeting. Walking into the interview room that day as his duty solicitor, Nick had been shocked by the sight of the burly brute of a man who sat at the table smoking. He wondered again how this man could be his father.

'My name is Nick, and I have been brought in as your temporary solicitor as you've sacked the last three. I have a duty to represent you... that is, if you want me to?' Spying him curiously, Nick paused, waiting for an answer, but none came. Billy looked bored and made a point of emphasising it with a yawn.

Trying to act as professionally as possible, considering what he knew about the man before him, he felt nervous. Now that he was in the same room as his biological father, he felt sick.

Billy Burke looked like a man who evolution had passed by. He was tall in stature and weighed around twenty stone. His enormous, tattooed arms rippled with muscle. They looked like two sides of beef. His shaven head was also covered in tattoos and his long bushy beard laid on his chest. The words 'Fuck U' were tattooed across his forehead and the words 'love' and 'hate' were tattooed across his very yellow knuckles.

'Sit down, laddie,' he barked, blowing smoke from his cigarette into the already smoky room, Nick did his best to hide his dislike of this obnoxious man.

Looking at him, he searched for any resemblance to himself. Nick noticed Billy's eyes were dead and empty like dolls' eyes, showing no emotion of any kind. Nick cringed inside; he couldn't imagine his mother ever lying in this man's arms, let alone having sex with him. It seemed beyond belief. Maybe he had looked better in his younger days, although Nick doubted it.

Stretching out his hands, which resembled two rough shovels, at last Billy spoke. 'You got any smokes on you?' His thick Glaswegian accent echoed around the empty room. Nick had gone prepared and threw a packet on the table before him. 'When are you going to get me out of here? I have business to see to.'

Realising it was an order, not a question, Nick opened his case and took out his paperwork. 'Mr Burke, you have been charged with robbery of a pharmaceutical warehouse. There were also two men shot at the site of the robbery and one of the guns has your fingerprints on it. Some of the drugs you stole have already been sold on the streets and the police have a full statement from a witness. Apart from that, Mr Burke, you are on camera, so no, you won't be leaving today.'

'What witness?' Ignoring everything else Nick said, Billy shouted again. 'What witness?'

'Personally, I think if you do have the rest of the drugs that were stolen, maybe if you handed them back it would reduce your sentence.'

Banging his huge fists on the table, Billy laughed out loud and scoffed at Nick. 'You're as green as grass, laddie, go home and play with your Action Man. You have to be fucking joking!' he bellowed. 'Do you know how much that stuff is worth on the streets, and what I went through to get it? Nay, laddie, that's my retirement fund. It's worth millions. A short stint in here is worth my pension fund.'

'I believe the witness is someone who was with you on the night of the robbery. He has decided to give a very detailed statement in the hope of reducing his own sentence.'

Pointing his finger directly in Nick's face, Billy almost spat, 'That witness is a dead man walking. You don't have to worry about him.'

'Do I take it you know where the drugs are, Mr Burke? There are three truckloads. The witness even implied there could be more?'

Shrugging his shoulders, Billy rubbed his sweaty forehead, creasing all of the lines on his head together.

'You're on camera, Billy! And two people have been killed!' Nick's voice rose but fell on deaf ears. This arrogant bastard thought he was above the law. As far as Nick was concerned, it was an open and shut case. Looking down at the paperwork before him, Nick saw that the witness was one of the men from the robbery who was still smarting after taking a drunken beating from Billy during an argument.

Billy was no gangland boss; he was a thug and a killer. He could be easily manipulated if he thought there was something in it for him.

'So you're the best defence they could come up with. You're still in short pants, for Christ's sake. What do you know about life?'

After a few more insults, Nick had left. He had been surprised that Billy hadn't dismissed him for another solicitor. But during the next couple of visits he had just let himself be known as 'Nick the lawyer'. Billy hadn't asked any more questions. He didn't care.

On one particular visit, it was clear that Billy was drugged up to the eyeballs. His pupils were wide and he was rambling. His usual barrage of insults came fast and furious. Angrily, Nick had spat out, 'My name is Nick Diamond.' No sooner had the words come out of his mouth, Nick could have bit his tongue. He was sick of the insults and in his anger he had blurted it out. His temper had always been his downfall. Now he had no choice but to take a chance and follow it up with the truth. On the other hand, Nick thought, Billy was so drugged up, it would seem like a dream.

Confused, Billy frowned and Nick gave him a moment for his words to seep through his brain. 'Diamond? I used to know a man by that name,' Billy slurred. 'A good friend of mine. We were lads together in Scotland. Not exactly a common name, is it. You're one of these soft southerners, how do you come by that name?'

'I have roots in Scotland. My nana was born and bred there and so was my father.' He could see that Billy was almost sobering up at Nick's revelation. At last, something was taking his interest.

'Your nana is Beryl Diamond?' Sitting back in his wooden chair, Billy took a long look at Nick. 'Maybe she is. You don't look like your father, but you have some of your mother's features. Vicky is a beautiful woman.'

The very mention of his mother angered Nick, especially as he used her name so flippantly.

'So Jack's son is a legal eagle and you've been sent to save my skin. Well, good for him. He was always a good friend. Although it could have been worse. You could have been a copper!' Laughing out loud at his own joke, Billy banged the table with his fists, almost tipping the table over.

Waiting for the laughter to die down, Nick swallowed hard before he dropped his next bombshell. 'I only took this job to meet you, Billy, especially since I found out you are my real father,' he said calmly.

A satisfied grin crossed Nick's face as he watched Billy's jaw drop. Now he knew he had the upper hand. Over the last couple of visits, he had found out more and more about Billy and his associates. Whether it was bravado or boasting, he had confided a lot in Nick, and a strange plan had formed in his mind. He was going to strip this man of everything he held dear. He would make him his puppet.

'My son? What makes you say that?' Stunned by this revelation, Billy's voice was more of a hushed whisper of disbelief.

'My mother. She told me everything. She didn't want me taking your job because it could drag up old skeletons. She was afraid it would compromise me. I'm not allowed to defend you in a case like this if I'm family.' Sorting through his paperwork, Nick avoided Billy's face and nonchalantly carried on as normal.

'So you've come out of curiosity to see what your old dad looks like, eh?' Billy's cold eyes glared at Nick, almost summing him up. It was clear to Nick that Billy had no real recollection of his night spent with his mother. 'Am I a big disappointment? Well, you don't look like you have gone short of anything. What are you after, years of past maintenance and Christmas presents?' Sarcasm dripped from Billy's mouth, as he shrugged. He couldn't care less about Nick. He was a self-centred drug addict who used brute force to get what he wanted.

Ignoring his sarcasm, Nick spoke again. For once, this was a serious conversation. It was low, almost a whisper, so no one could eavesdrop from outside of the door. 'Curiosity, yes, definitely. Wouldn't you be curious if you were me? But soon we will have to prepare a hearing and if anyone finds out we have any connection, I won't be able to represent you. That's the only reason I'm telling you this. The rest is up to you. You've sacked others before me and you can dismiss me too, if that's what you want...' Looking almost forlorn, Nick looked down at the table. He'd hatched his plan, now all he needed was for Billy to take the bait. Picking up his briefcase, Nick walked slowly towards the door. This was his gamble.

Deep in thought, Billy took another drag of his cigarette, hardly taking his eyes off Nick. The long trail of ash that hung on the end dropped onto the table and he brushed it away onto the floor.

'Wait, laddie! There is no need to be so hasty, you're as good as anyone and at least we're cut from the same cloth, eh? Family. I hate

England. Can't you suggest they send me back to Scotland, where my mates are?'

'Not for the time being, Billy. You were arrested here and will remain here until they deem otherwise.'

Stubbing out his cigarette in the ashtray, Billy stood up. 'Come and see me next week. I have something you can do for me, and don't get clever grassing me up. You're the one that sought me out and, son or no son, I will have a bullet put in your skull in the blink of an eye. I bet your dad doesn't know I'm your father. It would be a shame to spoil a good marriage.' His piercing gaze met Nick's. This was a standoff, and Nick knew there could only be one winner.

'You're my solicitor and whatever I tell you is in confidence, right?' Billy asked. 'Well, I have a job for you, that is, if you have the balls for it. Surely there is some of my blood in your veins. You will be rewarded, but I need a hand with some customs papers. Maybe you might know someone in the know. After all, you lawyers are more crooked than us criminals.' Laughing at his own joke, Billy lit another cigarette. His chewed fingernails were stained yellow and brown, making Nick feel even more sickened.

A warm sense of satisfaction filled Nick's body. This was what he had been waiting for. This was his chance to prove himself, to gain Billy's trust. It was easily done.

'What is in the trucks, Billy? If customs search the lorries, what will they find?' This was a simple game of cat and mouse and they both knew it.

'Nothing. If they haven't been tampered with, they will find nothing. All the drugs are under a false floor in the base of the lorry. The sides of the lorry are also false. Inside is just paint. Once we had adjusted them and put the false floor and walls in, we were ready to go.' Billy shrugged his shoulders and seemed agitated.

'Would it be such a loss if you couldn't get them through

customs? Maybe you should cut your losses, Billy.' Knowing it was a stupid question, Nick asked it anyway.

'Like hell I will. I worked hard getting that stuff. The drivers are just shit scared of getting caught. All they have to do is drive onto the ferry. If the papers are all in order, what's the problem?'

Nick had got onto it immediately once he had all the details from a reluctant Billy. For all his bravado, it seemed he had no one he could trust, and Nick was the answer to Billy's prayers, albeit the cause of future nightmares.

It had all gone smoothly and, much to Nick's surprise, he had enjoyed the adrenaline of sorting it all out. It had given that spark back into his life. And that was how it had all begun. Nick had been paid handsomely and he had enjoyed the power and the money... and the chase. But there had been too much money left over from the drugs deal and that was when Nick had decided Patsy could launder it through her salon. And when things had got bigger, he'd bought a pizza shop on Billy's advice to do the same. He knew a few men from prison who had been chefs and it was easy to set them up in business as managers. They kept their mouths shut and knew the rules.

As stupid as Billy was, he had a good criminal mind. Everything was kept in Scotland and Nick had been one step ahead of Billy and had bought the shops under the name Nick Burke. Well, he supposed he was entitled to the name, if nothing else. The paperwork was easily sorted, and Nick was surprised how easy it was to set up accounts in a different name and get away with it.

Billy had given him the idea to use the names of dead people at the cemetery and Nick got copies of their birth certificates, setting up new identities in their names. He'd even applied for lost national insurance numbers for tax reasons and opened bank accounts. Suddenly, he realised he had got a taste for this new life –

it was consuming him. Regrettably, he decided, he did have Billy's blood inside him after all.

The contacts Billy had given him already assumed he had something to do with Billy and followed the orders they were given without question. More out of fear than loyalty.

Nick had never shown his face. No one knew what he looked like or who he really was. The anonymity made him feel like special and he enjoyed this double life he was leading, but now his empire was enormous, and Billy was growing tired of being passed from one prison to the other.

But Nick had satisfied all of Billy's concerns and proved himself. Billy had to serve a sentence for taking part in a robbery; he knew that and accepted it. But it was nothing like what he would have done without Nick's help.

Now Billy had dreams of coming out of prison, boasting about his newly found 'son'. It disgusted Nick and he couldn't look his mother in the eye again. He stayed away from her as much as possible without Patsy becoming suspicious. Everyone was taking orders from him now. He held all the cards. He could keep them in prison, or send them back to prison if he wished to. They would even commit murder for him if he asked. Money talked, he'd learnt that. There was no loyalty when it came to money.

'Are you okay, Nick?' Patsy turned towards him and shook his shoulder gently, interrupting his thoughts, bringing him back to the present. 'Are you okay?' Resting on her elbow, she leaned over him and stroked his hair. 'You shouted out, but your eyes are open. Is it those dreams again? You've been having them for a while now. Maybe you should see a doctor? You're working too hard, Nicky.' She soothed and stoked his hair like a mother comforting a child.

Nick had had some kind of night terrors for a long time now, but they seemed to be coming to a crisis point and she was getting worried. He had sworn her to secrecy from his mother, and she had kept quiet, but something was seriously wrong and he wouldn't tell her what it was.

'Yes, I'm fine. Just a bad dream. Sorry I woke you, go back to sleep. You're right, maybe we will have a holiday or something soon. Sorry for disturbing you.' Kissing her gently on the lips, he opened his arms so she could lie her head on his chest with his arm wrapped around her. He knew she was right. Now was the time to get rid of Billy Burke once and for all before he went stir crazy! He was paying a high price for all the money he had made. For peace of mind, he had to rid himself of the burden he had made for himself. The whiskies he had gulped back were starting to take their toll and making him drowsy. Closing his eyes and listening to Patsy's steady breathing as she stroked the hair on his chest, he drifted off to sleep.

'Are you moving in?'

The residents of Thistle Park didn't like new faces. They were always sceptical. It had been known in the past for a plain clothes police officer to live in the flats to get information. 'Yes, my name is Natasha, but everyone calls me Tash.' Holding her hand out to shake Maggie's, the young woman looked embarrassed and flushed after walking the many flights of stairs with a child's buggy.

Maggie's years of wisdom and experience had taught her to interrogate the young woman as politely as possible without giving anything away. She and Beryl Diamond were the matriarchs of the estate, although Maggie had more dealings with the corruption surrounding the place than Beryl.

Eyeing up the nervous young woman before her, Maggie was certain this was no spy. She looked nervous, frightened even, standing on the concrete landing outside the front door of the flat she was viewing with a small child in a buggy.

'Would you like a nice cup of tea, love, and maybe I can fill up your wee one's juice bottle?' Maggie beamed a comforting smile and pulled her black cardigan around her shoulders.

'Don't go to any trouble, Mrs... erm... I'm just going to have a look around. The council have given me the keys this morning. I have to get them back to the office before they close.'

'It's no trouble, lassie, I was going to make one anyway. And as for the council office, that doesn't shut until 4 p.m., so I wouldn't worry. I'll be back in a jiffy, you start your tour.' Maggie winked and disappeared across the landing and down the stairs.

Putting the key in the door, Natasha opened it. The floorboards were scattered with all kinds of flyers and mail that had been put through the letterbox and she nervously kicked them aside and pushed the pram inside. The excitement bubbled up inside her, and she couldn't help smiling. This was going to be her new home. She didn't need the viewing, she was going to take it anyway. At last, she would have somewhere to call her own. The wallpaper was peeling off the walls in the hallway and the stench of the place was musty. But it was home.

Pushing the pram through the first doorway on the left, she looked around. This was obviously the lounge. The concrete flooring and the bare room made the sound of the wheels of the buggy echo. On the front wall was an oval shape on the wallpaper which showed there must have been a mirror or a picture there at some time.

Bending down beside the pram, she held her son's hand and kissed his cheek. 'What do you think, Jimmy? This is going to be our new home. All it needs is a good clean up. Shall we go and see your new bedroom?' Excitement bubbled up inside her and she almost laughed with joy. Taking her young son out of his buggy, she laughed as he ran around the room, pretending to be an aeroplane with his arms outstretched. They had never had so much space of their own. It was fantastic!

The next room led into the small kitchen. The back wall had been newly plastered by the council, a new kitchen sink had been put in and there was plenty of cupboard space. The lino on the floor was cracked here and there and the council workmen had left remnants of dust and plaster spilt from their bucket on the floor, but everything else seemed in order.

'Hello, lassie, are you there?' Maggie shouted down the hallway. Natasha had almost forgotten her in her excitement. Peering around the kitchen door, she saw Maggie holding a tray with two mugs on and some juice. 'I've brought us some biscuits and some crisps for the wee boy. Well, what do you think of the place?' Putting the tray on the floor, and handing Natasha her mug of tea, Maggie let out a deep sigh. 'It's not much, I grant you, and it needs a good clean, but it's only cosmetic, dear. A little splash of paint and some elbow grease will have it looking like new. And who are you, young man?' Smiling at the little boy running from room to room, Maggie held out the bag of crisps she'd brought.

Shyly, he half stood behind Natasha and looked at her and then at the crisps. 'This is Jimmy. Go on, Jimmy, say hello to the nice lady.' Natasha pushed him forward towards Maggie.

'Don't be shy, young laddie, we'll be seeing a lot of each other. That is, if you come to live here.' Looking up at Natasha's face, Maggie saw her smile, thinking how desperate she must be if she was pleased about moving into this dump. She didn't need to ask if she came from around the area, because it was pretty plain to see that she didn't if she thought this place was a palace.

Nodding, the young boy took the open packet of crisps and promptly started eating them.

'Oh, we're going to take it. I love it,' Natasha beamed, sipping the hot mug of tea.

Spying her and painting on a smile, Maggie looked around the room. It was clear to her the young woman didn't have a penny to her name. 'It will look better once you get all of your furniture moved in. New homes always feel cold and bleak without your furniture,' Maggie probed a little further.

'The homeless charity have got some furniture for us to start us off with,' Natasha stammered and then, realising what she had said, she blushed. Her face felt as though it was burning and highlighted her shoulder-length blonde hair even more.

'Don't you have much furniture, then?' A frown crossed Maggie's brow. She was more curious than ever to find out more about this pretty young woman before her. She looked very young, slim and naturally blonde. Dressed simply, in a pair of jeans and a denim jacket with a mustard-coloured T-shirt underneath, she lacked the usual cockiness of some of the young women on the estate. She was a shy young thing and already Maggie was warming to her.

'No, I'm from the kids' home. And then...' Looking down at the dusty floor, avoiding Maggie's eyes, she shyly carried on. She knew there was no point in lying. 'I've been living with an adult foster carer with Jimmy who shows you how to look after your child and stuff,' she stammered.

Ignoring her awkwardness, Maggie smiled with the same excitement as Natasha had shown regarding the flat. 'So this is your first home,' Maggie clapped her hands together, 'my, it's a whole new adventure. I remember when I got my first new home, I was beside myself with excitement.' Feigning excitement to raise Natasha's spirits, Maggie linked arms with her and walked around the rest of the flat. It was in poor repair, and there was damp on the bedroom ceiling, but even Maggie realised how precious this place was to Natasha. The poor lamb had nothing to call her own. 'What about wee Jimmy's dad, will he be coming along to see the place?'

'No, we broke up as soon as he found out I was pregnant.' Wrapping her hands around the warm mug of tea, Natasha looked around the rooms. She had been dumped by everyone she had ever met. She'd been in care homes for as long as she could remember and when she was eighteen and no longer the responsibility of the state, her social worker had found her an adult foster home, which taught them how to budget and be responsible for themselves. The foster carer, Lisa, had been very supportive and when she'd had Jimmy three years ago, Lisa and her social worker agreed to let her stay on a little longer. She'd taught her how to bathe and feed Jimmy, but Lisa had been asked to take on another young adult without a child to help them with the transition of moving from the children's home to living independently, and so the council had offered Natasha a place of her own. This was a fresh start, and the first time in her life she had ever lived on her own. She felt nervous and lacked confidence. There had always been someone on hand to ask for advice, but now it was up to her. It was just her and Jimmy and she was determined to do her best for him and give him everything she had never had. A mother's love.

'When Jock left this place, he left all of his furniture, although it wasn't much. It's such a shame the council tend to throw it all out before the new tenants arrive. It might have helped.'

'You know the people who lived here? Why did they leave?' Now it was Natasha's turn to ask the questions.

'Why yes, lassie, I've lived here all of my life, there isn't much I don't know about the place. The guy who lived here moved on to Edinburgh.' Drumming her fingers on her chin and looking up at the ceiling as though in deep thought, Maggie continued, 'He got a better job with better prospects, I believe. He was a bachelor, though, and they don't go in much for homemaking, do they?'

Breathing a sigh of relief, Natasha flashed a smile. 'Oh, that's good. At least no one died here. I would take it anyway, but it would be a bit creepy on my own if the last people had died in their sleep in the bedroom I'm going to use or something.' A nervous giggle escaped from Natasha.

'No, lassie, there are no ghosts or ghouls here. You're perfectly safe,' Maggie lied. 'And there are plenty of youngsters on the estate for young Jimmy to make friends with.' Seeing the smile on Natasha's face, Maggie knew she had made her feel at ease.

'What's that noise?' Natasha rushed to the front door and opened it, with Jimmy in hot pursuit.

'It's the mobile shop, dear.' The blast from the van horn surrounded the estate. Again and again, it rang out, letting the residents know of its arrival. 'It comes every day. It saves you having to walk all the way to the shops. He charges a little extra for the convenience, but it comes in handy… and when he knows you better, he sometimes gives you a little credit until payday,' Maggie prompted and nudged her in the arm with her elbow.

'Really?' Looking down from the landing to the white van that had been converted into a shop, Natasha looked on as people from all over the estate made their way to it. She had never seen or heard of a mobile shop before. 'I'm going to look for a job as soon as I can, but I need to see if I can get Jimmy into a local nursery first.'

Bending down and stroking Jimmy's chin, Maggie smiled. 'There's no rush in finding a job, love. You have a job already looking after this handsome young man. There is a nursery up the high street, maybe you could put his name down there.'

Mesmerised by people walking away from the van with bread, milk and other goods, Natasha looked at Maggie. 'Thank you. You've been very kind, Maggie. I don't know what to say. I admit, I was a little scared coming here on my own, but I feel better now.' Handing Maggie her mug, Natasha continued looking into the different rooms. She had never had so much space. There was never anywhere in someone else's house you could escape to. Now she felt like a real adult. Her mind was already wandering to the colours she would paint each room. She could see it in her mind. It looked fantastic.

'Then say nothing, Tash. I find that's always the best way. Come on, you had better get those keys back and make your arrangements. There are always a million forms to fill in. I'll see you both soon.' Maggie walked back into the flat, picked up her tray and mugs and left. Inwardly, she took a deep sigh. That poor wee lassie was as innocent as could be on an estate like this, without a soul in the world to care for her. It was like throwing a puppy to the sharks!

* * *

'Oy, Mags!' Fin was walking through the estate with a flat-screened television in a supermarket trolley. 'Who's the fresh meat with the kid?' Fin asked when he saw Maggie going to her own front door.

'Don't call me Mags, and she is not fresh meat. Well, not for you, anyway. Piss off and give her a chance to catch her breath! Fresh meat, indeed. You're disgusting. Whose house did you steal that from? Walking through here as blatant as could be and I bet you didn't put a pound in that trolley, you light-fingered bastard.' She knew the jungle drums were already beating with a new face on the block.

'I was only asking, no need to bite my head off. Someone was moving in their posh new home while I was passing, why would they leave the back of the removal van open if they don't want anything nicked? Must be worth a few pounds. And I have my pound token to put in the trollies. Do you need a television, Maggie?'

'Do I look like I need a television when I have idiots like you to watch? No, I don't, you weasel. Leave that girl well alone. The last thing she needs is a sorry excuse of a bloke like you sniffing around her. Have you been to the cemetery lately? Well, I have,' she barked and wagged her finger in his face. 'And any shit from you or your mates and I'll make damn sure there is a headstone with your name on it!' With that, she walked in and slammed the door, leaving a forlorn, shocked Fin standing there.

'What's up with her, Fin?' Beeny walked up to Fin and handed him a cigarette.

'Fucking old witch, she thinks she knows everything. Come on, Beeny, we have some distributing to do.'

'I wouldn't cross her, Fin, she seems to know a lot about the Undertaker. Nice television. What is that, fifty inch? Are you going to trade it with the mobile shop or sell it privately?'

'Shut the fuck up. No one says that name around here, apart from arseholes like you.' Fin shot Beeny a fierce look. That name was only ever whispered. And even though Beeny was part of his gang, he should know better than to say it so nonchalantly. 'You're a lanky bastard with a big mouth, Beeny. Do you ever take that woolly hat off your head? God, I bet you even wear it when you're having a shag!' Pulling Beeny's hat off his head, he waved it in the air.

'It's my trademark, Fin. Beanie hat. Everyone knows me by it, that's why they call me Beeny. Give it back, you prick. Fancy a beer at mine first, then we'll start dealing?'

'Yes, why not. I need to drop this off, anyway. I'm going to start on the pub corner, you can do the park with the kids. Did you pick your stash up from the telephone box?'

Tapping his denim jacket pocket with his little plastic bags of drugs inside, Beeny nodded. 'Yes, they've been dropped off as usual.'

'I was wondering how Steve's getting on. I haven't seen him lately, not since he started doing deliveries on that broken-down old moped. Those Albanians are always trying to step on our turf or steal our stuff off the delivery riders.'

'Stop worrying, you've got your own head to worry about. Steve's okay, he knows how to handle himself.'

Fin wasn't so sure; he hadn't heard from Steve in a while. He often saw him on his moped with his pizzas on the back, but Steve had never stopped to say hello. Even though they lived on the same estate, Steve seemed to be avoiding him.

'Come on, beer first, then business. Steve's his own worst enemy, Fin. You did your best and put yourself on the line against Billy Burke and his mates, speaking up for him and getting him a job. He's come out of prison like a born-again Christian or something. He knows the score, Fin, stop worrying about him.'

Even Beeny knew that was easier said than done. They had all been close friends and he often had a pang of guilt about stitching Steve up. He'd given Sheila a few pounds now and again without anyone knowing about it. It was survival of the fittest and he intended to survive the wrath of the Undertaker and his men, with or without Steve.

* * *

'Are you working tonight, Steve? I worry about you, especially when you come home battered and bruised.'

'Yes, Sheila, and don't worry about it. It's bringing in a wage and that's all that matters.' Looking in the mirror, Steve took a large intake of breath. He saw yet another black eye. Delivering pizzas was becoming more and more of a hazard. He knew his enemies hoped the other gangs dealing in the same areas would kill him. It was simple enough, the usual customers rang and placed their pizza orders, some wanted extra cheese. The extra cheese was code for the small plastic packet of cocaine underneath the pizza. On occasions, the other gang known as the Albanians, who cut their prices, would sometimes order pizzas and attack and steal the drugs off the driver, plus the money he had collected from other deliveries. Steve never knew where the next attack was coming from. It was a permanent turf war.

When he was delivering five or six pizzas to the same estate, it added up to a lot of money. Returning to the shops without money or drugs was the worst part. Having to explain himself to the manager usually turned into an argument and threats. His life was becoming a nightmare and there was no one he could tell. They had changed the code every so often and they had done the same to the Albanian drivers. To make things easier for himself, he'd decided to carry his old gun.

His old 'faithful', as he called it, had been buried. He had been surprised to find it where he had left it after all these years. Sheila loved plants and flowers and one day he had bought her a small rose bush and put it in a large ceramic plant pot outside on the balcony. It had flourished, but underneath that ever-flourishing rose he had wrapped his gun in plastic and buried it there. By now, it was taking up half the balcony and the roots were thicker than ever, and when he'd decided to tidy it up and put it into a bigger pot for Sheila, he'd been surprised with what he had found.

Carrying it around made him feel safer, although he knew if he got caught with it, he would go straight back to prison. When he had told his probation officer that he needed to work nights now and again, she had fought his corner and had the curfew tag on his ankle cancelled for two nights a week so that he could work. He'd explained that he had to work nights as part of the rota and if he couldn't, he could lose his job. Knowing how hard jobs were to come by, she had pulled some strings and, as long as he reported to the police station before and after his shift was finished, they were satisfied.

Some nights, he feared for his life, and no sooner did he go to some estate in the area, he could see them waiting for him. It was an ambush, and he always came off worse.

'You're dealing again, aren't you, Steve? Don't answer that with a lie because I know it.'

'I'm not dealing like I used to. I just deliver the pizzas with the stuff inside it. What am I supposed to do, Sheila? If I give up my job, I won't get a reference and I would have to answer a lot of questions to my probation officer. And where would I get another job?' He felt powerless and ashamed. As much as he had fought against the old regime, he'd been dragged back into it, kicking and screaming. He'd looked for other jobs but as soon as he told employers he was recently out of prison, their smiles had dropped and he had seen that familiar look on their faces which told him he didn't stand a chance.

'Well, since you doubled our interest on the mobile shop, the last thing we need is for you to lose your job.' Reaching across the kitchen table for his hand, Sheila gave him a knowing smile. Life had settled down of late, she knew he was doing his best to adjust, but at least they were more like a married couple now with two small daughters. It was nice to feel like a family again, even though lots of the people on the estate had ostracised them for his outburst at Midge. Everyone had to cover their own backs and take sides; Steve was just rocking the boat.

Lowering his eyes and clearing his throat, Steve couldn't help but ask. 'I've noticed you're not going out in the evenings much?'

'I know.' Standing up, Sheila picked up the dirty mugs and walked towards the kitchen sink. 'They won't give me the work, Steve, and I can't get credit any more. Not even my pick 'n' mix.' Sheila's voice tailed off. Some days, she felt life had got worse since he had got out of prison and not being able to get her hands on regular pills, making her go cold turkey, had made her snappy and anxious. Making a point of keeping busy, Sheila avoided Steve's eyes and kept her back to him while doing the washing up. 'I'm looking for a job, Steve. I thought I might be able to get some cleaning work or something. If you see any advertisements in windows or anything while you're out on your bike, let me know. It's easier now you're on shifts, we can split the babysitting and it won't cost anything.'

'Yes, sure, I can do that. Anyway, I've had an idea, Sheila. I've already spoken to the probation officer and she says she is going to write a letter to the council.'

'What letter? What are you talking about?' Throwing the wet soapy dishrag in the sink, making the water splash up and wet her face, she glared at him.

'I have asked her about a housing transfer. I explained things would get better if I was away from the old estate and the people I used to know. She thinks it's a good idea. If we can get away from here, Sheila, we can make a fresh start somewhere. Maybe even get something with a garden for the girls?'

'For God's sake, Steve, stop dreaming. Stuff like that doesn't happen to people like us! You're a criminal. Drugs and robbery is all you have ever known!' Rolling her eyes up to the ceiling, she sat at the table with him. Tears of frustration fell down her cheeks. 'I'm sorry, Steve, who am I to judge? I'm an addict, and I've sold myself to boot. But don't you see? People like us just don't get those kinds of things. It happens to other people, not us.'

Steve's voice dropped to a hushed whisper. The lump in his throat rose. 'Surely we're due a bit of good luck, Sheila. Let me try this. After all, they can only say no.' Looking up at her, he saw a smile cross her face and his heavy heart rose.

'You're right, Steve, love. They can only refuse us, and I'm used to rejection. But don't let it be known. Whoever is out there trying to make life difficult for you may do their best to prevent this happening,' she said seriously.

'Is it a deal, Sheila?' Steve held out his hand to shake Sheila's. At least they were on the same side. It seemed like a good idea and it was a goal. He didn't care where they moved to as long as they got away from here. He'd led his life, but for his girls he wanted better. 'Here's to a better life, Sheila. For all of us.'

'Absolutely, Steve.' Reaching forward, she cupped his face and kissed him, wetting his face with her soapy hands. She didn't want to destroy his dreams, but she wished he would come back into the real world. He must have spent night after night in his cell planning all of the things he would do when he got out, but even she knew it would all come to nothing. If anything, it was going from bad to worse.

12

CHARITY BEGINS AT HOME

'What the hell is all of that noise? For Christ's sake, it's still night-time!' Jumping out of bed, Steve ran to the windows. Vans were driving past the estate and parking on the old site near the community centre. Opening the front door for a better view, he saw that he wasn't alone in his curiosity. Being so high up on the twelfth floor gave him a bird's eye view. Bleary-eyed and yawning, one by one people came out, wrapping their dressing gowns around them to see what was happening.

Sheila came out and stood behind him. 'What is it? Why are all those vans going towards the old community centre at six in the morning?'

'Maybe they are going to knock it down, God knows it's a bloody eyesore. Kids are always playing on it, lighting fires and causing trouble. The junkies use it as their hideaway. Good riddance to bad rubbish, I say.' Rubbing his sleepy eyes and yawning, he leaned over the balcony for a better view.

'Yeah, I agree it's about time they did something with it. It surprises me the roof hasn't caved in yet and killed someone. I'll go and put the kettle on.'

Everyone was craning their necks to see what the commotion was as truck after truck made its way there, parking on the kerbside and up on the pavements.

'Christ, it looks like an invasion from wartime,' someone shouted and laughed.

Cupping his hands around his mouth, another one shouted across to the next block of flats. 'Anyone know what's going on?'

'God knows, they are probably looking for bodies!' someone shouted back. Everyone shouted across from their tower blocks to each other, but no one had an answer. It was a total mystery to all of them.

'I'll go and see to the girls, here's your tea. Let me know if there are any developments. I get the feeling it's going to be a long day, Steve.' Shivering at the early morning chill, Sheila turned to go in. The girls were already up and running to join Steve on the crowded landing of the flats to see what was happening.

Workmen were already emptying their vans and erecting metal fencing around the community centre. It was a hive of activity. Scaffolders were behind the fencing, setting up their long iron poles.

'Why would they put scaffolding up if they were going to demolish the place?' Confused, Sheila took the empty mug from Steve and handed him another one and a cigarette.

Frowning, Steve took the hot mug. He'd never thought of that. 'That's a fair point. I know they would want to make it safe, but they wouldn't put scaffolding up. Would they? I suppose they might,' he pondered. 'To make it safe.'

'No, there isn't a bulldozer in sight, and those workmen are not from the council, the vans don't have the council logo on the side. This is a private building firm.'

Steve could have kicked himself. He'd been too busy watching but she had seen the obvious.

'It takes a woman to think of these things,' Sheila laughed.

'Look at you with your jaw wide open. You're not a very good spy, love, are you? And where is the demolition lorry? Surely they would have come first?' And there are no gas men or anything to make the place safe so it doesn't blow up.' Enjoying her moment, Sheila laughed.

'All right, Miss Know-it-all, it must be hard work knowing you're right all the time,' Steve laughed. But Sheila was right, there were no demolition lorries. Workmen were filling newly arrived skips with rubbish. There was no point if they were going to knock it down. But why would anyone want to rebuild it? Steve shivered. It felt like someone had just walked over his grave. Why would anyone invest in that derelict old squat? It was a death trap and should have been bulldozed to the ground ages ago. Only someone who felt it could be put to good use would invest in that place. A sense of foreboding washed over Steve. He couldn't explain it, but felt whatever it was, it wasn't good news. Far from it.

* * *

An army of workmen seemed to have descended on the community centre. There were hard hats and men everywhere. Everyone from the estate looked on in awe as the scaffolding went up and all the old tiles from the roof were taken off.

'Someone is spending a lot of money on that place, Beryl. What do you think they are building?'

'No idea, Maggie. Is there no gossip about? I've never heard anything about building works. It's a shame, though. That old community felt like a part of me and now it's coming down like a discarded part of the past... I feel the same.'

'Oh, shut up, Beryl, there's life in you yet. You will outlive us all. Anyway, we don't know what they are building yet,' Maggie scoffed. Beryl Diamond had been supposedly dying for the last twenty years. If nothing else, she loved something to moan about. No wonder her family barely visited, she was a real miserable cow!

'I've found some things for you as you asked. They are in the spare bedroom. What are you collecting for?' Beryl was intrigued and she had been more than curious when Maggie had asked her if she had any old pots and pans she didn't need any more. Anything at all to make a house feel like a home. She didn't want to ask, because she felt Maggie should tell her. After all, it was for her benefit.

Walking into the bedroom, Maggie's face lit up. Good old Beryl, she might be a miserable cow but she had a heart of gold. The room was full of pots, pans, cups and plates. Even a rug and a lamp.

'A young woman is moving onto the estate and she hasn't got much.' Sitting down, Maggie let out a huge sigh. 'To tell the truth, Beryl, she has bugger all and she has a wee kiddie. I just thought we could show a bit of kindness and maybe find some things that we don't use any more. Maybe I'm going soft in my old age, but we've all started from scratch.' Smiling, Maggie took the proffered whisky canteen from Beryl and poured some into her cup.

'It's not soft, Maggie, it's human kindness and God knows we could all do with some of that. As you say, we've all had to start from scratch. What is she like, this new friend of yours?'

Maggie exchanged all the gossip she had on Natasha, and during the afternoon they had a really good natter about everything. After a few more drops of whisky from Beryl's canteen, they felt quite tipsy, laughing and reminiscing about the good old days. 'Here, Maggie, have a quick smoke of this. Our Nick gets it for me for my rheumatism. He's a good lad. He loves his old nana. He's the only bloody one that does.'

'I thought your Nick was some upright southerner solicitor. He doesn't seem like the kind of man that dabbles in this kind of thing.' Maggie took the joint off Beryl and took a drag.

'He knows someone who knows someone else, if you know what I mean,' said Beryl, tapping her nose. 'But he'd get shot and possibly lose his job if anyone ever found out.' The whisky was loosening her tongue and she couldn't help it.

'Beryl, you don't have to rely on young Nick to get you this stuff. God, people use it like teabags on this estate. Why didn't you say, I could get you some. It would save your Nick getting into trouble. Anyway, it's hardly a class A drug, is it? And it's for medicinal purposes, isn't it?' Maggie asked.

'I shouldn't ask him, Maggie, but this lot charge a fortune and I don't want the neighbours to know I use it sometimes. As I say,' Beryl emphasised, 'it's for my rheumatism.'

'Of course it is, Beryl. But he's taking a hell of a risk. Your Nick has done really well for himself. He's a nice laddie.' Maggie was genuine about Nick. No matter how well he had done, he always found time to say hello and pass the time of day with her whenever he visited Beryl.

'What makes you think this new lassie will move in, Maggie? Maybe she's changed her mind.'

'Because she has nowhere else to go. I get the feeling this is her one and only offer of a home. She'll come, rest assured, and when she does, I will bring her over to meet you. I'll get hold of a couple of young lads to bring that stuff over, if that's okay.' Maggie stood up and felt quite woozy as she left Beryl's house.

* * *

'Mr Diamond, you wanted to see me, sir.' Dressed in his suit, James McNally nervously stood in Nick Diamond's office. It was one of the few times he'd been here, but, even more surprising and worrying to James, he had no idea why he'd been asked here at all.

'Come in, James, sit down. There's nothing to worry about.

There's no easy way to say this so I'll just blurt it out and see what you say.' Nick had practised his speech many times, but he now he felt unsure. 'I have a very important client, James, and this client has been keeping an eye on you. I believe you know of him – Mr Burke?' Nick waited. He didn't want to sound familiar, so this vague recollection of Billy Burke suited his manner.

'Yeah, I know Billy Burke. Is he your client, Mr Diamond? What does he want of me? He can fuck off, I'm not getting involved. I'm sorry, Mr Diamond, I'm leaving.' Standing up, James was about to leave when Nick stopped him.

'Wait, James, Billy is not why you're here. Please... sit down and take a breath. I am not at liberty to discuss clients, but it has something to do with Mr Burke but not what he wants of you, but what my client wants.'

Shocked, a frown crossed James's forehead. He was puzzled about what client of Mr Diamond's wanted him, or better still knew of him. 'I don't understand, Mr Diamond.' Wringing his hands, James tried making sense of what Nick was saying. It all sounded a bit jumbled.

'This is a very confidential matter, and I am only passing on what my client tells me, but he feels Mr Burke has outstayed his welcome and his reputation. It's time someone else took charge of certain matters for him. But Mr Burke would not leave quietly or without a fuss and my client feels that if you wanted to take charge of any business transactions Mr Burke has, maybe given your history, you would encourage Billy to step down.' Nick's tie felt tight around his neck. With all his might, he hoped James knew what he was talking about. He wasn't a stupid man. On the contrary, he was very bright, which was why Nick liked him.

'Are you joking? The only way he would step aside would be if he was dead!' For a moment, they both paused, and their eyes met.

No sooner did the words leave his mouth than James realised what Nick was asking of him.

'He's guarded well, Mr Diamond, and he's a fucking animal! He may be getting on in years, we both are, but what this client of yours is asking is a lot. Do you know what kind of a man he is? It took four prison warders to hold him down once when he had a fight with another prisoner and two of them came away with bloody noses and broken ribs.'

Nonchalantly, Nick waved his hands in the air, expressing innocence. 'I really don't know much about this man, James. But as you say, it could be difficult persuading him to loosen his ties on his business dealings.' Nick laughed. He was doing his best to play it down, but he could see James was not taking the bait as he hoped he would.

'Take it from me, Mr Diamond. Billy Burke is bad news. The only way you are going to get close to him is if he's drugged with Rohypnol. He used to sell a lot of it at one time. Always got his hands on it and other similar stuff. He likes the prostitutes but now and again I know for a fact he's used that. He is low life. A fucking rapist!'

Nick felt stunned. His mind was in a whirl. He could see James's mouth moving but he wasn't taking in the words. Billy Burke drugged women and raped them. His mother had told him she couldn't remember what had happened once she was in his flat. She had also said they'd only had one drink. He'd raped Nick's mother! The bastard! Now it made sense. He could never quite fathom why his mother had slept with Billy, but now it all made sense.

Nick could feel the anger rising within him. Doing his best to remain composed in front of James, he sat motionless.

'Are you okay, you look a little pale?' Concerned, James pushed Nick's glass of water towards him. 'Mr Diamond?'

Breaking his thoughts, Nick forced a smile. 'Sorry, James. If that is what Mr Burke does with women and you know about it, why have you never reported him?'

'And say what without proof?' James shrugged. 'We argued over it, but the woman has to make the complaint, Mr Diamond. I could back up her story, but the complaint needs to be made first. Christ, all the police had to do was search his flat and they would have found the stuff. Don't blame me, blame that fat, druggie bastard.'

'Hey, I wasn't blaming anyone, James.' Nick held his hands up to stop James's outburst. 'I was only asking. Anyway, I just remembered I have an appointment and my work here is done. I will tell my client you're not interested in his offer.'

'Wait! Mr Diamond. Nothing is impossible, but what your client is asking is a big task. How do I know it's not a trap? A lot of palms would need greasing to convince them to turn on Billy. He always keeps his friends in money and drugs to keep them on side. He runs that prison, even the warders are on the take from him. Shit! They help him sell the stuff,' James stressed, trying to make his point. 'If it was that easy, Mr Diamond, I am sure someone would have done it a long time ago. And if what you're asking could be organised, it wouldn't be cheap, I hope your client understands that.' James gave Nick a knowing look. They both knew what they meant, but the words weren't spoken aloud.

'To start with, James, I'm not asking anything of you. I am only the messenger, so don't shoot me. This has nothing to do with me, but I am sure my client would cover any expenses you might have. I will leave you to think about it. You're obviously not the man my client thought you were. I'll say no more about it.' Picking up his briefcase, Nick walked to the door and opened it wide for James to leave.

'How long have I got, Mr Diamond? You know, to let you know if it can be sorted before you tell this client of yours?' James was already contemplating it, thinking about the money he could potentially make.

Looking at his watch and back at James, Nick's bored expression spoke volumes. 'Not long, I believe the matter needs sorting quickly.'

'Okay, leave it with me. Say nothing to your client for now, eh?' Once Nick had nodded and agreed, James left. And Nick knew he would agree. Why wouldn't he? He had James over a barrel. There was no choice. James was playing hard to get and Nick would let him if he felt it gave him some control, but the outcome would be the same. James would do as he was told and be pleased to do so. Nick had enough evidence on James to put him away for a long, long time.

* * *

Nick drove to the prison to see Billy. He was due to see him anyway, but he wanted to ask him about the drug James had mentioned. He wasn't sure how he would broach the subject, but he needed to hear it from Burke's mouth. Since leaving his office, all he could think about were James's words. He knew about Rohypnol and he needed to get to the truth. The traffic was heavy and he couldn't get to the prison quick enough. At last, he drove into the prison car park and looked up at the stone walls. He felt nervous and agitated. Most of all, if what James had said was true, he wanted to be sick.

As agreed, Billy kept up all the agreed presence in front of the warders. 'Mr Diamond, thanks for coming.'

Forcing a smile and handing over the usual packets of cigarettes, Nick sat down opposite Billy. He hated him with a vengeance. This loud-mouthed ape had raped his mother.

'I've spread the word, no one will steal anything from the community centre or cause any trouble while it's being renovated.

They will know soon enough that it has got something to do with me.' Sticking out his chest, full of his own importance, his arrogance annoyed Nick. Suddenly this brute of a man's bravado made him want to laugh. He was pathetic. A sixty-year-old man trying to hang on to his teenage years. It was like some theatrical tragedy. Billy had served his purpose and now his time was over, but first he wanted to hear the truth.

Nick should have skirted around it, but he couldn't. It was playing on his mind, the drive to the prison had been torture. 'Billy, I've been hearing you're quite the ladies' man?' Sarcasm dripped from Nick's mouth as he spoke. 'What's your secret, Billy? Personally, all that wining and dining wore me out, especially when there was nothing but a goodnight kiss at the end of it. If you know what I mean.' Giving Billy a knowing look, he watched as a loud guffaw erupted from Billy.

'I can't be arsed with all that, laddie. You're too posh for your own good. Women want sex, they just don't know it. Gagging for it, they are, that's why you need to give them a little shove in the right direction.' Folding his arms and sitting back in his chair, Billy gave Nick a wink and tapped his nose in a knowing way. It was as though he was sharing some boyish secret.

'What's your secret?' Nick didn't want to appear pushy and he had rushed the subject far too quickly, but he couldn't help himself. James had given him a lot to think about.

'I don't give my women a chance to say no, Nicky lad. When I want it, I take it. That's my motto. You'll learn, Nick, son. I can't be bothered with all that time and effort with nothing at the end of it. We used to sell a few drugs that helped things along a bit. It works a treat. You want to try it, son, it makes life a lot easier.' Billy laughed out loud at his own jokes, making Nick feel disgusted. Here he was a bold as brass, boasting about drugging women.

'I hope that doesn't include my mother, Billy.' His eyes bored into Billy's empty, lifeless ones. He felt hot and sweaty. As much as he wanted to know the truth, it made it all the harder, listening to this man joking about raping women.

Reaching forward, Billy slapped him on the shoulder. 'Not sure, Nicky boy, but something good came out of it, didn't it? I wouldn't have you if I'd never had my wicked way with your mother! She was always a bit uppity, but a few drinks down her and a shoulder to cry on made it all worthwhile. Come on, Nicky laddie, what's the big deal? Just drop a little of that stuff in their drink and they are yours for the taking!'

Disgusted, Nick sat there, stunned. This brainless oaf was actually laughing about raping his mother and any other woman who had the misfortune to cross his path. He wanted to shoot him there and then. Rip that evil tongue out of his head and nail it to the wall. He would make sure he had a sick painful death and then dance on his fucking grave!

Gritting his teeth, he ignored Billy's comments. Anyone could see he was drugged up to the eyeballs. Changing the subject back to the community centre, Nick informed Billy the builders had started their work. 'It seems someone is pissing on your parade, Billy. I've heard there's another man poaching around helping your friends out financially. He seems to be getting a lot of loyalty. You need to do something about it, never mind the community centre.' Nick dropped the bombshell that he knew would upset Billy, although he couldn't help himself.

The smile dropped from Billy's face. 'Who?' Who is it?' Billy's grim faced barked at Nick. Reaching forward, he grabbed Nick's tie and yanked him over the table, almost banging his head on it. Their faces were almost touching and Nick could feel the sweat from Billy's forehead against his own. 'Who the fuck is on my turf, Nick?' he rasped. 'We're partners and you should be looking after things on the outside. That's your job.' Billy's eyes widened, as though realising Nick's deceit. 'Is it you?' he shouted.

Shocked by this outburst, Nick hadn't expected Billy to attack him. He didn't know why, considering what he was like, but it hadn't crossed his mind that just sitting there opposite him he was in the line of fire. Struggling to pull himself away, Nick sat back down, straightening his tie and smoothing down his shirt. 'I'll find out,' he tried pacifying him. He wanted to get out of there unscathed. 'I have to go, I won't be around for a couple of weeks, and I have some personal things to sort out.'

'I'm fucking personal! Who is on my turf, giving orders? I made you a millionaire, I deserve your bloody time, you fucking upstart. Coming in here with your fancy suits. Now get me out of here or the next order I give will be you, that is, after I have told everyone you're my son and how corrupt you are!' Venom spewed out of Billy's mouth at Nick.

Coldly, Nick stared at him, now Billy's true colours were coming out. 'Who is going to believe you, Billy?' Nick's cold calculating eyes pierced Billy's and, for the first time since they met, he saw a worried look on Billy's face. He knew the odds were against him.

'I can tell them things about you and what you have been up to, isn't that enough?'

Nick gave a sneering laugh. 'Not in court. Evidence is the key and you have none, I have made damn sure about that. Save your threats, Billy, I am your only hope of getting out of here. You really wouldn't want any evidence, such as that CCTV recording that shows you murdered those men, suddenly turning up in the prosecution's hands.'

Billy's eyes widened with fear. He was angry and whatever drugs he'd taken were making it worse. 'Have you kept that tape?' he bellowed.

'Maybe I have, but rest assured, it will be in safe hands should anything happen to me.' Standing up, Billy knocked the table over, making it fly across the room, and lunged at Nick. Frightened, Nick backed away, his eyes wide with fear, but Billy's hands were around his throat, almost strangling him. His brute force pushed Nick against the wall and he could feel the pressure on his windpipe getting tighter.

Spit dribbled from Billy's mouth. 'If I'm going to serve a murder sentence, it might as well be you, you back-stabbing bastard.'

Nick brought his knee up hard into Billy's crotch, making him wince and loosen his grip slightly. Nick feared for his life – this angry, burly man could snap his body like a twig. 'All done here,' Nick croaked, rubbing his throat. Again, he shouted to the warders outside as loud as he could. Billy flew at him again, throwing the chairs towards Nick and around the room, as Nick tried to defend himself with his arms. Nick hammered on the door for the warder to let him out.

He was gasping for breath when the warders burst open the door and ran in. Billy was like a wild animal, going berserk, pulling at Nick, ripping his jacket and swearing. Throwing a punch, he hit Nick squarely on the jaw, knocking him off balance and banging his head against the wall, making him dizzy.

Through his dizziness, Nick could hear a bell. The warders had pressed the alarm button for back-up, and one of the two warders who stood outside the door grabbed hold of Nick's arm and dragged him outside, while the other warder was shouting at Billy to calm down. It was mayhem as Billy crashed around the room and tried pushing past the warder to get at Nick again.

A mob of warders filled the room, shouting at Billy and trying to restrain him. He was panting and his face was red with anger as he pushed the warders out of the way. More warders were running down the corridors. Leaving Nick outside, they closed the door to stop Billy's escape. He was like some angry lunatic as they pulled him to the floor, avoiding wild punches and kicks. Nick looked on through the window in awe. He was trembling. He noticed one of the warders was holding a small video camera, recording the proceedings. Curiosity got the better of him. 'Why is he doing that?' he asked the warder standing outside with him.

'Evidence, in case he makes allegations about how we restrained him. It covers our backs.' Seeing Nick's dishevelled appearance, he asked him if he was okay. 'What brought that outburst on, Mr Diamond?'

'I don't know,' Nick lied. 'He just flew at me.'

'You look pretty shook up, and bruising is starting to appear on that neck of yours. Come on, Mr Diamond, you'd better leave, I'll get the doctor to take a look at you, then the governor will want to talk to you about this. Are you sure you're okay?' Full of concern, the warder was about to escort him away when Nick took one last glance through the window. They had Billy on the floor, his arms behind his back, and he was handcuffed. One warder was sitting on him, while the others held his legs and continued shouting at him to calm down. Looking up, Billy saw Nick at the window, and his eyes bored into him. He was fuming.

Nick's legs felt weak as he followed the warder. It had been a near miss. A few moments longer and he would have been dead. The doctor checked him over in the governor's office and the governor wanted a full report about what had happened, although he could see Nick was in no fit state to do so.

Feigning all innocence, Nick repeated what he told the warder. 'Billy just lost his temper and lunged at me,' he repeated. He also dropped in that Billy was slurring and looked like he'd taken something... possibly drugs.

While sitting in the governor's office, he learnt that Billy had been sedated for his own good and the warders' protection.

Turning to the prison warders who had helped him, Nick shook their hands. 'Obviously, I won't be back,' he half smiled, 'he will have to instruct another solicitor. By the way, he told me he has a mobile phone sewn into his pillow and one in the woodwork room. What you do with this information is up to you.'

Weighing up the situation, the prison governor took a deep sigh. 'Don't worry, Mr Diamond, we'll sort this out. I think you had better leave now. We're used to Mr Burke's outbursts, it surprises me you lasted this long. You can press charges on this assault, if you wish.'

Nick gave a weak smile and shrugged. 'No, I won't be pressing charges, I'll leave everything in your capable hands.' Nick nodded and shook the governor's hand. Pleased to leave, Nick almost stumbled to his red E-Type Jaguar and turned to look back at the prison. 'Fuck you, Billy Burke, you fucking rapist. Rot in hell.' Once in his car, Nick lit a cigarette, his hands still trembling. He almost felt like crying with emotion at his near escape from death. He was glad to see the back of the place. Now it rested on James to get rid of Billy before he started spreading gossip and demanding vengeance. He hoped James would come good, for all of their sakes.

13

ICE-CREAM WARS

The mobile shop drove into the estate and blew its horn, waiting for the usual onslaught of customers. Today was benefits day, which meant payday. Midge picked up the credit book and flicked through the pages. There were rows and rows of columns showing what customers owed, not only for food but cigarettes and drugs too.

'Get out that holdall of cheap fags,' he said, 'this lot think it's Christmas day, getting cigarettes at four pound a packet for twenty. It certainly pays for all of those trips to Spain and back to pick them up. Cheap shit, they are, but this lot like them.' Opening the shutter, they could see the first of the customers coming towards them.

Just then, an ice-cream van drove at high speed into the fore-court and slid back its serving hatch, making Joe and Midge look up. A shotgun pointed directly at them. First it shot the tyres, the blast from the bullets making the van rock back and forth. The gunfire echoed around the estate as the shotgun carried on firing.

'Get the fuck down, Midge!' Groceries fell of the shelf, covering them both as they both scrambled for cover on their stomachs. It was mayhem. The bullets raining down on the van seemed never-ending. The whole van was being shot to pieces. Glass from the windscreen exploded. Joe felt his head and saw the blood on his hand. His forehead was bleeding. Midge lay on his stomach, his hands covering his ears. He was hardly visible, as he had hidden underneath one of the back shelves on the other side of the van, with all the bread and tins lying on top of him. Bottles of milk that had been in the line of fire dripped from the shelves.

There was a huge blast, and a ball of fire erupted into the air. 'For Christ's sake, Midge, they've hit the petrol tank. Get out!' Joe screamed at the top of his voice. Panic rose in them both as they scrambled to get out before they were burnt to death. They both heard the firing stop and the screeching tyres of the ice-cream van driving off as they kicked the back of the van open, almost fell out, and ran for cover.

The mobile shop, or what was left of it, gave out a second explosion and ashes from the groceries blew into the air, covering the ground like black snow. The explosions made everyone run in opposite directions, screaming in wild panic to save themselves. Midge and Joe were bleeding and covered in all kinds of food. Puffing and panting as they lay on the floor, they covered their heads with their hands. Everything had gone up in smoke, and what was more, so had the ledger full of creditors.

Black smoke filled the air and flames from the fire were nearly as high as some of the flats. Some neighbours on the ground floor had filled buckets of water and were stupidly throwing them at the bonfire in blind panic. 'The fire brigade is on the way,' someone shouted. 'Get out of the bloody way.' Other tenants on the top floor could hardly see anything from the balconies as the smoke rose into the air, making them cough and choke and shut their front doors for safety.

Loud sirens made them all breathe a sigh of relief. The fire brigade was close at hand. Soon this nightmare would be all over. Within a few hours, once the firemen had doused the raging flames with their hoses, all that was left was a steaming black mess of char-coaled metal. The van was a black, empty shell, hardly recognisable.

The police were hot on the heels of the fire brigade. Everyone knew there would be a lot of questions to be asked. Once the fire safety officers had looked the van over, they would see it was full of bullet holes.

The police knew it was a pointless cause because, as usual, no one around here would have seen anything. People were shocked, crying and rubbing dust and ashes from their eyes, making them red and sore, but no matter what happened in Thistle Park, the residents were blind, deaf and dumb.

Joe and Midge knew they would be at the front line of the questioning, but all they could tell the police was the truth. 'Well, well, well, if it's not little and large.' The policeman walked towards them where they were still cowering on the floor.

'Come on, you two, on your feet. What happened?' Ignoring their panic and pleas for help, the two uniformed officers stood there while Midge and Joe slowly got up, still shaking from the blast. 'Nothing to do with us, Sergeant Bates.' Their voices trembled with fear, but in their panic they couldn't stop rambling on.

'We came here as always with the shop, and some ice-cream van started shooting at us. That's all we know. And no, I didn't wait to see their faces, I was too busy running for my life!' shouted Joe. They knew the policemen, they had been arrested by them many times. This time they were actually innocent but who would believe them? They were a laughing stock. Whoever had done this would pay dearly. An ambulance eventually turned up and started attending to any casualties. Some had been cut by the glass, others were suffering from smoke inhalation. The policemen had to leave Joe and Midge while they were taken to the hospital.

They both knew they wouldn't have to report it to their boss; he'd have heard already and they would be in deep shit.

'We'll be seeing you two at the hospital. Don't think of going anywhere,' the policeman warned.

'Yes, well, don't forget my flowers and grapes, officer. Fuck, I pay my taxes, I know my rights. You would think we'd get better treatment than this. We've been attacked!' shouted Midge to the ever-growing crowd, as he hobbled into the back of the ambulance.

'Since when did you pay taxes, you haven't had a proper job in your life!' sneered the policeman. Shaking their heads, the police got back into their car and radioed back to the station what had happened. Starting the car engine, they headed for the hospital.

Throwing furtive glances at each other, the crowd that had gathered again slowly dwindled away. They felt foreboding at what was to come. Turf wars always affected innocent bystanders. It made them choose loyalty between each gang member. Either way, they couldn't win.

* * *

'Spider!' Fin shouted across the road to one of his mates. Puffing and panting after running up to him, he pulled out Spider's earphones. 'For God's sake, how do you do business if your head's full of music all day?'

'Because I don't need ears to do business! I sit in my car, people know who I am and know what time I deal. They come over and put the money through the car window. I whistle and that eight-year-old kid hanging around on the corner with his rucksack takes out a bag of crack or cannabis depending on what I have and hands it over. Job done. What do I need to listen to?'

'Go to the chicken kebab shop, you know, where Fatso Paul is the manager. Tell him Midge and Joe are at the hospital and the mobile shop's been blown up.'

Spider let out a low whistle and stared wide-eyed at Fin. 'You want me to pass on the bad news? Why me?'

'Well, with those things in your ears, you won't hear his anger, will you? Now go. Now!' Fin was half shoving him away. 'When the boss hears about this, he'll wonder why we haven't said anything, he'll know anyway, but I want him to hear it from us.'

'Okay, Fin, I'll keep you posted. Where are you going?'

'To the hospital to see if Midge and Joe need anything, though I must be nuts. That place is going to be crawling with coppers after this lot.'

Each of them ran their separate ways. Fatso Paul was one of the higher bosses in their establishment and was the main source of contact for the dealers. Fin knew he would pass the information on to the Undertaker and all hell would be let loose. And he definitely didn't want to be in the line of fire.

* * *

Joe lay on a hospital trolley, in a side cubicle. Now the adrenaline had left him, he felt groggy, dazed. Drifting off to sleep, he heard the curtain of the cubicle being drawn back, making him look up. Then his heart sank. 'How are you feeling, Joe? Do you feel up to making a statement?' Two police officers stood beside him and took out their notebooks.

Taking off his oxygen mask, he panted. 'Give us a break, sergeant. I'm not well. And to be honest, there is nothing I can tell you. We drove into the estate as usual, then the ice-cream van came driving in behind us and started shooting at us. What more is there to tell? I didn't ask their names, because I was too busy saving my own skin. Me and Midge could have been killed.'

'I know that, Joe, but why did they come gunning for you? Did you recognise the van?'

'Fuck knows, sergeant. They know we carry money, I suppose that's an idea. What do you mean recognise the van? It's an ice-cream van with pictures of ice-creams on it... how the bloody hell would I know?'

'All right, all right, Joe. When you're up to it, I want you to come down the station and make a proper statement. But I warn you, I will be making enquiries about this.'

'Ask Midge, he was there. We were too busy running for cover to stop and have small talk.' Joe was adamant. He too was puzzled; nothing like this had ever happened to him before.

'We have and he's gone home. He said the same as you. But we know there is more to it. There aren't too many ice-cream vans that serve shotguns.'

As the policemen left, Joe's mobile phone rang. He was surprised it still worked. 'Yeah, what?' His hands had been bandaged because of the minor burns to them. He could hardly hold his mobile.

'It's me, Midge. Get your stuff and come to the front of the hospital, I'm waiting for you. The police are sniffing around.'

Worn out and aching all over, Joe agreed. It made sense for them to meet up before they made their statements. 'They just left, okay, I'm on my way.' Rolling himself off the trolley and holding his ribs, Joe stumbled his way through the chaotic accident and emergency room. No one paid any attention to him. There were walking wounded everywhere, waiting for their turn to be attended to.

Walking through the doors, Joe looked around. It was dark outside and he couldn't see much. Then he saw the headlights of a car flash. It wasn't a car he recognised, so after looking around first, to see if anyone else had noticed, he slowly walked towards it.

Midge opened the window and looked out. 'God, you stink! Get in, will you. We have to get away from here. God knows, whoever tried to kill us might come back and finish the job. They know we're here.' Joe got into the passenger seat as Midge started the car.

'You don't smell so good yourself, I keep pulling sweets and cornflakes out of places I didn't know I had.' He half laughed, but it hurt his ribs.

'Yes, well, I got sprayed with eggs. Bloody awful.' Midge sniffed at his own jacket. 'Phew!' What with the smoke from the fire and the food everywhere, they looked quite a sight. 'That was a close call though, Joe. What the hell was all that about? We could have been killed. How's your hands, did you get burnt bad?'

'Stings like crazy! But rather my hands than my whole fucking body. We could have gone up in smoke. My head is throbbing. I don't know, Midge. This was a proper job. Not amateurs, they knew what they were coming to do, even down to the timing. This wasn't just chancers trying to rob us. We need to get to that van and make sure there is no trace of anything. I doubt it, but I want to make sure.'

'We'll go there now, the police will have secured it by now. We have to see what is left of the shop.'

'What the bloody hell is that?' Joe was looking down towards Midge's feet.

'What?' Looking up, Midge couldn't understand what he was talking about.

'Your feet! Why have you got two bricks strapped to your feet? Is that what the hospital did to you?'

Midge laughed. 'God, you are semi-conscious aren't you? Why would a hospital put bricks on my shoes? They don't put you on the rack these days, you fool. How do you think I reach the foot pedals in a car? I always strap a brick or a block of wood to the bottom of my trainers. Personally, I quite like those women's wedges. Those shoes are brilliant for driving in.' Midge nodded, not realising what he was saying, and definitely not seeing the shocked look on Joe's face.

Joe couldn't believe it. He felt too ill to take all of this in and felt pleased he was semi-conscious, but he couldn't help holding his ribs and laughing as Midge started to drive away.

* * *

'Fatso Paul!' Spider shouted as he ran into the kebab shop. Stopping short in the busy shop, he realised he'd said the wrong thing. The fat Greek man, wearing his white shirt and apron, gave him a daggered look and carried on serving his customer. 'In the back,' he thumbed to Spider.

Nervously waiting in the back room, Spider cursed himself for blurting out 'Fatso Paul'. That was what everyone called him behind his back.

The ham-fisted, overweight man pushed aside the multi-coloured striped blinds and walked in. Grabbing Spider by the throat, he pushed him against one of the lockers, banging his head against it. 'My name is Paulie. You can call me sir or mister, you little shit. Don't ever shout out Fatso in my shop again, you prick. Now what is it that is so important that you risk your life insulting me?' Still with his arm against Spider's windpipe, he waited.

Struggling, and trying to push him off, Spider eventually released himself from Fatso Paul's grasp and took a big gasp of air. 'The mobile shop,' he coughed. 'The shop was shot at by an ice-cream van. They shot the petrol tank and it's blown up. Joe and Midge just about escaped with their lives. They are at the hospital now.'

Frowning, Paul sat down on a wooden chair to rest his bulk of a frame, especially his stomach. Running his hand through his short, thinning black hair, he listened to what Spider told him. It wasn't much, but it was enough to make him roll his eyes up to the ceiling and back. 'Okay, you can get lost now,' was all he said, standing up.

'Any chance of a free kebab, Mister Paul, and maybe something to take the edge off the shock?' Spider fished hopefully.

'Sure, laddie. Hang on.' Paul walked to the front of the shop and came back. He had a handful of cold kebab meat and threw it at Spider, then he slapped him hard across the face, knocking him sideways. 'That's your free kebab, and the slap was for the shock. Now get out!'

Checking that the locker room was empty, Paul opened the floor safe and took out a mobile phone and dialled a number. 'Yes?' asked the voice on the other end.

Hearing the answer, Paul moistened his lips from their dryness and informed the listener what he knew. Once he had finished, the line went dead. Putting the telephone back into its hiding place, he walked back into the shop and started slicing the doner kebab meat. As usual, the shop was full to capacity.

The benches in the shop were for the customers to sit and wait while their order was being prepared by Fatso Paul. He saw to these customers personally and had his own serving counter. These were his usual customers for the cocaine and other drugs he sold. His customers would just come in and sit down without going to the counter. Instantly, Paul knew who they were and what they wanted and he would wrap up their kebab order with exuberance while slipping the packet inside the wrapping.

Slapping his huge hands together and clapping loudly, Paul beckoned his customer. 'Enjoy your meal.' He put the sixty pounds in his own cash register, which only he used. Tonight was no exception to business, whatever had happened. He'd passed on the message, it was up to them now.

14

A FRESH START

'Natasha, lassie! I thought you must have changed your mind, it's been ages, or it feels like it.' Maggie rushed forth and greeted Natasha in the forecourt of the tower block.

'Hi, Maggie.' Natasha smiled at the warm greeting. 'No, I haven't changed my mind, things just took longer than planned. I had to wait until the charity had a bed for me and Jimmy. It's all sorted now, though.' Natasha looked down at the floor and was happy at the distraction from Jimmy to break the ice. She felt embarrassed as Maggie watched the men empty the sparse small furniture van containing all of Natasha's worldly goods.

'I'll go and put the kettle on while you're busy, I suppose I had better make something for those two as well.' Maggie spied the furniture men doing their best, trying to carry a mattress up the many flights of stairs to Natasha's flat. Yet again, the lift wasn't working and so it was a daunting task for everyone.

'Thankfully, I haven't got too much for them to carry.' Blushing, Natasha looked up at Maggie under her eyelashes and pursed her lips.

'Nonsense, lassie, there is a whole host of things here for you. I tell you what, you take some bags up and leave little Jimmy with me. I'll make some tea and rally the troops to give those two a wee hand. Go on now, open the door before they blow a gasket carrying that mattress.'

Taking charge, Maggie waltzed off holding little Jimmy's hand as Natasha hauled up a suitcase. No sooner was she out of sight, the usual thieves gathered and stood peering into the back of the furniture van. 'Bloody hell, we wouldn't get twenty pounds for the lot of it.'

'Oy, you. Young Mathew. If you're going to hang around a removal van with those burglars, you can start carrying some of it up! And be careful, I'm watching the lot of you,' Maggie warned.

'What's going on, Maggie?' Steve was standing outside on the landing, smoking his usual morning cigarette, surveying the estate and catching a glimpse of the army of workmen at the community centre; lately it had become his morning routine.

'New young woman moving in, Steve. Poor mite, she has nothing to her name. I'm getting some of the lads to give those men a hand. God knows, they will have a heart attack climbing up and down those stairs all morning.' Pausing, Maggie looked at Steve. His fading black eyes and cuts spelled out his misery. 'How are you, Steve? We haven't had a proper catch-up lately.'

'I'm good, Maggie, you know me. I just get on with it. Do you want a hand?'

'Aye, that would be nice, thank you. Life outside not what you planned, laddie?' Reaching up, Maggie stroked his battered face. She'd known him since he was as little as Jimmy. His father had gone out for a loaf of bread one day and never come back with the change and his mother had died of cancer while Steve had cared for her in between going to school. In the end he had given up and got in with the wrong crowd. It was the usual story.

'And who is this then?' Ignoring Maggie, Steve bent down and came face to face with Jimmy. 'Hello, little man, what's your name?'

'This is Jimmy, Steve. Natasha's little boy. He's going to help me make some tea for everyone.'

'Well, wee man, it sounds like you're going to be busy. My little girls are at school. Maybe you could come around some time and play.' Steve laughed and joked with little Jimmy, much to Maggie's delight. She knew Steve had had a rough time of things lately, but he wouldn't complain. That wasn't his way.

'I'll go down, Maggie, before that van gets raided.' He laughed and walked away.

On her way to her flat, Maggie knocked on doors and told the occupants inside their help was needed and to get a move on. She didn't know why but she had warmed to Natasha and couldn't wait to surprise her with all the things she had collected from everyone to fill Natasha's flat and make it feel like home. She had begged some toys children had outgrown, and Beryl had even got her knitting needles out and started on a jumper for Jimmy.

The army of people finished the job in no time, even though they moaned about the flights of stairs. The furniture wasn't modern, but it was a start. 'I've got one of those pay-as-you-go electricity cards, Maggie. That means I won't get into debt or anything.' Wrapping her denim jacket around her to keep warm, Natasha smiled. Little by little, the beds were put up in the bedrooms, as Maggie supervised everyone.

There was a sofa and a mismatched armchair. A wooden cabinet for the living room and a small dining table with odd chairs. The charity had put aside an electric cooker for her, it had seen better days but a good wash and a scrub and it would look like new.

There was a cardboard box of miscellaneous plates and cups and two duvets. It didn't amount to much, but to Natasha it was everything. 'The council said I could go down to a paint and wall-paper shop they have a contract with and pick some stuff for decoration. I have a budget for each room, but it's just what this place needs, isn't it? A lick of paint.' Natasha's smile got bigger and bigger as the helpers laughed and joked with her.

'Come with me, lassie, I have a surprise for you.' Turning towards Steve and a couple of others, Maggie beckoned them. 'Come with me.' Natasha frowned and looked at Steve, who shrugged and laughed. 'We'd better go. Lead on, Maggie!' They all laughed.

Beryl Diamond had been looking out of her window, watching all the excitement. Maggie had spoken of nothing else over the last couple of weeks and seemed almost disappointed when there had been no sign of Natasha moving in. As Beryl watched everyone coming to her front door, she spied Maggie's excitement. She had known Maggie's granddaughter, the only kin she had left in the world since her daughter Michelle had dropped her baby off one night for Maggie to babysit and never returned. Although Maggie had received a note through the door one day from Michelle telling her that she was okay and that her new boyfriend had found it difficult having a baby in the way. Apparently, he wanted Michelle but not her extra baggage. Maggie had disowned Michelle for putting a boyfriend before her own child and Michelle had not been in touch since.

Maggie had loved Wendy like the daughter she wished Michelle had been. But poor beautiful Wendy had been tragically killed in a road accident on her eighteenth birthday.

It had been in all of the newspapers and Maggie had secretly hoped that Michelle would get in touch, but she hadn't. Nor had she turned up at the public funeral. Beryl had watched Maggie as she scanned the church for Michelle's face. But it was as though Michelle had forgotten she had ever given birth.

Maggie had gone into mental lockdown, especially when the people who had killed her granddaughter were to be given suspended sentences. Maggie had been distraught, almost suicidal.

Only the gang bosses that ran the estate and most of Glasgow had seen justice done. It couldn't bring her beloved granddaughter back, but it showed someone cared and gave Maggie peace of mind. The two men involved had been executed at point blank range and a photo had been sent to Maggie. It was gruesome, but it gave Maggie some kind of consolation. The gangland bosses who had helped her had Maggie's undying loyalty, even though she had no idea who they were. They contacted her via different sources and, whatever they asked of her, she did it without a second thought. Whoever they were, they had become family. They had cared more about Wendy than her own mother.

Beryl was pleased to see the softer side of Maggie again. This new Natasha woman seemed to have put a skip in her step once more.

'Here we are, Beryl.' Maggie burst into the lounge, full of excitement. 'This is Natasha and wee Jimmy. Natasha, this is Beryl Diamond. One of the longest residents on the estate.'

'I'm glad you said longest and not oldest, Maggie,' Beryl laughed. 'Go on, Maggie, this is your party. Everything is in the spare bedroom like before.'

Swinging open the bedroom door, Maggie stood there smiling. Natasha looked around the room at the boxes and black bin bags in the room and then back at Maggie. She was confused, she didn't know what she was looking at.

'It's for you, Natasha, lass. Everyone has chipped in and found some things they didn't need any more.' Pushing her forward, Maggie encouraged her to take a look.

'For me? All this stuff is for me?' Natasha stood in awe of the oddments of furniture and boxes in the room. Tears brimmed on her lashes and fell down her face, and she rubbed her nose with the back of her hand.

'Go on, lassie, take a look. Christmas has come early. Come on, boys, carry this stuff up to Natasha's flat.'

'Blimey, Maggie.' Steve popped his head around the door. 'There's more here than there was in the back of that van!'

Seeing the men carrying the boxes out, Maggie spied Fin. 'Hey, you, come here. And take that bored expression off your face before I wipe it off.'

'What is it, Maggie? I'm busy.' Fin tried his best to escape her, but she walked beside him.

'That television I saw you carting around the other day, do you still have it?'

A smile appeared on Fin's face. This was the kind of talk he liked. 'I do, Maggie, although I do have someone interested in it, I'm just waiting for their payday.'

'Don't talk bollocks to me, Fin. If you could have sold it, you would have done. I'll give you twenty pounds and that's it.'

'Twenty pounds? You must be joking!' Fin burst out laughing, until Maggie's slap around the face brought him to his senses.

'I'm not asking, I'm telling. Do your good deed for the day – take my twenty, make a young girl smile, and go and steal another one!'

'Why should I? Come on, Maggie, don't give me a hard time, you know it's worth more money than that.'

'Tomorrow is bailiffs' day, Fin.' Folding her arms in matriarch fashion, Maggie carried on. 'The moneylenders go around the flats and collect their money owed. If they take it in goods, such as taking someone's television away, they will sell it to another resident for cash. Just imagine what they would think if they thought you were selling on the estate. That's not how it works, is it, Fin?' Maggie's voice tailed off. She knew she had made her point when she saw Fin's face pale. 'Never mind, Fin, I'll come and visit you when you're in hospital.'

'I wasn't selling around here, Maggie, I swear. Those moneylenders are animals. A thousand per cent interest! No wonder no one can pay.' Fin held his hands up in submission. She had him by the balls and he knew it. The bailiffs not only lent money, they also sold goods. Usually it was crap, but if you took it, they made you pay for it.

'Well, that will teach people to read the small print. Good. Then twenty pounds it is, then. If only for my silence.' Maggie wagged a warning finger in his face. 'If they ever found out, you would be dog meat.' Maggie nodded and went back inside to sit with Beryl and Natasha.

'Here, lassie, put that throw over your shoulders, you look frozen to death.' Beryl pointed to the throw over the back of her sofa, which Natasha gratefully accepted. 'You might have no carpets, lassie, but there are a few rugs in that lot and that will do for now until you get on your feet.' Maggie impulsively wanted to give her a hug, but thought better of it.

'There's some cleaning stuff in that lot, too. Best get the beds made up first and get something to eat.'

'Thank you, ladies. Thank you so much, I don't know what to say.' Natasha reached forward and put her arms around Maggie. Beryl could see the pain in Maggie's face and a lump rose in her throat.

Once Natasha had left, Beryl took out her canteen of whisky, which forever seemed to be full and at her side. 'Take care, Maggie, love. She's not Wendy. I wouldn't want you getting hurt.'

'I don't know what you mean, Beryl. I'm just offering a little moral support to someone more unfortunate than ourselves.'

'Mm, of course you are.' Beryl poured the whisky into her own and Maggie's cup of tea as Maggie avoided her invasive eyes.

* * *

Once everyone had left her flat, Natasha pored over the boxes. Everyone had been so generous. Turning on the electric fire to warm the place up, she found the duvet covers that had been put in the boxes and made the beds up. All of the linen had been freshly washed and ironed, and she could guess who had done that. She thought her heart would burst, she felt so happy. This stranger, this Maggie woman, had done more for her in a short space of time than anyone had ever done for her in her whole life. She couldn't stop smiling.

Jimmy was amusing himself with all his new toys and someone had put a television in her flat while she was with Maggie and Beryl. It was her prized possession. Now Jimmy could watch all his favourite cartoons. She was going to be happy here. Already it felt like home.

15

THE ICE MAN

Tarpaulins covered the community centre, hiding it from public view. The noise that went on behind it was another matter. Day in and day out, workmen turned up in their lorryloads and worked noisily behind it, driving the residents crazy.

Even when the residents marched angrily up to the metal gates, rattled them and shouted abuse, they were ignored and turned away by one of the many security guards. Everyone was frustrated with it, but they could do nothing about it.

The police were still making enquiries on the estate following the explosion. Much to everyone's surprise, the police wanted to know where the burnt-out carcass of the mobile shop had vanished to. There was no sign that anything had happened.

It was all steeped in mystery, which only made the police want to dig deeper, but each time they failed. No one knew who had blown up the van and no one had seen it removed.

Joe and Midge had been informed by Fatso Paul that a new van was already being adapted into a shop and they would be on the road again by next week. In the meantime, they were to go door-knocking, collecting money owed, and make a new ledger for the people who couldn't pay up. Their task was an onerous one, but they followed orders anyway, hoping to ingratiate themselves again.

Although the explosion had nothing to do with them, they felt they would be blamed for letting their assailants get away without firing back at them. Only time would tell.

* * *

On the other side of town, in the suburbs of Glasgow, Albanian Noel drove up to his house. Parking on the drive and getting out of his car, Noel looked up at his house. It was late and dark. There were no lights on inside, which meant his wife and children were still at her sister's. After the day he'd had, he was pleased to have some time alone.

The conifer tree on his drive blocked his view of the front path slightly, but he could vaguely see something at the front of the house. Curiously, he cocked his head from side to side to see more clearly. As he got closer, he realised in horror what it was. Running up the path, he stared at his front door, then fell to his knees in shock. The gory sight before him made his blood run cold. 'Oh, my God!' he shouted to the open air, then quickly put his hands over his mouth to muffle his screams. Furtively he looked around, then buried his face in his hands. Raising his eyes upwards again, he looked at the warning that had been left for him and felt the bile rise in his throat, feelings of anguish and anger overwhelming him.

'Help me, Noel.' The weak, semi-conscious man half raised his head slightly and looked at him through the slits of his eyes. His breathing was laboured and his head hung limply to one side. His arms were outstretched and the palms of his hands had been nailed to the front door. Blood ran from the long, thick nails in his hands, down his arms and dripped onto the floor. His legs were astride and his feet had been nailed to the ground. It was a gruesome sight. On the man's forehead, someone had scrawled the words 'ice man'. It was barely visible, but the message was loud and clear.

Shaking, Noel ran around the back of the house. He had thought his brother Daniel was dead, but there was still life in him. God only knew how long he had been crucified to the door. This was abhorrent. Frantically searching through his toolbox in the shed for his claw hammer, Noel ran back around to the front door. 'Daniel, can you hear me?' he whispered and shook his shoulder. Looking around the street in the darkness, he saw no one was around. Obviously no one had seen Daniel, or they would have raised the alarm.

His heart was pounding in his chest and his hands were shaking. His mouth felt dry and he wanted to be sick, but he swallowed hard to keep it down. In the darkness, he saw Daniel nod his head slightly. 'I'm going to try to get these nails out, but it's going to hurt. The other alternative is to pull you away, but it will rip your hands to pieces,' he whispered. He could see Daniel was slipping back into unconsciousness and was grateful for it. He didn't know where to start. Firstly, he decided, he would get the nails out of his feet. Hopefully, they would come out of the concrete easier. He dreaded taking the nails out of his hands.

Kneeling down, he took hold of the claw hammer and, hooking it around the end of the prominent nail spouting from Daniel's bloodied foot, he heaved with all of his might to pull it upwards out of his foot, hearing the cracking of bone as he did it.

The darkness barely made the nails visible and Noel didn't dare switch the porch light on, but he did his best to see the end of the huge nail in Daniel's other foot and did the same. He realised he'd made a mistake when Daniel's legs almost crumbled beneath him, ripping his hands further, making him cry out in pain. He should have released his hands first.

Noel knew he had to work quickly and hooking the hammer

around the nail in Daniel's hand, he pulled for what seemed an eternity. Sweat poured down his face as the wet, bloodied hammer slipped out of his hands a couple of times and fell onto the path. The handle was slippery, and he wiped his hands on his trousers to dry them so he could grip the hammer tighter.

Eventually, Daniel's hand flopped down at his side and he hung at an awkward angle. Urgency carried Noel on as he struggled with the other hand, while trying to hold Daniel up with his own body. Blood dripped on him from the fleshy open wounds in Daniel's hands.

Noel was covered in blood and sweat. He cursed himself for this. He was the one who had ordered the turf war on the mobile shop. He was the one who owned the ice-cream vans. Everyone knew it. It wouldn't take a lot of deduction. That was why they had written 'ice man' on Daniel's head. That was the logo on his ice-cream vans.

He had wanted to own that Glasgow turf and take it over, instead he had brought horror and destruction on his family. He had undercut the Undertaker on prices of drugs and assaulted his pizza delivery men. Now it had all got out of hand.

Tears ran down his face; this was his young brother, he wasn't involved in this turf war. One last heave with the hammer and the nail in Daniel's hand finally came out and Daniel collapsed to the floor in a heap.

Stepping over him, Noel opened the front door and dragged Daniel inside. Closing the door, he switched the lights on. It was worse than he thought. Daniel had been badly beaten, and flesh hung from his hands where he had pulled the nails out, making the holes even wider and probably breaking his fingers or knuckles to boot.

His mind raced; how would he explain this at the hospital? He couldn't pass it off as a DIY accident. He knew he had to get him there, but wasn't sure how. In normal circumstances, he would call an ambulance, but he didn't think Daniel would last that long. Running into the kitchen, Noel put a cloth under the tap and ran back to Daniel, who was lying motionless. Washing the blood off his face, the water dripped down Daniel's neck, diluting the crimson blood into a pinkish colour.

In a blind panic, Noel ran back to the kitchen a second time and filled a bowl full of water before running back into the hallway. This time, he dipped the sodden cloth into the water and, standing above him, he wrung it out over Daniel's head. Apart from washing away the blood, it was bringing Daniel back to consciousness and he started to cough and splutter.

They were both soaking wet and bloodstained. 'Daniel, I need to get you to hospital. Do you think you can stand up and get into the car?' Noel knew it was a stupid question. He was asking him to do the unthinkable, with two broken feet!

Rolling from his back on to his side, Daniel summoned up as much strength as he had left in him to try to stand. His legs were weak, his feet throbbed, and his arms were numb. When he stumbled to get to his feet, holding on to Noel, he vomited.

'Come on, Daniel, lean on me,' Noel urged. 'Let's get you to the car.' Taking the full weight of him and putting his arm around his waist, they both staggered outside as Daniel dragged his feet along. The fresh air seemed to bring Daniel around, but now he could feel the searing pain in his hands and feet as he dragged one foot in front of the other. He started to moan and cry. His whole body had gone into shock and was shaking.

Noel shoved him into the passenger seat and watched him slip back into unconsciousness. 'Talk to me, Daniel, keep awake,' Noel shouted in panic. 'Sing something, for fuck's sake! Shout, howl. Say anything. We will be at the hospital soon!' Putting his foot down hard on the accelerator, Noel drove as fast as he could.

Noel's mind was in a whirl. How the hell was he going to

explain this when he arrived at the hospital? What if they called the police? Shaking the thoughts out of his mind, he decided to cross that bridge when he came to it.

Every traffic light he approached seemed to turn red, making him stop. The arduous journey was making him panic even more. He was frantically, shaking Daniel's shoulder and shouting. 'Wake up, for fuck's sake or all of this will have been for nothing!' Anxious and agitated, he drove on.

Approaching the front of the hospital, he took a sigh of relief and stopped. There were ambulances parked nearby, and the flood lights lit up the path. Pressing the horn and rolling the window down, Noel screamed for help at the top of his voice and jumped out of his side of the car. At last, nurses came running towards him to see what the commotion was. Once they saw Daniel, someone ran for a trolley and took over, pushing Noel out of the way.

Noel walked slowly into the hospital behind them all. He was shattered. He knew he looked a fright, but he didn't care. All he wanted now was for Daniel to survive his ordeal. He would wait while the doctors worked on him, but he needed to get home and clear the mess up. He knew this was his payment for his stupid impulsive ways. He was as guilty now as if he had hammered those nails into Daniel himself. Up to now, it had been a tit-for tat fight. But this was going too far. Who would be next? His young children? He had heard this so-called Undertaker was ruthless, and he had felt he could match him, but he didn't have the same sick ways as this man. He had tortured his brother and left him for dead. Sooner or later, someone would die and they would all end up in prison. It needed sorting, before it went any further, or they would all end up with nothing.

* * *

Nick was sitting at his desk when the telephone rang. 'Mr Diamond, is that you? It's James McNally.'

'I know who it is, James,' Nick laughed down the telephone. 'You gave your name to my receptionist who in turn told me who was calling. What can I do for you?' He felt free to talk. It wasn't unusual for an ex-con to ring a solicitor's office. James had been put straight through to him by the receptionist without a second thought. James had rung his office before, why should this be any different?

'Can I come and see you, Mr Diamond?' The anxious voice on the other end of the telephone made Nick smile.

'You can, I'll get my secretary to make an appointment for you.' Nick played ignorance. He had waited for this call. He had been on edge, waiting for James's reply, but didn't want to sound too eager.

'No, no,' James stammered. 'I would rather this not be on your appointment books. It's just an informal chat, if you know what I mean...' The silence on the end of the telephone convinced Nick it was good news. Why else would James be ringing him? If he wanted no involvement with him, he just wouldn't have answered. Instead, he wanted a secret liaison.

'Of course, James, why don't you just come to my office after hours tonight? I was going to work late anyway and everyone will have left by then. Does that suit you?'

'I will see you around eight, if that's okay. I'm sure your offices will be empty by then.'

Nick put the telephone down and smiled. His plan was beginning to come together, in fact all of his plans were coming together and that pleased him. It gave him a smug satisfaction. Nick wanted to laugh out loud. These men were supposed to be top crime bosses – they were a bunch of losers! But they were useful to his cause.

The community centre was well on its way to being finished. The army of builders had given him daily updates and he couldn't wait for them to drop the tarpaulin and show everyone the new renovated Diamond Community Centre. His nana would be so proud. It gave him a warm feeling inside, knowing she would be happy about it.

Nick had his finger in every pie now. All of Billy Burke's business associates took their orders from him, these days. They feared and respected him and they appreciated that he paid them their dues, unlike Billy, who was away creaming it off the top and short-changing them. Business was business and anyone who got in the way of that had better watch out!

Thinking about Billy Burke brought his mother to his mind. He needed to make peace with her. They were polite to each other in social gatherings, but there was always an awkwardness about their meetings. Nana's birthday party was the first time he had been there in over a year. He hadn't even remembered it was Nana's birthday or that she was visiting. He had been forced to go because Patsy hadn't answered his calls about the money. He realised now that that had been the sprat to catch the mackerel and get him to Nana's party. Over the last seven years, Nick realised, he had treated his mother badly, like a spoilt brat. Swallowing hard and consumed with guilt, he picked up the telephone and dialled her number.

'Mum? It's me, Nick. I wondered if you would like to have dinner this week sometime. We haven't had a catch-up in a long time.' His smooth, articulate voice wafted down the telephone to his mother's pleased ears.

'I'd like that very much, Nick. Would tomorrow night be too soon?' Victoria's hopeful voice made Nick feel a pang of guilt. She was a good woman and been dealt a rough hand.

'I'll come home, to Dorset'

'Home?' Victoria's voice wavered, she could feel the lump rising in her throat. He hadn't called it home in years. 'It would be nice to see you, Nick. Is anything wrong? Are you bringing Patsy?'

'No, I'd rather not, and everything is fine. I was just sitting here in my office, bored to death, when I thought of you. I'd like to get away for a while. Let's just have some "us" time, eh? And then Patsy won't scold me for eating too many profiteroles,' Nick laughed. 'I'll see you tomorrow.'

Concerned, Victoria asked again, 'Are you sure there is nothing wrong, Nick?'

'No, Mum, I'm just feeling a little homesick and want to see my mother alone.' Deep down, Nick knew it was true. Sometimes, he felt homesick and wanted to go back to familiarity, but he had been too stubborn to realise it.

His life had been crazy of late, and Patsy always seemed to have something to do. He felt quite emotional hearing his mother sounding so desperate. 'I do love you, Mum,' he whispered, while looking up at the window of his office, hoping the nosy receptionist wasn't listening.

He felt vulnerable. There was a silence on the end of the telephone and he felt himself blush. He felt like a young boy again.

'I love you too, Nick. I'll see you tomorrow, darling.' Sitting back in his chair once the call had ended, Nick pondered on his mother. He would tell her about the community centre and he would ask her to be with him at the opening. She would like that, even though it meant putting up with Nana for a few hours.

Taking a sip of his coffee, Nick reached for the telephone again. This time he would call Patsy. They hadn't seen much of each other lately.

Patsy sounded flustered when she answered the telephone. 'Nick, what's up?'

Rolling his eyes to the ceiling, he sighed. Why did everyone presume something was wrong when he was just making a social call?

'I'm just letting you know that I'll be going up to Dorset

tomorrow to see Mum. Are you around, do you fancy a late lunch before I go?'

The hesitancy in her voice said it all and he wished he hadn't asked. 'I'd like to, Nick, but I've promised some of the girls at the golf club that we'd go out. That's where I am now. By the way, I got your delivery, it's bigger than normal.'

'Not a problem, Patsy. Why would married couples want to spend some time together anyway?' He couldn't help the sarcasm, Christ, she could have suggested a coffee! 'And for the record, Patsy, any deliveries you have are not to be discussed on the telephone. I'll call you soon.' Slamming down the landline phone in his office, he felt angry. Patsy always accused him of not making the effort and now that he had, she had rebuked it. And as for the 'delivery' she spoke of... that angered him even more. Three holdalls of cash had been sent to her, hidden in boxes of salon products for her to launder, and here she was discussing it on the telephone. Sweeping his hand through his thick head of hair, he sat back and swivelled on his chair and looked at the pile of files on his desk. Picking one up, he scanned through it. Just as he thought, another innocent criminal to defend.

Nick felt restless, bored even. What was it about life? No sooner did everything go right in your life than there was something dragging you down. Maybe it was true. You can't have everything, and money didn't buy love.

16

THE MEETING

Fin and Beeny stood at the bar in their local pub. It was lunchtime and they were due to meet a couple of dealers who would give them another supply of drugs and pick up the money they had made. At least today they got their pay-out, that was the best part of the meeting.

Chalkie, as the landlord was known to everyone because his last name was White, turned a blind eye to the weird goings on in his pub. He was used to it and, as long as it didn't upset his other regular customers, he didn't care. Watching them going to the loo one by one amused him.

The dealer would come in, buy a drink, meet Beeny and Fin and then they would all wander off to a corner booth to talk. Fin, who seemed to be the self-appointed spokesman, seemed to do most of the talking. It was all hushed whispers and blatantly obvious to Chalkie that they were discussing something dodgy.

The drugs were usually wrapped in cellophane and put into the toilet cistern for collection. Envelopes were slipped across the table and the dealer would leave. Fin and Beeny would then go to the loo, pick up their stash and leave. Chalkie wasn't stupid, far from it. He was well paid for putting a sign on the door of the last cubicle in the toilets, stating it was out of order, for everyone's convenience.

'Oy, Fin, come over here a minute,' Chalkie shouted across the bar. He was polishing some drinking glasses, which made no difference as the cloth he was using hadn't been washed in years.

'What's up, Chalkie, mate?' Standing there in his jeans, leather jacket and sunglasses, even though it was a cloudy day, made Fin look like exactly what he was... a drug dealer.

'Did you pay for that drink?' Chalkie asked. His face never moved. He'd owned the Tartan Arms for years, and there was nothing he didn't know about Thistle Park and its residents. Lately, it had been busier than usual with the builders using it for their lunchtime watering hole. He seemed to be the only one pleased with the building works going on.

'You want me to pay for that pint? I might if I thought you cleaned the pipes once in a while. All your lagers are flat, why would I pay for that?' Turning to Beeny, Fin laughed. He was feeling light-hearted and cocky now he had a pocket full of money.

Without raising his voice, Chalkie raised an eyebrow. 'Because I said so, you little rat.' Reaching over the bar, he pulled Fin closer by his leather jacket. With his other hand, Chalkie reached into Fin's inside pocket and took out a wad of cash.

'That'll do, Fin,' he smiled. 'The rest will go towards all the drinks in the past you haven't paid for.'

'Hey, that's way too much. I'm going out clubbing tonight. Tonight is some woman's lucky night!' Trying to save face in front of the other customers, Fin could feel his bravery waning. Chalkie wasn't a man to cross.

'Well, you don't need much money then, do you? You always wait until ten minutes before closing time so you don't have to buy drinks all night for a woman, you cheapskate. And then you do laps around the dance floor, hoping some poor cow has got her beer goggles on and isn't too fussy.' A few of the other customers burst out laughing, ridiculing Fin.

'Yes, isn't there something about cruelty to animals? We've seen some of your girlfriends, Fin. Even the dogs' home wouldn't take them in.' Again, this was met by a great howl of laughter by the men at the bar.

'Well, this time you might be wrong,' Fin said, red-faced. 'There's a new bird on the estate and she fancies me. You wait until I bring her in, your jaws will drop. Come on, Beeny, I've had enough of this shithole with its flat beer. Whatever happened to the customer always being right?'

'Yes, but you're not a customer, Fingers Fin, you're a thief, and you'll drink my flat beer as long as it's free!' Chalkie shouted after him as he left. 'Right, laddies.' Chalkie turned to his old cronies at the corner of the bar who sat in the pub all day and made a pint of beer last just as long. Sitting there was cheaper than using their own heating and electricity, but as long as they bought a drink, Chalkie didn't mind. Displaying the wad of cash he had just taken off Fin like a fan in the air, Chalkie laughed, making his fat stomach wobble even more than usual. 'It looks like the drinks are on Fin!'

Once outside, Beeny pushed his woolly hat back, away from his eyebrows. 'Who's this new girlfriend, Fin, do I know her?'

Grinning, Fin swaggered cockily at the side of him. 'That Natasha bird. She fancies me, I know she does.' Sticking out his chest even further, he preened like a peacock.

'Has she said so?' Beeny couldn't believe it. He looked at Fin with admiration and slapped him on the shoulder. A wide grin crossed his face. 'You lucky bastard, she's well fit.'

'She hasn't said it in words,' Fin faltered, 'but I know she does. I'm just playing hard to get,' he shrugged. His ego was crumbling again. It wasn't turning out to be a good day. But now he'd thrown down the gauntlet to Chalkie, he had to find a way to get Natasha to go to the pub with him, whatever Maggie said. She protected that Natasha like a mother hen. God, Maggie got on his nerves sometimes. In fact, when he thought about it, she got on his nerves all the bloody time.

* * *

Nick had left his office door open when all the staff had left, it would be easier for James to let himself in when he arrived.

'Mr Diamond, sir.' Still knocking as he opened the door, James walked in. 'I saw the light on in here and presumed it was you.'

Looking up from his paperwork, Nick was shocked. James wasn't alone; behind him there was another man he didn't recognise. Doing his best to remain composed, he pointed at the chair. Looking up at the other man again, Nick waited for the introduction.

'This is Noel, Mr Diamond. A friend of mine.' James gave Nick a knowing look and a smile, but Nick still felt uneasy. He hadn't expected anyone else and James hadn't mentioned it.

'I'll get straight to the point, Mr Diamond. You say your client is instructing you on certain things regarding Billy Burke? You also mentioned that this client of yours would maybe like me to take things over once Billy is out of the way. I have looked into it and what he proposes is possible.'

Stone-faced and struck dumb, Nick nodded. He didn't like feeling this vulnerable and was uneasy with James discussing what he had said in front of this stranger. Clearing his throat, he decided to clear himself. 'As you know, James, my client is a very private man. I am bound legally not to betray his confidence. So whatever you and your friend think you need to discuss, please get on with it.'

'Noel and I both want to know if this is a trap or a truce. You see,

Noel here has had a bit of bad luck. He thinks it was possibly Billy Burke who tried to murder his brother by crucifying him to a door.' James shifted uneasily in his chair and looked at Noel, who said nothing. 'Billy Burke was on the same landing in prison when Noel served six months for possession. There were a few arguments and Billy threw his threats out to Noel. You know what he's like. He thinks he is the godfather of whatever prison he is in, Mr Diamond, and when he found out Noel was doing a bit of dealing, well, things just got worse. He even demanded Noel hand over drugs to him and get his family to smuggle them in.' James shrugged.

'Noel, here,' James continued, 'is head of the Albanian ice-cream vendors. There has been a lot of bad feeling lately between the dealers Billy Burke and the Undertaker use. When I told Noel about your client's idea of getting rid of Billy Burke...'

As a professional solicitor who had been in many difficult situations, Nick was calm, and held his hand up. 'Stop right there, James. I don't remember saying that. I am only the middle-man here.' Nick felt nervous. James was putting words in his mouth and he was in a dangerous situation.

'I know that, Mr Diamond,' James nodded, 'I just want to talk freely and properly, man to man so to speak, if that's okay.'

'Very well, James, carry on. As a client of mine you are also entitled to my confidentiality.' Sounding as professional as possible, Nick felt it was best to let James get whatever it was off his chest.

'As I was saying. When I told him about Billy Burke, Noel here, as a good-will gesture to your client, blew up Billy's mobile shop scam. It all went terribly wrong and you know the rest about Noel's brother. I feel,' James stammered and shifted uneasily on his chair, 'well, we feel that it's the Undertaker who wants rid of Billy Burke because he is becoming a liability. Would I be right? Does he also want rid of us?' James stammered and waited for Nick's answer.

Shaking his head and shrugging his shoulders, Nick picked up his glass and took a sip of water. His mind was working overtime. So, this was the ice-cream man he had heard so much about, he thought to himself. 'I don't know anyone called the Undertaker, James, apart from the ones at a funeral parlour. I'm afraid you have the advantage here.'

'We understand that, Mr Diamond. But if this man won't meet with us personally, we can only discuss business with you. Look, cards on the table.' James felt exasperated with this cat-and-mouse game and blurted out his plan. 'Noel here has a couple of lads doing a life sentence, so another couple of years on their sentence wouldn't mean anything. I have sounded out a couple of guys in the same prison as Billy Burke who hate his guts!' he half shouted and banged his fist on the table, nearly spilling the glass of water. Nick put his hand out to save it before it fell on his files.

'It comes down to money and security, Mr Diamond. These men don't mind doing their time, but they have families on the outside. Families they want to look after. I want the security that this isn't Billy Burke's joke and I'm the one who is going to end up dead. Noel here wants to make a truce. Maybe we could all work together. It would make life easier, don't you agree?'

Feeling a little more relaxed, Nick actually liked the idea. 'But as my client would be paying this money you're talking about and has a few more businesses than half a dozen ice-cream vans, surely you would agree he would get the lion's share?' Raising one eyebrow and spreading the palms of his hands wide at both of them, Nick waited. James and Noel put their heads close together and spoke in whispers while Nick waited. 'Yes, Noel agrees to that. The Polish brothels above the newsagents on the high streets are a good earner. The girls earn more money here than they could at home. They come over willingly and they live and work above the shops. It's not brilliant, but everyone is happy with the situation.' James gave a weak smile to both Nick and Noel, but their faces never moved. 'Three quarters of a million, Mr Diamond. That is what the men inside want to sort Billy out. There, I've said it.' James sat back in his chair and took a breath. He was all talked out.

Taking all of James's speech on board, Nick looked towards Noel. 'What about you? You're not saying much.' His broken English when he did speak explained to Nick why he got James to do the talking.

'We do this job, Mr Diamond, and our own people get hurt. Only soldiers hurt soldiers. Innocent people are now getting hurt. That's not good business. We do this to make money. My young brother is in hospital fighting for his life. He is a college boy. The first in our family to go to college.' Tailing off, Noel looked down and wrung his hands together.

'Can I ask what you two are together? How come you know each other?' Nick's curiosity was aroused.

'We met in prison, Mr Diamond. Billy stitched Noel up over a warehouse job. That is what I and Billy argued about. He got greedy and wanted to push Noel out of the deal. Noel got done and we both agree it was Billy who grassed him up.'

Summing up the situation, Nick felt it was his turn to speak freely. He was concerned that the Polish brothels had never come to his knowledge. 'Well, I have been instructed to agree a price regarding Billy and my client felt it would cost something. So I would agree to your price and make it a round one million.' Seeing Noel and James cast a glance at each other, he knew he'd said the right thing. 'As for you, James, I believe the offer for you to take over where Billy leaves off is a genuine one and you, Noel, make a good argument. It does make sense for everyone to work together as long as my client gets the lion's share. After all, it is you wanting the truce, not him. I will pass on what you say and get back to you. There is one thing I do know. Billy Burke's demise has to be painful and deadly and it has to be final. No being rushed off to hospital and made well to fight another day.'

'That would be guaranteed, Mr Diamond. Believe me, there is nothing more I would like to hear more than Billy take his last breath. It's a shame he's in prison. But these men would want money up front, or at least a retainer. They get nervous that people forget to pay once the deed is done. What about this son of his?'

A cold shudder ran through Nick, it was as though someone had just stepped on his grave. 'What son? I don't know what you mean.' Nick realised he really did need his poker face. What had Billy been telling everyone?

Spreading his hands jokingly, James laughed, 'I know he spread it about a bit, but he's been boasting about this son of his. Pretty well off and posh, apparently. He's saying they are going to be united once he gets out of prison.' James's laughter had suddenly turned serious. He wasn't a stupid one. He wanted no repercussions.

Shaking his head profusely, possibly more than he needed to, Nick stared wide-eyed at James and Noel. 'I haven't been told anything about a son. It seems you're up to speed more than me and my client.'

The room seemed to become hot and stuffy and almost claustrophobic for Nick, he felt he was playing with fire. James obviously knew more than he was letting on.

'Well, according to him, he has one and, funnily enough, he has the same first name as you. Nick. He's always boasting to fellow inmates about "my boy Nicky".' His words tailed off, as he paused while waiting for Nick's response.

Nick's tie felt hot around his neck, and he put his hand inside his collar to loosen it a little. He could feel the anger rising inside him. Nick knew that James had done his homework and come to all the right conclusions. Clearing his throat, again he denied all knowledge.

'Noel and me have been talking, Mr Diamond, and we just get a feeling that this son of his might know a little bit too much about every one of us. He could either put us in jail or have us all killed. It all amounts to blackmail. Noel and I would like some kind of assurance from your client,' James emphasised the word, 'that nothing would happen to us or our families if we went along with this scheme. Honour amongst thieves, eh, Mr Diamond?' Raising his eyebrows, James waited for the assurance he wanted.

Realising their half of the bargain, Nick felt better. He was dealing with businessmen and not that drugged-up Billy. Apart from their money, they wanted a full assurance that they would be safe. No more turf wars. He'd heard enough and standing up, he called the meeting to an end. 'I will see what my client says, gentlemen. But I am fairly sure we can do business.' Shaking both their hands, he waited for them to leave and locked the door behind them. Then, leaning on the back of the door, he gave a huge sigh of relief and pulled his tie off. He thought he was going to have a panic attack. Just what had Billy been saying while he was drugged up to the eyeballs and showing off to the scum of the earth? The sooner he was silenced, the better.

Nick's mind was working fast. He needed to get away for a while. Those few days in Dorset would do the trick. Picking up his briefcase and switching off the lights, he walked to his car. He'd already decided to give James the thumbs-up on the death of Billy Burke. He would wait and see if he achieved it, and more to the point he would make sure he was as far away as possible. Yet again, he would make damn sure he had a rock-solid alibi should anything go wrong.

Lounging on the Chesterfield with his feet up, Nick yawned. 'It's been just what I needed. A few days being spoilt by my mum, it's what we all need sometimes.' Nick had enjoyed the couple of days with Victoria. He'd left his suits and ties behind him. He couldn't remember the last time he'd worn jeans and T-shirts, even though they were designer. He felt at peace and, what was more, he felt the last few years of being at loggerheads with each other had come to an end. His mother had put up with a lot of sarcasm he had dropped into the conversation about cheating women when they had met in company and ignored it. She had been patient when his drunken tongue had lashed out at her for no other reason than his own anguish. He had felt like a pawn in a game. She had needed an heir to the Diamond fortune and gone out and got one. Now he knew the truth and was consumed with guilt at his childish behaviour. His mother had done nothing but shown him love and he had repaid her with spite. What a bloody fool he had been.

He had been stuffed to the brim with all his favourite foods and thoroughly enjoyed it. They had talked into the night and walked the Dorset countryside, taking in the fresh air. For the first time in what seemed an age, he admired the views.

When she had linked her arm through his during their walks, it had felt good. They'd had their heart-to-heart and cleared the air. 'Did you ever want to see Billy Burke again, Mum?'

'Good God, no.' Victoria looked at him, horrified. 'To be perfectly honest, I don't remember anything about that evening. I obviously can't take my drink, and I paid for it dearly,' she laughed. It seemed easier to talk while they were walking in the sunshine, surrounded by green meadows. It was peaceful and they could avoid eye contact. Squeezing his arm closer to her, Victoria shook her head. 'I must have fallen asleep or something...' Her voiced tailed off, as though trying to delve deep into her memories of that sordid night.

Anger rose within him. He knew exactly why she didn't remember that night. She had been drugged and raped. Thank goodness she didn't remember it, Nick felt sure it must have haunted her all of these years.

'That's why I hardly ever went back to Scotland with your dad, for fear of bumping into him again. I just couldn't face it.' Victoria looked sad and remorseful as they walked. 'Scotland reminds me a little of Dorset. Parts of it are beautiful with its wide open spaces. That beautiful castle in Edinburgh, steeped in history. You know I like history. Scotland has it all, but Billy Burke spoilt it for me in a way that can never be repaired. It's my own fault too, of course, but Scotland holds a lot of demons for me. I hope you understand that.' Stopping, she turned to him and wiped away a wisp of hair from his fringe that had fallen across his face.

'These things happen, Mum. Leave the past in the past, eh?' Squeezing her arm more tightly towards him, he pondered on her words.

'I love you, Nick, but I have always regretted being a fool and living a lie to your father. He didn't deserve it. Sometimes I felt he knew and sometimes... there were unspoken words between us. He didn't care, he had you and that was all that mattered. You were the light of his life. Mine, too.'

Nick looked solemnly around. The calmness of Dorset engulfed him as he watched the sheep jumping around. It felt like they were the only two people in the world. 'You didn't betray him, Mum. You never betrayed Dad. Billy Burke drugged and raped you. He used a date rape drug and he was well-known for using it on many occasions.'

Stunned, Victoria stopped walking. 'How do you know this?' Suddenly, it all came flooding back. Tears brimmed on her lashes. Her legs went weak beneath her and she had to sit down on the grass. Looking up at Nick, she asked again. 'How do you know that, Nick?'

'He's done it many times, apparently, and used to sell it at one point. So you can stop blaming yourself for that night. It wasn't your fault.' He wished he'd bitten his tongue and never said anything, but he thought this might help her have some peace of mind.

Tears rolled down her face, and she reached in her pocket for her handkerchief. 'All I remember from that night was one drink, then everything went blank. I've always had my suspicions, no one has that much of a lapse of memory,' she scoffed and wiped a tear from her eye. 'When I woke up, my clothes were dishevelled and undone and I had a shocking headache. Even when he walked me home and left me on the doorstep like a bottle of milk, I felt dizzy and weak. I went straight to the bathroom and threw up. Your father and Beryl didn't ask any questions. Looking back, I suppose they must have thought I had just stormed out and gone to the pub. Isn't that what people do?' Her face was solemn, as though recalling that awful night for the first time in years.

Nick sat beside her and held her hand while listening to her ordeal. He couldn't express the sorrow he felt. No woman should have to go through what she had. He was the only person she had confided in, and he was pleased about that. This was their secret and now it could be buried forever.

Carrying on, almost in a dream, Victoria's words were low and reminiscent. 'Your father and I were still in the middle of an argument and we didn't sleep together that night. I slept in the spare room. I remember lying down and falling asleep again, I was out for the count for twelve hours. I should have gone to the police with my suspicions, but what good would that have done? They didn't really believe in date rape when you were a baby, Nick. Only these days has it come to light.' Her voice wobbled as she spoke the words she had kept to herself for so many years.

Nick reached for her hand as she stood up. Standing beside her, he put his arms tightly around her and held her while her tears flowed freely. Her body was wracked with sobs. He felt closer to her now than he had ever been. All the barriers had been broken.

Now it was time to get back to reality. 'Don't forget, Mum. You're coming to the opening of the community centre. Billy won't be there and you are a strong brave woman. Don't be a victim.' He felt better when he saw the faint smile cross her face.

'I will definitely be there, if only to see Nana's face when she realises that it's you who has made her dreams come true. She'll probably have a heart attack.' Crossing her fingers, Victoria laughed. 'On a serious note, Nick, it's lovely to have something back in your father's hometown that bears his name. He would have been so proud of you. The Jack Diamond Community Centre, it has a nice ring to it.'

Arm in arm, they walked back to the house in silence. This talk had been a long time coming and she was pleased. She had her son back and that was all that mattered.

* * *

Before going home, Nick stopped off at his office and dialled James's number. 'I have all of the authority to grant you what you asked for, James.'

'What about the money?' On the other end of the telephone, James was sitting with Noel and gave him the thumbs-up sign.

'Come to my office in the morning, early, before the staff get here. Let's say around 6.30?'

'I'll be there.' James put the telephone down and picked up his pint of beer from the bar. 'All systems go, Noel. Drink up, we have things to arrange.'

'Thank you for doing this.' Noel didn't know how to express his gratitude. His brother was going to be in hospital for a long time. The police were hounding them both with questions. He didn't dare let his ice-cream vans onto the surrounding estates for fear of repercussions. He was losing money hand over fist, he needed to get things in order again and James was giving him that ticket out. He would be eternally grateful.

They had both played ignorant, but they knew the police were not letting this go so easily. A shoot out, a burnt-out van and a cruci-fixion? The pair of them left the pub and drove to Noel's house. They had a lot of organising to do. Murdering someone like Billy in prison was not an easy task, but it had to be done.

* * *

Early the next morning, Nick left the apartment and went to his office. Waiting for the cleaners to leave, he pulled back the carpet near the skirting board and started unscrewing the floorboards. Raising a couple of planks, he looked down. There were bags of all shapes and sizes, full of money waiting to be laundered. This, he had decided early on in his life of crime, would be his getaway stash, just in case it was ever needed. No one knew where it was and that was how he liked it.

Each block of notes held a thousand pounds. He neatly counted them out from his private safe. They were piled on top of each other like a stack of bricks. Nick took out the million and stashed it into two holdalls. They weighed a ton as he pulled them under his desk. Looking at his watch, he knew James would be arriving any minute.

Screwing the floorboards back down, he pressed the carpet near the skirting board down with his foot, to make sure it didn't look like it had been disturbed.

His heart was pounding as he heard the long-awaited knock at the door. Once Nick opened the door, he could see that James was alone. 'Not with your friend today, James?'

'No, Mr Diamond. Noel's English isn't very good, as you're aware, but he's had the shit scared out of him.'

'Is everything in order, James? My client is curious,' Nick asked. He wanted to know what they had decided about Billy but didn't want to make it too obvious. After all, he was only supposed to be the middle-man in all of this.

'Tell your client, Mr Diamond. Everything is in order and ready for Friday,' James assured him with a knowing look. 'Come midnight, it will all be over.' They both stood in silence for a moment and looked at each other. There was nothing more to say.

'This is what you came for.' Bending down, Nick pulled one of the holdalls by the handle and dragged it across the floor. 'There is another one. Are you going to count it?'

They both stared at the canvas holdalls in awe. 'I trust you, and if I don't, I shouldn't be doing business with you,' James snapped.

'I'm not a young man, Mr Diamond, and I have been around the block many times. I wouldn't be here if I didn't think you were on the level. Right, I'd better get the car loaded. I'll be in touch.' Heaving one of the bags, James went out to his car and then came back for the second. Shaking Nick's hand, he smiled. 'When shall I call you?'

'I'll call you. And don't think of running off to a life in the sun with all that booty, James, my client wouldn't like it.' Nick laughed, trying to make a joke about it, but the undertones in the sentiments were obvious. It was a big chance he was taking, and if they cut and run, who was he going to complain to?

'I wouldn't dream of it, Mr Diamond. We, that is your client and us, have a lot of business and a lot of money to make. I'm sure your commission in all of this is ample, or why else would you put yourself in this position? Apart from that, your client is like gas. He can't be seen, you can't smell him but he's as deadly as hell!' Nodding and shaking Nick's hand, James left. They had both said their piece and it was time for action.

Nick's mood felt lighter. For him, now, it was just a waiting game.

* * *

Natasha looked in her food cupboards and gave a sigh. Her benefits were not due for another two days. She couldn't keep taking plates of stew and stuff from Maggie. The horn of the mobile shop blowing in the forecourt gave her an idea. She'd only lived there for a month, and they didn't know her, but Maggie had said he gave credit sometimes. Taking Jimmy's hand, she ran down the flights of stairs. When she got there, she realised there had been no point in rushing – the queue was a mile long.

Eventually, it was her turn. Swallowing hard and looking around at the crowd behind her, she felt foolish. Going as close to the open window at the kiosk as possible, she half whispered to the man inside. 'Maggie said you give credit sometimes, I wondered if you could let me have a bread loaf and a tin of beans or something until I get my money.' Dropping her eyes to the floor, she felt ashamed and embarrassed. A small man came from the back and raised his head over the kiosk. 'Is that locket you've got on gold?'

Frowning, Natasha fingered the necklace idly. 'Only nine carats, it's not expensive or anything like that.'

'Hand it over. Joe, get a bread loaf and a couple of tins of spaghetti and beans.'

Joe put them into a carrier bag and handed them over. 'Benefits day, lassie, and we know what day that is. Its two pounds a day interest. If you can't pay, you don't get your locket back. Here, sign this.'

Confused, Natasha looked at the small writing book he was holding. 'What's that?'

'It says how much you owe and that you agree to give me the necklace in payment for groceries. If you pay your bill, you get your necklace back and this receipt.' Joe held his hand out as Natasha unclipped her necklace and handed it over reluctantly. Then she scribbled her name and door number underneath it. The groceries had been costly, but it had saved the day.

Grabbing the carrier bag, she lowered her eyes and walked away, almost running as she held Jimmy's hand tightly. Her face felt like it was burning as she looked under her eyelashes at the queue behind her, knowing she had just begged for a few meagre offerings. It felt like the whole world was whispering about her. She felt like bursting into tears, although she didn't know why.

'Who's next?' Joe shouted to the queue, rubbing his hands together.

'Can I have a ninety-eight cornet, please.' Midge took a cornet and started filling it with ice-cream.

'What's a ninety-eight, Midge?' Two police officers were walking the beat and following orders from the police station to keep a close eye on the new mobile shop.

Joe and Midge threw a glance at each other and then back at the sergeant and community officer. 'It's one without a flake, officer. An in-joke, you might say.' Trying to think on his feet, Midge gave a weak smile.

'Well, isn't that just an ice-cream?' Looking the crowd over, the other police officer looked around the mobile shop. 'Funny you had that trouble with the ice-cream van when you're taking his business.' The two policemen pushed their way to the front of the queue and spied Joe and Midge's uneasiness.

'Just a joke, officer, is that a problem? We've always sold ice-cream, that just a coincidence, wasn't it? There is business around for everyone.' Midge then proceeded to put strawberry sauce on to the ice-cream and handed it over to the customer.

'Isn't he going to pay for that ice-cream?' the policeman asked suspiciously., nodding towards the customer. The crowd started to dwindle away, the last thing they wanted was a run in with the police. Nodding to each other, the policemen knew they had achieved their goal. They knew it was a drug den, but they had no proof and they didn't have any excuse to search the van.

'Of course he is, officer, we're not running a charity, you know,' snapped Midge. He was feeling hot under the collar as well but it had nothing to do with the weather. He spied the cornet he had handed over. In the bottom of the cornet he had placed a small packet of cocaine. That was the code for it, a ninety-eight cornet.

Stupidly, the customer handed over two twenty-pound notes, without thinking, much to Joe's annoyance.

'Expensive ice-creams you two are selling. I'll have whatever he's having,' said the officer. Sarcastic and bored, the policeman knew they were up to no good, but whatever these people were buying, it was their own choice. 'Maybe we should look over this shiny new van of yours. It's a better model than the last burnt-out one you had. Did you ever find out what happened to it?' Again, the policeman yawned. He hated this estate. He had patrolled it many times and knew most of the inhabitants by their first names.

'No idea, officer, we thought you'd taken it. I bet those scrap metal guys stole it. I suppose it was worth something in scrap value,' Midge reasoned. 'Look all you like. Everything is above board.' Pouting and sticking his chin out to make his point, Midge looked at the officer who seemed to be taking a great interest in the ice-cream he had just handed over.

Quick as a flash, Midge leaned forward and knocked the ice-cream out of the customer's hand, making it fall on his T-shirt and on to the floor. Then he got out of the van and walked to where it lay. 'I'm cleaning it up, officer, don't worry.' Scooping it up, cocaine and all, Midge shouted for Joe to hand him some more paper towels to wipe the floor with.

Quickly Joe poured the officers' ice-creams and put a flake in. 'There you are, officers, on the house.'

'No, Joe, we don't take bribes, take this.' Putting his money on the counter, the police officer looked behind him at the solemn crowd. They didn't have much to say to each other in front of the police.

As the few customers that were left watched them walk away, there seemed to be a sigh of relief from everyone. Just the police being there seemed to put their teeth on edge.

'You! You silly bastard, come here,' Midge shouted to the customer when the police were out of earshot. 'Giving me forty quid for a fucking ice-cream?' Reaching forward, he punched him hard on the nose, knocking him backwards. 'Get out of here, you bloody fool.' Everyone seemed to turn a deaf ear to the proceedings, as the customer pulled down his baseball cap and wiped the blood from his nose with his sleeve. It wasn't their business and clearly Midge was upset.

Once they had served everyone else, they pulled the shutter down and drove on towards the building site. 'It's getting a bit tight around here at the moment, Midge. The police are crawling about every day.'

'Forget it, Joe, this van is in good condition, and we have licences. If they want to search it for no reason, that's harassment. What are they going to do? Search it every bloody day?'

'They would if they could, and don't forget you have a shotgun in the back of the van and a stash of gear.'

It was clear they both felt uneasy. Their silence spoke volumes. 'Changing the subject, who was that lassie with the necklace? I don't remember seeing her around before. What's her address?'

Midge reached for the credit book and looked at Natasha's name and address. 'Maybe she would like to pay her bills off at the cemetery. She's fresh meat, Joe. Nice and young, too.'

'How's business up there lately?' Joe was curious, he'd been taken off the usual patrol, collecting money from the usual punters. Something about being too much under the watchful eye of the police.

'Busy as usual. The van is always full of women paying off their debts and making a few extra quid. A blowjob and a quickie behind a headstone. What's the big deal? It's quiet and safe. Some even have their own patch, so to speak. It's better than walking the streets and they get brought home safe too. They are looked after. Think that new lassie would definitely make money.' Nodding at each other, they smiled like two Cheshire cats. They had their hooks into this Natasha woman already, it wouldn't be too long before she came cap in hand again and then they could suggest a way she could pay off her debts. After all, come benefits day, she would be short of cash again once she'd paid them and the interest she owed. It was a win-win situation, especially for Joe and Midge.

James and Noel had put all of their plans in place. Nothing could go wrong, this was a one-off chance to rid the world of this evil old bastard. The men they had chosen to do the job had been cherry-picked and handsomely paid and once they had been told by their families the money was safely in their accounts, they were satisfied. They were due to serve life sentences anyway for murder, what was one more added to this? They accepted their lot in life.

The noise in prison was deafening, the heavy boots of the warders permanently walking across the landings. Some of the inmates had nightmares and would shout and scream in the night, echoing across the staircases. The heavy cell doors slammed when the warders went to see what the problem was and, of course, there was the constant looking through the spy holes of their cell doors by the warders, checking up on them, no matter what time of night or day. There was no privacy, even when you were on the toilet. But most of all, it was the smell of the place, nicotine and disinfectant filled the air. They were miserable places.

Standing at the snooker table with his cue in his hand, Billy Burke shouted in turn for a partner to join him. He ruled the table as though it was his own. Hardly anyone got the chance to play without his say so.

He was still smarting from Nick's behaviour, although in his arrogance he knew Nick would have a change of heart and come crawling back. He'd been in solitary and his cell had been stripped of everything, especially his mobile phones, which had had been his lifeline.

'Hey, Billy, why not let us have a go?' Getting up, Ken, as he was commonly known amongst the inmates because no one could pronounce his Polish name, casually strolled over to Billy.

'Fuck off, immigrant! This is my table and my game,' he shouted. His thick Scottish accent bellowed around the room, like a lion protecting his own piece of land. Ignoring him, Billy pointed at another man, quietly playing draughts with his friend. 'Get your arse over here, before this lot muscle in.' His grim face sneered. Raising his tall stature even more and sticking his chest out, he pushed past Ken, knocking him sideways.

Not wanting a fight to break out, the prison warder walked up to Billy. 'Quiet, Billy, there's no need for that. Maybe you should go back to your cell.' Calmly the prison warder took the snooker cue from Billy and walked away.

'You!' Billy spat out at Ken. 'You skinny Polish bastard, you haven't heard the last of this,' he threatened, waving his finger in his face, his cold eyes burning into him. Everyone avoided Billy's wild stare. They didn't like being in the line of fire of Billy's anger. The room was still and everyone stopped what they were doing and cast glances towards each other nervously.

'You are also an immigrant, Billy.' Polish Ken smiled as he spoke the words calmly. 'After all, you're not from England either.' He was making his stance and throwing the gauntlet down. 'I'm ready for bed, keep your game.'

'Me, a fucking immigrant?' Billy shouted. Running towards Ken, he was stopped by a warder who barred his way. Billy's face turned red with anger. 'What the fuck are you lot looking at?' No one answered him and, seething, Billy watched Ken make his way up the metal staircase to his side of the landing where his cell was.

Billy knew he couldn't do anything about it now, but he was definitely going to make an example of Ken and his mates. They stuck together like glue, it made him sick. Making his way back to his own cell as instructed, he lit a cigarette. He didn't want to go back into solitary so soon after leaving it.

'You get out, I want the place to myself,' he shouted at his cell mate. Loopy Len scurried out of the cell, squirming as he passed Billy. Loopy Len was everything his name indicated. He was so far gone after his years on drink and drugs that he didn't know what day it was. He would sit in his cell and rock back and forth, talking to himself, driving Billy mad in the process.

Billy didn't mind sharing a cell with him, though; he never saw anything and he was submissive. Constantly saying the same sentence on a loop, no one took any notice of him, especially when he talked of the days when he stood in battle against Napoleon. Billy would throw him one good punch and that would leave him cowering in a corner for the rest of the night. Once done, Billy could get some sleep.

Just moments later, Ken and two of his friends burst into Billy's cell. One was holding a boiling kettle full of hot water and sugar that turned it into a thick, red-hot paste, and threw it at Billy. Shutting the door behind them to block out Billy's screams, he held his face, which by now was burning as the paste sizzled on his skin, making it blister and bubble as the skin slowly melted away. Rushing forward, Ken forced a pair of socks into Billy's mouth, as he held his head in his hands and rubbed his eyes, peeling the skin off his face. Billy was helpless; he tried standing to rush to the sink, but he could hardly see.

One of the men peeled off the machete that was sellotaped to his back under the plastic covering he was wearing and had been smuggled in the day before. Raising his arm, he brought it down heavily and sliced at Billy's throat with one swift blow. The sharp machete sliced through Billy's neck like a knife through butter. Blood spurted out everywhere as Billy fell to his knees, his screams ceasing as he fell to the floor. Handing over the bloodied machete to his friend, the Polish man nodded. 'Your turn,' he whispered.

Taking the machete, the man raised his hand. 'This is for Daniel, you bastard.' Raising his arm, the jagged edge of the machete sliced into Billy's neck, leaving his head hanging at an awkward angle. The cell floor was covered in a pool of blood. The walls were crimson-stained where the blood had spurted from Billy's neck and it flowed onto the bedding, turning this massacre into a sea of red.

Ken took his cigarette out of his mouth and flicked the lid of his petrol lighter upwards, waiting for the flame to ignite. Relighting his roll-up and taking a long drag of it, he then squeezed the small can of lighter fluid that had also been smuggled in towards Billy's bloodied body, squirting petrol up and down him, then throwing his lighter with its burning flame onto Billy's body, he watched him erupt into flames. He threw his cigarette on the bonfire for good measure. Pleased, he nodded at his friends. Their job was done. Billy was nothing more than a ball of fire.

Taking off the plastic waste sacks that they had stolen from the prison kitchens, they threw these onto the flames, too, then fled back to their own cells. The smoke and fire billowed out of the door of the cell, making the fire alarms go off.

The warders shouted for everyone to go back to their cells. 'Fire in the cells!' they shouted and pressed the alarm. Everyone ran in different directions as the prisoners looked up and saw for themselves the flames coming out of Billy Burke's cell. Warders fled to it with buckets of sand, but it was too much for them, as they stood in awe, looking at Billy's burning body. The heat was immense as Billy's charcoaled body lay there engulfed in flames, like a Viking burial.

One warder fought off the flames and jumped forward with a fire blanket smothering Billy, burning himself slightly in the process. Others followed suit with fire extinguishers and did the same with wet blankets, feeling the smouldering body beneath.

Sweat poured from them as they looked up through the smoky mist and saw the bloodstained walls, filling them with horror.

'The ambulance is on its way!' a warder shouted and burst through the cell door. 'I'd say he's definitely dead, no one could survive that,' he grimaced. The floor was awash with blood that the fire extinguishers had diluted and covered their shoes and trousers as they knelt beside Billy on the floor.

Peeling back the fire blanket, they looked at Billy Burke's charred remains. 'It looks like someone's cut his head off. Look for yourself.' Peering down, they nodded to each other. It was gruesome. 'Is everyone safe?' Bob, the chief warden, looked up to ask. He didn't know what else to say. He was lost for words. He'd seen riots in prisons before, but this was beyond belief.

'Yes, Bob. Everyone is okay. It's pretty contained in here. Leave everything as it is.' They were all panting and sweating from their ordeal. 'This is going to be one hell of an enquiry.' They all shrugged and walked out of the cell. Nothing was to be touched until the police arrived and the ambulance people had done their jobs.

Prisoners were making a racket and banging their cell doors and shouting to each other from their cells. The landings were in uproar.

'Hey, what's going on? Is Billy Burke dead?' they shouted to each other.

'I bet he's burnt to a fucking crisp.' In turn, they all shouted their questions and answers to each other.

'It couldn't happen to a nicer guy,' someone shouted at the top of his voice, rattling his cup against his cell door.

This was the bit of excitement they all yearned for. Something to keep them talking for days. Billy Burke was dead at last. Thank God for that! His reign of terror was over.

The warders shouted for them to calm down and be quiet but knew it was useless. This was just the beginning of a sleepless night for everyone. Soon the police would be here and the whole place would be filled with official visitors ploughing through the scene of the crime.

Nick had got what he wanted. A painful, horrible death for Billy Burke, with no second chances. Whatever happened now, the men who had done this had earned their money for their families. They knew there would be consequences if it was ever found to be them. They knew in turn all the cells would be stripped and searched. They knew the risks when they accepted the job, but at least their families would be safe financially, and Daniel had been given some form of justice. And Billy Burke was finally dead.

19

THE COMMUNITY CENTRE

Using a public telephone, Nick dialled James's number. The news was already reporting a major incident in the prison. They kept it very low-key in their reports, but it was enough to make a smile creep over Nick's face. 'Well?' Nick asked, once James answered the telephone.

'Cremated,' was all James answered. 'I'm getting a new mobile, I'll let you know the new number when I have it.'

Putting the receiver down, Nick winced. They had cremated Billy? How the hell did they get away with that? He was sure he would find out eventually, but for now they had to cover their tracks. Any contact between them had to be destroyed. Secretly wishing he could tell his mother, he thought better of it. More to the point, he wished he'd been there to see it and spit on Billy's charcoaled body. Surely, he mused, eventually the news reporters would let it be known that Billy Burke had been murdered and that would be enough for her.

Over the next few days, life just got better and better. James visited Nick at his office and gave him his new number. The gloves were off now, they both discussed in depth the terms of their agreement.

James and Noel were to take over the running of things, answering only to Nick. In turn, he would pass on information to his 'client'.

'Do we ever get to meet your client, Mr Diamond? Surely now would be a good time for us all to get to know each other?' Puzzled, James felt downcast. They had come so far together, but there was still no trust.

Trying to think quickly without causing offence, Nick took a deep sigh and sat back in his chair. 'My client is out of town at the moment, but he feels he would like to see how things go first. He is quite happy for you to organise the managers of the shops. If you wish to reshuffle things, that is also acceptable. Everyone answers to you. But be warned.' Nick's face grew stern and his eyes flashed green. 'My client makes the final decision. You will be working for him and Noel will be able to use his ice-cream vans to deal his drugs without any interference. Of course, there will be a commission to pay, which we have already discussed. This truce is based on trust and loyalty. Let's not get greedy.' Nick's piercing eyes bore into James's, making him squirm. Showing no emotion, Nick carried on. His articulate voice was barely above a whisper, although his threats were loud and clear. 'Let there be no mistakes, my client has made it clear to me. If he were to be betrayed in any way, this war would never stop until every one of his enemies was dead.'

James's jaw almost dropped, he was stunned. The suave sophisticated lawyer, with his designer suits and charming manner, suddenly made his skin crawl and made his mouth go dry. This was a totally different side to Nick Diamond than he had seen before. He was spine-chilling and threatening without raising his voice.

'We understand, Mr Diamond. We both know what your client is capable of. The only trouble he will get from us is what he causes himself.' James was trying to sound business-like, but under Nick's cold stare he could feel himself sweating, like a nervous schoolboy.

Lightening the mood, like the flick of a switch, Nick grinned from ear to ear. He knew he had made his point to James and there was no need to push it further. 'Actually, James, I have a little secret to share with you,' Nick said, smiling.

Quickly glancing up, James waited for this 'secret' Nick wished to share. His gut instinct told him he already knew what it was – that this cold, calculating man in front of him didn't have a client. His new, ruthless business partner was the Undertaker, also known as Nick Diamond.

Oozing with charm and friendliness, Nick ran his hands through his hair. 'I have some Scottish connections myself, James, and I am to be in Glasgow within the next few days. My wife and I have just bought the old community centre near Thistle Park and we're going to donate it to the people who live there. My grand-mother lives there, and they do say charity begins at home. So I'm sure we will be seeing a lot more of each other.' Knowing he had just pulled the rug from underneath James's suspicious feet, he was pleased to see the amazement appear on his face.

'That's you, Mr Diamond? I've seen all the building works going on, but it's all hidden. No one knows what it's going to be. Why would you do that?' James expressed his surprise, and mentally admitted he'd been wrong. This wasn't the secret he'd expected. He was barking up the wrong tree with Nick Diamond, he was just as much a puppet as he was. It did make him wonder what the Under-taker was blackmailing him about, considering he went to such lengths on his behalf.

'Not a word now, James.' Nick held his finger to his mouth. 'I want it to be a surprise for my grandmother. I have fond memories of a childhood in Glasgow, let's hope the community centre brings some fond memories to those who use it.'

'That's really nice of you, Mr Diamond, and it must have cost a fortune. The people around there have had nowhere to call their own in a very long time. But then a lot of it was their own fault. I don't want to piss on your parade, Mr Diamond, but you must have more money than sense,' James joked.

Nick raised his eyebrow and smiled sarcastically. 'The first part was my idea for tax purposes, and it is my roots. But our mutual friend put a lot of money up when he heard about it. We both have an added interest in it, mine is strictly sentimental, but my client saw an opportunity,' Nick smiled, hoping to convince James. 'It seems business is booming, he doesn't want to wait forever to get answers from messages. The community centre will also be a cover for a dookit. Do you know what that is?'

James frowned and suddenly laughed. 'Yes,' he said. 'In Glasgow it's pronounced ducket, but yes, I get it now. So you're going to have a messaging board or something? A drop-in messaging centre, is that what it's all about?' Suddenly the penny dropped. It was going to be a dealer's paradise, built in the name of charity.

'Not me, James, my client. The fine print is not organised yet, but it's better than street corners and Chinese whispers.'

'I like your line of thinking and it's a good cover.' James nodded. He knew Nick was going to object that it was his client's line of thinking, but he waved his hand to stop him.

'That's a bloody good idea, Mr Diamond, and you're the front man.'

'I will get my reward in heaven.' Nick laughed out loud and then looked at his watch. 'I'm afraid I have things to do, James, you understand. I will pass on your words to my client. I wish you well in your business venture together.' Standing up, without giving James a chance to speak, Nick held out his hand to shake.

Once James had left, Nick closed the blinds on his office windows, shutting out the reception staff outside. He felt very smug with himself. Now he had dropped the community centre on James, he would tell Noel and the circle would begin. This would be their messaging service in code. It was going to be one big notice board, but the workforce would easily find out where their drop-offs were and when. No one would find it strange all these people were visiting a community centre. After all, that was why it was there!

There would be multiple age groups visiting. Not just a gang of men or kids, looking suspicious, hanging around the streets, attracting police attention. There would be old ladies, young mums and their kids as well. Once opened, he felt sure Nana would be the self-appointed manageress of it all. After all, it was her son's name above the door. It would be cared for by the very person he trusted most and who would always watch his back.

* * *

After a short meeting with the other partner of the firm, Nick felt restless and picking up the phone, he dialled Patsy's mobile.

'Hi, Nick, what's up?'

'Nothing is wrong, I'm going to Scotland for a couple of days. I want to tell Nana about the community centre before it's public knowledge. Do you want to come?' He was feeling in high spirits, everything seemed to be going to plan and Billy was dead. Hearing the hesitancy at the other end of the phone yet again brought him back down to earth. Fuck! He cursed her under his breath. She had more excuses up her sleeve than a criminal going to court. He was sick of always being the bad guy for not being at home a lot, when in fact they were both as bad as each other. These days, all they had in common was sex, and even that was becoming mechanical.

'It's not the opening yet, is it, Nick?' Patsy took a deep sigh. She wasn't really interested in this mad idea of his, but if that was what he wanted, she knew he would do it anyway.

'No, it's not the opening. You're the one who is always complaining we never spend any time together. I'm offering you a couple of days away and all I get is a deep sigh. I'm seriously wondering why I bother.'

'Don't be like that, Nick. It's just short notice and I have interviews to do for the new shop. There is also the fact I want to be there when my new stock comes in.' She tailed off. They both knew that would be his next shipment of money to launder. 'I think it would be for the best if I was here, don't you, Nick?'

It had slipped his mind that he was due his next shipment of money coming in. He'd lost count now and, to be honest, he rarely even counted it any more.

'Yes, you're probably right.' His bright mood was somewhat dampened by her rebuke, but he accepted it. 'I'm going home to pack a few things and then I'm leaving tonight.' His light-hearted voice had suddenly turned back to business mode. At least when she whined and complained about how little time they spent together, he had the perfect weapon to throw back in her face. She had just given him the ammunition he needed.

Sometimes he wondered if she was having an affair, but for some reason the idea of it didn't bother him. The realisation that there was nothing left between himself and Patsy any more, apart from habit, suddenly overwhelmed him. They had both moved on.

Patsy was a good wife and businesswoman and she kept her mouth shut. Their brief sexual encounters were just a friends-with-benefits situation. She was a good woman but, like most people in marriages, they had just carried on regardless. There was no real love between them any more.

'I'm sorry Nick, you do understand, don't you?' she pleaded. 'It's just short notice. I promise I will be there for the opening, though. You spend some time with your nana. She would rather I didn't come anyway. She will have her little Nicky all to herself.' Nick felt that sounded like sarcasm. Fuck her!

'That sounds more like an excuse than a reason, Patsy. I have to go... bye.' He almost felt like throwing his mobile at the wall when the call was finished.

Picking up his briefcase, he nearly ran to the door. The last couple of weeks had been stressful, he was tired and needed time out. The long drive to Scotland would clear his head.

As Nick sped along the motorway, with the top of his car down and the wind in his hair, he felt better already. Listening to his music blaring out and having not a care in the world felt good. Free at last. Billy Burke had stifled him at times, he could now break free of those chains, without fear of being exposed.

A notification popped up on his smart watch from the supervisor of the building work. All was running to plan. A big grin crossed his face, he couldn't wait to tell Nana and see her surprised face when she found out she had got her community centre back.

Driving through the estate, he saw a young woman carrying two heavy shopping bags on the handle of a child's buggy she was pushing. Her long blonde hair attracted him first and he strained his neck to get a better look at her face. She was young and small framed, petite even. He felt tempted to offer her a lift, but, thought better of it, even though she had to be going in the same direction as him. Speeding up to pass her, he looked into his wing mirror to see her face... she was pretty. Very pretty indeed. Taking one last glance in his mirror, he drove on.

20

A BIG SURPRISE

'Nicky, darling! Why didn't you tell me you were coming? I could have cooked you something.' Throwing her arms around his neck, Beryl hugged him.

'Do I take it you're pleased to see me, Nana?' He opened his arms wide and, beaming, he almost lifted her off her feet.

No sooner had he been pulled inside, the kettle was on and Beryl was opening assorted cake tins. She was full of gossip and he couldn't get a word in. He couldn't stop laughing at some of her anecdotes. His warm genuine laughter filled the room, making Beryl smile. Her Nicky was home. Spying him, she thought he looked pale and tired, but a few days in the Scottish air would soon sort that out.

'I have something for you, Nana. Do you mind if I stay a couple of days?'

'Oh my goodness, laddie, you don't have to ask that, this is your home,' she squealed with delight and clapped her arthritic hands. 'You've brought me a present. There's no need for that, you are enough.'

'Well, I haven't exactly brought you a present. I'm going to have to take you to it.' He grinned mysteriously.

Frowning, she looked puzzled. 'When? Where are we going?'

'Get your coat, Nana, I'll drive you there.'

Slowly getting up, she took hold of the walking stick that was always beside her chair, although Nick knew she didn't need it. It was all for effect. She was as solid on her feet as anyone.

Putting her coat over her shoulders, he led her to his car and drove the short distance to the community centre. It was still covered in tarpaulins, and he had to wait for the security guards to let him in through the huge metal gates.

'What's all this, Nicky? We can't go in here, they've been building for weeks.'

'Aren't you curious, Nana?' Kissing her on the cheek, he walked her around the side of the building and pulled the tarpaulin aside. Seeing him, the supervisor jumped from his seat where he was having a quick sandwich and ran forward to greet him.

'Mr Diamond!' he almost choked on his sandwich. 'You didn't say you were coming today.'

Nick held out his hand to shake the supervisor's hand. 'I got your message and just thought I would pop along to see what is going on.'

'Well, it's getting late, sir, but mind your step now. Some of the paint is still drying. You don't want to get any on your suit.'

Nick just laughed, he felt relaxed and happy. Nana's idle chatter about the neighbours had lightened his mood and he was bursting to show Nana what he'd done. He just hoped it didn't look like a building site inside.

Harry, the supervisor, pulled the tarpaulin wider apart and held out his hand for Beryl to go over the step. 'Well, Mr Diamond. What do you think of the old place?' The smell of fresh paint and varnish greeted them first, as Harry looked around at the huge community centre which had once been an eyesore and now looked like new.

He beamed with pride and couldn't wait to show off all the hard work that had been done. Cleaners were milling around, while some of the workers were moving tables and chairs into place. Nick's eyes followed the laminate flooring all the way to the other end of the room. It had a built-in stage, with red velvet curtains at each side, Nick had insisted on it. He had decided that would be where Nana's bingo caller would stand. The machine was already fitted, full of numbered balls, already in place. Above it was a frame showing the digital numbers, larger than life. Obviously, the workmen had been playing around with it, but Nick didn't care.

At the far side were a few shelves and radiators beside two double doors. Beryl was quiet for once. Taking her arm, he steered her towards the doors and pushed them open. Harry was hot on his heels. Inside was a fully equipped kitchen area. Stainless-steel worktops surrounded double ovens and fridge-freezers. Industrial microwaves were fitted into the walls near the double sink units and dishwasher. There were boxes stacked up against the wall, and Nick turned to Harry quizzically.

'That's all the kitchenware, Mr Diamond. The ladies here are putting it all away in the cabinets, once they have finished putting all of the horizontal blinds up. Believe me, this place is huge and there are a lot of windows,' Harry said, pushing his flat cap off his forehead and adjusting the dungaree straps on his chest. 'You name it, Mr Diamond, we've got it, just like you said. I doubt there is a chef in the country with a better equipped kitchen.' Sticking out his chest, Harry was full of pride. 'Here's the serving hatch to pass the plates and cups through to the main restaurant area.' He lifted up a metal shutter with a flick of a switch, and Nick and Beryl looked through the hatch. Harry exhibited all of the fancy gadgets, including the huge glass cabinets that kept the food warm.

Beryl's legs nearly crumbled beneath her and she hung on to Nick's arm. Speechless, she burst into tears. Harry clicked his fingers and one of the workmen rushed forward with a chair for her.

'Don't faint on me, Nana,' Nick laughed, holding onto her. He had to admit it was amazing, considering the photos he had been sent of it in the beginning. The restaurant area was sectioned off from the rest of the centre with its red tables and chairs.

'Now for the best part, Mr Diamond. This was expensive, I'm afraid, we had to have it handmade and imported in.' Harry looked down at the floor. In the excitement of a free hand and an open budget, he had run amok.

'Lead on, Harry.' Raising his eyebrows with surprise, Nick opened the palms of his hands wide.

'Are you okay, madam?' Harry asked Beryl nervously. 'You really have to see this.' Harry looked at Beryl's ashen face as she stared around the room. Seeing her nod, he walked ahead of them.

'Come on, Nana, hold onto my arm.' Linking his arm with hers, they followed Harry.

Walking around the front, into the cold night air, Harry and another workman lifted the tarpaulin as much as they dared without the public seeing the display. Nick looked at the front of the centre and peered under the tarpaulin, but he couldn't see anything. Harry shouted across to another workmen, 'When you're ready, switch it on.' Suddenly the whole front of the centre lit up. The fancy sign hanging above the glass automatic doors burst into life. 'The Jack Diamond Community Centre.' It was all written in a fancy silver writing, except the word 'Diamond', which looked like silver glitter that changed colour in waves.

It was beautiful, and absolutely what Nick had seen in his mind's eye. Stunned, he stood beside Beryl in awe. At the side of it, built into the wall, was a photo of Jack Diamond and a plaque giving the dates of his birth and death. Fortunately, Nick had sent his favourite photograph of his dad. He had a great big grin on his face, in the sunshine, standing in a small wooden boat on a lake. He was wearing his favourite fishing hat covered in different coloured flies. He was holding up a fish he had caught with pride, with a small boy standing beside him, showing off his own small fish. It had always been Nick's favourite and he remembered being with him that day when his mother had taken the photo. He almost felt like crying. This was for his father, his real father – Jack Diamond. His mother was right, biology had nothing to do with it. Swallowing hard, fighting back the tears, he turned towards Harry. He didn't know what to say. The place was beyond his wildest dreams. They had all worked very hard to bring this derelict shell to life.

Coughing to clear his throat, Nick watched as Harry shouted for someone to turn the sign off. It wasn't to be seen yet and he didn't want to spoil Nick's surprise. 'It's a magnificent job, Harry. You and your workforce are looking at a hefty bonus for all your hard work. How long do you think it will take to get it all in place?'

Excited at the prospect of an added bonus, Harry shrugged. 'It's all cosmetic now. The paving outside is all laid. Couple of days, maybe less. We're waiting for the big-screen television to be fitted. We couldn't do it while the paint was wet.' Harry looked almost apologetic.

'And you have organised all the sports channels for the young men to watch?'

Harry nodded. 'I might come myself, my wife hates football – it interferes with all of her soaps.' He laughed. Noticing Nick didn't join in the banter, he quickly got back to business. 'Everything is just as you ordered, Mr Diamond. Once done, it just has to pass inspection to get the necessary certificates, which it will,' Harry assured him, 'and licensing for the bingo and stuff. They are due tomorrow, which is why we're working through the night. I have all of the paperwork.'

Suddenly an overwhelming feeling of guilt swept over Nick. It had all seemed like a good idea, but did he really want his father's name involved in drug dealing and prostitution? He felt unsure. This was indeed a memorial to his father, but had he been too hasty in his greed? It was too late now. Half a million had been sunk into this place. He'd gone overboard with everything. But suddenly, in the cold light of day, he was having second thoughts.

Beryl, who was in floods of tears, couldn't believe it. 'I can't believe you have done all of this, Nicky it's absolutely beautiful.' Mesmerised by the surroundings, she looked around again and shook her head in disbelief. 'When are you thinking of opening the place?' Her voice wavered.

'Just as soon as Harry here has it all polished and the certificates in place.'

'Can I show Maggie, Nick?' Beryl was beside herself with excitement. It was everything she dreamed of and more. 'Who's going to do all of the cooking and stuff? Will it all be free?' She fired question after question. Nick didn't know which one to answer first.

'This is your private viewing, Nana. Just us. Let Maggie see it in all its glory without the tarpaulin, eh?' Seeing her face drop somewhat, Nick tried to appease her. 'Just let Harry work his magic.'

'Too right, Mrs Diamond,' said Harry. 'You think it looks great now. Wait until we have properly finished with it, then you really will have something to show off to your friends.' Following Nick's lead, he could see that Beryl was satisfied.

'As for the cooking, I have a few chefs in mind.' Nick had already thought that a couple of the chefs from the pizza shops would do very nicely. This was a chance to give Fatso Paul and his brothers their vocation back. 'No, sadly it will not all be free, but it will be cheap. You can have your soup kitchen with any leftovers. Will that satisfy you?' He laughed as Beryl flung her arms around him and hugged the life out of him. He knew there would be no sleep tonight, she would talk his ears off. She was like a kid on Christmas Eve.

'Come on, Nana, enough excitement for one night. Let's get you home and in the warm again.' Steering her towards the exit, Nick turned towards Harry and shook his hand. It was heartfelt. 'You have done a magnificent job, Harry. It's much appreciated.' He winked.

Beaming, Harry nearly shook Nick's hand off. 'All in a day's work, Mr Diamond.' And as Nick left with his beloved nana, Harry breathed a huge sigh of relief.

21

A CHANCE ENCOUNTER

Arriving back at Beryl's flat, Nick was surprised to see a policeman knocking at her front door. His blood almost ran cold. Walking slowly, he waited for Beryl to comment, but when she did, he didn't know whether to be stunned or shocked.

'Terence! I forgot you were coming tonight. This is my grandson, Nicky,' she said, introducing Nick to the waiting policeman. Nick faltered. Obviously Beryl knew why he was there, but to him it was one big mystery. Who the hell called policemen by their first names?

'Is there a problem, officer?' Nick's voice was calm and articulate as he held his hand out to the policeman.

'No, Nicky love, come on, you two. I'll put the kettle on. I've made one of those lemon drizzle cakes you like, Terence. How's your wife?'

Nick couldn't comment, his brain felt frazzled. What the hell was going on?

'No, there's no problem, Mr Erm,' the policeman faltered. He could see Nick wasn't from around here. Not with that suit and that voice. He sounded like Prince Charles!

'Nick Diamond.' Nick introduced himself and smiled. He felt nervous. This was a weird meeting. All the while, Terence the friendly copper was following Beryl in her flat while someone from the police station was talking to him through his radio. Nick followed them in disbelief.

'Here you are, Terence, take a look at these while I put the kettle on.' Beryl handed him a plastic carrier bag and walked into the kitchen. Curiously, Nick looked on. This was a bizarre situation.

Terence emptied the bag on the sofa. Inside were a multitude of pink knitted baby garments and a blanket with pom poms on it.

Blushing slightly in front of Nick, Terence inspected them. 'This is just the ticket, Beryl. My wife will be well pleased,' he smiled. Looking up at Nick, who was hovering closely, Terence could see the puzzled look on his face.

'Your gran has done some knitting for me and the wife. We're expecting our third child and it's been confirmed that after two boys, the next one is going to be a girl,' he beamed with pride. 'I knew Beryl did some knitting for people and I asked her if she would knit something special for us. You know, to mark the occasion.' Embarrassed, Terence reached into his back pocket for his wallet. 'What's the damage, Beryl?' he asked.

'Don't worry, laddie, you supplied the wool. It gave me something to do.' Putting the cups on the coffee table before them, Beryl held up a plate with neatly cut slices of lemon drizzle cake on it. Instantly, Terence picked one up and started eating it, showing his delight.

'That's great, Beryl. Not only are you an artist,' he nodded at the hats and mittens she had knitted, 'you are a great cook as well.' Crumbs covered his thick black moustache as he stuffed it into his mouth.

Clearing his throat, Nick felt he should say something. 'Congratulations, officer. You both must be very pleased.'

'So what brings you to these parts, apart from Beryl here, of course?'

Nick didn't think it would take long before he stepped into 'copper mode' and started asking questions, but Beryl saved him the bother of answering and butted in. 'He's a solicitor, Terence, and he's just had the old community centre done up for everyone. It's a big secret...' She tailed off, looking at Nick in horror and slapping her hands over her mouth.

'You're behind the noise of the community centre?' Intrigued, Terence took his time and sat down to drink his tea.

'Well, yes. It's a secret, or rather it was until about an hour ago.' Nick strained to laugh. He felt uncomfortable at the interrogation he knew would follow. 'It's for Nana and also in memory of my father. This was his home and, like Nana, he was Scottish through and through.'

Terence nodded. 'I understand. Beryl talks of nothing else. It's a nice gesture but I think you're wasting your time around here. Thugs and hooligans, the lot of them. I would hate to see your efforts wasted. I hope at least some of them appreciate it.' Terence's genuine smile made Nick feel more at ease.

Oozing his usual charm, Nick laughed. 'Maybe, Terence. Erm, may I call you Terence? Or is that only reserved for the beautiful ladies on the estate?' Nick enquired politely and laughed.

'No, please call me Terence'. Once he saw him smile and nod, Nick carried on. 'Then please feel free to call me Nick. Maybe the youngsters are hooligans because they have nowhere else to go. That's how they get into trouble, isn't it? Plain old boredom. What is it they say... the devil makes work for idle hands?' Again, he laughed.

'Well, there are a lot of idle hands around here.' Terence joined in the laughter. 'If there is anything we can do to help, just ask. It's a good thing you're offering and maybe you're right. This place is like

Hell's Kitchen, the forgotten estate. This might just raise a few spirits. It's nice to think there are a few good people left in the world.' Raising his cup in the air, Terence nodded. 'Cheers, Nick.'

His genuine warmth made Nick smile. Mentally, he thought how everything was slipping into place. Now, he even had the police offering a helping hand. What a coup!

'We'll have a drive around now and again. Keep an eye on the place for you.' Standing up, Terence adjusted his hat and put the knitted pink baby clothes back into the bag. 'Are you sure I can't give you something for these, Beryl?'

'Don't even think about it,' she fussed as she walked him to the door and said goodbye. She waved him off like an old friend, even though there were a dozen curtains twitching in the neighbourhood!

'Well, you're full of surprises, Nana. I hope the people around here don't think you're some kind of mole. They don't take too kindly to the police, if I remember rightly.' Raising one eyebrow, Nick waited for an explanation. It's a wonder they hadn't ostracised her.

'Don't be silly, laddie. I knew his mum. She lived just across from here when he was a wee laddie. I probably knitted some stuff for him once.' As she busied herself clearing the tea things away, Nick was deep in thought. There had to be an angle here somewhere, he just couldn't think what it was. It was all a bit confusing.

After a good night's sleep and a hefty breakfast laid on by Beryl to keep his strength up, he told her he had things to sort out at the centre, made his excuses and left.

Dialling a number on his mobile phone, he waited.

'Yes, boss. What can I do for you?' Fatso Paul's voice replied.

'The usual meeting place in half an hour. I need to see you.'

'You're here?' Paul's voice wavered somewhat. He hadn't expected this when he got up this morning.

'Well, I must be, mustn't I?' Nick snapped. 'Half an hour, Paul.' Nick hung up. Paul, for all of his pitfalls in life, was a trusted employee and 'soldier'. He'd defended him once, as with all his associates, but Paul had more to lose and gave Nick his undying loyalty.

Sitting in the cemetery, in the memorial chapel, Nick was holding a bunch of flowers. Hearing footsteps, he looked up. There was Paul, bang on time.

'It's good to see you again,' he puffed, rushing towards Nick, his heavy weight making it harder for him to walk. His face was red and he was sweating slightly.

'You look like you've been running.' Nick's cold, sarcastic voice greeted him as Paul almost flopped on the bench beside him, breathing heavily. The wooden benches were scattered around the cemetery for people to sit on and think of their loved ones. It was a peaceful place, as with all cemeteries. But this one was special. It was always clean and cared for and, most of all, they were the best meeting places. No one could overhear your conversation, and if other people were there, they respected your privacy and spoke in hushed tones, while rearranging new flowers on their loved ones' graves.

Getting straight to the point, Nick spoke. 'You have heard about Billy, I presume?' Paul nodded. He didn't seem too distressed by it. Taking out his cigarette packet, he looked at Nick for approval.

Nodding, Nick carried on. 'You have done a good job keeping things in order with your brothers at the pizza shops. As always, your payments are on time, but it's time for you to move on.'

'Why? You have just said yourself, I have done a good job.' Panicking, Paul was almost pleading with Nick. His wide-eyed stare was full of fear.

'Hear me out, Paul, smoke your cigarette and don't interfere,' Nick warned. 'I have just made James McNally a proposition of a small partnership, to take Billy's place. He was becoming a liability. Do you know him?' Nick knew he did, but wanted to clarify it.

Puzzled, Paul shrugged and nodded. 'Yes, not very well, but he's one of the old crowd. Billy's age and his mate, by all accounts.' Suddenly the penny dropped and Paul sat there stunned, looking out at the perfectly cut grass in the cemetery. Taking a long drag on his cigarette, he realised Nick had given the order to murder Billy. The very partner he had built their empire with. What kind of man would do that to his long-standing partner? Paul was quaking in his boots and wondered what his own fate was. Rubbing his hands together, he looked around for who might be his assassin. 'He works with the Albanians who have been ripping you off. Why would you go into business with him?' Although Paul was frightened, he just blurted it out.

'Because it's easier than being ripped off, Paul, that is if we're all on the same side. We will all look out for each other. Don't worry, I'm still in charge,' Nick scoffed.

'Their ice-cream vans sell all kinds of dope and stuff. Aren't they the ones that blew up your mobile shop?' Shocked, Paul couldn't stop himself from asking the obvious questions.

Waving his hand in the air, Nick shrugged. 'That was all a misunderstanding. It's sorted out now. Anyway, back to business. I have a chef job for you at the new community centre, here in Glasgow, I have invested in.'

'What community centre?' Dumbstruck, Paul looked at Nick, frowning. He hadn't heard of one and he hadn't been informed of one in the area.

'You will see in good time. It has a small restaurant,' Nick carried on, ignoring Paul's confusion. 'I think you could run it. Your talents are wasted in the shops. It will also be a messaging service, for your dealers. They will know when to pick up and drop off. No one is going to pay a lot of attention to groups of people going into a community centre. Anyone can drop in for a cup of something and a chat. You and a couple of your brothers will see that it runs smoothly,' Nick warned. His voice was bordering on threatening. He waited for Paul to take in what he was saying. 'James and his ice-cream friend also have suppliers from Poland, which will make things easier. He is going to be transporting it in, not us. Our hands are clean. Any arguments over money with dealers and he is the one who gets shot.' Nick shrugged. 'His problem, not mine.'

Paul listened to Nick's carefully laid plans. It made his blood run cold, realising just how ruthless this man was.

'But you just said you were in partnership?'

'I'm partners with no one, Paul, you know that. Trust no one, that is my motto.' Sarcasm dripped out of Nick's mouth as he spoke. 'Haven't I always looked after you?'

'You have, Nick, I don't know what I would have done without your help. I would probably be dead now and my family would be destitute.' Paul's heart sank when he remembered how he had met Nick. He'd been a walking dead man and Nick had saved his life. Nick paid him very well for his services, he was more than gener-ous. On that he had no complaints. 'Who is going to look after the pizza shops, have you decided yet?'

'All in good time, Paul, just slow down, eh? Would you like a kitchen of your own again?' Nick smiled. 'A new beginning?'

Paul's head was spinning with all this information. 'Yes, I would like a proper kitchen of my own again.' Subdued, he looked down at the floor. It was simply game, set and match, and Nick held all the cards.

'That's settled, then.' Nick slapped Paul's leg for reassurance. 'James McNally will be making his presence known soon. He will be having a reshuffle. I told him he could. In the meantime, you sort out the best men you have to stay in the shops and who you want to work with you. The community centre will be a big operation and I don't want fools running it in my absence.' Nick assured him that his place in the line of things was guaranteed, unless he fucked up. Now that was a different matter. 'People around here know you, Paul, you have just moved on. They know you will carry on with your dealing. It makes sense. Oh, by the way, a copper called Terence will be popping in with his mates now and again. It's all under control, but be careful they are never off duty. Don't you agree?' Smugly, Nick grinned.

'You have the coppers on side?' Surprised, Paul shook his head. 'Nothing you do surprises me any more, Nick.'

'Good. That's just the way I like it. Don't want you thinking I'm a walkover.' The pair of them locked eyes for an instant.

'I don't think anyone would think that, Nick. You're always one step ahead of the rest of us.' Paul felt flattery was needed now. Some people would call it licking arse, but if that is what it took to stay alive, he would gladly lick arse!

'Right, well I have things to do and I am sure you do.' Nick stood up to leave.

'Nick, just one more thing,' Paul faltered. 'We're getting short of meth. Do you have any?'

Putting his hand to his chin, Nick thought about it. 'Yes, go and dig up grave 5021. It's on the left of here. It's the same as always, on the top of the old coffin in watertight bags. Make sure you put all the grass and everything back in place afterwards. Take two bags for now, that should sort it.'

'Thanks, Nick. Isn't that Billy Burke's mother's grave?'

'It sure is, Paul, who better to look after our money?' Nick laughed and walked away, throwing his bunch of flowers nonchalantly on someone's graveside and leaving Paul contemplating the conversation they had just had.

* * *

Walking back into Beryl's pristine flat, Nick could hear laughter and chatter and, walking into the lounge, he saw Maggie, Beryl's life-long friend, drinking tea from Beryl's china. His nana wouldn't use anything else. She liked a proper teapot, with cups and saucers. What captured him the most was the young blonde woman sitting at her side with a small child. This was the young woman he had seen walking onto the estate yesterday.

'Hello, everyone.' Oozing charm, he walked over to Maggie and kissed her on the cheek. They were old friends, and without knowing it, Maggie was an employee and an ally. Once Beryl had told him how Maggie's granddaughter had been killed, he had made sure justice had been served and sent her photos of their execution. She had become his eyes and ears without ever knowing it was him she worked for. Any orders he had for her were dictated down a long line of his trusted employees, like Paul, and she was more than happy to do what he wanted.

'Nicky! Beryl said you were home for a few days!' Maggie squealed with delight and hugged him.

'And who is this young man?' Avoiding staring at the young woman, Nick concentrated on the small boy, who was happily eating some of Beryl's homemade sausage rolls.

'This is wee Jimmy, Natasha's boy,' Maggie introduced them. 'They haven't lived here very long.'

Nick held his hand out to the young woman, he couldn't help admiring her beauty. She had captured his interest the day before and now here she was, sitting in his nana's lounge, as large as life. 'Nice to meet you, Natasha.' For a moment, they both looked at each other. It was a moment lost in time. Their eyes locked. Blushing, Natasha took Nick's hand to shake it, but instead he took it and kissed the back of it, making her blush even more.

'You old charmer,' Beryl scoffed. 'I will go and get you a cup.' She disappeared into the kitchen.

Maggie carried on filling Nick in on the local news, while he and Natasha kept glancing at each other, hoping it wasn't noticeable. Her long lashes were almost on her cheeks, he noticed, and her fresh, clear skin was like marble, highlighting her pink, perfectly formed lips. Their attraction was instant, and Nick could feel a stirring inside he hadn't felt in a long time.

Hearing the mobile shop blow its horn, Natasha stood up. 'I'd better go, there are some things I need.' Taking Jimmy by the hand, she shouted through to Beryl.

'Are you coming back?' asked Maggie, disappointed she was leaving.

'No, I have things to do,' said Natasha, almost tripping over herself to get out. Nick stood up.

'It was nice meeting you, Natasha. I hope we meet again.' Seeing a faint blush rise in her cheeks, he smiled. 'Here, get Jimmy some sweets.' Opening his wallet, Nick took out a twenty-pound note and handed it over.

Shocked, Natasha shook her head. 'I can't take that, it's way too much.'

'You can and you will. Get yourself some chocolate, too. I know you ladies like chocolate.' He laughed towards Maggie, who looked just as shocked as Natasha had at the money. 'Not another word, go on, take it, before that van disappears.'

Taking the money as prompted by Maggie, Natasha's voice was barely above a whisper as she looked into his green eyes adoringly and thanked him. As she was leaving, she turned around and took one last look at Nick, which made him smile even more. He knew that last backward glance meant she liked what she had seen too.

'Well, now she's gone, Nick, are you going to tell me about the community centre?' Maggie asked.

'Nana!' Nick moaned. 'God almighty, it's supposed to be a secret!'

'It's only Maggie, and her lips are tighter than a chicken's arse, Nicky!' They all burst out laughing. Beryl had such a lovely way with words.

22

KNITTING NANAS

Natasha stood in the queue at the mobile shop, waiting for her turn. A thought crossed her mind, but she felt guilty about it.

Joe stood behind the counter with his arms folded. 'What can I get for you, beautiful?'

Ignoring his comments, she said, 'Just a loaf of bread and a bottle of milk please.'

Putting them on the counter, Joe waited to see if she could pay. This was his chance to drop the hint about paying her debts by prostitution. All the women refused, disgusted in the beginning. He expected that, but as time went on, and they had time to think about it, they always agreed.

'And I'd like my necklace back, please.' Swallowing hard, Natasha handed over the twenty-pound note that Nick had given her. She felt guilty about using it and she would get Jimmy some sweets, but she didn't need any chocolate, she argued with herself. And who would know?

Joe and Midge glanced at each other, surprised. This wasn't how it was supposed to be. Midge searched around a drawer in the front of the van and found her necklace in a small plastic bag. 'You still owe us four pounds on top of that money. You haven't paid all of the interest.' Midge took her money and waited while she took her purse out and handed the money over.

'There you go, Natasha, if you need anything else, be sure to come back,' he shouted after her as she hurried away.

'Hey, Tash. I want you a minute,' Fin called after her.

'What do you want? It's Fin, isn't it?' Natasha was surprised he remembered her name, let alone used it so freely.

'Maggie was saying you were looking for a part-time job. I know there's one going at the kebab shop, serving and cleaning. I could put a good word in for you if you like.'

'Oh my God, yes! Oh yes, thank you. That would be great. Maggie has said she would always look after Jimmy for a few hours if I got a job. When will you know?' Pleased as punch, Natasha felt like hugging him.

'Pop in the pub tonight, I will let you know when my shift has finished. I always go straight in there for a pint before going home.'

Although Natasha didn't like the idea of going into the pub, she agreed. If that was the only way of keeping Fin sweet and finding out if she had a job, she would do it.

'Okay, about seven? I can't be much later, because of Jimmy, and it's short notice for Maggie to sit with him any longer.'

'Make it six-thirty, then, it won't take long and hopefully I will have some good news for you.' Fin felt he could be magnanimous on this occasion. Getting Natasha to the pub was his main goal, just to prove to that overbearing landlord Chalkie that he did have a decent-looking woman on his arm. He'd wipe the smile right off his face!

'Thank you Fin, I really appreciate that. I'll see you later.' Waving him off, Natasha was walking on air. She'd got her necklace back, and now she possibly had a job. On top of that, she had just spent a few minutes in the company of Mr Wonderful, Beryl's grandson. He was absolutely beautiful, she could still smell the waft of his aftershave in her nostrils.

* * *

'So, Nana. Is this all you do? Sit here and drink tea while gossiping about the neighbours?' Nick laughed.

'Cheeky bugger. You can't do much on a pension, you know,' she pouted, 'can you, Maggie? Some of my friends don't have a pot to piss in. That is why your community centre will be such a big thing around here. Somewhere for them to go without costing a small fortune.'

'I wouldn't know, I haven't got that far yet,' added Maggie, to make herself seem younger, 'but I know what you mean. Old Zena was telling me how skint she is. It's a shame, she's worked all her life and the state pension isn't much. That's why she makes those little dolls and things to sell at car boot sales and festivals. It all helps.'

'I've been helping her knit some soft toys to sell with my oddments of wool,' Beryl chirped up, not wanting to be outdone by Maggie. 'There are a couple of us, you know that, it keeps us out of mischief. And since that Terence saw the jumper I knitted for young Jimmy, he asked me to make him some stuff for his new baby.'

'Hang on a minute,' Nick interrupted. 'Are you saying you have a knitting circle and you sell soft toys?'

Maggie and Beryl both stared at Nick as though he was an idiot. 'Yes, keep up, Nick. I thought you were the one with brains,' laughed Maggie.

'Yes, sometimes door to door and stuff. Why?' Beryl was confused at Nick's sudden interest.

'Don't you need a trading licence or something?' Nick was

amazed. All these pensioners were selling soft toys door to door and no one stopped them?

'Nah! It's only a few bits and pieces, we're not down the markets or anything. But it does top up the pension a little,' Beryl stressed. 'People even come to us, like that copper Terence.'

'What do you stuff the toys with?' Now Nick's business brain was working overtime. This was a fantastic scam, and as it had been going on for however long, no one would pay a blind bit of notice to them going about their business as usual. Fill them with stuffing and drugs! Oh my God, they would fly off the shelves!

'Whatever we have. Sometimes it's old socks or dusters,' Maggie interrupted. 'Why?' They were both intrigued by Nick's sudden interest in their knitting circle.

'Maybe I could provide you with some wool and proper stuffing, instead of old socks!' he laughed. He was trying to think of a way to get Nana to agree to putting marijuana packets in the stuffing. That would be something he would have to tread lightly on. He was greeted by beams and thank yous for his generous offer, and felt that was a start in the right direction. Beryl was as proud as punch of her Nicky, helping everyone out. She loved boasting about him and this was a golden opportunity. As though hit by a thunderbolt, Maggie's next sentence nearly knocked him off his feet.

'As long as your nana doesn't make any of those fancy cakes of hers for your rheumatism,' laughed Maggie, 'full of marijuana, they were. Oh my God, Nicky, those old ladies, who constantly moan about their knees and not being able to walk far, were doing sprints around the block after a slice of Beryl's cake.' The eruption of laughter flew around the room. Beryl and Maggie had tears almost coming down their faces with laughter, they thought it was hilarious.

'Yes, yes, but in my defence,' Beryl butted in, trying to speak in between the laughter. 'Some of the women don't smoke, so how were they going to get some of that weed into them?' Nick was agog. Never in a month of Sundays did he think he would be having this conversation over tea and cake!

'I didn't think you ladies did that kind of thing. I'm surprised,' Nick coyly butted in.

Maggie's face grew stern and she folded her arms. 'We haven't always been this age, Nicky. We were doing that kind of thing before you were born. For God's sake, do the kids of today think they invented it? There might be snow on the roof, Nicky, but the fire is still burning inside of us. You cheeky sod!' Again, they all fell about laughing.

'Maybe you should put some in your soft toys, you'd get a better price,' Nick tentatively broached the subject.

'You're joking! With the prices the dealers charge around here? It wouldn't be worth it and they would cost too much. No one would buy them. There are old ladies queuing around the block for that stuff if the price was right, but they can't go to a dealer. They don't want their families finding out and who knows who the dealer is? Anything could happen to them. It's extortion!' Maggie complained, tutting.

Frowning, Nick sat upright on the sofa. 'So you're saying there is a market for this... with older people?'

'Old Sara has MS, she has a hard time and that stuff just eases it a little, but where is she going to get it from? To be honest, when you have given me some, I have shared it with her.' Beryl looked down at the floor, biting her bottom lip, she knew she had said too much. 'Maggie knows you help me sometimes, Nicky love. We have had some fun afternoons on it, haven't we, Maggie?'

'Haven't we just! Don't worry, Nicky lad. It's only special tea. I'm no one's judge and it stays right here.'

'I have a friend who sells that kind of thing, Maggie. That is how I get some for you, Nana. As you say, it eases the stress sometimes.

It's not exactly a class A drug, is it?' Spying the two women, Nick waited for their response. He was treading on dangerous ground, he knew that.

'Bloody hell, Nicky lad, London prices will be more expensive than here. We're all skint. Anyway,' Maggie continued, deep in thought, 'this is already someone's patch. We can't poach on it. Christ, they would have our guts for garters.'

Nick liked her loyalty, even now she was standing in the local dealer's corner, warning him off.

'It was just a thought, Maggie. The person I get it off is pretty cheap. If we knew who the main dealer was, maybe you could explain to him about the pensioners topping up their income. They are not exactly a threat, are they? A few pensioners, come on. Maybe he would provide you with something. It's just a thought.' Nick trailed off. He had said enough to make them both think. Now it was just a matter of time before he heard through the grapevine from Maggie. He could see she was interested but was being cautious.

'The dealers around here would want all of the money, Nicky, so it would be a waste of time.' Maggie shrugged. She looked down-hearted, but he could already see the plan forming in her brain. He thought she was probably cursing herself for not thinking about it before.

'Anyway, I must go. It's been a lovely afternoon with you both.' As an afterthought, Maggie stopped herself from getting up. 'Actually, Nick, I was going to ask you something. I know it's a secret about the centre, but Beryl mentioned you would need a caretaker and maintenance man, is that right?'

'Well, yes, the cat is out of the bag. So what of it?'

'I know a man who needs a change of job. He's been in prison a few times, but who hasn't around here? I believe he did courses in prison for woodwork and electrics at some time. He might be a decent caretaker for you.' Maggie had instantly thought about Steve. He had looked so tired and battered the last time she saw him. Hearing Beryl's revelation about the community centre and a caretaker had instantly brought him to mind. Maybe she could help him.

'If he has your blessing enough to put him forward, Maggie, that is good enough for me. After all, if it goes wrong, I know where you live,' Nick joked. 'What's his name?'

'Steve, Steve Marshal. He's just got out of prison. He's still on probation, so he will keep his nose clean. At the moment, he's a delivery man for the pizza shops up the road. He's having a bad time of it. Well, it's up to you.'

Nick almost grimaced when he heard the name. He didn't particularly like Steve. He'd been okay when he was an addict and a dealer, but he had just got too big for his boots! Making his own decisions, which is why he and Billy had set him up and got him sent to prison. They'd needed him out of the way. To make things better in Nick's twisted way of thinking, he had enjoyed hearing how Steve's wife, Sheila, had resorted to selling her body in a cemetery at night to make ends meet and becoming an addict to boot. That was where Steve's morals had got him.

To have his high moral standards in the community centre didn't fill Nick with glee. But he wasn't sure how he could refuse. Maggie was an old friend of Nana's and they would both want to know why Steve wasn't suitable. His back was against the wall here, and for once he didn't know how to get out of it without offending Maggie and his nana.

'Ask him to pop around sometime, Maggie,' Nick said reluctantly. 'He might not want to do it.' Nick crossed his fingers.

No sooner had Natasha run into the pub, looking bewildered, Chalkie the landlord approached her. 'Are you looking for someone, lassie?'

Breathless, she nodded. 'Yes, I'm looking for a guy called Fin, he said he would meet me here.' Gobsmacked, Chalkie looked at her in amazement. As far as he was concerned, the only people who looked for Fin were either coppers or bailiffs.

'Are you sure you have the right person? You're looking for Fin?' As though by magic, Fin's voice bellowed over to them. 'Tash, over here,' he shouted, waving from one of the corner tables. Chalkie and his mates at the bar all looked on as Natasha ran to Fin and sat down. She was all smiles and obviously pleased to see him. They couldn't believe it. 'What the hell does a nice wee lassie like that want with Fin?' Chalkie couldn't help commenting to his usual mates at the corner of the bar.

They all looked on in awe as Fin and Natasha sat huddled together at the table, laughing and joking. 'I got you a lemonade. I didn't know what you drank and didn't think it would be alcohol with your kiddie,' Fin lied. In actual fact, he'd only bought her a lemonade in advance in case she asked for something expensive.

'That's fine, thank you. Well, do you have any news?' Her face was flushed with excitement.

Casting a glance towards Chalkie, Fin was trying to spin it out a little longer. He didn't want her to disappear so soon, it wouldn't look good for his image.

'I've had a word with the manager and he said he needed someone part-time to help out. If you're interested, you can start Monday. He said you could pop around tomorrow and have a talk about times and stuff.'

Without thinking and much to Fin's surprise, Natasha threw her arms around his neck and hugged him. This was worth its weight in gold when he looked over her shoulder at Chalkie's face. Raising his hand, Fin stuck two fingers in the air, which said everything he felt.

While drinking her lemonade, she threw a multitude of questions at Fin about her new prospective job. Personally, Fin couldn't see the excitement of cleaning up in a pizza shop. He only worked there to deal his drugs, and it was a good cover. But to actually be happy about it without any bonuses, Fin really couldn't rise to that much enthusiasm.

'Come on, Tash, I'll walk you home.' Walking past the crowded bar, Fin stuck his chest out. 'Night, Chalkie,' he waved. He had proved his point and shut their mouths and he felt satisfied.

* * *

At Maggie's instruction, Beryl opened the door to Steve. Seeing him, Nick's heart sank. He would have to play this through, he had no choice. He had already decided that if Steve was under close watch from Paul and his brothers, he wouldn't step out of line, or they would kill him.

'Mr Diamond, Maggie said you might be looking for a caretaker for your new centre,' Steve stammered. Looking at the man before him, Steve felt more than underdressed. Nick Diamond, Beryl's grandson, had been the talk of the estate recently and now Steve could see why. The expensive grey suit he was wearing was obviously tailor-made and the fine silk shirt he could see underneath the jacket would cost him a year's wages.

His brown, collar-length wavy hair made him look younger than his years, but most of all Steve was mesmerised by those green eyes. His eloquent, low-toned voice made Steve feel like he was standing in front of royalty. This wasn't what he'd expected Beryl's grandson to look like.

'I am, erm, Steve, isn't it? Do you have references?' Nick was more than business-like. Maggie had already told him he was out of prison. 'Please sit down, there is no need to stand on ceremony and I can already hear Nana is making a cup of tea.' Nick smiled warmly, although he was gritting his teeth.

'I work at the pizza place doing deliveries. I know Maggie has told you I'm just out of prison and still on probation. But I can do electrics and woodwork, handyman stuff.' Steve blushed. It felt like he was in the head teacher's office.

Nick saw that he was squeezing his fingers into the palms of his hands, his knuckles were almost white. Steve really wanted this job, he obviously felt this was a step up and would get him off the streets.

Beryl walked in with the tray and Steve almost jumped up to help her. 'For goodness' sake, Nicky, put the laddie out of his misery,' Beryl pushed.

Taking a deep sigh, Nick knew he had no choice. 'Very well, Steve. Why don't we say a few months' trial? After all, you might not like it.' Spreading his palms out before him, Nick raised his eyebrows.

'I'm sure I will, Mr Diamond, thank you. When do you need me to start?' As an afterthought, Steve looked at Beryl, embarrassed. He hadn't asked the obvious question. 'How much is the hourly rate of pay?' he stammered, looking down at the ground.

Nick hadn't really thought about it, so stayed on level ground. 'Let's say the same rate as you get at your pizza job, but time and a half for weekends and late nights. Would that suffice?' He knew he had said the right thing when Steve's face lit up.

'It could be a lot of hours, Steve, especially in the evenings. It will close around 9 p.m. but you would have to clear things away and lock up – what about that tag on your leg?' Nick pointed. 'There could be special events and so on and I believe you have a young family.'

'That's fine with me, Mr Diamond. I'm sure I can sort something out with my probation officer and the coppers have been understanding about some of my night work,' Steve assured him.

'Let's give it a trial, but if it gets too much, feel free to call it a day. I wouldn't want you getting into trouble or anything. I would want you to start as soon as possible. The supervisor Harry, who has built the place, will give you an induction to the outside metal shutters to close up and everything and show you around. Do you have to give notice to your pizza shop?' Nick enquired innocently.

Nick had put everything possible in Steve's way to make it hard for him to accept the job, but it hadn't worked. Beryl was pouring the tea and grinning. His back was against the wall, he had to agree.

'Not a problem, Mr Diamond. I can sort that.' Again, Steve assured him everything was in order.

'Very well, Steve. I have just got myself a caretaker and you have just got yourself a job. Welcome to the Diamond Centre.' Reaching over to seal the deal, Nick shook his hand.

'Thank you, Mr Diamond,' Steve gushed, almost shaking Nick's hand off. 'You won't be sorry, I promise.' He was itching to get out of there and tell Sheila the good news. He couldn't believe his luck and he knew he owed Maggie a big favour!

'Aren't you going to finish your tea, Steve?' Beryl smiled.

Reaching for his small china cup, he almost gulped it back in one. 'Thanks, Beryl. I'm going to go and tell Sheila the good news. Thanks again, Mr Diamond.' Steve almost ran out of the door.

'Well, you really are the hero of the hour, Nicky. Did you see the smile on that boy's face? You've made his day,' Beryl grinned, not noticing Nick's hesitancy as he smiled back.

On the way back to his flat, Steve bumped into Natasha and Jimmy. 'Hey there, sheriff Jimmy,' he shouted. 'Are you going to shoot me?' He laughed when he saw Jimmy in his sheriff waistcoat with his badge on. This was their usual game and it had become a habit. Steve held his hands up in submission, making Jimmy and Natasha laugh.

Steve held his fingers up like a gun and pretended to fire at Jimmy, but Jimmy got in first. 'Bang! Steve, I shot you,' he giggled.

Falling to the floor, Steve played dead and waited for Jimmy to jump on top of him, then he would spring into life and tickle Jimmy while he roared with laughter. It was all good fun.

Getting off the ground, Steve could see Natasha was laughing, but she seemed happier than usual. 'You look in a good mood today, Tash.'

'I've got a job serving and cleaning at the pizza shop!' she squealed. 'That Fin put a good word in for me.'

Steve's face dropped. 'He's a good guy, Tash, but I wouldn't get too friendly with him.' He wanted to say more, but thought better of it. Changing the subject, he smiled. 'Well, that makes two of us, because I have just seen Nick Diamond and he's offered me the job as caretaker at his new centre. What a great day it is.' Steve almost punched the air.

'He's lovely,' Natasha blushed. 'Congratulations, Steve.'

Steve knew the signs. He could see the dreamy expression on her face, and even he had to admit that Nick Diamond was definitely a ladies' man. If he was that way inclined, he might even fancy him himself! He laughed. God knows, he smelled good enough to eat!

'Bring Jimmy over later to play with the girls, Sheila would like a catch-up. Bye, sheriff Jimmy,' he shouted, and held his thumb and finger up like a gun, almost running to tell Sheila the good news.

* * *

Nick had already leaked to the newspapers what all of the building works near the estate were about. It didn't take much. Everyone had seen what was going on, they'd been talking about it and suffered the noise for weeks, and they just didn't know what the big secret behind the tarpaulin was.

Now that Nick had spilled the beans, reporters were knocking on Beryl's door, asking her questions. Nick had welcomed them with surprise and admitted he was behind it all and it was in memory of his father, almost brushing a tear from his eye as he spoke. They had lapped it up.

He told them he wanted to give something back to the residents of the estate where his father had grown up and that it was all in the aid of charity. The local newspaper was amazed at this grand gesture, even though they thought he was crazy! But Nick reminded them that they couldn't get into the centre until its grand opening. Only Beryl Diamond could cut the ribbon that he would put across the doors.

His mum had suggested throwing a big opening day party for

everyone, especially the children, with a big bouncy castle at the front, to get the ball rolling. 'That will be good for publicity photos, Nick,' she said and he agreed. 'People like charity, they might even do a fundraiser or something. It's all in a good cause and for their benefit.' Nick had to admit it, his mother had been right.

Already, local food stores were offering hampers for the opening party. The local radio station had picked it up and praised the Diamonds for their charity. Interviewing Nick had been easy, his velvety tones wafted over the air waves explaining how much Scotland meant to his family. In his usual business manner, and in the promotional way it was intended, he'd thanked the stores that had sent hampers and toys for the children's play area. It was all good marketing and they had had free advertisements, which meant they would do it again in the future!

Hearing how well it had gone, Victoria suggested getting a monitor for the centre which would display advertisements. As the centre would be self-funding, they could charge for advertisements. It made sense and Nick had organised it. He was surprised at his mother's business brain and pleased she was getting so involved.

Once the day arrived and all of the tarpaulins and metal gates had disappeared, everyone gasped in amazement. They gathered outside in their droves to get a glimpse of the place they had all heard about. A large silver ribbon with a bow had been put across the door with a small podium and microphone for Beryl. She hadn't stopped smiling for the last few days and stopped anyone she saw and told them about the centre, like they hadn't heard it already, but she didn't care. She couldn't be prouder of Nick if she tried. She thought her heart would burst. She felt like a celebrity.

Over the last two days, Nick had constantly looked out of the windows for a glimpse of Natasha. He had seen her on odd occasions, and they had smiled and waved, but he never had a real chance to speak to her. He found himself trying to think up ways of instigating a meeting but felt it all seemed a bit cheesy. He felt like a teenage boy.

As promised, Patsy had joined him, which now annoyed Nick because he wanted to speak to Natasha. 'Well, you have gone overboard, Nick. My God, when you said a community centre, I didn't expect this. I'm impressed.' Patsy looked around the building with admiration. 'So, what's it all about, Nick? This is no patched-up bingo hall for your nana. Enlighten me?'

'Business and pleasure, Patsy love, plus somewhere for people to go in the evenings.' Nick could already feel the anger rising in him. After all these years, Patsy knew what buttons to press.

'You're going to be laundering money through this place, aren't you? For everyone who buys a meal, there will be an invisible customer with a receipt.' Mockingly, Patsy laughed.

'What do you care? You get your share. Look at you, standing there in a mink coat and pearls like the bloody queen. Did you really need to come here lording it over these poor bastards like that?'

Stroking her newly dyed blonde bob, Patsy smiled. 'I'm glad you noticed, Nick. After all, gentlemen do prefer blondes. Isn't that what they say?'

'They do when they are real blondes and not out of a bottle like yours.' His quick retort wiped the smile off her face.

Immediately, Natasha's natural blonde hair sprung to mind along with the fairness of her skin, causing a stirring sensation inside his body.

'Why the reception desk? What is all that about?' Patsy walked up to the reception area by the door and stroked her hand along the horseshoe-shaped desk.

'That was your idea, Patsy. Didn't you say people might want to book the place for birthday parties and those exercise classes? Well, how do they do that without telling a receptionist first? Who is going to book it... you?' his sarcastic tone made her wince when she remembered it had been her idea.

Changing the subject, Patsy could see Nick's anger rising. There was no point in arguing about it. 'The photographers from that local rag are getting restless, you had better give them your best smile.' Linking her arm in his, she walked towards the podium to join Beryl and Victoria.

'You look lovely, Mum. That is a nice touch.' Nick pointed to the blue tartan skirt suit she was wearing.

'I researched it, Nick. This is Diamond clan tartan. The real McCoy.' She grinned and kissed his cheek, while the photographers were snapping away like crazy. It was mayhem. The crowd was getting bigger and bigger.

Fin stood in the crowd, watching the display. 'Who the fuck does Braveheart think he is?'

'Beryl's grandson, by all accounts. Some top lawyer in London. I don't know him. Do you?'

Nick waved his hands to quieten down the crowd a little. 'There are refreshments inside for everyone, but most of all I want to thank you all for coming. This is your community centre in memory of my father, Jack Diamond. I hope you all enjoy it.' Nick stood down to a round of applause.

Helping Beryl up onto the podium, he put the microphone in front of her and gave her a wink. This was her moment. Looking to the side of him, he saw his mother smile.

'What is it?' he whispered in her ear.

'I was just wondering – when was the last time she was speechless and so nice to everyone?' she giggled under her breath, not wanting to cause attention.

'Thank you, everyone, for coming to this open day.' Beryl turned to Nick. 'Thank you, Nicky, this place means a lot to me.' Tears shone in her eyes, she felt so emotional. Turning to look at the sign as it began to flicker and light up, she shouted, 'Welcome, everyone, to the Jack Diamond Community Centre!' Beryl cut the ribbon to rapturous applause and whistling from the crowd. Nick was touched when he turned to his mother and saw her wipe a tear from her eye too. He knew how much she missed his father.

Everyone seemed to run through the doors in a stampede, inspecting everything. They looked on in awe at the newly refurbished place. It was magnificent.

'It looks more like a theatre with a restaurant,' Maggie commented. 'My God, it must have cost a fortune, Nicky!'

'You can't take it with you, Maggie. Are you alone, I thought you would have Natasha with you to see this?' Hoping his questioning didn't seem too obvious, he looked around the room at what seemed like a swarm of locusts taking the clingfilm off the many plates of sandwiches and eating their fill. The place was almost fit to bursting!

'She's on her way. She's popped into the pizza shop on the main road. She has a job there and starts Monday. Only a few hours here and there, but it will keep the wolf from the door. I'm going to look after Jimmy until a place comes up in the nursery. Though God knows when that will be. He will have passed his college exams by then!' Maggie scoffed.

The music started up to create a party atmosphere and instantly Nick walked towards Beryl. 'This is our song, Nana. Let's dance.' Beryl giggled like a schoolgirl as Nick started waltzing with her, to much applause from people who knew her. 'You look lovely today, Nana.'

'Thank you, Nicky, your dad would have been so proud of you. This has been one of the best days of my life. You're so generous, like him. He would give anyone in need the last penny in his pocket,' she beamed.

A pang of guilt stabbed at Nick's heart, as he wondered what his father would think of him. 'Ooh, that's enough for me, Nicky.' Beryl looked around at the table they had been sitting at. 'Natasha. Come and take my place, lassie. I need a sit down,' Beryl puffed.

Embarrassed, Natasha looked up at Beryl and then Nick and shook her head. Nick laughed. 'Are you really going to leave me standing here alone without a partner?' With more prompting from Beryl and Maggie, Natasha stood up as Nick put his arms around her. She almost trembled as Nick held her and they slowly danced. Their eyes met and locked. The chemistry was electrifying.

'I didn't think you were coming?' Nick's husky voice filled Natasha's ears.

Without thinking, in a hushed whisper, she blurted out, 'You're beautiful.' Then she blushed. 'I'm sorry,' she apologised, releasing her hand from his. She was about to walk away, when Nick held onto her hand tightly.

'You can't say something like that and then just walk away,' he smiled, furtively glancing around the room to see where Patsy was. He couldn't see her, and he was glad of that because he could feel himself blushing.

Natasha breathed in Nick's aftershave. It was intoxicating. Her heart was pounding in her chest. She had never felt like this before. 'I'm a married man, Natasha.' His crisp, articulate voice floated in the air, stating the obvious. They both knew this was just the beginning, but Nick wanted to make sure she realised he wasn't about to leave Patsy for some fling and lose half of everything he had worked for. Patsy would strip him bare if he left her for another woman. Confused, Nick couldn't understand why he was thinking this way. But it was how he felt at this moment. It felt like they were the only people in the room. He wondered how long you had to know someone before you felt this way. Was there a golden rule he hadn't heard about?

'Do I get to dance with the host of the party?' Victoria broke the silence and held out her arms. Reluctantly Natasha stepped away, leaving Nick and Victoria to dance. 'Someone had to break it up, Nicky love. You look like a dreamy schoolboy and you're dancing far too close for those photographers. She's pretty, isn't she?' Victoria raised her eyebrows and looked in Natasha's direction.

'I don't know what you mean?' The faint, tell-tale blush on his suntanned face told Victoria what she already presumed. Nick frowned and licked his lips to moisten them.

'Of course you don't. Just be careful. Those green eyes of yours flash like emeralds in the dark when you look at her and I am not the only one who will notice,' she laughed. 'Have you found a heart, Nicky love?'

'I'm a married man, Mum,' he scoffed, brushing off her mild-mannered interrogation.

'As long as you remember that, love.' Victoria kissed him on the cheek. 'But I've got a feeling you won't.' As the song ended, Nick followed Victoria back to the table where Beryl, Maggie and Natasha were sitting. Instantly, Natasha made her excuses and walked away with Jimmy, turning around for one last look at Nick.

'I need some air. It's got hot in here.' Rubbing his finger between his neck and his collar, Nick turned and walked towards the door. He spotted Jimmy in the children's play corner and scanned the room but Natasha was nowhere around.

The outside of the centre looked like some deserted ghost town. Everyone was inside, eating and drinking their fill. Nick wanted a moment to compose himself. He felt confused. Looking up, he saw Natasha standing in a far corner, and he could see she was alone.

'Hello, again.' Walking towards her, he couldn't think of what else to say.

'Hi.' Natasha almost jumped out of her skin. 'Did you follow me?'

'No.' Shaking his head, he laughed. 'I'm not a stalker.' Standing side by side, the silent pause was deafening.

'I'll always remember this opening, it's my birthday today,' Natasha blurted out. She knew she should go and see if Jimmy was okay, but she didn't want to leave this moment alone with Nick.

Nick's eyes widened. 'Your birthday? You should have said something, we could have got you a cake or something.' Nick cursed himself for the stupid things that were coming out of his mouth. A bloody cake! 'What have you got planned for your birthday? Did you get everything you wanted? Did that special man in your life buy you something nice?' he probed.

'Nothing special and no,' Natasha shook her head, 'there's no special person.'

'What would you like, maybe we can arrange something?' He didn't want to sound too obvious and he felt nervous.

Looking down at the ground, almost subdued, Natasha mumbled, but not loud enough for Nick to hear. He thought he'd heard what she said but couldn't be sure.

'I'm sorry, I didn't hear you,' Nick stammered. 'Well, I think I did, but do you want to say that again?'

'I said I would like to kiss you,' she muttered shyly under her breath.

Nick's heart was pounding in his chest as he glanced sideways at her. She was beautiful. Swallowing hard, he turned towards her. 'Go on, then.' Standing like a statue, he was surprised when she looked up at him and moved in closer. Tentatively, she pecked his perfectly formed lips slowly. Almost hovering over them. Gently rubbing her nose against his, she kissed him again. There was no response from Nick and she stepped away and smiled. 'I'd better go back inside,' she murmured.

The overpowering urge inside him surfaced. Reaching out for her arm, Nick pulled her closer. 'My turn.' He swept her up into his arms and their lips met, their passionate embrace knocking away all the barriers between them. Natasha's arms were wrapped around his neck, and she felt his muscular ones envelop her.

A deep stirring rose within Nick and he could feel his instant erection. He wished they were somewhere away from here as they clung to each other and kissed again. His tongue probed her mouth and sought hers as they were locked together. Suddenly they heard a noise and pulled apart. They were both panting and red-faced. Turning towards the wall, Nick adjusted himself and ran his hands through his hair, waiting for his erection to subside.

People were coming outside for a quick smoke, and Nick turned and walked back into the centre, hastily heading for the toilets so he could wipe away any traces of lipstick.

Putting his hands under the cold running water, he splashed his face with it. He needed a moment to collect his thoughts. He was being foolish, he knew that. But couldn't help himself. This was something different. He had never felt like this before. He was ashamed to admit it to himself, but he had never felt this way about Patsy and she had never kissed him so ardently in all of their married years.

Once Nick had composed himself, he went back into the centre to play the host and join in with the happy throng, while he searched the room for Natasha.

'Nicky, love.' Patsy sidled up to him. She looked bored. 'I've done my duty. I can hardly understand some of their accents, so I have just said yes and no in the right places. Would you mind if I slipped away?' She didn't want to let him down, but had had enough of the party. Scotland held no particular place in her heart. 'You don't really need me here, do you?' she asked, hoping he was going to let her off the hook.

Frowning, Nick couldn't believe his ears. It had only been a few hours. 'Well, that didn't last long, did it?' Nick looked at his watch, to press the point. 'If you want to go, Patsy, just go. The last thing we need is your bored face spoiling the party. For Christ's sake, this is for you as well, you know.'

'When are you coming home?' Patsy felt hurt at Nick's attack and tried appeasing him. 'You won't be staying much longer, will you?' Questioningly, she looked at him. 'You have set the place up, Nicky, and you obviously have put your plans in place. Why do you need to stay here? This is an awful place!' she barked.

'Don't even think of raising your voice at me in here,' he snapped under his breath. The last thing he wanted was an argument in front of all these people and he felt offended at her snobbish attitude. 'My father was brought up here... in this awful place!' he reminded her.

'Sorry, Nick. I meant no offence. I'll stay.' Subdued, Patsy looked up into his eyes, but was greeted by a cold glare. Pulling her closer to him, he whispered in her ear. 'Fuck off home. I'll come back when I'm ready,' then laughed out loud for effect, so everyone thought he had said something funny.

Tears mounted in her eyes and she sniffed. 'I'll go and say goodbye to your mum,' was all she said as she walked away. She realised now that she had just pissed on his parade and he was angry.

Seeing her leave, Nick felt better with himself. Suddenly he didn't feel guilty about his encounter with Natasha. She had wanted to be with him. No wonder he was confused. He'd made Patsy a millionaire many times over and put up with her sarcasm during his dealings, and she couldn't be bothered to put herself out for one day. Well, fuck her! Natasha was ready and waiting for him.

At last the day was over and Nick, Beryl and Victoria left their new caretaker Steve to lock up. Beryl had had far too much whisky out of her hip flask and was slurring slightly as Nick drove them back to her house. All in all, he was satisfied. It had been a good opening day and people were excited about it. They were already discussing when to meet up with their friends there.

Paul and his brothers had outdone themselves with the buffet. Nick got the feeling Paul enjoyed wearing his chef's whites again.

They all flopped down on the sofa and Victoria kicked her shoes off. 'Nicky, you put the kettle on and I think I should get Nana to bed. She's had enough excitement for one day!' She burst out laughing. Beryl was swaying back and forth as Victoria steered her towards the bedroom, thanking the gods that it was a flat and she didn't have to walk her up any staircases.

'I've made you a coffee, did she get off to sleep okay, Mum?'

Sitting on the sofa, Victoria put her feet up and rubbed them. 'She was asleep before her head hit the pillow. But you have given her one hell of a day to remember. And to think all this started from a few comments she made when she came home for her birthday party.'

'I think it will be a good investment and will pay for its own upkeep. And whatever else happens, I still own the deeds to the land. It's up to them now, Mum, isn't it? They will either ransack it or burn the place down or they will enjoy it for the purpose it's been given.'

'Well, from what I have seen today, I think they will nurture it. They don't get given much around here and I know there are some rotten apples around, but you can't tar them all with the same brush.'

'That's a nice way of putting it, Mum. Thanks for coming.' Taking his jacket off, Nick went and sat beside his mum on the sofa, lifting her feet up to put across his legs. He had taken his tie off and undone the top buttons of his shirt.

'Patsy left earlier than I presumed. Is everything okay?' Not wanting to interfere, Victoria had seen that Patsy was upset when she had left and knew they had argued in some way.

'You know Patsy, Mum. These are not her people. She doesn't understand. She couldn't get away quick enough. Do you think she has a bloke in the wings?' Nick laughed.

Soothingly, Victoria patted his arm. 'No, Nick, I don't think there is anyone else. As you say, she just doesn't like coming out of her comfort zone. She likes her salons and London. She doesn't understand what this means to Nana and you.'

'What about you, Mum? What does it mean to you? I asked a lot of you coming back here, I know that.'

'Truthfully, it makes me sad. I miss your dad, but something in his memory is nice. It keeps him alive. As for anything else you're talking about...' She looked at him over her coffee cup, they both knew what they meant, without having to say the words. 'I saw from the news that all that business is dead and buried. That is where you leave the past, Nicky. Anyway, I think I'm going to bed. It's been a long day and tomorrow you're going to have to replay it many times, especially when Nana decides to tell you all about it, as though you weren't there.' Standing up, Victoria kissed Nick on the cheek and went through to bed.

Closing the door, Nick rang James McNally. 'I'm in Glasgow. I want to see you tomorrow. Call me when you're here.' Nick was itching to get the distributors to work and sort out the message board for the community centre.

Standing up, he looked out of the windows at the estate. Some people's lights were on, other flats were in darkness. A small grin crossed his face as he looked around what was his empire now. Without knowing it, most of the people around here worked for him in one way or another. It was quite funny when he thought about it. Then another thought occurred to him. Impulsively, he picked up his jacket and quietly let himself out of the door.

Standing outside Natasha's front door, Nick now felt he had been too impulsive. It was nearly midnight and her flat was in darkness. Maybe he was being too presumptuous? He wasn't sure, but he was here now. Nervously, he tapped on the front door. He didn't want to knock too loudly, because he knew Jimmy would be in bed and the nosy neighbours would wonder who was knocking at this time of night.

Within a few minutes, the door opened. 'I knew you would come. I willed it and you heard me.' Natasha opened the door wider for him and instantly put her arms around his neck. Searching for her lips, he kissed her. Their embrace grew more passionate with each kiss. Their hunger for each other spilled over as they pulled at each other's clothing and their hands glided over each other's bodies on the way to the bedroom.

Natasha's soft nakedness beneath him sent passion soaring through him as they kissed and nuzzled each other's necks, clinging on to each other for dear life. Sliding his tongue down from her neck, he stopped at her pert upright breast and flicked her nipple with the tip of his tongue, making her gasp. Trailing his tongue down, he teased her thighs, as she opened them wider and took a sudden intake of breath, moaning with pleasure, as he teased and probed.

Natasha's head spun and she felt fireworks going off inside her body as she trembled beneath him.

Nick's body was on fire, too. He ached for Natasha. His manhood throbbed as Natasha wrapped her legs around him tightly and welcomed him. Their bodies were locked together in passion as their pleasure mounted, until at last they could hold back no more. A long moan escaped Natasha as Nick gasped for breath.

Lying there panting, trying to catch his breath, Nick reached out for Natasha and pulled her closer to him, lying her head on his chest. They were both satiated in their passion and the loving tenderness between them as they stroked each other and whispered words of endearment, until at last Nick could feel his blood rising again, lovingly turning Natasha on her back as their need for each other heightened their passion.

* * *

Seeing the digital alarm clock, Nick rubbed his face and turned to get out of bed. Opening her eyes, Natasha turned to him. 'Are you okay, Nicky?'

'Yes, it's six in the morning, go back to sleep. I have to leave before anyone sees me or Jimmy gets out of bed,' he whispered. Looking around, he searched for his clothes, which had been hastily discarded. Taking a backward glance into the bedroom, he yearned to get back in beside her.

With her blonde tousled hair, and her blue eyes staring up at him, he felt guilty for sneaking out like a thief in the night. 'I'll see you soon.' Leaning down, he kissed her.

'There's no pressure, Nicky. I'll be here. If you want me...' she tailed off, saddened by the fact that he was leaving.

Biting his tongue before he said anything foolish, Nick headed for the door. The cool morning air woke him up as he scrambled to button his shirt properly. He felt like punching the air and shouting for joy. Last night had been fantastic, he'd never felt anything like it.

Opening the door as quietly as possible, he was surprised to be greeted by his mum in the hallway. 'Wasn't the shop open for the milk, Nicky?' She stared at him and pointed her thumb towards the kitchen.

Stunned, but following her lead, he looked over to where she was pointing. He could hear Beryl in the kitchen. 'My, you're all early birds today. No, there wasn't any milk. I just came back to tell you, I'll take the car and drive further up the main road.'

'No need, Nicky love,' Beryl shouted through. 'That mother of yours must be as blind as a bat. Sending you out for milk when there is a perfectly good bottle here that I got yesterday. You poor thing. Sit down, I will make you something to warm your bones.'

Victoria looked Nick up and down, noting his dishevelled appearance. It wasn't her business, but she had a fair idea where he had been. Awkwardly, he smiled at her. 'I'll just pop to the bathroom.' Embarrassed, he walked away. He felt like a kid caught with his hands in the cookie jar. His mother had caught him sneaking in! God, how embarrassing was that? He was mentally prepared for the lecture she would give him later about Patsy, but for now he didn't care. He'd spent an amazing night in the arms of a beautiful woman.

Victoria had already decided she didn't want to get involved. She had only just got her son back. He was in his mid-thirties and so was Patsy. Neither of them made it easy for each other. Victoria felt last night was Nick's way of hitting back at Patsy for deserting him. Although that starry-eyed grin on his face made her wonder.

* * *

'Well, just look at you, Steve, with your keys jangling. You sound like a prison warder.' Sheila was all smiles this morning. For once, Steve had been home at a civilised time and he wasn't beaten to a pulp. She was pleased about his new job as caretaker at the community centre. She felt it was a step up. She had managed to get herself a part-time job at the launderette, too, and life seemed to be looking up for them. She still owed a lot of money, but they had decided that if they could live off what Steve earnt, then her wages could pay the debts. The normal benefits for the girls went into a Post Office account and Sheila had stressed that was only to be used for the girls' school clothes and presents.

They had sat down with Steve's probation officer and worked it all out, with a helping hand from the Citizens Advice Bureau. Sheila had hidden nothing and told them everything. There was no point in lying.

'Once you get your feet under the table, I might ask if they need any cleaners there or something,' she beamed. They'd had a rocky start but now things were looking up. She had a good feeling about all this.

'I tell you, Sheila, I owe Maggie big time. She put the word in for me. I am so glad to be off that moped, I was beginning to get saddle sores!' Sitting down with his mug of tea, Steve looked perplexed.

'What's wrong, you look worried?'

'No, nothing. It's just that Fatso Paul also works at the centre. He's going to be the chef there and in charge by all accounts. I just hope he doesn't start dealing in there.'

'Who's put him in charge?' Sheila felt as concerned as Steve looked but left it for now. There was no point in worrying about something that hadn't happened yet.

'Nick Diamond, I presume. The reception woman is Greek as well, I presume she is a friend of Paul's. You haven't met her yet, have you?'

Sheila shook her head. There were shouts and Penny and Sharon came wandering through to the lounge.

'Here's my girls.' Steve opened his arms to greet them. This was the home life he had dreamed of in prison. He did wonder whether he should mention anything to Nick Diamond about Fatso Paul and his drugs, but he thought better of it. Maybe Maggie had put a word in for Paul and he was still on probation with Nick Diamond. No point in rocking the boat.

Once everyone had had breakfast, Steve got ready to open up the community centre. 'I bet it will be busy today. Everyone will come for a proper look.' Greeting the postman as he opened the door, Steve noticed a letter from the council. The others were final demands. Quickly opening the council letter, Steve scanned it. 'Sheila! Sheila!' Almost jumping for joy, he waved the letter in her face.

'What? What is it?' she was almost panicking, but she could see him smiling, so it couldn't be that bad.

'The council have put us on their transfer list. We could be out of here anytime!' he shouted.

Suddenly Sheila's heart sank. 'Yes, just when we both have jobs. Now we're going to up and leave them? That's ridiculous.'

'It could be a long waiting list, Sheila, and we don't know where it will be. It could be a bus ride away. We'll cross that bridge when we come to it, eh? But for the moment let's be happy, and not a word in front of these two or the neighbours. Let's keep it between us.' Giving her a peck and shouting to Sharon and Penny, he left for his new life as the community centre caretaker. Things were definitely looking up!

* * *

'Is your mother still here, Nick?' Maggie stood on the doorstep with a cardboard box.

'No, Maggie, she's gone. Did you want her for something?' Nick couldn't believe it. He'd tried sneaking around all morning but everyone seemed to be out and about. For fuck's sake, didn't anyone sleep around here?

Glancing each side of the balcony, almost shiftily, Maggie replied. 'Good, because I have something to show you and Beryl.' Pushing past him, she walked into the lounge and put the box on the floor. 'Take a look inside that.' Maggie stood there with her arms folded.

Beryl looked up at her questioningly. She could see it had been opened. The brown tape across the seal was broken. 'It's not a dead animal or something, is it?'

'Nana, who puts dead animals in cardboard boxes and has the post deliver them? Look here. It's special delivery. Blimey, you have been watching too many gangster movies.' Nick shook his head in disbelief. He already knew exactly what was in the box.

Tentatively, Beryl opened the box. There was a mixture of wool and knitting needles inside. Confused, she looked up at Maggie.

'Keep digging, Beryl.' Maggie pursed her lips, and stood with her hands on her hips. 'I did what Nick said. I dropped a hint to that gormless Fin that he should maybe ask his boss if we could do a bit of knitting and maybe sell a bit of weed on his patch to raise the old girls' pensions and look!' Seeing Beryl's hesitancy to put her hand in the box, Maggie shoved her out of the way. At the bottom of the box in cellophane wrapping was a bag of marijuana. The bag was the size of a sugar bag. Beryl and Maggie stood looking at it, wide-eyed.

'Do you know how much that stuff costs an ounce, Beryl? Probably not,' Maggie scoffed. 'Well, a bloody lot, I can tell you. There must be two pounds of the stuff there. There is a typed note inside. Read it.' Again, Maggie almost threw the note at Beryl.

80-20 in your favour. Payable at the end of the month to Fin.

'What does that mean?' Beryl asked. She was totally puzzled by all of this.

'It means, Nana,' Nick butted in, 'that whoever Maggie asked has agreed to you selling on his turf and sent you the product to sell. Whatever you make, he wants 20 per cent for the stuff he has sent you. Let's be honest, Maggie is right. What this person hopes to make out of it won't clear the cost of that stuff for quite some time, will it, Maggie?'

Maggie looked worried, a frown appeared on her brow. 'Do you think we'll end up in jail, Nick? You're the solicitor, tell us straight.'

All wide-eyed and innocent, Nick looked from one to the other. 'If you're going to do this,' he said, 'you need to be tactful about where you get the stuff from and not advertise it. That means you, Nana. Who can you trust to do this knitting with you? Have you thought about that?'

Maggie and Beryl both nodded. 'Oh, yes, that's not a problem. The problem is where we all can meet up. It looks a bit suspicious us all meeting here. It's not as though we have a reading club or something.' Maggie paused.

A faint smile crossed Nick's face. Now he knew what she was getting at... just as he had predicted. The community centre. Maggie wanted the go-ahead from him.

Nonchalantly Nick shrugged, he was prepared to play this

game. 'I suppose you could always meet up at the community centre. Also, when you're knitting your soft toys or whatever...' Nick rolled his eyes to the ceiling, deep in thought. 'Why don't you put letters on them?' Seeing the puzzled look on their faces, he continued. 'You know what I mean. If you go through the alphabet, that could be the first letter of the name of whoever the people are buying it for?'

Clapping her hands with glee, Beryl nodded. 'I like that, Nicky. There are all sorts of cups and things with A, B, C and so on. People like that. It makes good presents. What a good idea.'

Everyone seemed satisfied with the idea, especially Nick. A was for acid. C was for cannabis. M was for meth. The line of drugs went straight through the alphabet. People would eventually know what they were buying under his tutelage.

Casting Nick a sharp look, Maggie couldn't believe a solicitor could be so easily dragged into this. Surely he should be telling his nana to steer clear of crime and not encouraging it. That was his job, wasn't it? Maggie felt there was something not right about this situation. It made her feel uneasy. Beryl's wonderful grandson Nicky had another side to him. He was as crooked as they come, but he disguised it well with his sharp suits and solicitor's status. For one brief moment, Nick caught her stare and the pair of them locked eyes for a split second. Although he was smiling, his cold green eyes shone like emeralds as he glared at her, challenging her to say something against him about his knitting ideas. Maggie's mouth felt dry and she swallowed hard, turning away to look at Beryl, who was totally oblivious to the atmosphere between her and Nick. Maggie didn't know what to think; maybe she was just being cynical and Nick was just appeasing his old nana. But Maggie felt there was more to this than met the eye. Her gut instinct, which was hardly ever wrong, told her something was amiss.

James rang him later that day. Nick was exhausted, he hadn't slept, and from the moment he walked through Nana's door, he was desperate to see Natasha. He hated the idea that he had just cut and run. He didn't want her to think that.

They met in the cemetery as instructed. 'Mr Diamond, it's good to see you.' Shaking Nick's hand, he sat down. 'This is an odd place to meet.'

'It's the perfect place to meet, James. Do you see anyone around here? Everything is up and running for you. I want a notice board putting up at the community centre, let's say for vacancies or something.'

The cemetery gave James the creeps, but he listened intently to Nick's speech, it seemed he had a lot to say.

'There is a circle of old women calling themselves the knitting nanas... they will be knitting soft toys and filling them with stuffing and packets of cannabis. Eventually, you will be stuffing them with other similar goods. Greek Paul,' Nick decided against calling him fat out of politeness, 'he will be the drop-off point for the distributor's money. They will pop in casually and hand their money over to him and him alone,' Nick stressed. 'I want to inspect Noel's brothels, my client has women from his own rackets that may be useful to him. The money-lending business carries on as before, but they answer to you. The pizza and kebab shops are your responsibility as well. Noel can have a couple of his men work there if he wishes, or as delivery men, but I want no creaming off the top and no trouble. There, I have said my piece. Do you have any questions?'

Surprised, James thought about it. 'It seems you have covered every corner, Mr Diamond. Are there premises above the community centre?'

'Yes, there's a flat I believe, why?' The flat above it had totally slipped Nick's mind. He hadn't even bothered to inspect it.

'We could use that as a brothel and a meeting place. Women walking in and out of the community centre won't raise too many eyebrows as long as they're dressed properly. Punters could pop in there too for a cuppa or a bite to eat, discreetly of course. I have to admit, that community centre is a really good idea. I don't know about a dookit. It's more like a ghetto.' James laughed, pleased that he had come up with an idea that Nick had overlooked. He liked Nick Diamond's business brain, and what is more he wanted to join forces, which made life easier. James felt he was an old man now, he wanted the money without the hassle. There was enough going around for everyone.

'That's a bloody good idea.' Then a thought occurred to Nick. He could have given the flat upstairs to Natasha. It would be their own love nest, away from seeing eyes, but would she want to move away from Maggie and Beryl? They had become close friends. And he couldn't be around all the time, he still had his life in London. He didn't want her to get lonely. No. Business was business, he decided. 'Come on, let's go and see the flat. The caretaker there is a man called Steve. Keep an eye on him, he's not my choice, but with one arm up my back I had to offer him the job.'

'Your client has given this a lot of thought, Mr Diamond.'

Weighing Nick up, James felt convinced there was no client. That this was the very man they all feared – the Undertaker.

Faltering slightly, realising his mistake, Nick agreed. 'He's been very thorough in our recent meetings, which is why I have rushed it all out to you in one speech. It was a lot to remember,' Nick laughed, trying to make light of it.

As they both walked into the community centre, James looked around and gave a slow whistle. 'Blimey, this place is fantastic!'

It was already filling up, people were ordering tea and coffee and sitting at the tables gossiping. Fatso Paul and his staff were cooking lunches. Nick felt proud of the place, it actually looked like it could be a going concern. 'Do you see what I mean, Mr Diamond? Who is going to be suspicious about people wandering in and out of here?'

'Let's go back outside, the entrance to the flat is around the back.' Nick led the way. He was curious himself. Fumbling around on his bunch of keys, he finally found the right one. The freshly painted flat greeted them. Harry had worked the same magic upstairs as he had downstairs. He had probably thought Nick would use it and had made special effort.

'You could rent this place out, Mr Diamond,' James suggested. It was a three-bedroomed flat, all it needed was furniture. The kitchen was all built-in and so were the wardrobes and when they opened the French windows, the balcony gave them a bird's-eye view of the area. Even Nick had to agree, it was a nice place. 'I also notice there are only CCTV cameras on the outside.' James had spotted that instantly. Old habits die hard, and from his old robbery days, that was the first thing he looked for.

'No cameras, no evidence. There are a couple, for insurance purposes, but they are not wired up to anything. I'm not sure I like the idea of people living above the centre. They would become nosy. No. I like your idea better. Get some beds and furniture sorted out. I'll get you a spare key cut.'

'I see your point, too many eyes and all of that,' James agreed. This was a special project and needed handling properly.

An idea floated through Nick's brain. 'I will have post sent here. Check the mail daily or have someone do it and just put it all together in a box, and I will sort it when I come back.'

'That's no problem.' James frowned and looked slightly puzzled. 'Do you intend coming back often, then?' He felt he'd been given a free rein, but there were a lot of conditions. He was beginning to feel like Pinocchio, with Nick pulling his strings.

'As often as needed,' Nick snapped. 'I do have family here, you know.' The icy glare that Nick threw James was enough to make James stop his line of questioning. 'Let it be known that this place is for storage, then it won't raise too many eyebrows,' Nick ordered.

As they walked back to Nick's car, they saw a police car outside. James stopped in his tracks. 'What the bloody hell do they want?'

Nick walked into the centre to see what was going on and was greeted by Terence and his colleague. 'Mr Diamond!' Terence shouted from across the queue at the tea bar.

Casually, Nick walked towards them. 'Terence, how nice of you to come here.' Turning towards one of Paul's brothers serving at the counter, he said, 'The officers don't wait in the queue. They are busy men. Make sure they get served first and it's on the house.' His charming manner pleased the two policemen. This was going to be their drinking hole for their tea breaks daily, Nick was sure of that. They wouldn't want any other coppers muscling in on their freebies.

Shaking their hands and accepting their gracious thanks, Nick and James walked out of the centre. 'That's a bit dodgy, isn't it? Coppers using the centre. That will have people on their toes, Mr Diamond.' James didn't like that side of things.

'People don't always see what is under their noses, James. And I agree, it will make people more cautious in their dealings. Keep your enemies close. If the dealers get caught being stupid, it's their funeral, not ours. I want no sloppy ways, this is a professional set-up and I wanted it treated as such.' His cold manner and sharp tongue was enough to convince James that he was right about Nick. He was the Undertaker. He had murdered Billy Burke and he was certain he would have James murdered, too, if he decided to.

As they parted company, James agreed with Nick. Keep your enemies close. That was exactly what Nick Diamond was with all his fancy suits and charming smile. A wolf in sheep's clothing!

James felt he needed to speak to Noel about his concerns. He had been a good friend to James when others turned their backs on him, and he wanted to repay his loyalty. Going to see him, he wasn't sure if he was doing the right thing. He told Noel about his meeting with Nick. After all they were all partners.

'What is it, James, what ails you?' Just by James's body language, Noel could see there was a problem.

'I think,' James stammered, 'and this is only my gut instinct. But I think Nick Diamond is the Undertaker, which means he was the one who ordered Daniel's crucifixion. I'm not sure, so don't do anything hasty. Let's continue with this truce and take his money. Let's not start a war. Don't make me regret sharing this with you!' James warned.

'Nick Diamond? Are you sure? He seems very reasonable. Do you trust him?'

'No, I'm not sure, and I wouldn't trust him as far as I could throw him. He thinks he's untouchable. It wouldn't surprise me if he wanted us all dead. He killed Billy, who's next. You? Me? Just leave it for now, Noel. I could be wrong, but we will work this out. Let's fight fire with fire. Not emotions,' James warned, although he could see the angry look on Noel's face. Had they got themselves in too deep?

* * *

On his way back to Nana's, Nick took a chance and went to Natasha's flat. He was disappointed when she wasn't there. One of the neighbours told him she had a shift at the pizza shop when he told them he was passing a message on for Beryl.

'What's all this?' Walking into Beryl's flat, he was greeted by half a dozen old women sat around drinking tea. It looked like a pensioners' tea party! There were walking sticks scattered around the room and the odd Zimmer frame in the hallway. Taken aback, he looked towards Nana for an explanation, while all the women shouted hello and waved in unison, smiling at him.

'My knitting pals, Nicky. We're having a meeting. Maggie will be here soon, she is looking after young Jimmy until Natasha gets home.' Beryl smiled innocently. She couldn't see what the problem was. After all, it was all agreed, wasn't it?

Trying to find a spare chair, Nick sat down. He was astounded. What a bloody day he'd had.

'You do all realise this has to be kept firmly under wraps? You could be arrested for this and the police would want to know who is providing you with the stuffing!'

'Yes!' they all shouted at once towards him and nodded.

'We might be pensioners but we're not stupid and the extra money will come in handy. And how can we tell them who's supplying when we don't know ourselves? Only that stupid Fin bloke, it's his problem. He'd better pass the money on,' one muttered.

'Maybe we should get receipts from him,' said another.

Receipts? Nick's brain hurt. How the hell were they going to ask for receipts? He wasn't even sure Fin could write, let alone give this lot receipts!

'Mondays and Fridays, we are going to meet at the centre for our knitting session and tea, before the bingo starts. Glenys, Stella and Moira are going to go door to door delivering it. We might get a few regulars and that would help, they have mobile scooters and it's easier for them to get around. Josie and Maggie are doing the stuffing,' Beryl announced. It was a perfectly laid plan.

Nick couldn't believe his ears. It had been organised with military precision. Everyone knew what part of the production line they were on. It was fucking crazy! He needed a lie down, this was too much for him to take in. 'Just out of curiosity, Nana. How much are you charging for these knitted animals?'

'Thirty pounds. Maggie says the stuffing is anything from ten pounds upwards and we have overheads to pay.'

'What overheads?' Stunned by the casualness of it all, Nick was puzzled.

'Well, we have our 20 per cent to pay and a little wool and we want to make some money for ourselves. Time is money, Nicky, and those toys take time,' Beryl stressed.

'You do realise they can get it for less than that?'

'Yes, but not so easily accessible and delivered.' Another woman butted in. they all turned to each other and continued with their meeting, ignoring him. Then Maggie walked in. 'Hi, Nicky. Well, ladies, what have I missed?' she enquired.

Dumbstruck, Nick walked towards the bedroom and threw his jacket on a nearby chair. 'What the fuck have I done?' The last thing he needed was to become a laughing stock to his colleagues when he was representing a bunch of old ladies in court for dealing!

After a short nap, Nick felt better. Getting up and showering, he was pleased to see the house was empty and Beryl was happily cooking dinner for them both. He was starving. He couldn't remember the last time he'd eaten.

As the night drew on, he could see Beryl was falling asleep in her chair and convinced her to go to bed. No sooner had she gone, he slipped out of the door to Natasha's flat.

Nick was surprised that the door was ajar. Pushing it slightly, he walked in and down the hallway. The bedroom door was open and Natasha was lying in bed. 'I left the door open for you, it's better than knocking. Come here.'

'That's a hell of a risk around here,' he smiled, slowly peeling his clothes off to join her in bed.

'What we're doing is a risk. Well, it is for you.' Natasha's eyes were cast downwards at the duvet. 'Who cares, you're here now.' Reaching out for him as he joined her on the bed, they kissed, each one more ardent than the last. Already Nick could feel the fire rising inside him. He wasn't sure how long he could hold back, he was already at boiling point.

'Now, Nicky, I want you now,' Natasha urged him on and once again they were locked together like a jigsaw, engulfed in passion. No sooner had one encounter ended and they caught their breath, they stroked and teased each other's bodies again with expectancy of more excitement to come. They couldn't get enough of each other. Their soft endearments to in the darkness of the room as they kissed urged them on for more. Eventually, Natasha laid her head on Nick's chest, roaming her hands through his hair. His muscled arm wrapped around her made her feel warm and safe. She knew she was punching above her weight but was happy for the here and now. Thoughts of Nick and their stolen nights together made her happy. Remembering his soft kisses during the day put a smile on her face. It felt so natural, being in his arms, like they had known each other a lifetime.

* * *

Nick had stayed in Scotland longer than anticipated. He had been there for two weeks and knew he had to leave. Natasha felt like an addiction to him. He couldn't get enough of her. In the end, he had given up hiding it if they met during the day. No more was it a polite hello like strangers after they had spent all night in each other's arms. He didn't care any more. He was happy. They both were and that was all that mattered. Didn't he deserve some happiness in his life?

They spent as much time as possible together. He took her out for candlelit dinners and they lay in each other's arms afterwards, satiated by their lovemaking, while Maggie babysat. She had raised an eyebrow at the situation but said nothing.

Although their affair became neighbourhood gossip, Nick didn't care. He checked in with Patsy every couple of days to make sure the money deliveries were in order and made excuses for his prolonged stay. All he wanted was his illicit nights of passion with Natasha and to make every second count.

26

During their last night together and their heart-breaking goodbye, the words finally escaped Natasha's lips. She had said them so often in her head and now she couldn't hold them back any longer. The raging tide was held back no more. 'I love you, Nick,' she whispered, while they lay in each other's arms, satiated by their love and lust for each other.

Her faint Scottish accent filled his ears as he lay in the darkness, stroking her soft blonde hair with his hand, while looking up at the ceiling. He was tempted to say the words himself, but bit his tongue. Each time he held her, the words formed in his head, but he was afraid to say them.

'Don't, Natasha. I have to go home, you knew that before all of this started. Don't make me feel guilty.' The huskiness of his voice hid the trembling he felt inside. He didn't know what to do. His feelings for Natasha were strong, but he had to leave. He had wondered if it was some kind of holiday fling and only time would tell. Time and his departure. They were worlds apart. If you love something, you have to let it go. If it comes back to you, then it's yours for life, he reasoned.

Turning on her stomach, she propped herself up on her elbows. 'I don't want to make you feel guilty, Nicky. I just didn't want you to leave without me telling you. I know you're married, but I love you and I wanted to say it out loud.' Leaning across, she kissed his lips.

A lump rose in Nick's throat. 'Would it help if I said I loved you too? Or would you think I'm only saying it because I feel guilty? I do love you, Natasha, rest assured of that.' Swallowing her up in his arms, he held her tightly and breathed a sigh of relief. He had got it out of his system. He, too, didn't want to part without saying it, but he didn't want to give her promises he couldn't keep.

'Just leave in the morning, Nicky. No goodbyes, let's just have tonight together.' The heartache she felt knew no bounds. He was walking out of her life and she might never see him again.

'I'll be back. I promise. And it's not Patsy I'm going home for. I have a job, responsibilities,' he stressed, trying to make her understand.

'Make love to me, Nicky,' she whispered. A tear had formed in her eye and with all her might she fought to hold it back. She wanted to feel his warm, athletic body heighten the love she knew they both felt. Emotions ran high as they reached for each other in the darkness.

Leaving her asleep, Nick crept out as quietly as he could. He felt sad, leaving the warmth of her body. Their lovemaking had been slow and passionate and every word of love they felt for each other had poured out with each kiss. For the first time in years, he felt like crying. To Nick, it felt like he had everything but nothing. None of it mattered any more. He needed the long drive home to clear his head. Everything had happened so quickly. He wanted to be the man she thought he was.

'You look down in the dumps, laddie. Is there anything I can do?' Beryl hugged him tightly; she had loved having him stay with her, even though she knew it wasn't just her prolonging his stay.

'Yes, Nana, there is. Here is a bag of things for Natasha. One is a mobile phone, if she wants to use it to call me, she can. It's up to her. It's got plenty of credit. There are a couple of other presents, but there is money, too, and I will be sending some regularly to her. I didn't want to give her it myself. I didn't want her to think I was paying her off. I'm not, Nana, believe me, I'm not. I'm just trying to help her the only way I can. Explain that to her for me. She needs a new bed,' Nick laughed, trying to make light of it. 'That bloody spring keeps sticking in my arse. Sorry, Nana, I didn't mean to be crude.' He kissed her on the cheek.

'I know, love. And yes, I will explain and fight your corner.' Stroking his face, Beryl was saddened as she saw Nick's sunken shoulders as he walked to his car.

* * *

It felt strange being back home; it cast a new light on things, even though it had only been for a short while, it was like he was seeing things through different eyes. Patsy wasn't home, there was no surprise there, even though he had told her when he would be arriving. She must have really missed him!

There was a note on the dining table from Patsy saying she would meet him at a local restaurant tonight and have a proper homecoming. Flinging it in the bin, he poured a long-awaited whisky and ran the shower. He felt hot and sweaty after his long journey and was glad of the time alone to relax. Once he had done that and ordered something to eat, he would call the law firm to see if there were any messages and let them know he would be back tomorrow.

Walking into the restaurant where he knew Patsy would be waiting, he tried his best to raise some enthusiasm. It wasn't her fault he'd met someone else. 'Patsy, you look well.' Leaning over to her side of the table, he kissed her on the cheek. He had to admit, she looked like she had made a special effort. Her bobbed blonde hair had been newly done, but then, with a host of hairdressers at her fingertips, it wasn't surprising. The black Chanel dress she wore clung to her slim figure, doing her ample bosom justice.

'You look well, Nicky. Have you been eating a lot of Nana's Scotch broth?' she laughed. 'I've ordered you a drink. It's good to see you.' Nick's heart sank. Patsy sounded genuinely happy to see him, almost to the point where he could feel her eyes roaming over his body and lingering slightly at his face.

'Just a lot of last-minute business to attend to regarding the community centre. But you wouldn't be interested. Anyway, I'm back now, although I will have to pop there from time to time to check up on things.' Nick thought he would get the word in early about going back to Scotland regularly.

'You're back and yet you're talking about going away again so soon?' Patsy felt deflated. She had missed him but didn't want to sound like a nag. She had already planned to be at home to meet him today, but one of Nick's money deliveries was due and she had to be there.

Flippantly, Nick waved his hand in the air. 'I'm just talking, Patsy. That's what people do over dinner, isn't it?' Raising one eyebrow, he nodded towards her and took a sip of his drink.

'Well, I need to talk to you.' She rolled her eyes around the room, searching for the right words. 'The shipment today was much bigger than normal, Nick. It will take longer to sort it.' Licking her lips to moisten them, she picked up her glass of wine and took a sip. She knew Nick hated these conversations, especially in public, but it had to be said.

'For God's sake, Patsy, will you never learn?' Nick snapped. This time he picked up his whisky glass and gulped it back in one.

'Come on, get it off your chest, and make sure the guy at the next table hears you!' he barked.

'You need to come and see it for yourself, Nick, that's all I'm saying...' Tailing off, Patsy could see the anger rising in Nick's face. It was time to change the subject. 'Look, let's enjoy our dinner. You must be tired after your journey. We don't need to talk business now.' She smiled and flirted with him and, in normal circumstances, Nick would have followed her lead and looked forward to dessert. Patsy was definitely offering it on a plate. But things had changed since he'd met Natasha.

They talked and laughed over dinner like old friends. Nick didn't hate Patsy or anything like that. He supposed in a way he loved her, but not in the same way he loved Natasha. That was a very different love. He didn't want to hurt Patsy, but they had just outgrown each other and times like these and when they shared a bed together were just habit. He was sure Patsy was having an affair of her own. She was barely around these days and never questioned his absence. They were just playing at being married for appearance's sake.

Looking over the candlelit table, Patsy reached out for one of Nick's manicured hands and held it. The heady scent of his aftershave wafted towards her. Breathing it in, she felt her own desire rise. 'I'm sorry we argued the last time we met. Let's put all that behind us now.' Patsy waited for his answer.

Taking a deep sigh, Nick squeezed her hand. 'It's all forgotten, Patsy. We were both stressed, and it was a busy day for all of us,' he smiled. Whether it be how much he had drunk, or the ambience, Nick could feel himself being drawn into Patsy's flirting. Suddenly his mobile vibrated in his jacket pocket. Excusing himself, he took it out and looked at the text message.

I miss you.

Nick could see it was from Natasha. He felt sick. His stomach turned somersaults, content that she had contacted him, but he felt guilty sitting here flirting with his wife.

He hastily typed back:

I miss you too darling.

'Is everything okay, Nick?' Patsy asked, noticing Nick's uneasiness.

'Yes, everything is fine. Just business. Nothing for you to worry about. I'm just a little tired, that's all.' A faint smile crossed his face.

'Well, I hope you're not too tired, Nicky. Why don't we go home?' she asked hopefully.

'It's been a long day and a long couple of weeks. Even your seduction techniques couldn't tempt me tonight.' Seeing the disappointment in her face, he asked the waiter for the bill. Trying to keep two women in his life was bloody hard work!

* * *

Days turned into weeks and then months. Normality had crept back into Nick's life. A day never passed without talking to Natasha. When possible, they would have Zoom chats. One of the presents he had left Natasha was a laptop, with specific instructions that she used some of the money he had given her to get the internet installed. They would talk for hours, and she would send him photos of herself outside the centre with Nana and Jimmy, making him laugh. He itched to get back to Scotland. His body yearned to feel her arms around him again, but each time something came up.

Reports from Fatso Paul and the receptionist were fantastic. Patsy had been right, people had enquired at the centre about birthday parties and one was for an evening Zumba class. It would all go to the upkeep of the place. James's regular reports were even more staggering.

The knitting nanas had held a charity tombola, selling raffle tickets and giving prizes that people had donated, including their soft toys as samples. James had to admit they were doing a roaring trade. He'd laughed out loud when he'd told Nick that their mobile scooters went up and down all the housing estates in the area selling their soft toys and knitted hats and scarves, and no one paid a blind bit of notice. The weekly soup kitchen that Beryl insisted on was a hit. Homeless people from far and wide visited the centre for a hot meal.

Although this had confused Nick, once James explained, it made perfect sense. Most of the homeless people who milled through the doors were new faces. The police couldn't keep up with the number of strangers coming and going. It was all a smokescreen concocted by Maggie and Beryl. James had opened the brothel above the centre, but during quiet periods, rather than have the prostitutes sit around waiting for custom, he had them waitress or clean the community centre. It all made perfect sense and the regular visitors got used to seeing the girls who worked in the brothel in the community centre. Everything was coming together perfectly – even James sounded amazed.

Only Fatso Paul had an axe to grind. Nick had given him £6,000 as his share and Paul felt it should have been more. He explained that he had his brothers to pay too, but Nick had rebuffed him and told him the next payment would be much bigger. If he didn't like it, he could always leave, was Nick's attitude, knowing full well Paul wouldn't.

Noel was happy with his lot, trade was good and his brother was due out of hospital soon. He had put a few of his own Albanian staff in the pizza shops and on deliveries. The money was rolling in. There was no more fighting. Everyone had their share and was happy with it. James informed Nick there was some mail in the flat, but it wasn't addressed to him. It was addressed to a woman. What should he do with it?

A big grin crossed Nick's face. He was waiting for this. 'Just put everything in a box, James. I will sort it out. I'm coming up to Scotland next week.'

Immediately, Nick telephoned his accountant. 'Tom, it's Nick. Just a quick word. Do you remember me telling you about that partnership I was going into with Karen?'

'Yes, of course I do, Nick. We're just waiting for her paperwork and stuff.'

A few days before he had left Scotland, Nick had undergone his usual practice of picking a name from the cemetery and applying for copies of the birth certificate. A plan was forming in his brain, but in order to make it happen he would need a new business partner. So he decided to invent one. Karen. It seemed post was already being sent to her. She had an address, a birth certificate and a national insurance number. He would organise a bank account over the telephone and drip-feed as much money as possible into it.

This would be his private pension, without Patsy knowing. He had thought about how he would live if he left Patsy. She would strip him bare of every penny, but she couldn't if she didn't know these accounts existed. His business partner, Karen, would own everything he could get away with, should he decide to make a run for it with Natasha. When Nick had seen Karen's name, it had made him laugh out loud. She was a French woman with British citizenship, which meant it would not be suspicious if Tom or anyone never met her, because she lived abroad.

Nick had already sorted the legal side of the paperwork, stating that she had bought half of his pizza shops and owned half of the land the community centre stood on. One of his colleagues had signed the papers and they had been witnessed, once he had greased their palms. He had taken a photo of a woman from the internet and downsized it to a passport photo. When he had all the relevant information and a bank account to pay for it, he would apply for her passport and upload the photo.

'Apparently, everything is in order. I am going to Scotland next week to finalise things.' Nick was feeling very pleased with himself. Patsy would be okay, she had her shops. He wasn't leaving her penniless.

Nick wanted a chance of happiness. He wanted out of everything now and to just live a peaceful life with the woman he loved. If she would have him.

* * *

Steve felt perturbed. He knew Paul was dealing at the centre and he felt loyalty deserved loyalty. Nick Diamond had been good to him and he knew the man had a right to know what was going on. After talking it over with Sheila, he felt he should warn him what was happening behind his back. It could ruin it for everyone who enjoyed the centre.

'He could close it down, Steve, and then you wouldn't have a job. Have you thought of that?' Sheila warned him. She was frightened. Their lives had improved lately and now Steve could ruin it all.

'That's why I'm doing it. I could lose my job anyway if it gets raided or closed down.' They both agreed to make the call to Nick. Maybe they could salvage something out of it. Sheila sat beside him as Steve made the call.

'Mr Diamond, sir, it's Steve Marshal, the caretaker at the centre.'

'Yes, I remember you. What's the problem?' Nick snapped. He couldn't understand why he was ringing him.

Steve went on to tell Nick what he suspected. Holding the telephone to his ear, Nick's blood ran cold. He was stunned. This man who he had given a job to was about to grass him up. The bastard! He couldn't just be happy and turn a blind eye. Nick was angry but kept his composure. 'I'm coming up to Scotland next week. We will discuss it then. I have to go.' Nick was blazing. Steve just couldn't keep his nose out. He hated him! The sooner he sorted him out, the better.

Steve felt he had done his bit for Nick Diamond. What he decided to do with this information was his business.

'That voice, Sheila. There is something about Nick Diamond's voice. Especially after that call, he almost snarled at me. I have heard that voice before but I can't think where.'

'Maybe it's just one of those things. I wouldn't worry about it,' Sheila shrugged. 'I'm going to the launderette. The kids have been playing on the balcony, tipping over that sandpit you made out of a paddling pool. It's a bloody mess. Leave it, I will clean it up later.'

Although she shouted as she left, Steve hardly paid attention. He knew he had heard that voice before. Nick Diamond's voice was distinctive and the sarcasm that had drawled down the telephone from Nick had set something off in his memory, but he couldn't think what. Hopefully, it would come to him soon. Maybe Sheila was right, it was just one of those things. But he wasn't sure and he suddenly had a bad feeling about it all.

27

Nick telephoned Natasha, but he could tell by the tone of her voice something was wrong. She wasn't her usual chatty self. He pressed her to tell him what the problem was, almost shouting at her in the process, causing an argument.

Natasha started to cry and apologise. 'I'm pregnant, Nicky,' she shouted back at him. Shocked, Nick almost dropped the telephone. She couldn't be pregnant. He wasn't able to have children. He'd been married to Patsy for fifteen years and she'd never once fallen pregnant!

'Who is the father?' he shouted. He felt disgusted and betrayed. This was the woman he was going to spend his life with. He was going to give everything up for her and now she was pregnant with another man's child.

'It's yours, Nicky. I could never look at another man after you. I love you! I've only just found out. I swear, Nicky, I'm having your baby,' she cried and sniffed down the phone. Nick's heart was pounding, it wasn't possible. She had to be lying.

'I can't have children, Natasha. In all of the years I have been married, Patsy has never been pregnant.'

'Well, maybe that's Patsy's fault, because I'm telling you, Nicky, I am definitely having your baby. I have taken five tests and they all say the same. I'm pregnant,' she shouted at him.

Nick frowned. This was the last bombshell he had expected today. 'Look, Natasha. I'm coming up to Scotland for a few days next week. We'll talk about it then.'

Ending the call, the realisation that he was about to become a father stunned him and he could feel himself shaking. He couldn't believe it. His legs felt weak and he had to sit down. Pouring himself a drink first, he thought about what Natasha had said. Was it possible? Could she really be pregnant? The more he thought about it, a smile appeared on his face. He was going to be a father! A warm feeling spread through his veins. He was going to be a father. He cursed himself for losing his temper with her. She needed to keep calm and not get stressed. She was a pregnant woman in a delicate situation. He needed to get to Scotland. Impulsively he picked up his car keys and slammed the door behind him.

* * *

'Nicky! Nicky!' Natasha ran to him and threw her arms around his neck. Their kiss was long and passionate, as they clung to each other. She couldn't believe her eyes when she saw him.

Nick's body ached for her, and he could feel his manhood rising instantly. It was a flying visit, he just needed to see her quickly. 'I'm only here for a few hours. I have to be back in London tomorrow. I just needed to see you. Are you okay?'

'I am now you're here,' she grinned. 'I don't care for how long. You're here and that's all that matters.' She pulled him towards her again, and they kissed and walked towards her flat. Consumed with passion, they tore at each other's clothes, they wanted nothing between them.

'Is it okay?' Nick stopped. 'Are we okay to do this?' A thought occurred to him. In his passion he was pulling her around the new bed she had bought. He wanted her.

'Yes, Nicky, it's fine.' Taking his hand, she placed it on her stomach. 'I will always have a part of you here with me.'

Stroking her stomach, Nick felt tears brim on his lashes and fall down his face. 'My baby. When is it due?' His voice was choked with emotion. He had never realised how much he wanted to be a father up until now. He had just put it to the back of his mind. What you've never had, you never miss.

'You work it out,' she laughed. 'It's been three months since you have been here. Around June. I have something for you.' Running into the lounge, Natasha came back, holding a photo. 'This is a scan of our baby. This is us.'

Taking hold of the picture, he couldn't quite make it out until Natasha prompted him. 'Can I keep it?' He didn't know what to say as he stared at the little figure in the photo. He couldn't explain the joy he felt. His grin was wider than his face. Reaching for his wallet, he put it inside carefully and then turned towards Natasha.

Consumed with a deep hunger for each other, they made love. Afterwards, as they lay in each other's arms, Nick sat up. 'I have to pop out to the community centre. I won't be long.' Dragging himself away from her, he left.

Walking into the centre, he was surprised to see it was packed and in the far corner were the knitting nanas. 'Well, ladies,' he beamed at them. 'There are flames coming off those needles.' They all jumped up to greet him.

Unexpectedly, Terence walked up to him. 'Mr Diamond, it's good to see you back!'

'Hello, Terence, just a flying visit, I have some business to finish up. It's erm...' Nick was trying to think on his feet. 'It's regarding the kids' Christmas party I'm giving.' Thankfully, it was early

December and that was the best he could think of to satisfy this nosy copper.

'A kids' party? That sounds great. If there is anything we can do to help, be sure to let us know. This place has been a real godsend to the kids around here. The streets are clear and there has been no trouble since it opened.' Terence and the community officer grinned. 'I've just popped in for one of those pink elephants the girls here knit. My dog is chewing its way through every soft toy we have in the house. Bloody thing. I want to replace the pink one. I've just picked this one up, Beryl, from over there. How much?'

Nick saw Beryl's face drain of colour and the women all glanced at each other furtively. 'Take it, Terence, to replace the one your dog has chewed, but keep it away from him this time, eh?' Not knowing how to get out of this, it was the only thing he could do. It dawned on him that the pink ones were full of marijuana. Jesus Christ, he couldn't believe it.

'Oh, thanks, ladies, I appreciate that,' Terence laughed. 'And yes, this one is going straight into the nursery. Those pink ones are flying off the shelves. Everyone around here must be having girls!' Nick waited until Terence had left.

'What the bloody hell are you doing, leaving them lying around?' he demanded.

'He's supposed to ask,' Beryl snapped. 'Just picking them up to suit himself, cheeky bastard!' She was interrupted by Maggie's laughter.

'What are you laughing at, you silly cow?' Beryl shouted.

Trying to control herself, Maggie wiped away a tear from her eye. 'I was just thinking about his dog. If it chews that toy, it's going to be as high as a kite! The dog is an addict.' They all burst out laughing, but Nick didn't have time for this now.

'Are you really going to throw a party for all of the kids around here?' Nana asked.

'Yes, of course. You organise a tree and stuff and I'll pay. I need to speak to Steve. Where is he?'

Beryl pointed her knitting needle in the direction of the fire exit. 'He's mopping out the back.'

Striding outside, Nick caught sight of Steve. 'Steve, I believe you have a problem with working here.'

Shocked at seeing Nick, Steve stopped mopping the floor. 'Careful, Mr Diamond, I haven't put the hazard sign up yet and the floor is still wet.'

'Just answer the fucking question, will you?' Nick was already flustered from the drive and Terence's marijuana-chewing dog. Why did Scotland always end up in a drama?

'No, Mr Diamond. I like working here. That's why I thought I should tip you off. If it gets raided, those coppers will close the place down. I thought I was doing the right thing?'

'Well, it seems to me that you're sticking your nose in where it's not wanted. But I'm glad you told me first.'

Steve paled in disbelief and stood there wide-eyed at this sharply dressed, articulate man who was his boss. Suddenly, he wanted to be sick. That voice, that threatening voice! That bloody voice. Suddenly, it all came back to him. He'd received a call when he hadn't killed that young kid years ago, threatening him. This was that very same voice. The call had only been a minute or so, but it had sent chills down his spine the way it did now.

'It's you. You're the Undertaker. You ruin people's lives, you bastard!' Walking towards him, Steve wanted to strangle him. He was blazing with anger.

Nick smiled sarcastically. 'I don't know what you mean.' He laughed. The cold, hard expression on his face made Steve stop in his tracks and squirm as those green eyes bored into him.

'You know exactly what I mean. I will tell the world who you are. Mr Fucking Nice Guy. You're a murderer!' Steve couldn't help himself. This man had ruined his life and had turned his wife into an addict and a prostitute.

Nick's calm soothing voice now held threatening undertones that made Steve tremble. With his once charming smile dropping, his face was like granite as he spoke. 'Tell them what?' Nick raised one eyebrow innocently, throwing Steve an icy glare. 'You're the criminal wearing the ankle tag. Who would believe you? I have no blood on my hands. Now, be a good boy and think about it.'

Nick's voice was barely above a whisper as he spoke. 'Evidence is key, Steve, and you have none. You're going to rant and rave about an Undertaker in an interview room with two detectives. It's laughable and so are you. As I am in a good mood and short of time, I will let you think about it. Turn a blind eye and mop your floors, or there will be repercussions, I promise you that. I could shout for help now – my good friend Terence the sergeant is through there drinking my tea, I'm sure he would arrest you if I told him you were threatening me. Do you fancy spending Christmas in prison? They will take you back there, Steve, I guarantee it.'

Steve stood there like a statue. Nick's cold words filled his ears. Clenching his fist together, he was about to throw a punch. He was angry and couldn't help himself. Seeing this, Nick laughed. 'Go on, I dare you. Assault and threats. How old will your daughters be when you see daylight again?'

Knowing he was beaten, Steve relaxed. His head was throbbing and his mind was racing. It was true, he had no evidence to prove his words. And not only would he finish the sentence he was tagged for, this man would have him charged with assault. His heart was pounding in his chest. What would Nick do to Sheila and his girls once he was out of the way? There was no telling. This man was pure evil, he cared for no one. 'Fair enough. I presume you want me to leave quietly, but this isn't over by a long chalk, Mr Diamond.'

'Stay if you want, I really don't care.' Nick waved his hand in the air nonchalantly. 'How are you going to explain your unemployment to your probation officer? But keep out of my business. I will give you the week to think about it, and I will be back. Don't do anything silly, Steve, after all, I know where you live.' Nick's laugh made Steve's blood run cold. On the face of it, to anyone in the centre, it looked like they were having a friendly chat and joking. He couldn't win. 'I will put my orders in place and even if anything happens to me, they will still be carried out. How are your wife and children?'

Realising Nick's threats were against his family, Steve knew he had him firmly by the balls. 'People will realise what you are eventually, they don't need me.' Subdued, he looked down at the floor. 'I will finish after Christmas.' Although Steve's body was raging with anger, he knew there was no way out.

Nick shrugged and walked away, leaving Steve rooted to the spot. Feeling the bile rising in his throat, he leaned over his mop bucket and vomited. 'I will kill you, Nick Diamond,' Steve vowed to himself.

Once his shift was over and he had locked up, Steve almost ran home. He was going to rid this world of that bastard once and for all. Nick was coming back to Scotland in a week. He couldn't wait. All he had to do now was bide his time and work things out properly in his head. He didn't want to get caught out and he had no intention of going back to prison and leaving Sheila to fend for herself.

'Whoa, hold your horses, mate. Where are you going in such a hurry?' Fin held his hands up and moved out of the way before Steve ran into him.

'I need to get home,' was all Steve said.

Seeing the panic and worried look on his face, Fin stopped him. 'What you need before going home is a drink with me. You look shocking. What's the matter?' Come on. You can't go home like that.'

'I've had some bad news, that's all.'

'I can see something is wrong. Come on, Steve, we're old mates. What's wrong? Come back to my place, it's empty.' Steering him towards his flat, Steve followed. Fin was right, he needed a moment to compose himself before going home. He had bottled up his conversation with Nick all day and it felt like his head would explode. Whatever had happened between them, Fin was a good friend.

Entering Fin's flat as he unlocked the metal door, Steve ignored the mess and sat down. He felt like crying. Fin got them both a can of lager and handed him one. He had never seen Steve in such a state. 'Come on, mate, you can tell me.' Concerned, he urged him on to tell him.

'Nick Diamond. He's the Undertaker,' was all Steve said. 'He's almost admitted it to me and threatened my family.'

Stunned, Fin sat there, trying to take in what Steve was saying. This was way beyond what he expected. 'You must be wrong. Braveheart is respectable and not from around here. What did he say?'

'The community centre is a drug den. The whole place is a drop-off point and messaging point. That façade that he was doing something for the community is a fucking joke,' Steve spat out. 'All he is doing is creating a smokescreen for dealers.'

Fin went quiet, he didn't want to admit to Steve that he knew what the centre was being used for. He was a part of it. 'Nick Diamond? Are you sure?' Fin couldn't comprehend it. It didn't make sense. 'You must have misunderstood him, Steve. It's not possible. He's a lawyer.'

'Yes, well, he's a fucking crooked one. He's at the bottom of all of this and I'm going to kill him.'

'Don't be hasty, Steve. You could go away for a long time if you're thinking about murder. Don't even think about it. Be sensible. I know you have history, but for fuck's sake, Steve, I beg you. Leave it. Leave well alone.' Fin was almost pleading with him, while trying to make sense of it all.

'I am, Fin. Look what he's done to us. He's ruined my family.'

Steve took a few gulps of his lager to moisten his dry throat. His teeth were on edge.

'No, you're not, Steve. You're thinking about you. You're angry, yes, and him – well, I can't believe it. But if you kill him, what happens to Sheila then? You're looking at a ten-year stretch, minimum.'

'Is that it, then? I just forget about it and carry on? For fuck's sake, Fin, grow a pair. This man has terrified you for years. Don't you feel the same as me?'

'Yes, course I do. We have all been conned. Who else knows this? Nick Diamond was the last person I would have thought of, and so would the police,' Fin stressed, trying to reach some kind of reason in Steve. 'Let it go, Steve, he's not worth it.' Fin could see his words were falling on deaf ears, and he didn't know what to do. This was his friend, but if he went ahead with this vengeance, he couldn't help him. Finishing his drink, Steve stood up to leave. Without thinking, Fin moved towards him and put his arms around him and hugged him. 'Be lucky, mate, and don't do anything rash. Brothers, eh?'

'Always, Fin, but rest assured. One day, you will feel like I do now.' Trying to hide his anger, he left.

Fin didn't know what to do. He couldn't call anyone about the conversation he had just had. If Nick Diamond was the Undertaker, he was the only other person who knew. He was a dead man walking. No way would Nick Diamond give him the chance to unmask him. He felt nervous and sweaty. Sitting down, he drew a line of cocaine from the coffee table. He needed something to take the edge off.

* * *

Sheila was in the kitchen when Steve got in. 'Egg and chips do you?' she shouted.

'Yes, that's fine.' Going to the French windows that led on to the little balcony outside their flat, he couldn't believe his eyes. The rose bush where he hid his gun was in a different pot, it had been changed. Now he was panicking. 'Sheila, what happened to your rose bush? Isn't that a different pot?'

Walking into the lounge, Sheila laughed. 'Blimey, what big eyes you have, grandma. Shut the bloody doors, its freezing, and you're letting all the heat out!'

Closing the doors, Steve asked again. 'Yes, but I'm right, aren't I? That is a different pot, isn't it. Why did you change it?' Mentally, he was trying to weigh Sheila up. Had she found his gun? If she had, she wasn't shouting at him for having it, he would have expected that.

'I told you, cloth ears,' she laughed. 'The kids were playing in that paddling pool you filled with sand you stole from the builders at the community centre. The pot got smashed, so I replaced it this afternoon. Why?' She thought it was odd that he was making such a big deal over a plant pot. 'Come on, food's on the table.' Following her to the kitchen, Steve took a backwards glance towards the balcony. He was sure he'd put it back in there when he stopped working for the pizza deliveries. Maybe his mind was playing tricks with him, he'd had a lot to think about this afternoon. Pondering, while listening to Sheila and the girls, he wondered if he had left it in his locker at the pizza shop. He had to get it back. He was going to shoot Nick Diamond, he was determined about that.

Waiting until Sharon and Penny finished their dinner and went to watch television, he sat with his mug of tea at the table. Whatever happened, he felt Sheila deserved an explanation. 'Sheila, I have something to tell you. Close the door and sit down.'

'This sounds serious.' Puzzled, she did as he asked and sat

down.

'Do you remember when I said I thought I had heard Nick Diamond's voice before? Well, I have.' Steve unfolded the whole sorry story to her, as she sat in stony silence. Apart from the shocked look on her face, she said nothing.

'Say something, Sheila.' He paused. He had been waiting for an outburst or discussion but none came.

'What's it got to do with us where he deals? We knew it was someone, so why not him? You're earning good money, you don't come home battered and bruised any more, and you're not delivering his drugs. We have just got on our feet, Steve. The debts are being paid off and we have the chance of being transferred out of here. Why do you always have to defend the world against evil? It's nearly Christmas, the tree is up, the decorations are up and we have presents stashed away for the girls. Believe me, it's a far cry from the situation I was in last year. It's not our business. You tell him you were mistaken and let sleeping dogs lie.' Standing up, she started to clear the table and wash up. She wasn't interested. All that bothered her was her own family.

Smarting inside, Steve heard her out. As far as she was concerned, the matter was over. But there was still the missing gun. He needed to find it.

'Don't you understand how I feel, Sheila? He ripped our family apart.' Although she had her back to him, he got up and slid his arms around her waist. Kissing her on the cheek, he felt the wetness from tears falling down them.

'You did that, Steve, when you happily worked for him. I've given blowjobs in a cold cemetery on my knees to pay for his tailor-made suits. If I can let it go, so can you,' she murmured.

Her words almost broke his heart. She wanted to put the past behind her. All her reasoning was right. Sighing, he turned her around and kissed her. 'You win, Sheila. It was my mistake.'

* * *

Over the next few days, an enormous tree arrived at the centre, which Steve helped to decorate. Nick had given Nana £1,000 to buy some assorted presents for the boys and girls, and they had also organised for a Father Christmas to come and deliver them to the party. Everyone was looking forward to it and was in a festive mood.

The knitting nanas were clacking away, knitting Santas, filling them with their own surprises. The regulars asked Beryl if she would be baking any of her special brownies, with that added touch of seasoning they had sampled at her fundraising. With eyebrows raised in wonder, Beryl nodded. 'Maybe, what do you think, Paul? You're the chef.'

'That sounds like a very good idea, Mrs Diamond,' he laughed. 'They will make the party go with a swing. I was thinking of organising some kind of firework display for the kids too. What do you think?' he shot back at her.

Everyone shouted with joy. 'Yes, absolutely!'

'Oh, this is going to be a Christmas we'll never forget.' Nana clapped her hands together at her friends, who were as excited as small children.

* * *

'Have you remembered, Patsy, I am going to Scotland tomorrow? It's the kids' party.'

'Yes, I was thinking of coming with you. Would you like that, Nick?' Seeing his face drop, she let out a sarcastic laugh. 'No, you wouldn't, would you? It would spoil your break with your Scottish tart!'

Shocked, Nick shot his head up and looked at her. 'What do you mean by that, Patsy?'

'Don't take me for a fool, Nick. I know you. I also saw you very indiscreetly with your tongue down that blonde woman's throat on the day of the opening. It looked like you had her head in your mouth!' Patsy was very calm and very matter-of-fact about it.

Nick blushed to the roots of his hair and stammered, 'She's pregnant, Patsy. She's having my baby.' Now it was Patsy's turn to be shocked. She hadn't expected this. She had presumed it was just a fling.

'Well, that puts a different slant on things, doesn't it?' she snapped at him, upset. This revelation was a bolt from the blue. 'What about us? Is that it, I'm just going to be cast aside while you play happy families? What about me? What about the money?' she barked.

'Oh, now we're getting to the truth of the matter,' Nick laughed. 'You don't give a shit about me as long as you can still live as you always have. To be fair, Patsy, I would like to carry on our arrangement if possible. We have been good business partners. Why should anything change?' Standing up, Nick poured them both a drink and sat down in the armchair opposite her. 'We can go our separate ways, Patsy, but that is up to you. Think about it. I will be back after the party and that will give you time to think.'

Listening to Nick's cold manner, Patsy realised she despised him. It sounded like he was breaking up a business partnership, not a marriage. It seemed he had already made his mind up. When was he going to tell her? Was he just going to cut and run without an explanation? She had known their marriage was over for a long time. But she had once worshipped the ground he had walked on. To be just discarded like this hurt her pride.

'How far pregnant is she? Are you sure it's yours?' she asked calmly.

'Three months. And yes, it's definitely my baby.' Then, looking down at the floor, he felt sorry for her. He had never intended for any of this to happen, but he was glad it had. 'I'm sorry. I never wanted to hurt you, you must believe that.' Nick was genuine, he had respect for Patsy. But now they were both still young enough to find new lives and move on.

'I must believe nothing, you bastard! Nick's in love and the rest of us can just fuck off, is that it? Were you going to tell me, Nick? Didn't I deserve that?' She threw her glass at him and Nick held his arm up to shield himself.

'Stop it!' he shouted. 'Stop this right now. Be careful, Patsy, don't push me too far. You have lived well enough and you're as greedy as I am.' Venom spewed from his mouth as his green eyes flashed at her, while he watched her rub her red face.

Shaking, she nodded. She was crying but could see it made no difference. Where had her Nick gone? Over the last few years, he had changed into a monster.

'I will be leaving early. Have a think about it, Patsy. A good long think, and I will be back a couple of days after the party.' Storming out of the house, Nick realised time was not on his side. Going to his office, he locked the door and pulled the skirting board and carpet away. Underneath the floorboards was his getaway money. Bags and bags full of hoarded cash no one knew about. Buried beneath them was a gun. He intended to sort Steve out himself. Ignoring the staff, he took out the bags and loaded the boot of his car. After four trips, he was shattered and sweating. By his reckoning, there must have been around four million in those bags and they were bloody heavy! Pouring himself a well-earned drink from the whisky bottle he had stashed in his filing cabinet, he sat back in his chair and drew breath.

Going back to his apartment, he was glad to see Patsy wasn't there. It was getting late and he wanted to pack. He considered going to Scotland tonight, but he had been drinking and the police were always on the alert at Christmas, it wasn't worth his driving licence. He would go first thing in the morning, he decided. Tonight, he would get some sleep.

* * *

The missing gun disturbed Steve. He was sure Sheila didn't know anything about it, or she would have mentioned it. She had said something about the kids playing on the balcony and breaking the pot, so maybe it had fallen out. While she was out, the next morning, he ransacked the place. He needed to find it, but it was nowhere to be found. God! What if it had been there and she had just scooped it all up with the rubbish? It was fully loaded and ready to fire. It would be in the bins downstairs, he would have to check the skips. Then a thought struck him: what if he had left it in the drawer that all of the delivery moped keys were kept in? It was fit to bursting. Some nights he had been so tired when he returned the keys to the shop, he couldn't think straight. He knew that it was a stupid thought, because it would have been seen by now, but in his panic he wasn't seeing reason. Maybe he could ask Fin to check it, just to ease his mind.

Ringing Fin, he explained the situation and asked him to look for it. Fin agreed, but wanted guarantees that Steve wasn't going to use it. This was just for safety's sake. Checking his watch, he realised it was time for him to open up the centre. Over the last few days, there had been a lot of excitement.

Everyone had clamoured to see the Christmas lights and the large pine tree. Paul was cooking Christmas dinners and preparing the buffet for the party. He seemed to be in his element, bossing all the kitchen staff around. There were trifles galore. It seemed like everyone had something to do. It had been mayhem.

Running along the landing, he saw little Jimmy standing outside. Natasha's front door was open and he had come out for some fresh air. Steve smiled; as usual, he was wearing his sheriff's waistcoat and badge, with a Stetson hat. Steve knew what he had to do. 'Oh no, Sheriff Jimmy. You've caught me.' Standing there with his hands in the air, Steve laughed. It was the same scenario every time. Jimmy laughed and pointed his finger and thumb at him like a gun. 'I'm quicker on the draw than you, Sheriff Jimmy.' Pointing his own fingers at him, Steve was surprised when Jimmy ran in. Puzzled, he hoped he hadn't scared him. He was about to go in when Jimmy came out. 'I've got a gun,' he laughed.

Steve looked down at the little boy in horror. The heavy gun wobbled slightly in Jimmy's hands as he pointed it at Steve. 'Where did you get that from?' Trying to hold his composure, Steve didn't want to frighten Jimmy.

'From your house. I found it.' The penny dropped. Steve suddenly realised that Jimmy had seen the gun from the smashed flowerpot and taken it without being seen. Jesus Christ! Steve cursed himself. Keeping his voice steady, he knelt down, so that he was face to face with Jimmy. 'Give that to me, Jimmy, please, mate. I will get you a bigger one, then we can play,' he whispered while he looked down the barrel of the gun pointing directly at him. As those tiny fingers hovered over the trigger, Jimmy's hand wobbled slightly, as he fought to hold the weight of it.

'Nooo,' Jimmy laughed. 'I'm the sheriff and you're going to die.' Without a second thought, Jimmy's little fingers pressed tightly on the trigger, knocking him backwards, banging his head on the floor. The shot echoed around the estate. It had been a direct hit in Steve's forehead. He was dead. Blood poured from the hole in his skull onto the landing as he lay in a crumpled heap.

Natasha flew to the front door and looked out. She saw Jimmy first, crying and trying to stand up. Then she turned and saw Steve. A huge scream erupted from her as other doors opened to see what the noise was. Seeing what had happened, someone was immediately dialling the emergency services. Someone else was kneeling and shaking Steve, but they could see the bullet hole. It was useless. They all looked up at Natasha for an answer, but there wasn't one. She was pale and shaking. Sobs wracked her body as she reached for Jimmy and held him close to her. She felt numb, like this was all a bad dream. Pulling apart from him, she started shaking him frantically by the shoulders. 'What have you done?' she shouted in panic. 'What the hell have you done?'

Jimmy began to cry again and shouted for Steve to wake up. 'Steve, it's tickle time,' he shouted, escaping Natasha's clutches and bending down beside him, waiting for Steve to burst into life, like he had so many times before, but nothing happened.

'There is the gun. Nobody touch it,' shouted one of the neighbours.

'Where the hell did he get that from?' the neighbours shouted angrily at Natasha, who by now had fallen to her knees in despair. All she could do was shake her head while she cried. She couldn't talk.

'Where is Sheila?' someone asked. Emotions ran high as everyone was panicking and shouting. Only Natasha and Steve were motionless.

Hearing what had happened, Maggie rushed puffing and panting to Natasha's side. 'What happened, Natasha? Where did Jimmy get that gun from?' Natasha shook her head and fell into Maggie's arms. She was distraught.

'Careful now, dear, you don't want to lose the baby.' Maggie tried soothing her. She was as shocked as everyone, but was doing her best to keep everyone calm. The sirens from the police burst into the forecourt, followed by an ambulance. All they knew was that someone had been shot.

Maggie was angry; maybe she could have got someone to sort this out without the police. 'Who rang them?' she shouted angrily but she knew it was pointless. No one answered and the police were already running across the landing.

Seeing Steve's body, the police pushed the gathering crowd out of the way. They asked what had happened and immediately rang through to the station. The police steered Natasha and Jimmy into the flat and sat them down, followed by Maggie. They would have to wait for the detectives to arrive. 'What happened, miss?' They looked up at Natasha.

'I'm the sheriff and I shot cowboy Steve.' Snot and tears ran down Jimmy's face as he confessed with all innocence. 'Is he all right?' he asked. The policemen stared at each other. How the hell could they arrest a four-year-old for a shooting? Tentatively they asked him, 'Well, sheriff, where did you get the gun?' They did their best to put him at his ease. It was an awkward situation and all they could do for now was calm the situation.

Wiping his nose with his sleeve, Jimmy told them he'd got it from Steve's house and hid it. 'Did you know about this?' they fired at Natasha.

'No, I swear, I didn't. I really didn't,' she cried.

'Were you hiding it for him?' they enquired.

Maggie intervened. 'Look, officers, this has been a tragic accident and she is a pregnant woman,' she snapped. But even she couldn't believe what she was hearing.

Two detectives stepped through the door and introduced themselves. After a brief chat, they took Natasha and Jimmy down to the police station. Steve's body was still on the landing, awaiting forensics, and they had to step over him to get past. Natasha shielded Jimmy's eyes from the sight as she held him to her trembling body.

Frantically, Natasha pulled at Maggie's arm. She was frightened and panicking. 'Call Nick, Maggie. Get him to come to the station, he will sort this out. Tell him what happened! It was an accident!' Natasha screamed, as she was bundled into the back of the car.

Nick was in high spirits as he sped up the motorway. Everything in his life was going right. His mobile was ringing constantly and, when he glanced at it, he didn't recognise the number, so he switched it off. He had better things to think about. Tonight, he would have Natasha in his arms.

Nick's mind wandered to his baby; he wondered what it would look like and what sex it would be. He couldn't help smiling when he thought about it and a warm feeling spread through him. He loved Natasha and they were having a baby, and with all the money they had behind them, they would live the dream.

Pulling off the motorway, he drove into one of the local towns. Seeing a jeweller's shop, he stopped. He wanted to buy Natasha an engagement ring. That would prove to her he was serious.

It would be a romantic gesture, proposing at Christmas time after the kids' party. He hoped Patsy would be sensible about it all, the last thing he wanted would be for her to have a terrible accident!

Business was business, she would see sense, and he felt sure of that. He just needed to get rid of Steve and nothing more would give him greater pleasure. As far as he knew, Steve was the only person who knew who he really was.

He was pleased he had invited his mother; she was due in Scotland anytime today and she had been delighted when he had asked her to the kids' Christmas party. This time next year, he would have his very own child to buy for. The future looked hopeful.

Parking around the back of Nana's flat, he opened the door. He didn't think she would be in but wanted to make sure. Taking the bags of money with the gun out of the boot of his car, he stashed them in her empty wardrobe in the spare bedroom. Walking across to Natasha's flat, he was shocked to see all the police tape outside. Panic gripped him. What had happened to her? There was no one around, so he went to the community centre.

'Nana!' Bursting through the doors, he shouted for her. 'Where's Natasha and what is all that police tape doing outside of her house?'

'Calm down, Nicky.' Maggie greeted him first. 'She's at the police station.'

'Police station. Why? Has someone hurt her? There is police tape everywhere.'

'Didn't you get my messages? I left loads on your mobile phone, I have been trying to call you all day.'

'No, I was driving. It's switched off!' Grabbing Maggie by the shoulders, he squeezed her. 'Where is Natasha and what's happening?'

Stunned, Nick listened to Maggie's story of the day's events. His jaw almost dropped and he felt dizzy when she told him Jimmy had shot Steve. 'Come and sit down, you're as white as a sheet.' Maggie's eyes brimmed with tears. She was visibly shaking.

'No, I have to go to the police station, where is it?' He felt hot and suffocated in this room, he needed to get to Natasha. Lost and confused, Nick looked around the centre for answers. He was in a blind panic.

'I'll come with you,' Maggie volunteered. Just as they were leaving, he bumped into his mother coming through the doors.

'Nick, love. It's lovely to see you.' Then she noticed how pale and shaken he was. 'What's wrong? What's happened?'

'Natasha. She's at the police station,' he shouted. 'I have to go.' Pushing past her, he ran out of the doors to his car, pulling Maggie alongside him.

'Why is she at the police station?' Victoria shouted, but it was too late, he had already gone.

* * *

When they got to the station, Maggie told him to stop babbling and take a breath. 'You're her only hope, Nick. God knows what is happening in there. You need to remain calm.' Sweeping his hands through his hair and straightening his tie, he nodded and took a huge breath.

Inside the police station, he introduced himself as Natasha's lawyer but was told she already had the duty solicitor and she was being interviewed now. He would have to wait until they could get a message to the detectives.

Slamming his hand on the desk, his anger rose at the desk sergeant. 'I am her lawyer. Are they charging her? I demand her release now!'

The sergeant disappeared. Maggie pulled Nick to one side. 'Well, that went well,' she glared at him. 'Pull yourself together, Nick, you're making things worse.'

A detective came out and introduced himself. 'Come with me.' Maggie and Nick stood up. 'Is she your secretary?' He pointed at

Maggie. When Nick shook his head, he looked at Maggie. 'You stay here.'

'What happened? Why are you keeping her?' Nick demanded. He felt more in control of the situation now.

'We're holding her for twenty-four hours. Possession of a firearm is very serious. A man has been killed, Mr Diamond.'

'Yes, but she didn't shoot him, did she? She didn't even know the gun was there.'

'You seem very well informed.' The detective raised his eyebrows and shrugged. 'Come on, Mr Diamond. They all deny knowledge of things in their house when they are arrested. How can she have not known?'

'Can I see her?' Nick was doing his damndest to remain calm. He could see his bad attitude wasn't getting him far.

'She has a solicitor. You can talk to him and possibly see her. Five minutes, while you all decide who her lawyer is.'

The detective walked him to the interview room and let him in. Natasha's face was red and puffy from crying. When she saw him, she jumped up and ran to him, flinging her arms around his neck. The duty solicitor in the room looked at them both, locked in an embrace, and gave a false cough to break them up. Nick turned to look at him. Holding out his hand, he introduced himself. 'Nick Diamond, I'm her lawyer. What have they said so far?'

'Larry Kavanagh If you don't mind me saying, Mr Diamond, it's not going to help your cause, if them outside know you're lovers. You can't defend her.'

'Just tell me what has happened.' Nick sat down.

'Possession of a firearm. They are waiting to do a video talk with Jimmy in one of the playrooms. Social services have been called. Jimmy will be put into temporary care while they sort things out. They are keeping her here for twenty-four hours, no matter what.'

'My family will have Jimmy. That's not a problem. Why are they holding her?'

Hysterically, Natasha shouted, 'Don't let them take Jimmy from me, Nick. Help me, please!'

Larry waved his hands in the air. 'Can we all calm down? Natasha, this is just procedure. You have no family and social services have been informed. A man has been killed here, can't you understand that? Your son has killed him. It's an accident, a bloody tragic one. But there is the question of the gun. He's going to need a lot of counselling and therapy for most of his life. Nick, tell her. You know I am right.'

Sighing Nick took a breath and nodded. He had to think with his lawyer brain now. 'They haven't charged you with anything yet, Natasha, and I doubt they can. But they can hold you here for questioning without charge. All we can do is wait until tomorrow or if they let you go in the meantime. How is Jimmy, Larry?'

'He's fine,' Larry assured him. 'He has no idea what is going on. He's had burger and chips and he's being looked after. You know they have special friendly rooms for kids. What a fucking mess.' Larry let out a deep breath, and sat down. In all of his years, he had never come across a four-year-old killing someone. 'I think I should carry on with this interview tonight, Mr Diamond. You're in no fit state and you're too emotional. Let's not rock the boat, eh?'

'Are they going to put her in the cells?' Nick frowned. He felt helpless, but he knew Larry was right.

'Yes. All being well, she should be out in the morning. Apart from...' Larry tailed off. He hadn't told Nick the worst of it.

'What? What is it?' Nick demanded.

'Her fingerprints are on the gun. She says she saw it in his toy box the other day and picked it up. She thought it was a toy someone had given him, not realising it was real, but somehow her fingerprint is on the trigger,' Larry shrugged. It all seemed hopeless.

'Only Jimmy can help her, Nick, otherwise it could look like Natasha shot Steve and is using Jimmy to cover it up.'

This was worse than Nick thought; no wonder they were holding her. He had to get through the next few hours until tomorrow, to find out if they were charging her with anything.

'I'll come back tomorrow, Natasha. There is nothing I can do tonight. Don't worry, it's always darkest before dawn. I will sort it out. Jimmy will tell them what happened. Don't worry,' he stressed. He was in turmoil, he didn't know what to do. It was a waiting game. He was heartbroken – for her, for Jimmy and most of all for himself.

Thanking Larry and agreeing to see him tomorrow, he hugged Natasha and kissed her. 'Be strong, darling. I will see you tomorrow.' Her forlorn look as he left the room would haunt him forever.

Maggie fired question after question at him when he saw her. She had expected Natasha to be with him. On the drive back, Nick told her about the fingerprints on the gun.

'Well, how would she know if the gun was real or not? That could have been any one of us. I have been in Jimmy's toy box many times.'

'We have to wait until tomorrow, Maggie. It's serious. It all depends on Jimmy's testimony.' Nick hated Steve more than ever now, when he thought about it. So Steve had a gun, did he? Well, he could only guess who he was going to use that on. Nick knew it was for him. Yet again, even in death that bloody man was annoying him. Still, he mused to himself, Jimmy had saved him a lot of trouble.

'What's that noise?' Nick looked up as they drove towards the estate. There were shouts and loud music.

'It will be the Christmas party. They couldn't cancel it. You have to be there, Nick, and so do I. Come on, it might help us take our minds off things. You said yourself there is nothing we can do now. I bet you could use a drop of Beryl's whisky. You're the host, Nick, you have to go,' Maggie pushed.

Pulling up outside, he walked in with Maggie. He was in no mood for partying, but Maggie was right. There was nothing he could do tonight. And he sorely needed Beryl's canteen of whisky.

The room looked fantastic. Paul had laid all the tables next to each other with red tablecloths and crackers. It looked like Santa's grotto. Some people were a little sombre, but they were putting on brave faces for the sake of the children. Seeing Nick, they all looked up at him for answers, but he had none. Children were piling through the doors, laughing and putting on party hats of all shapes and sizes.

'Don't spoil it, Nicky.' Beryl squeezed his hand. 'The wee ones have looked forward to this all week. It's not their fault what has happened. What are you going to do, sit at home all night and wallow in pity?' she asked.

'Don't lecture me, Nana, I really don't need it.'

Victoria joined them. 'Nicky, you really need to paint a smile on that face of yours. Stay for an hour and then leave. Father Christmas will be here soon. Just one hour, eh?' Soothingly, Victoria did her best to appease him.

Nodding, Nick agreed. Mustering up every bit of enthusiasm he could, he smiled and greeted everyone in typical host style. The cheers and laughter from the children were deafening. They were all pulling crackers and eating their fill as Christmas songs filled the room.

Victoria pulled him aside. 'Patsy phoned. She told me you're leaving her. Is that right?'

'Jungle drums banging early? What else did she have to say?' Swigging back Beryl's canteen, he waited for another lecture, as the whisky warmed his thirsty throat.

'I'm only asking. You love this Natasha girl and you're having a baby. I'm pleased for you, Nick, but I would have liked to have heard it from you first,' she smiled. 'She already has a little boy, doesn't she? Are you going to be okay bringing up another man's child? They will both be your children. Treat them equally. And please be kind to Patsy. This isn't her fault.'

'My father managed it, didn't he? He brought up someone else's kid!' Nick spat out. Victoria winced at Nick's cruel remark and moved away.

'Nicky, have you finished with my whisky? Give it here, I will top it up.' Turning sharply, Nick hadn't noticed Nana standing behind them. Handing over the canteen, he smiled. 'Sorry, Nana, it's been one of those days.'

Fin strolled up to Nick. 'Evening, Mr Diamond. Nice party.' He grinned, remembering what Steve had told him. 'You've heard what happened to Steve the caretaker, then. Does that mean there is a vacancy?' He laughed. It seemed he too had been drinking too much.

'Shut the fuck up, you fool, and as for Steve, it couldn't happen to a nicer man. As for you, you can't even deal drugs properly, let alone look after a place like this. You're a fucking clown and always have been. Go back to your squat and sniff something!' Nick hissed.

Fin's face drained. Now he knew that Steve was telling him the truth, otherwise how would Nick Diamond know so much about him? 'Steve was my mate and I know you set him up.'

'Good for you. Enjoy your last evening of freedom before you join him in the morgue. Nobody speaks to me like that.' Nick's anger was getting the better of him.

Fin was just about to take a swing at him when Beryl stepped in. 'No fighting in here. I don't know what it's all about, but anyone can see you have both had too much to drink. You, Fin, go and help the wee ones and you, Nicky, go and see where that Father Christmas is. The sacks of presents are over there for him to give out. Now sort it, the pair of you. Go on, scoot!' she shouted.

Glaring at each other, they parted and did as they were told. Going outside into the crisp night air, Nick could see the snow beginning to fall from the clear night sky. Seeing a car's headlights, he looked up, expecting the very late Father Christmas. He was amazed when he saw that it was Patsy's car.

'What are you doing here, Patsy?'

'I have as much right to be here as anyone else. I am Mrs Diamond. That's still my family name above the door, isn't it?' she hissed at him, slamming the car door. 'So where is she, then, the woman who has stolen your heart? How come you're outside on your own? Has she dumped you?' Patsy couldn't contain herself any longer, she was angry that Nick was playing happy families so quickly behind her back. She felt like a fool.

'If you have come for an argument, you've wasted your time. She's in police custody. Her kid shot someone today.'

Concerned, Patsy stopped her bickering and asked if Natasha was okay. 'No, I mean it, Nick. Is she okay? And what about her child?' Maybe it was age, Patsy couldn't help but feel concern.

'No, she's not. Look, just go inside, will you, I want a minute to myself.' Taking out his cigarettes, Nick lit one, ignoring Patsy as she entered the centre.

Throwing his cigarette butt on the floor, he walked back into the centre. 'Paul, over here.' Carrying his huge bulk before him, Paul walked towards Nick.

'Great party, Mr Diamond. Look at the kiddies, they love it.'

'There is no sign of Father Christmas. The bastard seems to have let us down. I think you should start the fireworks around the back in a minute.'

'Sure thing, Mr Diamond. I'll get them all ushered through.

That will give us time in case he is stuck in traffic. It's Christmas, the traffic is bad and the roads are icy.'

'Yes, well, I wish you had a red suit, you fat bastard!' Nick barked and slurred, his green eyes flashing with anger. 'We wouldn't need any stuffing. Are you still pissed off because you think I short-changed you?' Nick was taking his anger and stress out on everyone that approached him, he couldn't help it.

Surprised at the attack on him, Paul frowned. 'Mr Diamond, I have done nothing wrong. And as for the money, yes, we expected more, you know that.' Paul walked away, muttering something in Greek under his breath.

Lighting another cigarette, Nick stood there alone. This wasn't how it was supposed to be. He had envisioned tonight as special. The snow falling and everyone in high spirits would have made it the perfect night to ask Natasha to marry him. He was gutted. He could hear the loud bangs of the fireworks and squeals of delight around the back of the centre and their colourful display as they shot into the sky, filling it with colour.

As he turned to walk in, deciding to hand out the presents himself, he was shocked to see Father Christmas standing before him.

'Where the fuck have you been? Everyone is waiting for you!' he shouted. He stopped short when the person in the Father Christmas suit raised their arm and pointed a gun at him. Shocked, he was rooted to the spot. He was just about to say something when, without giving him a chance to speak, the figure fired the gun. Nick staggered back then fell to the floor, clutching his chest. Dazed, he opened his palms wide, and saw the blood drip from his hands and through his fingers. The searing pain in his chest led to a burning sensation in his head. Blood poured from the bullet hole in his chest. His breathing was laboured as a black mist forced him to close his eyes.

Before the darkness consumed him, he saw his assailant stand over him and fire the gun once more into his head, finishing him off. Father Christmas then fled into the night, leaving Nick's lifeless body lying there with the snow gently falling on top of him, as his blood turned it pink. The snow fluttered in the air like cotton wool, covering his assailant's footsteps and any evidence.

No one had heard the gunshots over the firework display. A group of people were walking towards the centre. When they saw Nick's body lying there, they ran over to him. Only the outside lights of the community centre lit up the night sky. At first, they thought he was drunk, and knelt down to get a closer inspection and pick the poor man up. Startled, the woman of the group cried out when she saw the blood on her hands. The snow had turned crimson from Nick's bloodied body and she started screaming and shaking. Then they spotted the bullet holes, especially the one in his forehead. For a split second, they looked at one another in shock, then panic gripped them. Scrambling to their feet, their clothes were wet from the blood-soaked snow.

'Help!' they shouted hysterically, barging through the automatic doors and running into the community centre.

Everyone came rushing out and surrounded Nick Diamond's lifeless body, sprawled on the floor. Victoria rushed forward and shouted his name, but there was no response. Others held her back as she cried out. The sound of Slade boomed out of the doors and echoed around the estate.

Terence the policeman had been at the party and came out. Seeing Nick's body, he bent down and checked him over and instantly radioed to the police station. 'Everyone stand back,' he shouted to the gathering crowd. 'Go back into the centre. Get your kids out of here! This is a crime scene now! Get back,' he shouted over the hysterical screams of the shocked crowd. Victoria rushed forward, sobbing, but Terence stood up to stop her. 'Go back into the centre, Mrs Diamond. Leave this to me.'

Patsy stood there in shock, looking down at her husband. She felt numb. Instinctively, she held onto Victoria. She felt faint, her legs were trembling while doing their best to hold her up. 'Please go back into the centre, ladies, and take Beryl with you,' Terence stressed. Thankfully he could hear the sirens of emergency vehicles coming to his aid. Turning to her side, Victoria saw Beryl standing there with tears running down her face. Reaching out for Beryl's hand, she held it tightly as Terence ushered them back into the centre.

In the dark December night, everyone looked on in awe and shock. The crowd grew silent as they watched the police cars and ambulance pull up beside them. Terence was relieved when the police got out of their cars and started ushering people back into the centre. Standing in a half circle surrounding Nick's body, they were motionless. Christmas tunes were playing loudly, but time had stopped. The burning question on all their lips as they cast glances at one other was: who had killed Nick Diamond? And why?'

ACKNOWLEDGMENTS

Thanks to Sue, Avril and Julie Charles for all of their help and support.

Thanks to the Boldwood team for all of their advice and support.

Thanks to all the readers and bloggers for their support.

Many thanks to Emily Ruston, my editor, whose patience knows no bounds.

MORE FROM GILLIAN GODDEN

We hope you enjoyed reading *Diamond Geezer*. If you did, please leave a review.

If you'd like to gift a copy, this book is also available as an ebook, digital audio download and audiobook CD.

Sign up to Gillian Godden's mailing list for news, competitions and updates on future books.

http://bit.ly/GillianGoddenNewsletter

Gold Digger, the first in the series, is available now.

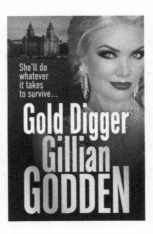

ABOUT THE AUTHOR

Gillian Godden is a Northern-born medical secretary for NHS England. She spent thirty years of her life in the East End of London, hearing stories about the local striptease pubs. Now in Yorkshire, she is an avid reader who lives with her dog, Susie.

Follow Gillian on social media:

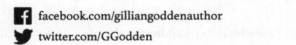

facebook.com/gilliangoddenauthor
twitter.com/GGodden

ABOUT BOLDWOOD BOOKS

Boldwood Books is a fiction publishing company seeking out the best stories from around the world.

Find out more at www.boldwoodbooks.com

Sign up to the Book and Tonic newsletter for news, offers and competitions from Boldwood Books!

http://www.bit.ly/bookandtonic

We'd love to hear from you, follow us on social media:

facebook.com/BookandTonic

twitter.com/BoldwoodBooks

instagram.com/BookandTonic